The Cavalie

By
Eleanor Swift-Hook

County Durham, April 1643

For the second time in less than a year, Sir Nicholas Tempest stood watching a lead-lined coffin lowered into a vault.

His father was dead.

Heroically, they said, leading a charge at Tankersley Moor.

But Nick knew it had been an act of self-immolation. His father had been permitted by the Earl of Newcastle to retire to his house near Durham and sit out the hostilities due to ill health. Instead, knowing he was mortally ill, he chose to leave life on his own terms, in the heat of battle. But that changed nothing for Nick.

Anger at his father for leaving him to take responsibility for the family at the age of twenty-two overwhelmed his grief. His stepmother stood with her children clustered around her. A clutch of ducklings dropped into a storm-tossed pond, their secure lives broken apart and looking to him to mend it all. The three youngest, wide-eyed and not understanding it all, the two older girls, eyes red from weeping.

It didn't help matters that his brother Henry, a man now at twenty-one, was there, steady as a rock, anchoring them. He could afford to be sanguine. He wasn't the one left to bear the burden of two estates and the security and prospects of five children and their mother whilst fighting a war.

And then there was the Covenant.

The secretive cabal to which his ancestors had bound the Tempest family and the weight of whose yoke now fell onto Nick's shoulders along with the rest.

Nick had seen the golden blond hair of the man he knew only as Gabriel, stark against the black he habitually wore and accompanied by a retinue that was clad as soberly as he was. He knew there was going to be a reckoning of some kind. For the man to come here from London on such short notice, through a country torn apart by conflict bespoke great need.

1

And Nick had no doubt that apart from the death of his father, the main topic of their conversation would be the fact that Nick had managed to misplace his wife.

That thought turned his guts. He had trusted Lieutenant Daniel Bristow with his life many times. Trusting him with bringing Lady Tempest from Howe in Weardale to Nick's new quarters in York had seemed no issue. But instead of escorting her, willing or reluctant, from Howe to York, Bristow and his men had vanished into thin air and so had Christobel.

Of course, when they failed to return Nick sent to Howe and was told that Lieutenant Bristow and his men had indeed arrived, stayed one night in mid-December and set out the next day with Lady Tempest. Nothing had been heard from them since. Had it been anyone else, Nick might even have been persuaded that they had been swept away in a torrent crossing a river or frozen to death in a snowdrift or been captured by the enemy.

But this was Danny Bristow. Nick had never met a more resourceful or capable man. He knew that no matter what might have befallen them, Bristow would have found a way through it—or a way to get word to him somehow. That it had now been over four months, told Nick he had been betrayed. Betrayed by the man he had trusted completely.

Worse still, Nick had been unable to do anything about it. He was at the disposal of William Cavendish, Earl of Newcastle and commander of the King's Army of the North, and it was the will of the earl that Sir Nicholas Tempest and his men remained to strengthen the York garrison.

Nick had spent a lonely Christmas in York.

Back then he had still nurtured a hope that Bristow might yet return. The months since had been trying at best and dull at worst. He had protested his confinement on more than one occasion. The last time he had been told it was his duty to help ensure the security of Her Majesty Queen Henrietta-Marie until passage south to her husband could be achieved in safety.

Meanwhile, the earl's army was active with the clever and experienced Lord Goring, winning battles at Seacroft and Tankersley, and Nick was left checking supplies, inspecting ditches and overseeing the training of recruits. Then came the news of his father's death and he and Henry had been granted the time to take his body back to Newhall, the Tempest family home. There to do what might be done, in the span of a few days, to set their family's affairs in order.

Those attending the funeral, thinned in ranks by the demands of war, left. Nick found himself unable to put off meeting with the Covenant man. It was in the same room where he and his father had met with the Covenant before, the grand parlour with its tall windows looking out over the grounds and the fields beyond. That time there had been two men, known to Nick as Michael and Gabriel. This time it was only Gabriel.

Henry appeared put out when Nick excluded him from the meeting saying it was private business. But, being Henry, he had gone to look to their stepmother and half-siblings with a modicum of good grace. Nick, bolstered by anger at his father's abandonment, went to face Gabriel alone.

He tried to be polite.

"I apologise for keep—"

"There is no need for niceties, and no time for them either," Gabriel interrupted him. "I'm required urgently in London, but have, perforce, to come here all because of one man's stubborn pride."

Nick blinked. "I have not been stub—"

"Not you," Gabriel snapped. "I was referring to Sir Richard Tempest."

"My father was always—"

"Well, that is the point of my visit."

Something in the strangeness of those words made Nick's blood run cold.

"What do you mean to imply, sir?" he demanded.

"I am implying nothing," Gabriel told him. "Why do you think it was so important to us that it was you and none other who wedded and bedded Christobel Lavinstock? Did you really think we cared if the ignoble and irrelevant house of Tempest climbed the steps of the throne?"

Nick was staring at the golden-haired man now, feeling as if someone had taken the floor from beneath his feet and left him tumbling.

"You need to speak plainly," he said, hearing his voice begin as a snarl but crack on the last word.

"Are you truly that much of a fool?" Gabriel sounded incredulous. "Sir Richard Tempest made a compact with the Covenant. On condition that it was never spoken of in his lifetime, he agreed to raise you as his own son."

Nick felt sick and dizzy. What was he saying? Did he mean…?

"But he always spoke to me of the family, of the future… Of the importance of blood..."

"Of course. How could he do otherwise? Besides, I think he'd convinced himself it would never need to come to light. Why do you think he was so keen to make an end to Sir Philip Lord and the Covenant?"

"But I look—"

"Like a Tempest?" Gabriel sounded contemptuous. "So has every Coupland for the last three generations. The Couplands and Tempests are so inbred as to be near incest. Your mother was a Coupland, in case you have forgotten."

It made no sense. Or perhaps it did. He was the one sent to live at Howe as a child, he was the one told of the Covenant, he was…

"And Henry?"

"Has been a useful stick to beat you with but he is a Tempest. When your father's will is examined, you will find he is to inherit Newhall here and all the unentailed Tempest lands on the sound basis that you already have Howe."

There was an odd twinge of relief in that. If Henry had Newhall, then most responsibility for their stepmother and her brood would fall to him also. But it was a small storm-blown rock of compensation in the sea of confusion.

"So who am I?" Nick asked. "Am I of…?" his mouth was suddenly too dry to speak.

"Of the bloodline?"

The bloodline. A bloodline that went back to Queen Mary and Philip of Spain and held the possibility of an alternative, legitimate monarch to the present Stuart dynasty whose right to rule was being challenged in this war. The bloodline the Covenant existed to protect and foster—or perhaps, more accurately in Nick's view, to exploit as best suited their ends. Except exploiting the man who embodied that bloodline today, Sir Philip Lord, had proved to be beyond their ability so far. Which was why they had tried with Christobel, Nick's missing wife, who was also of the bloodline if illegitimate.

"Am I?" he asked, his stomach tightening.

"No. Of course not," Gabriel sounded as if he thought the idea ridiculous. "No more than I am, or we would not need your wife, would we? Oh, do not fret, your name stays Tempest and will do unless times shall change."

"Then I don't understand—"

Nick had seen this man be even-tempered and moderate, even kind and condescending in the past. But now he was full of fury.

"You have no need to understand." Gabriel crossed to the window and looked through it. "Good God, I sometimes wonder if it is worth it."

It struck Nick then that this explained why his father—no, not his father—why Sir Richard had done what he had done at the end. Perhaps ashamed, unwilling to face Nick knowing he would soon learn the truth.

Gabriel was still talking. "You are a son of the Covenant. If you can show that you have the steel needed, there is a chance for you to advance your position, to take up your rightful place within our hierarchy."

Nick considered. He had learned to loathe the Covenant and its unholy grip on his life, had seen and felt the power these men could wield. But to be a part of it? To be one who wielded such power…?

He made his decision.

"What is it you want me to do?"

Chapter One

In over seven weeks since Sir Philip Lord married by church rites, he had spent less than five full days in the company of his wife. One of those was his wedding day itself.

Even given that these were far from normal times that seemed intolerable to Gideon. But then Sir Philip Lord was better known as the Schiavono, a mercenary commander whose name had resounded across the battlefields of Europe and the waters of the Mediterranean. War was his business and England was at war. That meant Sir Philip was fully engaged, helping to prosecute that war alongside Prince Rupert and Prince Maurice the king's nephews.

In stark contrast Gideon, though employed by Sir Philip, was a man of law. He had been a lawyer in London this time the previous year. Gideon Lennox, a well-thought-of and up-and-coming man. But circumstances had forced him to abandon his identity and become Gideon Fox, clerk and legal advisor to Sir Philip Lord.

At least that meant he was able to spend every day in the bittersweet company of the woman he loved. Zahara, companion and maid to Lord's wife. The bitterness came from knowing they might never be wed, for between them lay barriers of faith and history which seemed insurmountable. But for Gideon, and he hoped for Zahara, the sweetness of what they had was precious beyond price.

Perforce, he and Zahara had been close in recent weeks, as they shared just three rooms in Christ Church College in Oxford—and those three rooms were occupied by four other people. They were rooms granted by the king to Lord for his use and that of his household as he was a valued commander of the king's forces. The rooms were therefore home to Lady Catherine Lord and her small household, of which both Gideon and Zahara formed a part.

So did Shiraz, Zahara's self-appointed guardian since he had rescued her as a newly orphaned child from floods in the city of his name. As close to her as a brother and just as loyal to Sir Philip

Lord. He was Persian by birth and a man of some standing. Or he had been until he fell afoul of political enemies who had robbed him of his tongue. He still understood more languages than Gideon had ever learned and communicated fluently with his hands to those who understood that silent language. He was also deadly with sword and bow and was undoubtedly one of the most dangerous men Gideon had ever encountered.

The rooms were also presently home to Christobel, made Lady Tempest by her forced marriage, but who preferred to be simply Mistress Lavinstock. She had escaped to Oxford from Howe Hall in Durham, where her husband Sir Nicholas Tempest had held her prisoner.

Under Lady Catherine's benign rule, the household, though cramped, managed passably well day to day. The most menial tasks fell to their maidservant, Martha whilst Zahara had control over ensuring their needs from food to laundry were met. Shiraz was a silent presence, and often an absence, as his duty was to ensure their broader safety and his self-appointed task was to keep the horses they owned well exercised. Kate, as Lady Catherine wished Gideon to call her, often expressed the desire to be able to do so as well. However, an injury sustained from a bullet wound meant riding was no longer a safe possibility for her. But it was something Gideon and Christobel were both happy to assist with now and then.

Their main work, though, was in dealing with the news, intelligence and other communications which came to them in Oxford from various sources on behalf of Sir Philip and the Palatine princes. There were newspapers and pamphlets from London and abroad, letters addressed to Sir Philip from his far-flung network of correspondents, as well as encoded messages and other urgent communications carried by scouts, or smuggled to them from—and often by—Kate's spies, most of whom seemed to be women.

It meant that all of them, but Kate and Gideon in particular, spent much of their time reading, digesting, collating, deciphering and copying documents, assisted at need by some carefully selected clerks. A messenger was sent daily, sometimes twice in a day, bearing the fruit of their labour to where it was needed.

A few days after his wedding at the end of March, Sir Philip had left Oxford as part of Prince Maurice's command. With him went two men Gideon had come to view as friends: Daniel Bristow, Lord's Lieutenant Colonel, an expert in artillery, siegecraft and military engineering, and Major Anders Jensen, who was a Danish physician-surgeon. Behind them marched the men of Lord's mercenary company—now become Sir Philip Lord's regiments of horse and foot, under Captains Roger Jupp and Argall Greene.

They had orders to halt the advance of Sir William Waller, made Lord-General of Parliament's Western Association, who was seeking to fight through from his base in Bristol and join up with the Earl of Essex's forces presently advancing up the Thames Valley. Prince Rupert had set out around the same time to march north and secure the Midlands for the king and so prepare a way for the queen and her precious convoy of munitions to get through to Oxford from York.

Word reached Oxford that both princes had been successful. Rupert took Birmingham and Nantwich. Maurice, with Lord at his side, defeated Waller at Ripple. But then before their victories could be properly consolidated, both princes and their armies were summoned south again.

Reading had been besieged by Essex, placing Oxford itself under threat.

The need for speed meant that no reunion was possible then. Although Anders had come by with the reassuring news that all were well, and they would come as soon as Reading had been relieved.

But things hadn't quite worked out like that.

The governor of Reading, Sir Arthur Aston, had vowed he would hold the town to his final breath. However, he had been badly injured and the acting governor, Colonel Fielding, negotiated a truce. When the king and the princes arrived to attempt a relief, Fielding refused to break his given word and at the end of April, he surrendered the town regardless. So, far from returning, Sir Philip Lord and his men were kept busy for the next three weeks helping to secure the outlying defences left between Reading and Oxford.

"Meanwhile, in our absence, whilst we were busy not-relieving Reading, all our good work in the Welsh borders was undone. Hereford fell to Waller," Danny said ruefully.

They had just finished a meal celebrating the return of Lord and his men to Oxford and were receiving a first-hand account of the events they had so far only heard from the messengers.

"That's what comes of leaving a man like Lord Herbert in command," Lord said. "The man is useless. Just because your father is the Earl of Worcester does not mean you are a capable military commander."

"No," Kate agreed. "But when your father *is* the Earl of Worcester and is almost single-handedly funding the war effort thereabouts, providing both money and troops, then you can get away with just about anything."

"I offered to stay to give Herbert guidance and backbone," Lord said, picking up his cup from the table and taking a drink before going on. "Prince Maurice would have none of it, saying his brother wouldn't forgive him if he failed to return with me."

"So Herbert got the command," Danny told them. "And he didn't even wait for Waller to appear before running. The dust of our hooves must still have been within sight of the city defences when he was off like a hare. He claims he came here to Oxford to seek reinforcements and to appeal for more funds, even though he knew before he set out that we had been recalled precisely because there were none to be had. The craven left no one in Hereford with the rank and authority to organise a defence."

Lord shook his head at the folly of it all. "I am sure Sir Richard Cave tried. He is a damn good soldier. But you cannot defend a city with too few men when the citizens themselves have no will for any defence. And because he surrendered to save the town—a town he couldn't hold—Cave gets to be court-martialled and Herbert goes free of any blame." He sounded bitter.

"It is Herbert who should have been court-martialled. Waller only wanted to plunder Hereford anyway," Danny said. "He couldn't hold the place himself. We've already got it back."

"So now," Lord concluded, "Waller is sitting in Gloucester with three thousand men, all the wealth he has gathered and the munitions to both hold it and create havoc in the countryside about."

That was something Gideon could speak to. "It seems Waller might be planning to repeat what he did in Hereford at Worcester," he said, and Kate nodded.

"We've had several reports that strongly suggest as much," she said.

Lord inclined his head. "Reports, you will be pleased to hear, the king is taking seriously. Which is where we come in." He reached into his doublet and pulled out a folded paper, which he opened and spread on the table.

Gideon peered curiously at what clearly depicted a city, with the old walls and newer earthworks and fortifications marked and lines projecting where more might be built.

"The city of Worcester," Lord said. He tapped the map. "*The ditches must be deep; the counterscarps narrow and steep; the walls made high and broad...* This is a plan Danny has supplemented from his recent reconnaissance, to show both its existing defences and those which we will need to add. It is not an easy place to secure. There are hills here which could command the city if well used and it has no less than seven gates none of which are in good repair."

"*We* will need to add?" Christobel asked.

Lord favoured her with a smile and Gideon was reminded yet again of how similar they looked. "Indeed so."

"You are taking us on a military venture?" Christobel sounded doubtful.

"This will be an exercise in diplomacy and engineering as much as a military operation." Lord turned to Kate who was sitting beside him. "You may have encountered Sir William Russell who is presently here in Oxford?"

She nodded. "The Baronet of Whitely. A saturnine gentleman. One much concerned with his status and fierce for the king's cause. He all but lost his home at Strensham when Essex took and pillaged it to the bare walls, or so he tells anyone who will listen."

"I suspect he'll make up the loss somehow," Lord sounded unsympathetic. "He is High Sheriff of Worcestershire and Governor of Worcester. All the taxes and gifts collected to support the king's cause in the county will pass through his fingers." He refilled his cup and took another drink. "Russell is here both seeking reinforcements and to complain against one Colonel Samuel Sandys who has raised a regiment of foot for the defence of the city. It seems the two commanders mutually loathe and detest each other. So too do their men who have taken to fighting in the streets given the slightest provocation."

"We are sent as peacemakers to the warmongers?" Kate asked.

"We are sent with a list of tasks to accomplish. Including things as diverse as keeping the peace between those two factions, improving the defences, securing the city from Waller and expanding black powder production there."

"You have the authority? You are made governor?" Kate sounded suspicious, but then she knew Lord better than anyone.

"That is where we have to be diplomatic," Lord said. "The king is reluctant to remove the local men as he feels they command greater loyalty from the local people and have more chance of recruiting effectively as a result. So, for the time being, I am placed in the strange case of having authority from the king—and hopefully, *force majeure*—to compel Sandys' cooperation, but without actual rank or authority over him. Thankfully, Russell is being kept in Oxford for now so I will only have one of the two to dance with."

"Let me get this clear," the thread of anger in Kate's tone was marked. "You are made the unofficial advisor to the man who is the unofficial governor?"

Lord looked thoughtful then nodded.

"That about sums it up."

"Philip," Kate sounded aghast. "That is—"

"The king's command," Lord told her. "*But that the heavens appoint I must obey*."

"Even so," Anders said, in the silence that followed, "it is a bold mouse that makes her nest in a cat's ear."

"I am sure we will manage well enough," Lord said cheerfully. "If I had any doubt, I wouldn't be asking you all to come with me."

"Asking?" Danny feigned surprise. "Do you mean I could have declined your recent invitations to engage in mad dashes about the countryside at all hours, sleeping in ditches and dining on stale bread?"

Lord laughed. "You were not sleeping in a ditch at Tewksbury when Prince Maurice lauded you for your bridge of boats across the Severn. There was no stale bread on the table when we were feasted by the good people of Worcester after we saw off Waller at Ripple last month. There was claret, sack, white wine, meats..."

"That was last month," Danny protested. "Before the mess at Reading. And I very much deserved that after we chased down Hazlerigg's lobsters and slaughtered most of them. Besides, you forget that whilst you, the prince, Cave, Herbert and the rest were toasting each other's military prowess in claret and sack, I was going around the outskirts of Worcester, arguing with the utterly undelightful Dudd Dudley and making sketches and notes for him so he could take the credit for building *my* defences."

"A good job you did of it too," Lord told him. "Your talents would have been wasted at the celebration—no one could have given you a decent game of cards."

That made everyone laugh.

"When do we leave?" Zahara asked as the laughter subsided.

Lord smiled at her. "There are a few matters to arrange, but within a week."

Later, as Anders left for his own accommodation elsewhere in Oxford, Lord took Gideon to one side.

"I have recently learned that Sir Edward Kelley, his brother, Thomas, and their sister Lydia, were born and raised in Worcester. It is where both Lydia and Thomas were last known to be."

That was news indeed. Because Sir Philip Lord had not returned to England from the continental wars to fight in this one. He had returned to use the confusion of war to find proof, if it existed, of his birth and heritage.

He had been brought up under the control of a shadowy conspiracy, the Covenant. Their original grand design was to provide a legitimate ruler who could unite a Europe torn apart by religion. They even had a new vision of Christianity, Rosicrucianism, which they intended would heal the schism between Catholics and Protestants.

Those plans had long since floundered. But the Covenant endured, striving to promote its power and seeing in this civil war their chance to take control of England. They believed they could offer Parliament an alternative monarch, one with a pedigree that could displace the Stuarts. But for that, they needed either Lord himself. Or Christobel, who looked so like Sir Philip with the same white hair and turquoise eyes that she was surely his close relation.

Lord had been taught he was the descendant of a bloodline which had begun with Queen Mary Tudor and Philip of Spain. He was the man they would make king. But Lord had made it clear more than once that he only wished to know who his parents were.

A series of clues led Lord and Gideon from a secret chamber in Howe Hall in County Durham, where Lord had spent his childhood, to another in a house in Mortlake where he had been born. That house had once belonged to Dr John Dee, the man who seemed to be a founder of the Covenant. But there the trail had ended except for the existence of a partially destroyed genealogy which gave the name of the woman who might be Lord's mother, Madinia, and her date of birth in fifteen ninety, making it very possible she might still be alive. But there had also been some evidence that perhaps the family of Sir Edward Kelley, who had once scried for Dee, might yet hold the documents Lord sought.

"You think the Kelleys still live?" Gideon asked.

"They would be in their seventies or eighties," Lord admitted. "But it is not an impossibility. When we get to Worcester, I will need you to see what you can find. My hands will be tied by the work I must do."

Three days later they left Oxford, making the sixty-mile journey in easy stages, slowed by their baggage and small artillery train. It was coming towards the end of May, roads were drier and travel less difficult even for the heavy wheeled vehicles they escorted.

Worcester was a fine city on the banks of the River Severn, with the prominent tower of its cathedral dominating the place and a largely broken castle beside it. Within the walls and recent earthworks it had well-set houses and flourishing businesses.

They were met at the Sidbury Gate by the acting governor, Colonel Samuel Sandys. He was a tall gentleman in his late twenties, with strikingly blond hair and nut-brown eyes. His whole demeanour betrayed that he regarded the new arrivals as an unnecessary imposition and a slight to his own ability. However, upon seeing the king's warrant which Lord produced, he reluctantly agreed to their making an entrance, on the condition that he and his men led the way.

To Gideon, they looked like sparrows heralding peacocks.

The orderly ranks of Lord's foot and horse were clad in uniform blue and grey coats. The horse proudly followed an azure banner with a white cat's head looking out of it. The infantry, bearing muskets, marched behind a large flag with the same blazon. The thump and tuck of the drums kept the soldiers in step and the sharp notes of a fife played a melody that was both jaunty and yet menacing. The tune they played was officially called 'Sir Philip Lord's March' though Gideon had heard the men refer to it with the kind of jesting affection they held towards their commander and paymaster, as 'The Schiavono's Strut'.

At their head was Sir Philip himself. He was resplendent in azure silk threaded through with silver and decorated with silver braid and gemstone adorned points. The lace of his collar was white cotton, and his hair was just as white in the spring sunshine, where it emerged from beneath a broad-brimmed blue hat with a white feather. His armour was polished to gleam, from breastplate to tassets and his silver-spurred boots were of white leather as were his gloves, upon which glittered more silver and flashes of blue.

Gideon could admire Lord's appearance at close quarters because he rode just behind him. Danny, clad in a humbler version of the same outfit, was beside Gideon, with a broad grin splitting his freckled face.

"We *do* look *gorgeous*," he enthused as they marched along Sidbury, passing fine and prosperous-looking buildings and being watched from their windows by fine and prosperous-looking people. "Silver threaded samite and sapphires. The good citizens of Worcester must surely be won over. They are a city of drapers, clothiers and glove-makers after all. You can see them all pricing up his outfit—and that's before they even *glance* at his horse."

Danny had a point. Dazzling as was his dress, the horse was worth many times the value of Sir Philip Lord's clothes. A cremello stallion of fine Italian stock, a gift from the king, battle-trained and hardened, as much a weapon of war as a means of transport. Hooves lifting in a proud gait, neck curved, and head held back, the creature was truly magnificent.

But to Gideon's mind, those of the citizenry of Worcester who had turned out to watch the display Lord was providing, were not looking all that impressed or even friendly. They undoubtedly held a grudging admiration in their collective gaze, but then they were maybe more used to seeing men in ill-assorted items of clothing carrying anything from a billhook to a fowling piece marching as soldiers.

Gideon looked back as they turned the corner, past where Roger Jupp held his place as Captain of the horse, beyond Argall Greene's infantry, to the small, spring-slung coach which had recently been repainted in Sir Philip Lord's livery and in which sat Kate and Christobel, with Martha. Behind the coach, he caught a glimpse of a face that lifted his heart. Sitting on the pillion of a powerful black gelding ridden by Shiraz, was Zahara, her apricot hair secreted beneath a tightly set coif and a lappet cap. Beside the black gelding, Gideon recognised his own little chestnut mare, now lent on a permanent basis to Anders who rode her. After them, came a collection of women and children who belonged with the soldiers and at the rear of their procession, a selection of field artillery, carts and wagons, with its escort of infantry armed with flintlocks to avoid the fire hazard of matchlocks near supplies of black powder.

The baggage train also carried tents that Lord had brought with them so that there would be no immediate demands on the city for the quartering and support of his troops. There was an open space called the Pitchcroft to the north of the city beside the River Severn where musters and other public events took place which Gideon knew, from conversations on the march from Oxford, Lord intended his regiment to occupy. But first, they needed to make themselves known both to the people of Worcester and to its existing garrison and high command.

Their arrival had been orchestrated by Lord to make an impression of his authority, grandeur and the discipline of his men, upon the people of Worcester. Gideon was sure that after months of military occupation by troops from both sides, the city was not going to be throwing open its arms to any new soldiers who arrived.

"They should like us more than the other lot," Danny said as if reading his thoughts.

"Which other lot?" Gideon was confused. "You mean Russell's and Sandy's men?"

"Those too, I'm sure. After all, we're so much prettier." Danny grinned and fluttered his eyelashes. "But I meant they should like us more than Parliament's soldiers. Last autumn Essex occupied the city and let his troops behave very badly. They smashed up the cathedral and treated the town as malignants. All our side has done is demand money with menaces. We're *much* nicer to them."

"I can't think they will appreciate our presence as anything save an extra burden," Gideon said. "They already have troops billeted on them." He was wondering how much the people of Worcester had been called upon to pay at a time when their trade would be severely restricted by the stringencies of the war.

"Gentlemen," Lord's voice held admonishment. "Let us save our opinions for private moments and present a smiling beatitude as our public face."

Chastised, but not even slightly subdued, Danny continued grinning. To Gideon's amusement, he took to responding to the cold stares with a gracious bow of his head and swept off his hat most gallantly to a pair of elderly ladies who seemed to be particularly disapproving of this invasion of their city.

They continued their circuit of the streets. Led off by a handful of Sandy's men, the baggage train and artillery left by the Water Gate to establish their camp on the Pitchcroft. The coach and its outriders, including Shiraz and Anders, continued to follow the troops. Having completed a loop about the city, they turned

16

through a gate to the cathedral. There Lord's men formed into disciplined ranks behind their commander. Lord waited until all were in place then made a gracious bow to Colonel Sandys, lifting his voice so it would reach the crowd of citizens who had assembled.

"Colonel Sandys. His majesty bade me commend you on the excellent work you have been doing here on his behalf in prosecuting his cause and helping to protect the city. I believe the people of Worcester are blessed in having your service."

But Sandys' expression remained tight. Gideon had the distinct impression that the acting governor was not in any way mollified by the excess of praise even if offered so publicly. Lord turned his attention to the crowd itself.

"True, loyal and faithful people of Worcester, your devotion to your king is rewarded by his devotion to the safety and security of your homes and families. He has sent to you myself and my men to assist Colonel Sandys, bolster your defences and help ensure that none of your fine buildings within the walls will be made to suffer as your beautiful cathedral was made to suffer."

"I wonder," Danny said in a low voice pitched for Gideon's ears only, "how he plans to break it to them that we will, however, be demolishing some of those fine buildings that are *without* the walls?"

Whether Lord heard or not, he didn't show it, his focus still on the small crowd, his voice lifting easily to reach them.

"I am not going to ask that you open your homes to my men here, we have brought our own accommodation with us. I am not going to ask that you pay more money for our support, as long as you are paying your due assessment you already contribute heroically to the support of his majesty's armies. My only request is that you are willing to give of your time and effort if we need to call upon you, to help improve and extend your defences so that the city will be kept safe from all who might covet it."

"He makes it sound so easy," Danny murmured. "You can be sure upon whose shoulders will fall the main work of those defences and it won't be Dudd Dudley."

Gideon frowned. It was the second time Danny had mentioned the name. Lord was still talking, saying things about cooperation and unity.

"Who is Dudd Dudley?"

Danny rolled his eyes heavenwards.

"You may regret asking that question because now I feel duty-bound to introduce you to the man, and that is something that, under other circumstances, our friendship would have prevented. Remember, you have brought it upon yourself."

Lord had finished speaking, if not on a rousing note, then one of sufficient enthusiasm that the crowd gave a muted cheer. Then he made a slight gesture with one hand and the tuck of the drums started again followed after a few beats by the fifes playing his march, and the infantry and most of the cavalry headed back along the street to follow the baggage train out onto Pitchcroft. A group of eight of the cavalry remained formed up about the coach.

As the crowd drifted away, Lord spoke to Sandys who was sitting stiffly on his horse as if stuck to the saddle by a spear down his spine.

"I thank you for that, colonel, it is not easy to stand by when another seems to take your place. I promise you I'm not here to do so. I wanted this to be presented to the people as being under your auspices—you are the acting governor, and I am merely here to give strength to your hand. My purpose was to make the nature of that strength apparent to all."

"I don't understand why the king even sent you here." Sandys frowned. "Did Russell– ?"

Lord spoke firmly across him.

"I assure you Sir William made no complaint to which his majesty has given ear. But he did ask for men to help protect the city. My scouts encountered evidence of pillaging raids from Waller's force on our way here and local people tell me he has sent men as close as Powick."

Sandys' jaw tightened.

"I'm fully aware of the danger to the city and have put all in order." Then he frowned. "You've set your men to camp on the Pitchcroft. Surely they will be vulnerable there?"

18

"That is why I have placed them there for now," Lord said. "It is to show the city how much confidence I have in its security."

"But if Waller should attack then—"

"Then my scouts will let us know and my men will move within the walls. Since Waller will come from the south there will be time to do so. Meanwhile, we must work on improving the defences, so my confidence is not seen to be misplaced."

"Improve the defences?" Sandys bridled. "We've spent a fortune modernising them. Colonel Dudley has assured me that they are comparable to the best to be found in Europe."

Danny gave a whoop of laughter and then tried to pretend he had a coughing fit instead.

"I am sure Colonel Dudley will have made good use of the funds the city provided," Lord said, his tone tactful. "My own engineer will further reinforce what has been done."

There was a grudging silence from Sandys. "I'll arrange accommodation for you. Evict one of the more prominent citizens who has been less than forthcoming with their assessments."

"I have no wish to inconvenience any citizen here needlessly," Lord assured him. "I have seen several inns and I'm sure one will be suitable to host myself and my household."

Sandys looked surprised.

"I—" He started, then stopped himself and inclined his head. "Our experience of professional soldiers here hasn't been—" He stopped and coloured as if suddenly aware he was insulting the man sent by the king.

"This is England," Lord said. "I try to fight gently here."

Gideon wondered that the irony was not obvious to Sandys, but the man just nodded as if he took the words at face value.

"Then I would recommend The Talbot, or there is The Cardinal's Hat, which is where we often hold our committee meetings. They are close by, and both are large and comfortable establishments."

Having inspected both, Lord settled on The Talbot. The sight of gold coin secured the goodwill of the host, and they settled in.

Chapter Two

Gideon wasn't surprised to find he was sharing accommodation with Danny but, much as he liked Lieutenant Colonel Daniel Bristow, he was not an easy man to share a room with. He fought a nightly battle with sleep and was inclined to try and recruit any about him in that cause to play cards or dice until the candle had burned down.

But before Danny even had a chance to see the room they were to share, Lord summoned him for a private talk. When he joined Gideon there a short time later, he was looking thoroughly subdued.

"It seems my sense of humour wasn't appreciated," he said by way of explanation. "I am forgiven, though. Our commander and his lady have been invited to supper with Sandys, his wife and some senior officers. You, me and Anders get to go too."

Gideon had been hoping to spend time with Zahara, but when he suggested as much as they were about to depart, Lord insisted.

"We need to impress," Lord said. "My bringing two professional men of indubitable probity will achieve that." He had changed his clothes and now wore crimson and white, which matched the robe Kate was wearing as he handed her into the coach. Then he turned and pulled a folded document from his doublet. "And Danny, I have this for you."

Gideon could see Prince Rupert's signature on it and Danny's expression shifted as he unfolded it and read the text.

"I am made General of the Ordnance for the City of Worcester and a full colonel?" He frowned at Lord. "What's this about?"

"I insisted as that was the only way to be sure Dudd Dudley couldn't override you. Now you are his equal in military rank and in overall control of the guns and defences here. I'm sure he will argue that point, but he has to listen to you."

"I don't think he would care if I were a major general," Danny said.

"No. But this means he won't be able to dismiss what you say."

"We could just ignore him completely." Danny had a wistful note in his voice.

"He is General of Ordnance for Prince Maurice," Lord said, impatience in his tone. "So no, you cannot and must not ignore him completely." He ended the conversation by getting into the coach after Kate and closing the door.

"I don't think it would be possible anyway," Danny said ruefully as he rode with Gideon and Anders behind the coach. "Dudd is the kind of man it's impossible to ignore. For a baron's bastard, he has an excessively high opinion of himself."

"That is the tragedy of his condition," Anders observed. "The nobler the blood, the less the pride. A man who is base born will always feel the need to demand respect and will run much faster and further than most to obtain it. It is not an easy life for such a man."

"Perhaps," Danny said, his sympathy clearly not engaged. "But I don't see why that means the rest of us have to suffer as well."

The Sandys had a pleasant house within the cathedral precincts and not far from The Talbot. They made an impressive arrival. Kate descended from the coach, skirts unfolding elegantly about her and walked into the house, looking queenly on Lord's arm. Danny and Anders followed, both holding military rank and dressed appropriately, and Gideon—a mere civilian—brought up the rear in more sober, professional, garb.

Inevitably it was a predominantly male gathering. Gideon tried to line up names and faces, but of the ten or so men there, only a couple stayed in his mind. One was Martin Sandys, brother to the acting governor who was only eighteen but already colonel of the city militia. He kept glaring at Gideon as if taking offence at his presence. The other was Dudd Dudley, who had the loudest voice, the loudest laugh and the most to say of anyone there. It wasn't hard to see why Danny despised him.

There were two women present aside from Kate. The older of the two, in her mid-twenties, was Sandys' wife Mary. Gideon found himself sitting beside the younger. A petite and slender woman in her late teens, introduced as Mistress Ursula Markham a cousin of Mary Sandys. Gideon realised that the reason the younger Colonel Sandys was casting hostile looks was that he coveted the place beside Mistress Markham. She on the other hand was cool towards Martin Sandys putting her shoulder towards him as much as she could.

Tired from the journey, resentful that he was sitting beside the wrong woman, irritated that yet again he was being introduced by his nom-de-guerre of Gideon Fox rather than by his true name of Gideon Lennox, and with scant interest in adding to the talk flowing about him anyway, Gideon restricted himself to the minimum conversation politeness would allow.

From the opening sallies which eulogised the king, something Gideon found difficult to agree or approve, to a discussion of the tactics that had won the battle at Ripple about which he knew nothing, the talk moved onto the construction of the defences. At which point Dudd Dudley became even louder and more self-adulating, whilst Danny could be seen visibly biting his tongue under a Baltic glare from Lord.

"We're fortunate that the garrison has the support of many of the citizens here," Sandys said then smiled at Gideon's neighbour. "Mistress Markham has been doing sterling work in motivating the wives and daughters of Worcester to assist the men in their travail."

Ursula Markham smiled but didn't blush at being singled out. She had been talking to Kate for much of the meal and Gideon had heard her express some forthright opinions.

"I try my best," she said. "Digging ditches is hard work and the least we women can do is help out with fetching and carrying to support the men."

"It's also most excellent for morale," Sandys added. "Before the women began going to the earthworks it was difficult to persuade the soldiers that it was part of their work to dig. Having the women there encourages them to do so most enthusiastically."

"If you would allow it, Mistress Markham," Kate put in, "the women of Sir Philip Lord's regiment would be most pleased to join your ranks. Most are quite experienced in supporting such work."

Which Gideon knew to be an understatement. He wouldn't be surprised if collectively the regiment's women could design, dig and even defend such fortifications too.

"I'd be delighted to have their assistance, Lady Catherine." Ursula Markham smiled at Kate and then her lips tightened. "You see, sadly not all the women who would like to help us can do so. Some husbands and fathers have strong opinions that women shouldn't be doing such work."

"You speak of Nehemiah Fisher?" Sandys sounded contemptuous. "The man is a Puritan of the worst kind. Not only must his own soul be spotless, but he must compel others to polish theirs to his satisfaction. I can't abide the man. I find I agree with Middleton: *I'll sooner expect mercy from a usurer when my bond's forfeited, sooner kindness from a lawyer when my money's spent, nay, sooner charity from the devil than good from a Puritan.*"

There was laughter from around the table and Gideon studied his plate.

"But Reverend Fisher always has a full congregation to hear his sermons," Martin Sandys said. "There are those in the city who are not fully committed to the king's cause, and most are of Fisher's congregation."

"They are but of the middle rank of people," Dudd scoffed. "None of any power or eminence takes their part."

That was met with more nods from most about the table.

"Indeed, individually they have little voice," Mary Sandys said, her own voice quiet. "But the city is strong in trade. If you look at who sits on the council most are of that middle sort, our clothiers, hosiers, glove makers…" She trailed off clearly aware her view wasn't being well received.

"The council is under the dominion of the Commissioners, indeed one or two of them even sit on it," one of the bluff officers said, his tone dismissive. "Besides, they know better than to try and cause any problems. Even Fisher is careful to trim his sails to our wind. As Dudley said, middling people of little account."

"I believe Mistress Sandys makes an important point," Lord said. "The city's wealth is in the hands of those middling men and if we wish to keep that wealth flowing to our support it is not wise to ignore them."

Dudd Dudley coughed loudly and cleared his throat.

"I would have thought you of all men would be master of ensuring the reluctant open their purses, Sir Philip. Weren't you once a pirate?"

There was an awkward silence in the wake of his words, Danny gave an audible groan and Lord smiled.

"In my youth, I was many things," he agreed. "However, I strive to ensure my men are supplied from above not from below."

"Well, I hope you haven't lost the ability to squeeze gold and silver from the recalcitrant," Dudley ploughed on. "I've not been paid for the last shipment of ordnance I made to Sir William." He glared at Samuel Sandys as if it was his responsibility.

Lord tapped his glass with one finger.

"If money due is unpaid I will certainly help collect it," he said. "I will also visit the leading citizens and speak to them about the importance of their contribution to fund strong defences. Even those who are not our ardent supporters must remember how they were treated when the Earl of Essex came to visit."

Mercifully, it was not long after that the evening came to a close and they were preparing to make the short journey back to the inn.

"I swear I'll kill him," Danny muttered loudly enough for Anders and Gideon to hear. They were waiting for Lord who had been held back by their host.

"I know the herb patience does not grow in every man's garden," Anders said, "but our commander is not delaying our return deliberately. I am sure he wishes to be gone to his bed too."

Gideon saw from the glint in Anders' eye that he knew the real target of Danny's chagrin, but Danny himself was too caught up in his ire to realise he was being teased.

"God no, not Philip. As ever he was approaching sainthood in his equanimity and tolerance. I mean that bastard Dudd Dudley. He turns my nerves into lute strings and knows exactly which to pluck to rile me—and takes pleasure from the doing. He found every way he could to cast aspersions on my ability whilst assuring everyone of his own extreme competence. He even claimed my designs as his own and the idea is now so rooted in the opinion of those men that to disavow it would make it look as if *I* were the one trying to steal another man's work."

"You worry too much, my friend," Anders assured him. "The whole world can see what kind of man Dudley is."

"Except the whole world doesn't have to work with him. I do."

Lord emerged from the house and climbed into the coach beside Kate. A few minutes later they were back at the inn and handing off their mounts to the stable boys there.

As they were heading into the building, Lord intercepted them.

"Danny, your card game will have to wait and Gideon, you will have to contain your desire to see Zahara a little longer. There is something important I need to share with you both that I had from Sandys."

Anders gave them a smile of sympathy and left for the room he was sharing with Shiraz. Gideon envied him. Already tired, after talking to Lord it would be too late to find Zahara.

"Is there wine?" Danny asked, hopefully.

"There is wine," Lord assured him, propelling them both towards the stairs. "But for the love of God, you may not try and persuade Kate into a game of Piquet."

Perhaps fortunately, Kate had already retired into the closed curtains of her bed, so Lord picked up the wine and cups and carried them through to the room Gideon and Danny were sharing. There he poured the wine and served them himself.

Danny sat on the tester bedstead and took a drink. Then he lay back across the bed, the wine cup set on his ribs held from tipping by the fingers of one hand. "So what did Sandys have to say that is so important?"

"There is someone well placed in the city who is working for Parliament."

Danny sat up, lifting the wine cup as he did so and managing not to spill so much as a drop in the movement. "It's a city. You can't hide the troop numbers or the defences from anyone in it. Any carter going in and out with eyes to see and ears to listen would know—and Waller has likely sent people in as well."

"That's not what Sandys is concerned about."

25

"He has other plans brewing," Gideon suggested. "Less public plans?"

"Yes. It seems the king has 'other plans' which Sandys has been charged to carry out—plans his majesty didn't trust Sir William Russell to see through." Lord picked up his glass and sipped the wine. "Before we left Oxford the prince told me that Russell was something of an agitator in the past—ten years ago he stirred up riots against the disafforestation of some land the king sold. The king is not a man to forget such things. He might trust Russell to keep Worcester, but he prefers to look to men he sees as more reliable for anything sensitive. That's why Sir William has been encouraged to remain in Oxford until this matter is settled. Details of things such as sorties and the movements of troops and supplies, which have only been known about by the governing council here in Worcester, seem to be getting to Waller. Either that or he is disturbingly good at guessing the times and places they will be."

"Movements will be known about from elsewhere," Gideon pointed out. "They take organisation—planning."

Both Danny and Lord looked at him as if he was missing the obvious.

"Let me give you a simple example," Lord said. "We travelled from Oxford with no attempted attack from Waller though had he known we were there, he could have intercepted us with three thousand men. Our presence was—deliberately—not advertised in advance. No one here knew we were coming until just before we arrived. On the other hand, a shipment of cannonballs was attacked and diverted by a strong force from Waller and the organisation of that was done here in Worcester."

"So where do we come in?" Danny asked.

"We come in as outsiders with no local prejudices. You and I get the delight of investigating the senior officers, no doubt with help from Kate." He shifted his gaze to meet Gideon's. "You may recall Edward Blake?"

It would be hard to forget the man who had been Prince Rupert's clerk. He had been a Parliamentarian spy, instrumental in the capture of Kate by Essex and her gaining the injury that meant she could now no longer run and ride as she once had.

"You think Sandys' man of letters is the traitor?" Gideon asked.

"He'd be well placed to be so as he clerks for the committee as well. A man called David Collins. You can talk to him and see." Lord hesitated before going on. "There is another investigation I want you to take on as well."

"Which is?"

"Whoever our traitor is, they will be part of a wider group. There are many malcontents here in Worcester. The spiritual needs of that community are undoubtedly being met by the Reverend Nehemiah Fisher. Your father was, as you tell it, a man of similar passions so you should not find it difficult to persuade Fisher that you adhere to his views."

Gideon was so shaken by the demand he answered before measured reflection could prevent him from doing so. "You expect me to feign my beliefs? To pretend to accept a view of God that I don't hold? It is one thing to practise deceit in worldly matters but in matters of faith I—"

"I'm not asking you," Lord said curtly. "I'm giving you an order."

His tone and assumption were fuel to Gideon's outrage. "You cannot demand that of me. I will investigate Collins, but I draw the line at such pretence with Reverend Fisher."

Gideon set his jaw, meeting Lord's glare with determination and aware that Danny was looking between them with an expression of intense curiosity. Lord let out his breath in a sharp sigh.

"A man of principle is a dangerous creature. Very well. Someone else shall take on Reverend Fisher. Someone more sure of the unblemished sanctity of their soul and less concerned by whatever outward mumblings might be made around it." He drained his cup and put it down then strode the few paces to the door. "Goodnight, gentlemen."

The door was closed behind him before either could respond and Danny turned to Gideon, eyes wide.

"You said 'no' and yet you still stand there untouched and not struck down. I am impressed and doubly so." Danny swept into a deep bow as he spoke. "You have my profound respect. Had it been me, he would have turned me off in the instant. He has done so in the past. More than once. What is your secret?"

Gideon found his throat constricting with an unknown emotion. "It's no jest," he said. "It's a matter of conscience."

Danny's expression changed. "I don't recall saying I thought it a jest. But bear in mind Philip was raised to see all kinds of religion as part of the same faith. He sometimes forgets others mark clear divisions between Lutheran, Laudian, Calvinist and Catholic. If you'll take my advice, walk softly for a few days and don't mention this ever again. Especially not in front of anyone else. Philip will tolerate anything from his friends, except humiliation."

That was the thought Gideon carried to bed. Unsurprisingly, Danny was suddenly no longer interested in sleep and took himself off to try and find someone to play cards with despite the lateness of the hour. Lying in the dark, after his prayers had been murmured to the night but before sleep claimed him, Gideon wondered why no mention had been made of the other reason for their being in Worcester. Investigating Parliamentarian spies was one thing, but wasn't he supposed to be looking for the Kelleys?

He woke to find Danny sitting on the far side of the bed and pulling on his boots, presumably having returned at some point in the night and slept.

"Zahara was asking for you." Danny greeted him cheerfully. "I think she was going with Shiraz to the camp to bring the women to help with the defences. With any luck, their presence will get more volunteers out and digging."

That was all the incentive Gideon needed to be up and dressed in a couple of minutes. When he got to the common room, Danny had already gone, but Zahara was still getting ready to leave. He presumed Shiraz would be seeing their black gelding saddled and setting the pillion seat. Zahara smiled as he reached her, and the shadows of the previous evening were scattered from Gideon's spirit as clouds chased away by the sun.

"I am glad you are up before I need to go," she said, rising to greet him and taking both his hands in hers, a gesture he knew was as intimate to her as if they kissed. "It is fortunate I was delayed.

28

Martha was nervous and unused to the finery she was wearing today to go out with Lady Catherine and the Schiavono."

Gideon barely heard the words, holding her hands and revelling in her smile.

"May I go with you?" he asked.

Her smile grew warmer. "Of course. If you have the time." Then her expression changed, and her brows drew into a frown of concern.

"You are troubled," she said, and it was not a question. "Something has happened that has disturbed you."

Gideon tightened his hands briefly on hers and then released them. How could he explain to Zahara, whose religion was not even Christian, what he had refused Lord and why?

"It is something between you and the Schiavono," she divined. "He was in a short temper this morning until Lady Catherine spoke with him after which he seemed much restored. You should talk to the Schiavono once your anger and upset have faded. He will listen."

Gideon could say nothing to that. Yes, Lord would listen—if Gideon were offering an apology or bending to his will. He was spared having to muster a reply by the unexpected arrival of Christobel, dressed modestly, her hair hidden as tightly as Zahara's under a coif with a plain bonnet and collar.

She greeted Gideon before turning to Zahara. "We should go if you're ready."

Zahara nodded and touched Gideon lightly on his arm.

"We have an escort as well," she said.

Christobel looked as if she might object, then smiled.

"Of course, if you have the time to spare whilst we go shopping."

Gideon was confused now.

"Danny said you were going to the camp to engage the women in helping with the defences."

Zahara laughed.

"I did that as soon as I had finished my prayers. Shiraz took me. And Brighid will be bringing the women, or already has, to meet with Mistress Markham and the women of the town who are willing to help."

29

"Then where are you going now?"

Christobel exchanged glances with Zahara.

"I have some business to see to," Christobel said. "But you are welcome to accompany us to explore the shops here first. That would be most helpful. Then you can excuse yourself and we will go on."

Curiosity urged him to ask what it was they were intending to do, but politeness restrained him. He presumed it would be something acutely feminine or they would be content for him to remain in their company.

They spent a pleasant hour looking at the business side of Worcester. Christobel, he knew from experience, had a solid head for good value and quality, and bargained determinedly with a draper to place orders for some cloth. Zahara admired a pair of gloves with such delight that Gideon waited until she was distracted and then purchased them, hiding them in his coat and surprising her with them when they had walked on.

Worcester was a very different city from London.

It was nowhere as big, but like London, it had the river and was a port, with boats taking and receiving trade from the coast at Bristol. The streets were clean, and the houses were well-built. Some had escaped beyond the boundary of the city walls, a mark of how long England, here and further south, in particular, had known peace. The Scots might regularly invade and harry the north of the nation and unwalled coastal communities might endure raids, but a city such as Worcester had not required that its citizens be restricted to its defensive perimeter for over a century. Gideon wondered how much of that expansion Danny would be able to protect with his defences and how many homes might be left to the chances of war or even demolished to ensure the security of the city.

"I so hope this war will be over soon." Christobel might have been reading his thoughts as they walked along the street. "But whichever side wins, there's a generation of anger and hate being fired in this forge, I cannot see that passing tamely into history."

"Wars never pass tamely into history," Zahara said, her voice quiet. "They leave scars in the souls of those who have suffered them. Like the fights between children, pitiless and contemptible, for little reason and less gain."

"Oh, there's always gain," Christobel retorted. "If there was no gain then wars wouldn't happen. The point is, surely, that the amount of gain to the victor is invariably less than the destruction it leaves in its wake."

"And what is the gain of this war?" Zahara asked, her tone holding a real curiosity.

Christobel shrugged. "As I see it, this war is the king and his wealthy men, against parliament and its wealthy men, fighting for who between them holds which reins of power. The gain to the victor is in deciding how we worship, how we are taxed and what that money is spent on."

Gideon found himself staring at Christobel with his mouth slightly agape. He had become used to her plain-speaking and frequently scathing humour over the last few weeks, but this was different. She was putting forward a view he had heard spoken only by the most extreme of his London friends.

She caught his look and heaved a sigh. "I mean it is a war in which the just and fair rule of the king is being threatened by the arrogance and overweening ambition of a parliament seeking to usurp his divine mandate."

Zahara laughed and covered her mouth quickly.

"But you stay with Sir Philip Lord," Gideon pointed out. "He makes his living from war."

"We women cannot change the world," Christobel said. "We can only live in it as it is arranged by men. I have no one else who will protect me from the man who forced me into marriage, so what right do I have to judge my benefactor?"

It was an increasingly uncomfortable conversation and Gideon was glad when a few minutes later, Christobel and Zahara made their farewells, going off in the direction of the market cross. It was broad daylight, both were plainly dressed, and many women were out with just a female servant to attend them, so Gideon pushed down his concern at the two being unprotected and found himself reflecting uneasily on the truth in Christobel's words.

He made his way back through the town, intending to call on Colonel Sandys to see if he could gain an introduction to David Collins. The Sandys had a house on the Cathedral Close and as Gideon walked into the cathedral precincts, he heard a low groan as if a man was in extreme pain. The sound came from the other side of the wall that protected the private grounds of one of the houses.

The sound came again, and Gideon crossed quickly to look over the wall which reached his shoulders. A man crouched on the grass beneath an ornamental tree that grew beside the wall further along from where Gideon stood. Then he saw that sprawled on the grass under the tree was a woman and the man's hands were at her throat. The woman was Ursula Markham. She lay as if thrown there, discarded, her clothes awry and her head at an unnatural angle, her murderer still holding her by the neck.

Gideon had no conscious awareness of scaling the garden wall before he was over it and running, drawing his sword as he did so. He could feel his teeth bared in a feral snarl, but it was only as he reached the dead woman, he recognised the man who had been crouched beside her and was now on his feet. Colonel Martin Sandys, the younger brother of Samuel.

Sandys reacted to Gideon's charge too late and tried to pull his sword free then changed his mind and started to run. But Gideon was faster. Before they had reached halfway to the house, he caught Sandys and forced him to the ground, the point of his blade pressing to the young man's ribs through his clothes. This was the lure of wild justice, of settling a score with his own hands. It took him considerable effort to hold himself back from completing the thrust and running the man through.

"You will hang for what you've done," he snarled.

Martin Sandys was shaking his head, his eyes wide with fear and another emotion that Gideon struggled to reconcile with what he had seen.

"I didn't kill her. I would never hurt Ursula. Never." He sounded vehement, but Gideon had met many who protested innocence whilst harbouring guilt.

32

They must have been seen from the house because several men came running out and Gideon realised then, swiftly but belatedly, that this was Sandys' home. And in any confrontation, Sandys' men would, inevitably, take his part against Gideon. Stepping back, he put up his sword and saw with relief that amongst those coming towards him was Sir Philip Lord as well as Samuel Sandys.

It was Samuel Sandys who spoke, frowning at Gideon.

"You can explain yourself. Holding my brother at sword point. What is this argument about?" Then he looked at Martin and his lips tightened. "This is not some affair of honour over a woman, is it?" From his tone, Gideon gathered that if it had been so, then it wouldn't have been the first.

"In a manner of speaking it is," Gideon said tightly.

"Then you most certainly do need to explain yourself," Lord spoke softly but a cold shiver touched Gideon's spine.

"Mistress Markham is dead," he said, hearing the bleakness in his own voice. There were audible gasps from most present. Lord's eyes widened as if in sudden understanding. "She lies at the back of this garden, close by the wall. I came past to call on Colonel Samuel Sandys and I saw this man crouched down beside her body, his hands still on her broken neck."

Martin Sandys struggled to his feet. "That isn't true. I didn't harm her. I found her lying there. I was trying to wake her. I just bent to shake her shoulders, but… but she… she was…" he concluded with a dry gulp and covered his face with his hands.

Lord's expression was now speculative.

"Is that a possibility?" he asked his gaze on Gideon.

What could he say to that? Of course, it was a possibility. Except that wasn't how it had seemed at the time. But then, at the time, he had been inflamed with truly feral rage.

"His hands were on her neck."

"You must believe me," Sandys protested, turning to his brother with a look of appeal.

"I think, before any of this goes further, we should see if Mistress Markham is where these men tell us she is," Lord said, asserting his authority. "And whether she is indeed dead." He gestured to Gideon. "Fox, show us where she lies. Colonel Sandys will remain here with his brother's men. As he asserts his innocence, he will not flee. To do so would be to condemn himself."

Gideon led the way. Ursula Markham was as he had seen her before. As Lord and Samuel Sandys stood grim-faced, he answered questions in a monotone, his emotions caught like a lump in his guts.

"If you wouldn't mind, colonel," Lord said after the questions ceased, "I would like to bring my physician-surgeon to see if he can cast some light on the cause of death."

"We can see how she died," Samuel Sandys said. "Some monster tried to strangle her and broke her neck. Why would you have a physician examine her? This is not their work."

"Humour me if you will," Lord said, then lowered his voice, "As things stand it would be hard for your brother to avoid being found guilty. If you think—as I do—that he is innocent, then this is a way we might be able to show that he is. My man Fox is a lawyer by training. He will do what he can to show that your brother is not the man who is responsible for this."

Gideon wanted to speak up. To say that in his opinion Martin Sandys was most certainly the man responsible, but a glance from Lord held him silent.

Sandys chewed on his lip and then nodded.

"Very well, I agree. But surely we can move her to a more—"

Lord put a hand on Sandys' shoulder.

"I will see to it. You need to go to your wife. Tell her what has occurred. But keep your brother close. Until this cloud is lifted from him, he needs to be seen to be cooperating, not resisting. That way his innocence is demonstrated."

After Samuel Sandys had been persuaded to leave, Lord turned to Gideon, suddenly urgent.

"Find Anders. I only hope he can answer our questions."

"I will," Gideon agreed. "But how can you say you think Martin Sandys is innocent when—?"

"I have no idea if he's innocent or not," Lord said, cutting across him. "I do know that the best way to be able to prove his guilt—if

34

he is guilty as you believe—is to provide more than just your word. The only way his brother will allow any proper investigation of this killing will be if he is convinced it will exonerate his brother. To prove his guilt, we need to espouse his innocence." Lord looked again at Ursula Markham and his expression hardened. "Now go, I have other urgent matters I need to look to today."

Gideon went.

Chapter Three

"She cannot have died long before you found her," Anders said as he and Gideon walked back into the house behind a small procession that bore the slight body of Ursula Markham. Awaiting her arrival by the door was Mary Sandys, whose face was pale. Sir Philip Lord had already left saying he had to meet with the mayor and some leading citizens. Even murder did not interrupt the business of war.

"So the man I saw holding her neck killed her?"

Anders stopped walking as if weighing the balance of that in his mind.

"His hands were at her neck, yes?"

Gideon nodded. The image was clear in his mind.

"It was that which made me go over the wall. I thought…" He trailed off.

Anders put a hand on his arm briefly.

"There was nothing you could have done. You see, I believe she was killed by a blow to the head from behind, not by her neck being broken. It was hard to see under her hair, but there was a wound there. It seems to me whoever killed her undid her hair to cover that up."

"Martin Sandys hit her from behind and—"

"You are quick to assume it was him," Anders said, frowning again. "That is like discussing the quality of bread that is not yet out of the oven. I noticed she was wearing fine gloves, one of which was torn with scratches and there was white blossom—may blossom—in her hair and over her clothes."

It was Gideon's turn to stop their progress.

"Hawthorn? But there's none in the garden here."

Anders nodded. "It is a strange thing."

Gideon tried to put the puzzle pieces together in a way that left Martin Sandys the murderer.

"Which means either someone chased her through or by a hawthorn, or they hit her, perhaps, so she fell into one and…" Then another thought followed on and he started running towards the house, leaving Anders to follow in his wake.

Asking urgent direction to where Martin Sandys might be, Gideon found him closeted with his brother in the colonel's private cabinet. Anders had caught up with him by the time Gideon was admitted. The cabinet was a small room, one wall lined with shelves, and another occupied by a large Dutch kast, with engrailed double doors and balled wooden feet. The remaining space was taken by a writing desk with two chairs, one of which was occupied by Martin Sandys.

The two Sandys brothers wore identical expressions of grief and anger. Martin, a younger reflection of Samuel. He was sitting by the window that overlooked the gardens. When Gideon entered, he got to his feet quickly, joining his brother who was standing a short distance away from the window, with his back to the kast.

"You have news." Samuel Sandys did not make it a question.

"I have," Gideon agreed, "of a sort." He gave his attention to the younger brother. "Colonel, if you would please allow me to inspect your hands and your clothing."

Martin scowled. "What is this? Do you still think I'm guilty?"

Gideon kept his true thoughts to himself.

"I may have a way to show you were not involved in the killing," he said.

Martin looked to his brother who gave a curt nod.

"Sir Philip asked us to cooperate with Mr Fox and said he will do his best to uncover the truth."

Reluctantly Martin gave his brother a stiff filial bow then turned to Gideon.

"What would you have me do?"

"Just stand here, in the light from the window, and allow me to examine your clothing."

It did not take long. There were no signs of scratches or snags such as hawthorn might provide on either Martin's clothes or his hands and there were none of the tiny white flowers either, which would have been starkly visible on the dark blue he was wearing.

Disappointed, Gideon exchanged a look with Anders who shook his head.

"Well?" Sandys demanded. "Does it show I am indeed innocent? As if anyone could ever imagine I would have hurt…" He looked away.

"Would you tell me what you were doing in the garden?" Gideon asked.

"I was… was…" he looked up embarrassed.

"Just tell them, Marty." Samuel Sandys sounded long-suffering.

"I was composing poetry." The younger Sandys' face was now bright red. "I like to walk in the garden here and compose poetry. It was a love sonnet. Then I heard a noise like something heavy falling from a tree, so I went to investigate, and I found… I found…" He stopped talking and swallowed hard, then turned to look out of the window, perhaps unaware that his reflection was still visible to Gideon as his face crumpled.

"Are you satisfied with whatever you wanted to ascertain?" Samuel Sandys was cold.

Gideon nodded.

"Good then, perhaps you can leave us and—"

"No." Martin Sandys spun around, heedless that there were tears visible on his face. "No. I want to know what you think you can do to find the monster who murdered my Ursula."

Gideon bit back the urge to point out that she was not and had never been that. He had little liking for this man whether he was guilty of murder or no. Instead, he gestured towards Anders.

"Dr Jensen can explain what he thinks happened."

Anders made a polite bow. "I am only speculating, but I think with solid grounds to do so. You see, there are scratches over Mistress Markham's hands and may blossom caught up in her hair and clothes. There is also a wound beneath her hair where she had been hit heavily and that blow, I think most likely to have killed her."

"I do not see—" Samuel Sandys was frowning, so Gideon quickly picked up the account.

"We believe it most probable that the man who killed her did so elsewhere—somewhere with hawthorn."

"You mean she wasn't murdered in the garden?" Martin Sandys looked relieved. "I don't think I could have faced walking in it, looking at it…"

It was as well Anders spoke because Gideon found his anger restored at the young man who seemed more concerned for his own feelings than the death of Ursula Markham.

"It seems unlikely," Anders said. "I suspect the noise you heard of something falling from a tree was the murderer who had carried Mistress Markham here. Then, for whatever reasons of his own, dropped her into the garden, which led to her neck being broken."

"Dropped her into the garden? When she was already dead?" Samuel Sandys sounded appalled.

"She was small and light. A man of not much more than average strength could have managed it."

"The back wall separates us from the cathedral precincts," Samuel Sandys said. "I have seen hawthorn growing there. Perhaps you should go and see if there is anything there?"

Gideon went with Anders, and it wasn't difficult to find hawthorn. The problem being there was a lot of it. After braving some promising-looking points of ingress and finding nothing, they gave up.

"I do not think it was Colonel Sandys who killed the young woman," Anders said, brushing the small white flowers from his clothing as they went back through the city.

"He had reason to though," Gideon said. "He was obsessed with her, and she spurned him. We saw that at supper last night."

"That may be true, but love is one-eyed, and hate is blind. He seemed to think, against all evidence, that his poems and persistence would yet win her heart. I believe she was slain by someone who was ruled by hate for her, not by love."

Which, Gideon thought, probably said more about Anders than about the murderer.

"Perhaps she had just told him his efforts were in vain and he was angered. Who else would hate her?" he asked.

They had reached the Water Gate where their ways would part with Anders going to his work with the company. The Dane stopped and put a hand on Gideon's shoulder.

"That, my friend, is the key to this, I think."

It was only after Anders had gone his way and Gideon was walking back to The Talbot that he recalled something from the conversation of the night before. Something Ursula Markham herself had said. *Some of the men have strong opinions that it is not the place for women to be doing such work.* It was possible, Gideon thought, that he should be going to speak with Nehemiah Fisher after all.

Lost in thought and speculation he took the wrong turning and found himself, quite suddenly, in a very different sort of Worcester. This was the Worcester that became the docks and was no longer a city of prosperous houses but huddled and densely packed ones. In amongst them, the occasional alehouse or ordinary poked a gaudy sign onto the street like a beckoning finger.

Raised voices on a doorstep ahead drew his attention and that of a small crowd. Two men were being harangued in the street by a woman who stood in her doorway but seemed to be giving as good as they got. The familiar smell of nightsoil filled Gideon's nostrils. He passed a hand cart which carried a covered tub and was half full of what looked like mud, but stank vilely, and realised that these were saltpetre collectors.

Gideon knew little about the manufacture of munitions—the casting of cannons happened in a foundry and muskets were made by gunsmiths. But the match needed to fire them was made from cord soaked in saltpetre and saltpetre was also used—somehow—in the making of gunpowder. And saltpetre production needed urine and excrement-soaked soil, such as could be found under the floors of outbuildings and hovels, where the mess of the human or animal inhabitants congealed over time. Gideon recalled Lord saying that one of his tasks in the city was to expand upon the production of gunpowder there, which meant that such scenes as the one playing out before him would become more frequent.

These two saltpetre men were having to face the ire of one of the locals of Worcester, who took understandable exception to rough men forcibly entering her house and digging up the floor of her home. The woman, in her middle years with greying hair, a heavy body and a look of grim determination, blocked her doorway.

"You can't come in," she yelled, even though the men were less than three paces from her. "My mother is over eighty and I'm not letting the likes of you upset her by tearing the place apart."

The small crowd that had gathered were calling encouragement in a way that if Gideon had been one of the saltpetre men, he would have found intimidating, but these two seemed hardened to such abuse.

"If you don't let us in, we'll get the soldiers and they'll make more of a mess than we will," one of them snapped.

"And you'll be arrested and fined as well," the other added.

"You do that then," the woman repeated. "I'm not going to let you—"

Then the first man lunged at her, and she screamed. Gideon moved as fast as he was able, pushing through the crowd, sword coming into his hand as soon as he was past them. He could see in the surprised wide eyes of the saltpetre men the impact of having someone who was clearly a gentleman appear in front of them wielding a sword.

"You have no right of entry here," Gideon said, his sword as steady as his voice. The saltpetre man who had grabbed the woman released her and stepped back.

"We have," he protested. "In the name of the king. We work for Mr William Richardson. Take it up with him if you have a problem."

"As a lawyer, I can tell you that the law grants you the right to dig in outhouses, barns, stables, dove-houses and such but not in a private house. *And they cannot dig in the Floor of any Mansion-house which serves for the Habitation of Man."* Gideon quoted, hardening his tone. *"It is very necessary for the Weal publick, that the Habitation of Subjects be preserved and maintained.* You have no right of entry to this good woman's dwelling." Somehow, he had a feeling that Coke had not been thinking of such a humble residence when he made that statement, even assuming the woman owned the house she lived in. And he was sure that in these times of war, such niceties were suspended anyway. But he doubted these men would know that. Besides, he was the one holding the sword.

The saltpetre men glared at him with venom. One of them cursed and spat on the ground and walked back to the handcart. "Leave it, Josh. Cart's full enough anyway."

The small crowd that had gathered, jeered and the other saltpetre man turned and made a rude gesture as they went off along the road.

The woman whose home Gideon had just protected was still standing in her doorway, mouth open and looking at him as if a creature from myth had landed on her threshold.

"Who are you?" she demanded, then she flushed. "I mean, thank you for defending me, sir. But don't they have the right?"

"I promise you what I said is the law," Gideon told her, returning his sword to its scabbard, "They shouldn't enter any private dwelling, only outbuildings."

"Thank you, then, sir." She managed a small smile. "You were most kind."

Gideon nodded, but in his heart, he knew it was not that simple. It had been something more complex, to do with hearing a woman scream when seized by a man and the too vivid memory he had in his mind of Ursula Markham, who may even have screamed, and no one had come to her aid.

. "If I'd any coin to pay you, I would gladly do so, sir. Had they got in, I swear that would have been the death of my mother. It would have broken her heart to see the house she loves all destroyed and dug up."

"Your mother need have no fear now," Gideon told her, hoping that was true. He was about to make a brief farewell and go his way when he realised what she had said earlier. "Your mother, you said she is over eighty, is she in good health for her years?"

"Very much so, sir. Although she is not so strong at walking now, and her sight is not what it was."

"Her memory is good?"

The woman laughed.

"She can still tell the tale of how when she was a girl Queen Elizabeth visited the city, saw a pear tree and commanded three black pears be added to the city's arms. Oh yes, her memory is excellent."

"Would she speak with me?" he asked, then seeing the confusion on the woman's face he went on quickly. "One reason I have come to Worcester is to discover what happened to the relative of a client of mine who lived here forty years or more ago. Your mother might remember them. My name is Gideon Fox, and I will happily pay your mother for the chance to ask her a couple of questions."

The woman still looked uncertain but seeing Gideon was serious, stepped aside so he could enter. "After what you just did, we'll not take your coin, sir. You'll have to mind your head as you're a bit tall for in here."

Inside the house was small, dark and low-ceilinged, as he had been warned. It also smelled foul. He wasn't surprised the saltpetre men thought this might be a good place to dig. The woman's mother sat by a small window at the back of the room, a distaff at her shoulder and her hands busy with spinning on a spindle. She stopped when her daughter addressed her, peering short-sightedly at Gideon with watery eyes in a wrinkled face.

"Mother, this is Mr Fox. He's a lawyer. He made the saltpetre men go away and he'd like to ask you some questions to try and find someone's relative who used to live here forty years ago."

If Gideon had any doubts about the mental acumen of the old woman they vanished as soon as she opened her mouth, although her words were a bit malformed through a lack of teeth.

"Someone lost a fortune, eh?" she asked. "That would be the only reason to look for a relative you've not thought about for forty years."

"Well, no." Gideon wondered how open he should be. "My client hopes to find they are still alive. He didn't know they were relatives until recently."

The woman made a noise of disbelief.

"There'll still be money at the root of it, mark my words. What'd he be paying a lawyer for otherwise? But that's not my affair, it's yours. Ask your questions. If I can answer you I will."

"Thank you. Do you recall the Kelley family? There were three siblings, Edward, Thomas and Lydia."

That was met by a long silence and Gideon was about to rephrase his question when the old woman spoke.

"A wild one, Edward. Went off to foreign parts, I heard. Sir Edward Kelley, they made him." She fell silent again and seemed to be thinking. Gideon was about to prompt her when she went on. "Elizabeth she was. The sister. They called her Lydia. Always close to him. But it was Tom who went off with him to foreign parts. Of course, she was married by then. She'd show people a small piece of gold she said Ned made."

Gideon's pulse had picked up as she spoke.

"You knew them?" he asked, unable to keep the excitement from his voice.

The old woman shook her head.

"Not well. But in those days, we all seemed to know each other. Not like today. Everyone then was more friendly. Helpful. Now it is all argument and fighting. Of course, I had a nice house then too on Forestreet. That was before my Frank died. He was not a careful man, and his debts took everything." She sounded wistful.

"Do you know where Lydia—Elizabeth—is now?"

"She was older than me so likely she's dead." The old woman gave a little laugh.

"You're not certain though? Why's that?"

"Because she left Worcester." The old woman had resumed spinning. The spindle rotated back and forth. "It would have been a few years after the queen passed, God rest her. We'd heard by then that Edward—Sir Edward as he'd become—had died. Thomas came back and took Elizabeth off with him. She was a widow by then of course."

"Do you know where she went?" Gideon was finding it hard to keep his excitement in check.

There was another silence, just the whisper of wool between her fingers and the squeak of the wood against the thread.

"I don't recall I ever heard. A shame as that's what you want to know, isn't it?"

All the hope of a short time before drained away from Gideon, leaving him feeling hollow. It was a bitter draught to swallow having held certainty so briefly in his grasp.

"Yes," he said flatly. He reached into his pocket for a coin. It wouldn't be fair to allow his disappointment to deny her some reward for taking the time to talk to him.

"Then you should ask her daughter," The old woman said. "I'm sure she'd know."

Gideon's hand froze.

"Her daughter?"

"Oh yes, she had a big family. But only her daughter is left now. That's Joan."

"This daughter still lives in Worcester?"

"Yes." The wool whirled about the spindle and ran through her fingers. "She married Naomi Brown's son."

Gideon was beginning to feel as if he was having to tease out the information as the old woman was teasing out the wool from the distaff.

"Where do the Browns live?"

The spinning stopped.

"Oh, Joan's not a Brown," she said as if Gideon must be a little slow not to have worked that out. "Brown was Naomi's name before she married."

It was like trying to bring water from a rock.

"What is her name today?"

"Fisher," the old woman said firmly. "Joan married a man called Nehemiah Fisher."

Chapter Four

Nehemiah Fisher.

Gideon was beginning to feel haunted by the man.

He was thinking about what he should do, walking back through the better part of Worcester, when he saw the familiar figures of Zahara and Christobel on the street ahead of him. He increased his pace to catch up with them and as he did so, realised they were walking beside a tall, spindly, man, clad in a sober charcoal grey that avoided the showiness of true black. He had a dramatic brush of grey hair that stuck out from under his sugarloaf-crowned hat at right angles to his head.

He seemed to be declaiming in a serious mien and the two women were nodding, and then he said something that made Zahara blush and Gideon increased his pace. But whatever had been said it had been by way of a parting shot because by the time Gideon caught up with the two women, the man had extended his long stride and was already a good way further along the street.

Zahara greeted him with a smile as he reached them.

"You have good timing," she said. "We are just returning to the inn for dinner."

"Who was that you were talking to?" Gideon demanded.

Christobel looked as if she wished Zahara would say nothing, but Zahara seemed unperturbed.

"That was the Reverend Nehemiah Fisher. He is a man who is very strong in his faith. But his faith is hard, proud and unyielding. It is like a fortress with high walls and parapets from which he looks down on those who have less certainty or who see more of love and less of fierceness in their relationship with God."

"You are too kind to him," Christobel said. "He is so busy trying to remove the mote from the eye of his neighbour he has completely missed the notion that he might have an entire stack of planks in his own."

Gideon felt a sudden ugly suspicion.

"Why were you talking with him?"

46

Zahara was about to say something, but Christobel cast a sharp look at Gideon and spoke first.

"Let's get back to the inn. Talking in the street makes us appear as idle gossips, against which we have just been warned, and besides, I am hungry."

She was right in that the street was not the place to challenge the two of them on what they had been doing in company with Nehemiah Fisher. But from Christobel's reaction, Gideon was now convinced his suspicions were well founded and he walked with them in angry silence, Zahara sending him a puzzled look.

Gideon commanded a private room to dine in and was less than pleased when Danny appeared with a face that looked as if it was aching from the effort of keeping a grin in place. For the man to whom a grin was second nature that was an odd notion and bespoke a trying morning's work. Danny instantly launched into a blow-by-blow account of that morning, spent in the irritating company of Dudd Dudley.

To be fair, Danny made it humorous, often at his own expense as he described how Dudd had been demonstrating the solidity and strength of his breastworks by jumping on it, inviting Danny to do the same. Despite being a good stone or three lighter than the portly Dudley, Danny was the one who fell through as the breastwork collapsed and took a tumble down the glacis.

When they stopped laughing it was Christobel who became serious first.

"You could have been badly hurt. That man is dangerous."

Danny's smile in response to her concern was warm and happy.

"That was when I'd had enough and headed back here," he admitted. "I am finding Dudd a difficult challenge." He looked at Christobel. "How did you get on with your own challenge?"

Christobel must have seen Gideon's expression change because she gave him a brief look and explained.

"Sir Philip asked me if I would go along to Reverend Fisher's church and let it be known I follow his views, in the hope that I might be able to discover who within the community is openly aligned with Parliament. Zahara went with me as my maidservant. Unfortunately, that didn't go as well as we wished." Before

Gideon could react, she turned to Danny and continued her account. "We were in the church praying quietly, thinking just to be seen so that we might become accepted. He stormed into the building in high agitation and, upon noticing us, went straight into a sermon upon the rightful duties of women and quoting St. Paul. *Let your women keep silence in the churches*."

Zahara nodded. "And John Knox," she said.

Christobel changed her stance, adopted a glower and crashed a fist on the table. "*Their strength, weakness: their counsel, foolishness: and judgement, phrenesie.*"

"He told us we must leave," Zahara said.

"When we walked back, he walked with us denouncing Eve and all her daughters." Christobel shook her head and laughed. "Then, as he left us, he said he hoped he would see us in church on Sunday to hear his sermon."

Danny found that hilarious but in Gideon's mind was a stark image of the body of Ursula Markham and how easily it could have had the face of Zahara.

"How could Sir Philip put you two in the way of danger like that?" he demanded.

"We were in no danger," Zahara told him, "Shiraz was with us. You would not have seen him any more than Reverend Fisher would have seen him. He will now be following the minister since he left us, to see where he was going."

"Not," Christobel said tautly, "that we needed any protection by Shiraz or otherwise. We were quite capable of going to sit in a church all by ourselves. In broad daylight. In the morning. In the middle of Worcester."

"You have your work cut out with Fisher then," Danny observed. "I am glad Shiraz was with you because I get back and am inundated with tales of a woman done to death by Colonel Sandys. He apparently ravished her in his garden, then murdered her after."

Zahara's eyes widened, and Christobel's mouth formed a bleak, tight line. Danny's gaze switched.

"Gideon, why am I so sure you will be able to enlighten us as to the truth of it?"

But then Gideon was the only one of them who had not reacted with shock at the news.

"You sound as if you think I am somehow responsible," he said.

Danny's eyebrows rose.

"Not at all. But you always seem to take an interest in discovering the why, who and wherefore behind any dead bodies we chance to come across."

"This was not just a dead body'," Gideon said, disliking the levity with which Danny was treating the matter. "It was Mistress Ursula Markham, with whom we took supper yesterday evening."

Danny closed his mouth, his expression bleak. "Martin Sandys was very attentive to her, and she cold to him. Is he taken for the crime?"

"When I found her in his brother's garden, he was crouched beside her," Gideon said and explained what Anders had discovered that exonerated him.

"Wasn't Mistress Markham the one who's been leading the city women with the preparations for a siege?" Christobel asked.

Gideon nodded his thoughts on the intelligent and determined young woman he had sat next to at supper who had been snatched from life so cruelly. "You would have liked her."

"Without her, the women will falter," Christobel said. "Whoever murdered her will have killed the spirit of the city."

That wasn't something Gideon had considered.

"You're right. Perhaps she was killed because of that," he said.

"If so, it is vital her work continues," Christobel said. "I must speak with Sir Philip and tell him Reverend Fisher won't listen to a woman. That will free me to take on what Mistress Markham was doing."

"No," Gideon spoke so harshly that all three of them looked at him in surprise. "I won't allow it. Isn't it enough to have one woman dead?" He glanced at Danny. "You agree this is much too dangerous."

Danny swallowed a mouthful before he replied.

"It would be dangerous," he said, and Christobel's brows drew together. "But Christobel is right. This isn't just a murdered woman, this is the womanhood of Worcester being bullied and threatened. And from a strictly military perspective, if the women retreat now, the men will lose much heart. Sentiment for the king here isn't as strong as any of us would like. Most of the traders and craftsmen are more inclined to oppose than support us. A decent push from the other side and we'll find the citizens in more open opposition. Then we'll be fighting on two fronts when Waller comes."

Gideon stared at Danny in disbelief.

"You're not suggesting Christobel should take over from Ursula Markham and risk suffering the same fate?"

Danny considered.

"If it's what she wishes to do," he said. "I can think of no one better to take on the role. I can arrange for her to have an armed guard at need."

The look of surprise on Christobel's face was replaced by one of such warm affection towards Danny, that Gideon felt he was intruding to witness it. Danny, he concluded, had only agreed to please Christobel. Which was madness. Surely no sane man could stand by and allow a woman he cared about to walk into such danger?

But before he could say anything, Danny stood up.

"I need to talk with Ned Scarlett, the city's chief cannoneer. He'll know the individual idiosyncrasies of his guns. That will determine how we use them and where. Once I get the artillery set right, we can keep Waller at arm's length if he comes. We have all we need here to manufacture munitions at need and there are decent stores already."

Christobel was on her feet too.

"I'll come with you and see if I can find who is organising the women now and lend her my support."

"Brighid Rider will know," Danny said. "She's been out there helping all morning." He held the door for Christobel, made a brief bow towards Gideon and Zahara, then left closing the door behind him.

It was quiet after they had gone. Gideon noticed that when he was alone with Zahara it always seemed quiet and peaceful.

Zahara said nothing until she had finished carefully stacking the empty dishes and plates and sat back down.

"You are angry with the Schiavono."

It wasn't a question and Gideon, unable to lie to her, nodded.

"He asked me to approach Fisher. I refused as it would mean pretending to a faith I do not hold. I draw the line at lying about that. Then when I found Mistress Markham today…" He broke off. "Don't you see? That could be Christobel. That could be you—if Lord had…"

Reaching over the table, Zahara gripped his hand.

"When you went to Paris, to London, those were dangerous things and not things you liked to do, but you still did them."

Gideon stared at her wondering what she was trying to tell him.

"I went to Paris for Kate and Anders. I went to London for Sir Philip. I wanted to do what I could to help them."

Zahara rewarded him with a smile.

"Christobel is no different. She wants to help."

"But—" Gideon broke off. Why was it so hard to explain how very different that was? "I am a man," he said at last.

Zahara lowered her gaze and Gideon knew he had somehow disappointed her. He wondered how to explain.

"You went with her," he said. "Something could have happened to either of you—both of you. I couldn't live if anything happened to you."

Zahara's eyes flashed, and she surged to her feet.

"You think it is different for me?"

Gideon had never seen her angry like this before. It left him disoriented.

"Of course not."

"But you still do what you do and do not stop to think what I might feel about it. You do not ask me before you put yourself in danger."

Gideon found his mouth had dropped open.

Zahara went on. "Would the Schiavono tell Lady Catherine what she may or may not do in such matters?"

"It is different for them," Gideon protested. "They are different. Their marriage is different."

51

The anger faded from Zahara as quickly as it had risen, like a summer storm. She sank back to her seat.

"Yes, it is," she admitted. "I would not want to live as they live in a marriage. But I would not want to stop being myself in one either."

"I would never ask you to. Not in any way," Gideon assured her, feeling lost in the conversation they were having. He had thought it was about Christobel, but somehow it had become about himself and Zahara. "I am trying to understand," he said.

Zahara took his hand and leaned forward.

"You do not always need to understand," she said softly. "You just need to accept."

"You make it sound simple."

"It is." She got to her feet again and this time used the hand she still held to draw him up with her. "You will find who killed that poor woman. I know you will."

Shaken by the confusing conversation, Gideon saw in her gaze the faith she had in him. He wanted to merit that faith more than anything in this world.

"I'll do my best," he promised. Then something occurred to him. "You said that Fisher only came into the church once you were in there and he seemed agitated when he arrived?"

Zahara nodded.

"He was most distressed and disturbed."

"Did you notice if there were any small white flowers on his clothing? Or scratches on his hands or face?"

Zahara wrinkled her brow in thought, then shook her head slowly.

"I do not recall anything like that. He was sober and precise in his dress." She tilted her head, remembering. "He was upset. As if he had wanted to prostrate before God and finding us there meant he was unable to do so."

"That speaks of guilt," Gideon said, suddenly realising that he would have to do what Lord had asked of him after all, to bring a man to justice for murder. But he vowed to himself he would find a way to do so that didn't require him to lie about his faith.

A soft tap on the window made Gideon whirl around. Shiraz was outside and Zahara crossed swiftly to see him. Shiraz's hands moved, weaving words in the air that Gideon couldn't understand.

Zahara turned back to Gideon.

"Shiraz says he followed Reverend Fisher back to the church. He was praying. He kept saying 'Oh God, help me' over and over."

"That speaks of guilt."

Zahara gave a small nod.

"I must go," she said. "I promised Brighid I would join her working with the other women on the fortifications as soon as I was free to do so."

"I'll—"

But she was already shaking her head. "Shiraz will take me. You need to speak to the Schiavono."

She smiled so warmly that the tightness of misery the morning had placed upon him seemed to release. But when she left the room, it was as if the sun had gone in behind a cloud.

Sir Philip Lord, Gideon learned, was out and there was no certainty he would return to the inn until the evening. Meanwhile, the matter of Nehemiah Fisher was complicated by the fact that Gideon needed to talk with Fisher's wife about something else entirely. Joan Fisher would hardly be willing to speak to him about the whereabouts of her mother if Gideon had just had her husband brought to trial for murder.

That thought lent him purpose. If he was going to get the information Lord needed it would have to be before there was any move to question Reverend Fisher. Asking the host of the inn where the Fishers lived, Gideon got directions to a house on Angel Lane.

Worcester was no great size and even though his destination was at the opposite end of the city from The Talbot it wasn't a long walk to get there. Angel Lane turned out to be little more than an alleyway with the houses so close they almost met overhead.

It was only when he turned into the narrow lane, he realised he was being followed.

He had seen the two men talking together across the road when he left The Talbot and thought nothing of them. But now they were close behind him, moving with intent and picking up their pace, leaving little doubt as to their purpose.

Gideon had no idea who they were or what they might want with him, only that they seemed set on pursuing him. To call on the Fishers might be to bring violence to their threshold or even across it. So, instead, he picked up his own pace and was not surprised when they matched it.

Whilst it was narrow, Angel Lane was not a blind alley. It ran straight for about fifty yards, then turned sharply to the right. After which Gideon had a wall on one side and houses on the other—and ahead perhaps a hundred yards away was the busy Forestreet.

Gideon broke into a run.

He might well have won the race. After all, he had a lead on the two men, and he was longer-legged than either. But what defeated his attempt was a door opening and a modestly dressed young woman stepping out with a basket over one arm. The narrowness of the footway meant that he would have cannoned into her had he not taken the only alternative and stopped but stopping meant he also had to turn to face his pursuers, which he did, drawing his sword as he spun around. He heard a gasp from behind him.

"Get back in your house and lock the door," he said, not looking to see if the woman obeyed. If these men succeeded in their attack, they might decide that the woman too should suffer the same fate being witness to their deed.

The two men had slowed when Gideon turned, clearly not liking that he held a sword. They were armed with cudgels and knives. Had it been a year before, they would have swiftly overpowered him. Then he had been as ineffectual and unskilled a swordsman as most of his profession. But even as he turned and spoke, he could feel his body preparing for a fight. That was the legacy of those who had worked to train him—men like Jupp, Olsen and even Lord and Danny on occasion.

Because of that training, he attacked without hesitation, with extreme ferocity and went for the man who had the weapon with a longer reach. His chosen target was taken by surprise. But then Gideon must have looked little threat. He was dressed as a civilian and had run like a hare when the two made their presence felt.

Gideon advanced again, which was too much for one of the two who turned and ran, leaving his friend at the mercy of Gideon's swordsmanship. The cudgel was unwieldy by comparison to the deft blade in Gideon's hand and as the man tried to swing it, Gideon drove the point of his sword into the arm that held it. The heavy thing fell to the ground. Its wielder yelped and would have run too, but Gideon had moved so the man was trapped against the wall on the side of the lane opposite the houses. He wanted to ask who they were and why they were after him.

That was when Gideon made his one mistake. He stepped in too close before bringing his sword up and staggered back from a hard kick, the breath driven from his body. It was good fortune that the man decided upon flight as Gideon was doubled over, winded and gasping and would have been pressed to defend himself. He could only watch through watering eyes as the man took off back along Angel Lane at a healthy sprint.

"Are you alright?" The voice belonged to the woman Gideon had almost run into. With her was a man, a servant from his dress and demeanour, who carried a stout stick.

Gideon managed to nod, words being beyond him and accepted her offer to step into her house and sit down. He was helped into a modest but tidy parlour by the servant.

"Forgive me for asking, sir—" the woman started to say.

"I'm Gideon L—Fox, a lawyer from London," he said, the words gasped more than spoken. He was grappling with a tight sick feeling inside as well. If it was known who he was in Worcester to the degree that men were sent to attack him, then what chance did he have of carrying out his intention to uncover the murderer?

"You are a lawyer?" She sounded delighted. "I am Phoebe Young. Oh, this is such an irregular way to be introduced, but I couldn't leave you out on the street after those two men…" Her voice trailed off and she shook her head at the horror of it. "And you were so brave in my defence."

Her eyes held a warmth that startled him.

"It was my own defence too," he said quickly, but the luminous gaze remained strong.

"I am sure so," she said, "But here is a small cup of aquavitae and herbs. My mother swears by it as a remedy for anyone who has had an injury. Forgive me for not introducing them, but my parents are both out."

Gideon sipped the fiery liquid, then drank more confidently when he found that whatever herbs had been added were not ill tasting.

"Valerian, Chamomile and Lavender," she told him. "And honey."

"Thank you. I feel better already," Gideon managed to muster a smile.

"You are most welcome. It's the least I could do." She seemed to glow as he smiled. "Did you know those two men who attacked you?"

"I've never seen them before. I was in Angel Lane to call upon Reverend Nehemiah Fisher and his wife."

Phoebe Young clasped her hands together in front of her and sank onto a chair.

"Then it was indeed God's will that I should encounter you like that. The Fishers are my parent's friends. There has even been talk of…" She broke off and flushed bright red, then dropped her gaze demurely. But she was subdued only a moment before she was on her feet. "I can take you to them but—those men, they work for Mr Richardson. I recognised them."

Richardson. Where had he heard that name recently?

Gideon remembered and stared at her. "They were *saltpetre collectors*?"

Phoebe Young nodded. "So now you know you can bring them to justice."

A weight lifted from his shoulders. He had feared the Covenant had somehow found him, Instead, he had earned the ire of the local saltpetre men. Though it was unlikely that William Richardson would know of the attack. Most probably it had been undertaken by his thwarted employees, concerned lest Gideon repeated his defence against them at other properties and make their work harder. They wouldn't have intended to harm him, merely intimidate him into leaving their business alone. No wonder they had run off when he turned on them with a sword.

He thanked Phoebe for the information and agreed that, yes, it would be most kind was she willing to present him to the Fishers.

"Reverend Fisher knew my father, who was a minister in London," Gideon explained, inventing as he spoke. "My father mentioned his name once or twice in a way that suggested they were quite well acquainted. Being in Worcester on other business, I thought to take the opportunity to pay my respects."

"Your father was a minister?" Phoebe's eyes grew large and round as if he had said his father was an earl. When she carried on talking her voice was breathy. "That is such a wonderful thing, I must tell my father. Are you staying long in Worcester, Mr Fox?"

Chapter Five

Phoebe was a complication Gideon could have done without. However, to his sense of shame, he took advantage of her.

They walked the short distance to the Fisher's house, accompanied by Phoebe's servant, only to find that the Reverend Fisher was out visiting the elderly and Mrs Fisher was out visiting the sick. As he was with a family friend, Gideon pushed his luck. Hoping for confirmation of Fisher's guilt, he expressed surprise, saying he had called at this time as he had been advised that the Reverend was out in the mornings. That was met by a confused look from the maidservant who had answered the door.

"He was in the house until near dinner time," she said. "He was with Mr Young and two others for a prayer meeting and Bible study. I took them refreshments." She sounded affronted as if Gideon was suggesting her master was less than fully attentive to his calling.

Gideon was disappointed. She had no reason to lie, and it seemed Reverend Fisher had not only been at home at the time that someone was killing Ursula Markham, but he also had three men and a maidservant who could vouch for the fact.

"My father said at dinner that the reverend was called away from the meeting a few minutes early and he was looking rather distressed when he went out," Phoebe said, and Gideon could have kissed her hand. "Is everything alright?"

The maidservant looked uncomfortable. Then her face cleared.

"I could ask if Mr Ezra Fisher will see you."

Phoebe reacted as if she had been stung. "Oh no. We'll come back another time."

Gideon was left with little choice except to withdraw with her.

"I apologise," Phoebe said, her eyes downcast, suddenly demure as Gideon walked her back to her house. "You see, my family have it in mind that Ezra and I… that he and I… that…" Her lips tightened. "And it is completely unsuitable," she finished as if that was obvious. Before he had any need to think of a response,

Phoebe gushed on. "But if you wanted to present your respects to the reverend you could come to supper tonight. The Fishers always join us for supper on a Thursday. I am sure my father would wish to meet you too, Mr Fox. Especially when I explain how you were so brave in my defence. Besides, Father is often talking of London and how he wishes Worcester was more akin in spirit to it. He is always keen to read any of the discursive pamphlets that come to us from there."

To say that accepting such an invitation would be unconventional was an understatement. Had Gideon not been desperate to progress his work of uncovering both a murderer and the whereabouts—if still living—of Lydia Kelley, he would most certainly have made a polite excuse and refused.

It was only as he saw the devastating smile of delight on Phoebe's face at his acceptance that he realised that she might well be reading a different interpretation into it. But by then it was too late. He left Phoebe Young at her door and made his way back to The Talbot feeling uneasy within himself.

Sir Philip Lord had returned in his absence. Gideon found him alone in his room reading through a message. He put it down when Gideon closed the door.

"After a most interesting morning in the company of a man who loves the king but loathes those who support him here, I am returned as the pigeon to his roosting only to find. Kate has gone abroad to offer what she may of comfort and assistance to Mary Sandys." Lord studied Gideon's face with mock intensity. "You have the demeanour of a man who believed he sucked on an orange but then found it was a lemon. Am I about to be lambasted?"

"You sent Zahara and Christobel to speak with Reverend Fisher."

Lord inclined his head.

"I did."

"You put them in danger."

"Now that," Lord said, "is a matter of conjecture. I consider that having Shiraz close at hand more than mitigated any real peril."

"Yes, but—"

"Do you feel Christobel and Zahara are incapable of making such judgements regarding their own activities?"

That was an unanswerable question.

"It's not something that should be an issue ongoing," he said, avoiding it. "I have decided I shall undertake the task as you first requested."

He had the satisfaction of seeing Lord's eyebrows rise in surprise.

"What's brought about this change of heart?"

"I was too hasty in my rejection," Gideon admitted. "I'm sure there is a way I can do what you ask."

"Welcome back from the ranks of saints and martyrs to the human race where we embrace imperfection and give grim necessity its due at need," Lord said piously. Then his expression changed. "But you have been delving already. Has the tragic death of Ursula Markham put your principles into perspective?"

Which cut too near the bone for Gideon, so he ignored it.

"I had a chance encounter," he said, which once spoken somehow seemed more of an excuse than an explanation.

"Chance," Lord echoed. "*Who would trust slippery chance?*"

"Well, it *was* chance. I mistook my way and came upon two saltpetre men who were trying to invade the home of an unfortunate woman."

"And as Sir Galahad you leapt to her defence. She was young and comely?"

"She was past middle-aged and not so, but the saltpetre men had no right to go into a private dwelling."

"Ah, so it offended your legal principles. I see." Lord shook his head. "The king needs gunpowder. Gunpowder needs saltpetre. The necessities for saltpetre have to be recovered from wherever such may be found."

"Then they should make good any damage they do," Gideon retorted. "That is what the law says, *the Ministers of the King who dig for Saltpetre, are bound to leave the Inheritance of the Subject in so good Plight as they found it.* They are just digging it up and leaving the mess. Huge gaping holes in floors."

"Your outrage does you credit," Lord said. "If you wish me to lay my heavy hand upon the shoulder of the man concerned, give me his name and I shall gladly do so. But I suspect that was not the focus of this tale."

"No. Not at all. But because of my stepping in to help her, I discovered that the woman's biggest concern was that her mother, who was over eighty, should not be disturbed."

Lord turned his gaze on Gideon with widening eyes.

"You chanced upon Mistress Kelley?"

"No. But the old woman did know of her. She said that she is no longer living in Worcester. That she left with her brother many years ago. But her daughter still lives here."

"Her daughter?" Lord's gaze was intense. "Tell me."

"You will like it as little as I did. Her daughter is married to Nehemiah Fisher."

Lord stared at him incredulously, then chuckled as if at an excellent joke. "So that's why you have overcome your nausea for dealing with the man?"

Gideon felt his lips tighten into a line.

"No. That is because he might be our murderer."

It took little time to tell the basis of his suspicions and recount his encounter with William Richardson's saltpetre collectors on Angel Lane—something that made Lord frown and state coldly that he would take action on it. Gideon explained how, with the help of Phoebe Young, he discovered Reverend Fisher had witnesses who could say for sure it was not he who did the deed.

"But from his behaviour since, I'm not convinced. What Shiraz overheard in church suggests a guilty conscience," Gideon said.

"And thanks to fair Phoebe you will have your chance to meet with him and his wife. I wish I could speak with Goodwife Fisher myself. The risk is if she shares her husband's views, she would regard me with hostility and contempt. So I will trust you to find what coin will purchase the information I need. Whatever it may be, if it is mine to bestow, she may have it." He picked up his hat, which had been carelessly discarded on a chair, and set it back on his head. "Now. With me, Mr Fox, if you please. We shall seize the moment and speak with William Richardson about improving his business practice."

As Gideon had suspected, William Richardson had little knowledge and less care about how those who retrieved the muck from which the precious crystals of saltpetre could be produced went about their work. Having begun with swagger, bluster and denial, after a five-minute conversation with Sir Philip Lord in which no threat was uttered, nor even an imperative deployed, Mr Richardson agreed to review his men's collection techniques. He promised to ensure they understood the obligation to make good in any property they entered, regardless of whether the householder concerned was wealthy or otherwise.

It was a work of social alchemy which Gideon could only watch with admiration. Then he played his part, saying he had no intention of seeking the arrest of the wayward men who had attacked him, or those who had tried to impose on the household he had defended. The implication plain that if any further such incidents occurred, then Gideon would review his decision. But again, it was left unstated and the sheen of sweat on Richardson's brow as he showed them out surely owed nothing at all to the polite conversation they had just had with him.

"You did not instruct him to keep his men from domestic dwellings," Gideon observed as they left the fine house Richardson had acquired from stolen filth.

"I did not because I would not ask the impossible. As I already told you, the army needs saltpetre, and the raw material for it must be dug up wherever it may be found. What might inconvenience a householder might save the lives of my men in the field." He was mounting his horse as he spoke. "I believe there will be less antipathy to his collectors doing their necessary work if Richardson uses a little more of his high profit in redress to those he must inconvenience."

Gideon could only hope he was right.

"I need to see Sandys and then redeem Kate," Lord said, as they rode away from Richardson's fine house. "You can accompany me to make the acquaintance of David Collins. I will make some excuse for the two of you to need to work together."

The excuse Lord provided was to have Gideon and Collins go over the assessments for payments due to support the troops and garrisons in Worcestershire and create both a list of all defaulters and a shorter list of those who were the wealthiest of them. Gideon supposed the work they did that afternoon was useful, determining who might receive a visit from a troop of cavalry in the near future, but in terms of providing any evidence that David Collins might be a Parliamentarian sympathiser, it was fruitless.

Lord and Gideon were outriders to Kate's carriage for the short journey back to The Talbot. Gideon took the opportunity to report what he had found.

"I'm not sure that was time well spent. Collins' loyalty and devotion are to his family—about whom he talked at great length. Since his father and three brothers fight for the king, and he has two sisters wed to men serving as soldiers who do likewise, I think he would be an unlikely traitor. He told me he would fight if he could, but he has a twisted leg and he sees his work as being a way of supporting what they do."

"It was time well spent," Lord said. "Being able to cross a second name from the list is valuable."

"A second name?"

"Danny's opinion of Dudd Dudley, expressed with an extreme regret, is that he is utterly incapable of any kind of surreptitious dealings and too full of himself to be our traitor."

Once back at The Talbot, Gideon had a little time before he needed to depart again. He used it to ensure he was appropriately clad, and his face and hands were clean, before heading out of the door.

He was surprised to find Lord waiting for him clad in modest servant guise, skin darkened, and hair concealed beneath a grubby-looking Monmouth cap, sword discarded in favour of a long-bladed knife.

"It's as well our host is not the most observant of men," Lord told him with a wry expression. "He came to the door with a message when I was halfway transformed. Thank heavens for Kate, although she couldn't stop laughing."

"You know this isn't going to be a supper held at the Fishers'?"

Lord inclined his head and made a gesture with one arm to suggest Gideon went ahead. "Indeed so. But I'm sure you will be able to persuade the good reverend to invite you to his house and I, established as your servant, will accompany you when you do. In the meantime, I shall acquaint myself with whatever I may about the reverend and his faction from the view beneath, which in my experience often offers great insight."

When they arrived at the Young household, 'Thomas' was promptly escorted to the kitchen. Gideon was introduced to Jacob Young and his wife Esther by their exuberant daughter. They welcomed him so warmly, he felt a twinge of guilt at practising deception upon them.

"We hear we owe you our thanks for protecting Phoebe from ruffians in the street," Mr Young said. "That is a sad indictment of these times."

"I fear it was my fault those ruffians were there," Gideon said.

"Indeed so?" Young's tone made it clear that was not the impression he had been given by Phoebe herself, but she seemed utterly unabashed and just smiled at her father.

"They were running at us with cudgels and knives," she said. "Mr Fox put himself between me and them and told me to go back into the house. Then he fought them and drove them away." Her gaze shifted to Gideon and became luminous. "He was so brave."

Jacob Young cleared his throat. They were still standing in the small parlour that served also as an entrance hall.

"Please, come through to the supper, Mr Fox, then you could tell us why the men were pursuing you."

The supper was patently more than this household would usually put on and from the rather anxious looks he was receiving from Esther Young, Gideon realised that was on his account rather than the Fishers. He offered a reassuring smile and complimented the room, although it was simple, and took the seat he was offered. But before he could recount his tale, the Fishers arrived and there was another round of introductions and apologies for the absence of their son Ezra due to mild ill health, which brought a look of stark relief to Phoebe.

Nehemiah Fisher wore the same charcoal doublet with its small pewter buttons as he had when Gideon had seen him in the street before. But apart from that, there seemed little here of the man who Shiraz had described to Zahara as prostrating himself before God in misery. He glared hard at Gideon.

"I'm sure I know you from somewhere," Fisher muttered as if he was addressing himself rather than making a comment to the company.

"Perhaps because you knew my father at some point." Gideon found the lie came easily—too easily. "He spoke of you a few times."

"Name?"

"Len—" Gideon caught himself just in time. "Leonard Fox. He was a Presbyterian minister. He came from Scotland to London with King James."

Fisher's brow creased.

"And he spoke of me, you say?"

"I believe so. He spoke of a man with your name who lived in Worcester."

Fisher's face cleared.

"That would have been my father. He gave a sermon to some of the Scots when they came through Worcester." That thought seemed to satisfy him because he nodded a few times. "My father. That explains it."

Gideon's smile was genuine, relieved that his hastily crafted lie had found some solid purchase in the mind of this odd man.

"I am pleased to make your acquaintance, even so," he said and received a terse nod in return.

After prayers at the table, once the supper was served, he turned his attention to Joan Fisher. She was a stark contrast to her husband. Where he was long-limbed and sharp-joined, she was rounded and small with a kindly expression that seemed willing to overlook or forgive all the myriad faults in human nature that her husband seemed intent on seeking out and destroying. Gideon had to wonder how they got along. He had pictured any wife of such a man as Fisher as being a shrivelled shrew, with a scowl to match his. Before he could engage her in some conversation, Jacob Young spoke.

"Mr Fox was about to tell us what happened to him today," Young said. "According to Phoebe, he was quite heroic."

Gideon launched into the tale of losing his way in the streets of Worcester and encountering the saltpetre men. His account of ordering them away with legal insistence brought an open-mouthed look of adoration from Phoebe, and nods of agreement from the rest of the company.

"They think they can go where they will, those men," Esther Young said. "Go into someone's house and turn it upside down."

"You did well to make a stand against such an ungodly profession," her husband agreed.

"Is that why you were set upon?" Joan Fisher asked. "Those saltpetre men are rough. I could see them being keen to dissuade you from further opposition."

Gideon nodded. "I believe that is what happened," he said. "They followed me, determined to ensure I wouldn't interfere in their work again."

"William Richardson is a greedy and grasping man," Nehemiah Fisher pronounced and brought his fist down hard on the table as if to underscore the point. "A greedy, grasping sinner and it is written: *The wicked flee when no man pursueth: but the righteous are bold as a lion.* Bold as a lion you were, Mr Fox." Then his eyes narrowed as he looked at Gideon appraisingly. "I think you are of the righteous, Mr Fox and we are in sore need of such in this city in these troubled times."

What was he supposed to say to that? Then Gideon recalled how his father conducted such conversations.

"*Evil pursueth sinners: but to the righteous good shall be repayed,*" he said firmly as if that was an explanation rather than a simple statement of divine truth.

"Amen. Amen." The word echoed around the table.

Fisher cleared his throat and there was an expectant hush.

"I believe perhaps you are sent to us, Mr Fox, and your name is a sign of it."

Fox? Gideon was about to protest but Fisher went on.

"This king, Charles Stuart, is like the priest, Aud, claiming to be greater than God's true people and by his wealth and tawdry earthly glory, blinding them to the truth as Aud did with his sorcery. And as Gideon was chosen by God to deliver the children of Israel from the Midianites, so I see God's hand in your presence here. We in Worcester are under the oppression of these godless troops and you have come to us."

His words were met by silence, in Gideon's case an appalled one, which he hoped didn't show on his face. Phoebe appeared enraptured and her parents looked uncertain. Joan Fisher nodded vigorously.

"Amen and amen," she said and that prompted another chorus of 'amen' from the Young household, with varying degrees of enthusiasm.

Gideon said nothing and Fisher leaned towards him.

"You think you are unworthy to be an instrument of the Lord?"

"I'm just—"

But Fisher gave him no time to finish.

"Think of Jonah who ran from God as he did not feel worthy. Think of Gideon himself who would not believe until he had received signs."

"I'm not sent here by God," he protested. This was exactly the sort of situation he had wished to avoid.

Joan Fisher smiled and spoke kindly.

"Do not disturb yourself, Mr Fox. My husband means only that we cannot know God's will for us betimes. Is that not so, Reverend Fisher?"

There must have been something in her tone which penetrated Fisher's vehemence because he stared at her then gave a slow nod.

"Yes. Yes, of course, my wife. It is given only to the few to be sure what is God's will for us." Then he turned back to Gideon. "Tomorrow. You will come and speak with me. I think we have much to discuss."

Mercifully, after that the conversation turned to other things, guided by the determination of the two wives. It fell to talk of Gideon's life in London and his prospects as a lawyer, and he found himself speaking as if he were the man he had been a year before.

"And you have no wife?" That was from Joan Fisher. "Surely such a presentable young man as you with such good prospects, would have by now? Or a young lady in mind?"

There was an awkward silence. Of course, what was it Phoebe had said? Something about her family wanting her to marry Ezra Fisher?

"I have no one in London," Gideon said honestly and changed the subject by complementing the meal. That worked to navigate past the shoals and a short time later the evening was over, and the Fishers were rising to leave. Gideon made his farewells at the same time and Esther Young said she would fetch his man.

"I see you have taken some thought to your safety," Jacob Young said as they were at the door. Lord had appeared, the dutiful servant, ready to escort him back. "This fellow looks as if he might hold his own in a brawl even with Richardson's bullies."

Avoiding Lord's eye, Gideon mustered a nod.

"Indeed so. I feel much safe—"

There was an odd, strangled noise from Fisher, who had been waiting just outside the door as his wife bade the other women goodbye.

"I knew I had seen you before." Fisher's tone was accusing, and he pointed a finger at Gideon, stepping forward to poke it into his ribs. "You were with the forces of Babylon. You came here with the Midianites. I saw you riding behind that puffed-up, coxcomb son of Belial." His voice trembled. "*They shall lay hold on bow and spear; they are cruel, and have no mercy; their voice roareth like the sea; and they ride upon horses, set in array as men for war against thee, O daughter of Zion.*"

Gideon felt his blood chill and beside him, Sir Philip Lord's hand moved towards the long-bladed knife he wore.

Chapter Six

"You are not mistaken, Reverend Fisher," Gideon said quickly, then as that led to sharply indrawn breaths, he went on: "But do not take that at face value, I beg you."

"Explain yourself," Fisher demanded, his face glowering beneath heavy brows, inches from Gideon's own.

"Gladly. You know I am a London man, the son of a strict Presbyterian minister, a man devoted in religion. Yes, I am presently in the employ of Sir Philip Lord, but that is not as it appears. I am sure here in Worcester you have men of faith who work hand in glove with the Governor and Colonel Sandys and yet are not of their party—men who must come and go in some secrecy so they may serve…" he hesitated and glanced around as if reluctant to speak out "…whom they truly serve."

"How can we be sure of you?" Young said, his voice now catching and hoarse, no doubt more than aware of what would happen to himself and his family if they were shown to have any inclination to be less than loyal to the king.

"If I were Sir Philip Lord's man, I would have had men ready to seize you should you betray yourselves." He gestured to Lord. "Instead, I brought only Thomas as he too is of my persuasion."

Gideon thought he had failed. The overbright gleam in Fisher's eyes had still not faded when he began speaking again.

"*Enquire not ye of mine act: for I will not declare it unto you, till the things be finished that I do.* You." Fisher stepped back suddenly. "You are as true in the service of that base, vain and ungodly man as Judith was in the service of Holofernes. Were you loyal to the malignant man you rode in with, you would indeed have done as you say and have no cause to deny it."

Gideon nodded as relief washed over him.

"You will visit me tomorrow and we shall talk about it," Fisher said, "Tomorrow." Then he turned to Joan. "Come wife, we must go home."

It was as if Fisher's judgement was absolute. The Youngs looked much relieved, and Phoebe was smiling again. Lord's hand had relaxed.

"I'll see you safely to your house," Gideon said, surprised the Fishers had no servant to light their way. Presumably, Fisher trusted God to protect him from any earthly dangers.

The Youngs seemed pleased to see him go, except for Phoebe who had to be pulled within by her mother so the door could be closed.

"I think Phoebe likes you, Mr Fox," Joan Fisher observed as they walked along the narrow lane. It was just wide enough that Gideon could walk alongside the Fishers, with Lord behind the three of them.

"She seems a godly young woman," Gideon replied, deciding that was a safe enough response.

"She is a little flighty, in my opinion," Joan said. "Too much so for my Ezra. Ezra is a very stern and strict man in matters of godliness, as is his father."

Gideon was glad it was too dark for the flush of colour that suddenly warmed his face to be seen. The assumptions around himself and Phoebe seemed to be escalating. Worse, Joan Fisher seemed to sound more approving of Phoebe's 'flightiness' than of her son's strict religious attitude.

"Hush woman," Nehemiah rumbled. "Such things are not to be spoken of."

"Peace, my husband, I only say what all Worcester knows, and here is our door. Thank you for your company, Mr Fox."

There were brief farewells then Gideon and Lord extended their strides to head back through the darkened streets of Worcester. A patrol of soldiers was making its way along Forestreet, and Lord pulled Gideon urgently into a side turn.

"There is a curfew by my orders," he said speaking in an undertone. "I don't want to endure the comments we would have to put up with if we needed to call on Danny to vouch for us and free us from custody. He would never let me live it down. Being called a 'puffed up coxcomb son of Belial' would be mild by comparison."

They waited then, in silent concealment, pressed against the side of a building to avoid the pools of light that would be cast by the lanterns of the patrol. Only when they were sure the soldiers were well past and away did they continue along the empty street. Sounds of a brawl a few streets away disturbed them but they made it back to The Talbot without incident.

There was an untoward amount of activity there. Danny appeared beside them, face grave and grabbed Lord's arm.

"You'd better get changed fast. I've said you're with our men, but Sandys is impatient. I offered my services, but he's convinced only the great Sir Philip will do."

Then he was gone before he could draw any attention to them, and Lord cursed quietly.

"We'll have to talk tomorrow," he said. He moved off, invisible in his servant guise, making for the stairs.

Gideon searched for Zahara, but she was nowhere to be found and no one was in the room Anders was sharing with Shiraz. Heading back down to the common room, Gideon met Danny coming up the stairs.

"Anders and Zahara went to tend some at the company camp. I doubt they'll return tonight. Kate and Christobel have retired to bed, and I've been greasing the wheels of high command to stop a major incident whilst you and Philip were being entertained by the locals."

Danny steered Gideon towards their room as he spoke and closed the door, sweeping off his hat, ran a hand over his brow, pushing back the hair from his eyes as he did so.

"In the absence of the Governor, Sir William Russell, his Lieutenant Colonel Adam Davies feels it is incumbent upon himself to uphold the honour of Russell's regiment to the point of backing his men even when they were clearly in the wrong and were the aggressors in a drunken brawl with some of Samuel Sandys' soldiers. Since Argall Greene's men were both witnesses to the event and the ones who separated the two sides, Sir Philip Lord is also pulled into the heated fray." Danny dropped his hat on the bed and sat to begin removing his boots. "I am now, mercifully surplus to requirements." He finished taking off his boots and reached into his doublet. "So, Piquet or Primero?"

Gideon resisted the response that he had no wish to play either and gave in to the inevitable with as good a grace as he could muster. It was over two hours later that Danny was summoned by Lord and Gideon was finally able to get to sleep.

The following morning Zahara and Anders still had not returned and Gideon rose to an invitation from Kate to join her to break his fast in her room, with Martha serving them.

She greeted him with a warm smile.

"I thought I would have to eat breakfast alone. Have you tried this drink before? Oh, you really must, it's called chocolate and I have it on the finest authority that not only is it delicious when well sweetened, it is also fortifying for the humours."

Gideon dutifully tried it, finding the bitter undertones not so much to his taste.

Kate lifted her cup of chocolate in a toast then went on. "Philip and Danny went out with our cavalry to collect the plate from the local defaulters and stiffen their resolve. They may well be away all day. Zahara sent word that she and Anders should be rejoining us later today and Christobel left early to go out with the women working on the fortifications. There. I have been your news sheet." She smiled at him and set down her cup. "Oh, and Philip asked that you await his return before visiting the Reverend Fisher again. He seems keen that he should go with you."

Which was not entirely unexpected after the lengths Lord had gone to in establishing himself with Fisher the previous evening. Gideon was telling Kate what he had learned so far about the murder and where his suspicions lay when Martha came in with a folded note which she said had been left with the innkeeper and was addressed to 'Mr Fox'.

Kate glanced at the handwriting and her eyebrows rose a little.

"Really Gideon? A *billet-doux*? What would Zahara think?" But it was clear from her teasing tone she had no doubts at all regarding his romantic loyalty.

Gideon unfolded the paper.

THE CAVALIER'S OATH

Please meet me behind the church. I have found out something important that I think you should know about the men who attacked you.

Phoebe Young.

Gideon passed the note to Kate, who looked thoughtful.

"From what Philip told me, that young lady carries a torch for you."

A warm wash of embarrassment flushed Gideon's face.

"I've done nothing to encourage her," he said.

"I think defending her from attack would qualify in her eyes." Kate smiled and handed the note back. "What will you do?"

"I shall have to go and see what she has found out."

"Be careful," Kate cautioned. "You don't wish to compromise the girl. I'd offer to come with you myself, but I think if my arrival in a coach didn't terrify the poor child, my presence would undermine your play with Philip against the Fishers. The same if I sent Martha with you." She clicked her tongue in irritation. "Of course, everyone else is otherwise engaged. But yes, you can hardly leave her standing in the churchyard waiting for you. I assume you know which church, since she neglected to specify?"

"Not for certain but I am assuming she means the Reverend Fisher's church. It would be secluded to the rear so the perfect place for a private meeting."

"Or an assignation," Kate said, smiling. "Be kind to her, Gideon, kind but firm. She must understand not to put herself in such a place again. She is fortunate that you're the last man on earth to take advantage of her naivety."

Leaving Kate to enjoy a second cup of chocolate, and Martha delighted that she was allowed to have the one he abandoned, Gideon left. He paused on the way out of the inn to ask how the note arrived. It had been delivered by a servant who matched the description of Paul, the man who had accompanied himself and Phoebe to the Fishers. Gideon set out determined to make it clear to Phoebe that she must avoid such behaviour in the future. He could only assume that as he had been a guest in her parent's house, she now felt she was free to communicate with him as if he were a close family friend.

The churchyard, such as it was, had the shelter of a wall, some bushes and a couple of trees. There was one tomb, weathered and covered with moss and lichen and as Gideon went through the small gate at the back of the building there was no sign of anyone. He felt a lift of relief. Phoebe Young had either changed her mind or left already.

As he turned away, he caught an odd splash of blue from the corner of his eye, from behind the tomb. It was so out of place he turned back to look more closely.

It was blue cloth.

A sudden chill clutched at Gideon's stomach.

Oh, God. No. Please. Surely not.

The silent prayer spoke itself as he forced his feet towards the tomb, the awful certainty of what he would find almost paralysing him.

Phoebe Young lay like a discarded child's ragdoll, her eyes gazing up at the sky, arms bent, and legs folded as if she had stumbled then collapsed face down before someone had lifted and turned her to look up.

Gideon stumbled himself and went to one knee beside her, his hand touching something sticky. Looking without really seeing, he picked up the stone, heavy in one hand, which had blood on one end—blood and skin and hair. Gideon stared at it, slowly piecing together in his mind that someone had hit Phoebe from behind with this stone and killed her.

The scream shook him back into reality. He turned to see two women and a man who had walked around the side of the church. He got to his feet, thinking to ask one of them to fetch help. Then his numbed mind reminded him there was no help now for Phoebe Young. But he would still need Anders.

"Murderer!"

The woman shrieked the word as Gideon took a step towards the group. She was pointing to his hand. The stone. The blood was on the stone he still held and on his hand.

74

"No, you don't understand," Gideon said, shaking his head and taking another step. The three cowered back and the women screamed again.

It was inevitable that screams in Worcester at that time, with the city so well garrisoned, would result in the appearance of soldiers. Unfortunately, they were not Lord's men. It was only because there was an officer with them he wasn't killed on the spot. Instead, he was seized roughly and despite the officer's orders, he was subjected to some covert blows, the last of which was to his head after which everything became a blur.

Afterwards, he recalled repeating denials, trying to explain. No one listened. He was hustled through the streets towards the castle which was also the prison, with people staring and shouting. Once there he was taken down the stone steps to be left in the common pit, a circular chamber perhaps twenty feet across, already well occupied. There he slumped by the wall, his aching head in his hands, the stench of piss and shit churning his stomach.

But bigger in his mind than his own plight was the image of Phoebe Young, her eyes like dull glass, staring and empty, meeting his gaze in silent accusation. For it was his fault, surely, that she was dead.

The same eyes had looked at him with such vivid, warm and luminous adoration the evening before. If he hadn't tried to use her interest in himself to secure an opportunity to meet the Fishers, then she wouldn't have sent word to meet him alone. She wouldn't have been in the churchyard at that time to become the vulnerable victim of a vicious murderer.

A hand brushed his leg and with the reactions of the swordsman he was becoming, he grabbed at it, catching a slender wrist in his grip. Even in the gloom of the circular prison room, he could see the would-be thief was a young woman. She squealed as if he had hurt her and shouted abuse at him.

Gideon was too emotionally battered to respond and released her instantly, hoping if nothing else he had shown his fellow prisoners that he was not an easy target for their attention. But it was a warning to him to keep his eyes open. Here no one would stop him from being beaten and robbed. If Worcester was anything like

London, the gaolers would only intervene if the violence became disruptive enough to disturb their games of cards or dice.

Having seen his speed of reaction a couple of the men who had been edging closer, turned away from him as if in disinterest, but Gideon was sure they were all wondering why a gentleman had been thrown in amongst them. It came to him that he should bribe one of the guards to get word to The Talbot. Once it was known he was detained here, there would be those with power and influence moving heaven and earth to set him free.

Once his legs agreed to support him, he crossed to the gate and called to the guard asking to see the gaoler. But the man said he would have to wait until Colonel Sandys had seen him before he could expect such a privilege. Then he tried to bribe the guard to take a message for him. The man took the coin then laughed, saying he was too busy to go anywhere but would maybe do so when he was off duty.

Frustrated, Gideon tried to tell himself that it made little difference. Lord would hear what had happened. The whole city would surely be talking of it. But unless he could think of a way to show the world that he was indeed innocent of the death of Phoebe Young, even Sir Philip Lord could do nothing. He couldn't protect Gideon from the working of justice if it was deemed that he had been guilty of murder. The problem was Gideon knew all too well how such things ran. Why should they look further for a killer when they had someone who could be placed so neatly into the role?

He reached into his coat and realised that the note Phoebe had written was still there. It was perhaps evidence in his favour. The servant would surely admit to having taken a message to The Talbot for her even if he had no idea what the message contained. Then it struck him. The note she had written had said that she had information for him about William Richardson's men. If she had come by something incriminating about the saltpetre men, perhaps they knew she had and had acted to stop anyone else from finding out.

It stirred a small flame of hope in his breast, and he tried to nurture it by thinking through the scene as he arrived behind the church, trying to recall every detail to see if there was anything he might have missed. But every time he tried to picture the small churchyard, all he could see was the tomb, the splash of blue and the cold, sightless eyes looking up into his own as if in accusation.

He squeezed his eyes shut trying to banish that image when a slight sound close by made him open them again. One of the men was crouched close beside him and there was a small knife in his hand, the kind a thief might use to cut purses.

"Give me your purse and I'll leave you be," the man hissed, his expression invisible in the gloom.

"Very well." Gideon moved as if reaching for his pocket but instead kept his momentum going and used his forearm to knock the knife away against the wall, ploughing a fist into the man's exposed torso. It was not as powerful a blow as it would have been had he been on his feet, but it was enough to wind the man and Gideon quickly claimed the knife from the nerveless fingers. He held it up, ready to use if needed.

"Leave me alone."

Still choking, the man retreated rapidly.

Gideon put the knife down, suddenly shocked by how naturally such action had come to him. Whatever the last year had done, it had made him as much soldier as lawyer, perhaps even more soldier. It wasn't a pleasing thought. On its tail came the realisation that if he was in here for long, he would need to sleep, and his fellow prisoners would take full advantage of the fact. He just had to hope he would be redeemed soon.

An hour or so later food arrived, but it seemed only those who could pay were permitted anything other than slop and stale bread. Gideon counted the number of people and found an angel in his purse. He held it up by the bars so the gaoler could see, eyes glittering greedily in the thin light.

"This is yours if you bring a decent bowl of pottage and a good piece of bread for every man, woman and child here—myself included."

It was a large sum for him to be spending feeding the dregs of Worcester, the vast majority of whom he was sure fully deserved to be incarcerated. But somehow he lacked the stomach to be able to sit and eat decent food whilst those about him had scraps or nothing.

When it came an hour later the food was barely decent, perhaps a small piece of bacon fat to flavour every bowl, but it was warm and better fare than he was sure most here had eaten in a while. For a time, there was nothing but the sound of eating and then a few swift brawls as the stronger stole the bread of the weaker, but that was not something Gideon could do much about.

He had not expected gratitude from his fellow prisoners, he knew enough of human nature to know that even as they would devour the food, he purchased for them they would still resent him and the fact that he could afford to purchase it and they could not.

It grew dark, the only light coming from a single lantern on the other side of the barred door. Gideon began to wonder if he was to be left in that place indefinitely until he was dragged out to attend the inquest where he would be formally accused.

His absence from The Talbot would have been noted by now and the fact of his arrest brought to Sir Philip Lord's attention. But still no one came. Perhaps Lord had decided that to intervene in local justice was not within his remit when he needed the goodwill of the city. Perhaps he thought Gideon deserved to suffer for his foolishness in being taken as a murderer. Perhaps he thought Gideon guilty of the murder. Perhaps...

Whatever the reason, he had given up hope of redemption that night and begun to think how he could somehow secure himself to risk sleep when the gaoler came down the stairs.

"Fox," he called. "Is there a Fox here?"

That led to a few loud jokes about the name and a rising catcall as Gideon got to his feet and walked to the door. The sense of relief as it swung open and he was permitted to step through it was physical, as if he'd been released from pressing stones set upon his chest.

He followed the gaoler up the steps, counting each one as he went, twenty-six steps up from purgatory, from Hades, from—

Zahara was there. Swathed in a cloak, her face pale with concern. From the way her expression grew more grave, Gideon could only assume that in the raucous flicker of the fire in the hearth and the candles about, she saw nothing to reassure herself in his appearance. Shiraz stood behind her, folded woollen cloth in his arms.

"I came as soon as we found out," she said. "The Schiavono and Daniel will not return tonight. They sent word they have had much work to do and further afield than they originally thought would be needful. Lady Catherine has sent word to them and has been doing all she can to see you free, but Sir Samuel is not heeding her. She managed permission for someone to come and see you and he had not wanted to grant that." Zahara gestured to Shiraz. "I brought you a warm cloak and some blankets."

Gideon found it hard to breathe. He turned to the gaoler and reached for a coin.

"Surely we can have some privacy," he said, holding out a shilling.

The gaoler took it and gave a brusque nod.

"Only a few minutes," he said then left, closing the door behind him and locking it.

Zahara moved into his embrace, and they clung to each other briefly before she stepped back, and he released her.

"They are saying you killed Mistress Young—and Mistress Markham."

The air in Gideon's lungs was sucked away.

"I am accused of murdering *Ursula Markham*?"

Zahara nodded.

"You are accused by Colonel Martin Sandys. He says you were so quick to blame him to hide your own guilt. Now you have been caught red-handed having slain Mistress Young, which shows you are the murderer. Both women were killed with a heavy stone so whoever killed one is likely who killed both. He claims you lured both women to an isolated place where you could kill them."

Gideon reached into his doublet and found the note.

"The Youngs' manservant delivered this to The Talbot," he told her. "It is proof that I didn't lure Phoebe there. Give it to Kate. She was there when it came. And ask her to discover if any of the saltpetre men were unaccounted for at the time Phoebe was killed."

Taking the note from him, Zahara read it and slipped it out of sight before taking his hands in hers.

"I will do so," she promised. "Lady Catherine spoke of that note and tried to persuade Colonel Samuel Sandys to release you, or have you removed to a room of your own, but he refused. But as soon as the Schiavono is back things will be different. He will make Colonel Sandys listen and you will be freed." She smiled up at him and squeezed his hands as if the pressure could push reassurance into him. "God is good. He will not let you suffer for a crime you did not commit."

Gideon wished he could share her conviction. In truth, he had known of too many miscarriages of justice to be too optimistic in his own case. But he did take heart from the knowledge that in one thing she was certainly right, when he returned Lord would do all that could be done. It was a sliver of comfort in the despair he felt.

Shiraz had put down the cloth he carried and spoke silently to Zahara with his hands. She nodded and replied to Shiraz in a language Gideon did not understand. Shiraz responded with a few more gestures and Zahara nodded again before turning back to Gideon.

"Shiraz says I should tell you that if you wish he will bring you from this place. I told him that you would not want to oppose the law, but he says that sometimes the law is wrong. He says that you are a good man, and he will not stand by and see you falsely confined and condemned. He is concerned that they will try and enact their 'justice' on you before the Schiavono returns."

Shiraz nodded as she spoke. Somehow Gideon didn't doubt that given the element of complete surprise and the skill of Shiraz, he could indeed affect an escape. He also had to wonder if Shiraz was right about the Sandys' intentions. After all, if they could condemn Gideon quickly it would free Martin from any further suspicion.

It was a terrible thing for Gideon to feel that the law would fail him when he most needed its protection. If he went along with what Shiraz suggested, it would mean the end of his life as it was now, but at least he would still have life. He was certain that between them Lord and Kate would find a way for him to leave the country. Perhaps he could go and live in Saint-Léon-du-

Moulin or one of the other estates Lord had. Perhaps Zahara would go with him and perhaps they could be happy.

The sound of the key in the door heralding the return of the gaoler brought him back to earth. To escape would mean killing their way out. To escape would not only mean becoming an outlaw himself, it would also make Shiraz one—and Zahara too. He couldn't do that to them. To escape would mean turning his back on every conviction and principle he held dear and to abandon those would be to become nothing in his own estimation. Life on such terms was not a life he could contemplate.

He looked at Shiraz, who still had a hand on his sword, and who touched his coat with his other hand pulling back the fabric so a pistol butt could be seen. Gideon shook his head.

"I thank you, though. It means more than you may know that you offer such for me."

Shiraz held his gaze and must have seen Gideon's determination because he inclined his head in understanding and, Gideon thought, something of respect.

Just before the door opened Zahara reached up and brushed his cheek with her fingers.

"God keep you safe," she whispered. Then she stepped back, demure, as the gaoler entered the room. Gideon put the cloak they had brought about his shoulders and scooped up the blankets, unable to look back as he left the room.

There were twenty-six steps down to Hades, to purgatory—to hell.

Chapter Seven

That night was one of the worst Gideon had ever endured. He couldn't risk sleeping. He had no allies here, only predators who wanted his purse and wouldn't care if they had to take his life to get it.

Not that sleep was much of an option anyway. He had given away one of his two blankets to a woman with a baby which was crying incessantly until the warmth of the blanket soothed it into a fitful sleep. But then three more men were thrown in to join them and two of those were drunk and shouting. A fight broke out and blood was shed. Gideon kept to himself as much as he could even when the barging mass of men came close. The thick cloak and the blanket Zahara and Shiraz had provided brought him some comfort.

The interminable night passed and not long after dawn had slipped slender fingers through the bars of the one window, they came for Gideon. He was bleary from lack of sleep, filthy and stinking. This time he was taken into a room he assumed was used for the administration of the gaol, because there were bags and strings of documents on the walls and a battered desk.

The one chair was occupied by Colonel Samuel Sandys, his brother, fresh-faced and beardless standing beside him. They wore near-identical grim expressions. The older Sandys' opening sally set the tone right away.

"You can make this all a lot easier on yourself if you confess to your crime, Fox."

"I've committed no crime," Gideon said in his most professional and confident voice. Whatever his appearance, he could still carry himself as the lawyer he was.

"You are a despicable liar." Martin Sandys moved, hand lifted to strike.

"No." His brother's arm shot out at chest level to stop him.

"When is the inquest into the death of the two women?" Gideon asked, keeping his professional calm. "I would like to give evidence there."

"There is no need for an inquest when the matter is so plain," Samuel Sandys snapped.

"I beg to correct you, sir," Gideon said. "It is required for any death under suspicious circumstances. Sometimes the *prima facie* appearance of the case is not the whole truth and that is the function of an inquest."

Samuel Sandys scowled.

"Do not think to lecture me in the law when you are the one who has broken it."

"I haven't broken the law," Gideon insisted. "Someone murdered those two women, but it wasn't me."

"Then how do you explain that you were there on both occasions?" Martin Sandys demanded. "You came over the back wall right after I found poor Ursula who had been thrown over it and you were caught with the stone still in your hand by the body of Mistress Young. How do you explain that?" His voice shook with anger.

"If you recall, *I* found *you* by the body of Mistress Markham," Gideon pointed out. "And I was in the churchyard as I had been summoned to see Mistress Young. If you speak to the Youngs' servant he will tell you how he carried a written message for her to The Talbot, a message which the host then passed on to me. The message said that she had information regarding two saltpetre men who had attacked me outside her house in Angel Lane yesterday— nearly attacked Mistress Young too had I not stood my ground and defended her. Maybe it is those men you should be questioning, not me."

"Saltpetre men? What the—?"

"As I said, the *prima facie,* in this case, is not the whole story."

"How can you stand there so calmly?" Martin Sandys snapped. "The women are dead."

Gideon met and held his gaze. "Because I am innocent of their deaths and, like you, I want to find out who is guilty of them."

In truth, he surprised himself with how calm he felt. He knew he walked on treacherous ground, but he also knew now that whilst these men might try and bend the law, they couldn't disregard it completely. Their tenure was too fragile. Samuel Sandys was only acting governor of the city and was ultimately accountable to Sir William Russell. He also could not afford to offend Lord. Which was, of course, why he was so keen for Gideon to confess. He wanted a quick and tidy end to these murders. Justice seen to be done. Martin Sandys, on the other hand, simply wanted someone to blame for the death of the woman he had idolised.

Samuel waved a hand as if brushing away Gideon's inconvenient denial.

"You say there was a written message?"

"There was. I told you what it said and that both the innkeeper at The Talbot and the Youngs' servant can confirm that it was sent. I made no assignation with Mistress Young."

"Then where is this message?"

Gideon felt brief gratitude for the prescience he had in placing it safely in Zahara's care.

"I showed it to Lady Catherine Lord, and she has it now for safekeeping. I am sure she will have mentioned it to you."

Samuel Sandys frowned. That was something he obviously found inconvenient. Lady Catherine Lord was not a person easy to set aside.

"I have not seen it. Regardless, you will be detained pending your trial."

A trial might not take place for weeks or even months during which time Gideon would, of course, be held prisoner. Despite himself, Gideon shivered.

"I hope investigations into the killings will continue in the meantime," he said. "Since I did not commit them, whoever did is still at large and might kill again."

Martin Sandys snorted.

"I think we have the right man. The women of Worcester are safe as long as you are kept locked up."

"And that is precisely what will continue to happen," his brother said, expression hardening. "I think we are done here."

When Gideon was pushed back into the dungeon, it was to find both his blanket vanished, and the place he had left it, occupied. He might even have sought to reclaim the spot, but the new occupants were two children with eyes as round as saucers who stared at him in mute misery and fear. So he left them there, glad he still had the cloak.

He found another place, but this one was less isolated. He had to be on his guard much more against the men there. Morning went to afternoon and Gideon dozed, waking abruptly if anyone came to close. It was starting to get dark when the door of the dungeon was flung open and Gideon shot to his feet.

Sir Philip Lord strode in, eyes blazing and face demonic in the swaying lantern light, radiating narrowly controlled fury. Danny Bristow was at one shoulder holding up a lantern, with a tight-lipped Colonel Samuel Sandys a couple of paces behind, alongside two of Lord's soldiers. Lord stopped short of Gideon, who suddenly found himself alone. Those who had been near him tried to lose themselves in the shadows. No doubt they feared drawing the attention of this terrifying figure who had burst into the prison like a creature of vengeance.

"Mr Fox," Lord said, his tone cold, but Gideon, knowing him better than most, could hear in it the fine thread of relief. He turned sharply, hand on his sword and those left closest to Gideon, cowered away. "Colonel Sandys, you will release this man into my custody immediately. You have my word he will present himself at any legitimate inquest or trial."

Sandys looked unhappy, but he set his jaw and nodded. "If you insist, Sir Philip."

Lord gave him a brief bow.

"I do and thank you. Colonel Bristow, take Fox to my lodgings. I have some urgent business with Colonel Sandys."

Then Lord swept from the prison, Sandys a pace behind.

"I wouldn't wish to be the one wearing Samuel Sandys' boots right now," Danny said after they left. Then he gestured to the door, held open by one of the two men Lord had brought. "Shall we go?"

Gideon needed no second bidding and as the door was locked behind him, he stopped and closed his eyes to offer a silent prayer of gratitude for his deliverance. Danny gripped his arm.

"Are you alright?" He sounded genuinely concerned.

Gideon opened his eyes and nodded.

"Yes. It is just... just…"

Danny gave him a lopsided grin.

"I know. Believe me, I know." He steered Gideon up the flight of steps to the fresh air. "We came as soon as we could. Philip is furious. You should have heard him lecturing Sandys about how you were the one he had set to find the killer and any accusation of your involvement in such could only be malicious. He ordered that Anders be permitted to examine the dead woman and set a guard on the place where she was found until he can look there too. Philip seems to think our physician has some ability in knowing the how and why of a murder from such things."

Danny's speech took them up the twenty-six steps and into the main body of the castle where Gideon stopped. There was something he needed to do.

"I must speak with the gaoler before we go," he said.

"We have your sword. The man took something else of yours you want back?"

"In a manner of speaking.".

Of course, now Gideon was standing on the same side of the bars as the gaoler himself, he was smiling and obsequious.

"How can I help you, good sirs?"

"I believe you owe some money," Gideon told him.

The gaoler looked puzzled.

"I don't think—"

"I gave one of your men a golden angel to provide a good meal for every prisoner and he served but a thin gruel and a small piece of bread."

Danny's eyes widened. "You paid this man an entire angel? For that?"

"I did," Gideon confirmed. "As I see it, he still owes me a decent meal for those prisoners."

Danny's expression hardened, his hand resting on his sword. "I agree. He does."

They left the gaoler promising to provide a good meal for all his charges. It was little enough, but it went some small way towards salving Gideon's conscience that he could walk free whilst, beneath his feet, his fellow accused, both the innocent and the guilty, were left to rot in the dark.

Arriving back at The Talbot he received a hero's welcome.

Zahara embraced him, even before he had changed out of his filthy clothes. Kate insisted they have a special meal to celebrate and sent Martha to arrange for a room and the best food and drink the inn could offer. Shiraz was smiling and Danny regaled them with a hilarious account of Philip Lord taking Colonel Samuel Sandys to task for daring to imprison Gideon in the first place.

Gideon went to get changed. He was delighted to feel the touch of fresh linen on his skin and glad to be rid of the stench of the prison. It was fully dark outside by the time he was sitting on the side of the tester bedstead doing up his shoes and a knock at the door announced the arrival of Anders.

"I wanted to be sure you had taken no harm in that place," he said, putting his large leather medical bag down.

"None so far as I know," Gideon assured him. "A few bruises where the men who took me were less than gentle, but nothing worse."

"I am glad that Sir Philip got you out of there," Anders said. "I had no idea you had been thrown into the city prison until this afternoon when matters were already being put in hand to see you set at liberty. I was with our men last night."

"Did you manage to see Mistress Young?" Gideon asked.

"I did, but only because I had the authority and armed force to insist on it." Anders looked pained at the memory. "That does not make me feel proud, but her parents were set against anyone doing so. They seem good people and they loved their daughter. But the fire doesn't care about the owner of the coat that is burning."

"She mentioned saltpetre men in her note, do you know if any enquiry was made?

"Lady Catherine did so herself. But all the men working as collectors in the city have been accounted for. None could have been in the churchyard alone at that time."

Gideon felt his heart sink. He had been so sure.

"Was there anything…?"

"She was killed by being hit with a rock from behind," Anders told him. "The same as Mistress Markham. However, I would say that unlike Mistress Markham she was not running or even concerned for her life. There was no sign that she tried to fight or flee. It is as if the man either crept up behind her and struck her without her knowing he was there, or she knew him and had no reason to fear to turn her back on him. I was able to offer that small comfort to her parents, that she would not have known fear or pain."

"But nothing which exonerates me," Gideon said, unable not to sound bitter.

Anders spread his hands.

"I can only tell you what I observed. But tomorrow when it is light, I will look at the place it happened and see if that adds anything more to what I may tell you of her death." He picked his bag up just as the door burst open. Danny exploded into the room, his face blanched beneath the freckles in an ugly contrast.

"Anders. It's Christobel."

The Dane was out of the door a pace behind Danny. Gideon felt his heart lodge in his gullet as he ran after the other two men, taking the stairs three at a time.

Please, he prayed, *please, please not Christobel too...*

Christobel was in the room that had been prepared for their celebration of Gideon's redemption. Her complexion, always naturally pale, had a grey tinge to it as she sat in a high-backed chair. Zahara was holding a cloth which smelt powerfully of medicament, over a place on the back of her head. Brighid Rider was soaking another cloth in a bowl of the pungent-smelling liquid and Kate was standing beside Christobel, talking to her in a calm and cheerful voice. She turned, smiling with her lips if not her eyes as they entered the room.

"...and here is Anders," Kate said and stepped back, sinking into a chair herself.

A tidal bore of relief rushed through Gideon's veins. Christobel was alive. She had not been murdered like the others, although it was apparent someone had tried.

Christobel managed a weak smile but those startling eyes, the twin to Lord's, looked dull. Anders asked both her and Zahara various questions and examined the head wound.

"Gideon, you do realise what this means?" Kate asked.

"It means I was right to fear for Christobel's safety," he said, unable to avoid a bitter bite to his tone.

"It means," Kate said with emphasis on the second word, "that you are exonerated. You couldn't possibly have attacked Christobel." Kate beckoned Brighid over. She left the cloth soaking in the bowl and made a brief curtsey. "You must tell Gideon what happened. There might be something he thinks needs doing right away so we can find the man who attacked the two of you."

Brighid nodded, her dark eyes meeting Gideon's gaze.

"We were walking back with a group of women who'd been helping with the new eastern defences Colonel Bristow has in hand. There was a dozen of us. It was getting to twilight, and we'd come up along the earthworks from Friar's Gate to Martin's Gate. We'd just heard how you'd been taken for the murderer and Christa was—" She broke off and flushed, her dark complexion darkening further into a blush. "Mistress Christobel was angry and saying how it was plain to see it wasn't you. We decided to let the other women go ahead. Chri—Mistress Christobel said she wanted to see if she could lure the murderer out so we could prove—"

"Wait." Gideon held up a hand as he spoke the word "The two of you *planned* to get attacked?"

Brighid nodded then flushed again and dropped her gaze. "But it wasn't like that."

Kate gripped his arm.

"It is done, Gideon," she said in a tone that left him no room to object. "Let us take from it what we may. Recriminations, if required, can come later."

Gideon closed his mouth and held it closed by willpower as Brighid sent Kate a grateful look and went on.

"The thing was," she said, "we didn't mean it to be then. You see we were going to go back and ask Roger so he could follow us. But we'd no chance because that was when it happened. There's a stand of bushes by the back of Martin's Gate and a cut-through behind the houses as it turns into Glovers Street, and we were just passing when a stone flew out from the bushes and hit Mistress Christobel. Before I could do anything, it was followed by a man saying something about it being an abomination to wear men's garments, though what he meant I don't know as we were both clad in skirts." She lifted her shoulders in a shrug. "Anyway, I don't think he saw me as we had to walk one by one through the cut there. I had my knife and stabbed him as he went to hit Christa again. He yelled. Then other people came running. He fled back into those bushes and was gone. I would have been after him, but Christa was hurt I had to look to her."

Gideon tried to set aside his concern for the danger the two women had been in so he could concentrate on what Brighid was telling him, as Kate had said there might be something needed to act on quickly.

"Did you see this man—his face? Or anything about him?"

"He was tall but his build I couldn't say. He had a dark coat which made him hard to see and the light was poor."

"Where did you stab him?"

"I think the arm or shoulder."

"Did you cut him deeply?"

"I felt the knife go in, but it was through cloth, and it came out as he pulled away so it can't have been bone deep." She shivered at the memory.

"You heard him speak, was he a local?"

"He was English, but I'm not sure of anything else."

At least the man they were looking for was marked. He had been stabbed.

Anders was still tending to Christobel, mixing something in a small bowl and explaining as he worked.

"...what Ambroise Paré calls *commotio cerebri*. It is usually temporary but causes headaches, nausea and even slight memory loss. The good news is that the skull itself is not broken, but I have treated it with his suggested remedy for injury to the skull of rose oil, egg white and turpentine." He looked across to Christobel and smiled. "You will be fine in a few days at most—perhaps even tomorrow, God willing."

Christobel looked dazed but gave a small nod to show she understood. Danny scooped Christobel into his arms, a turban of bandaged dressings about her head, and carried her upstairs. Zahara and Brighid followed as Anders repacked his medical bag.

Kate gave Gideon a small smile. "I am sorry this has spoiled our celebration for you," she said. "However, we all need to eat so I see no reason not to go on with the meal. Philip always has enough appetite for three men anyway."

"If you will excuse me," Gideon said. "I should first go and see where the attack occurred. There might be something there that could help identify the man we seek." He got to his feet.

"You mustn't go anywhere alone," Kate said quickly. "Aside from your safety, you need to take Danny with you so you cannot be apprehended again."

Which was an uncomfortable reminder of the fact that he was at present free solely under Sir Philip Lord's grace.

"I will come too," Anders said. "That is if Lady Catherine is willing to delay the meal to which we are all so generously invited?"

"Lady Catherine is content to do so," Kate agreed. "Although she is not able to promise the food will be as good as if served at the time she requested."

Anders left quickly to return his bag to his room. Kate leaned forwards and took Gideon's hand in her own.

"It must have been harrowing for you to find poor Mistress Young like that. She was enamoured of you and that always places a sense of responsibility on those of us who care about how we pass through this world."

Gideon shook his head but not in any form of denial.

"She was young. Vulnerable. I exploited that to meet the Fishers. If I hadn't—"

"If you hadn't, she would still have sent you that message," Kate assured him. "Ever since you defended her, she was looking for an opportunity to have your attention." Kate released his hand and sat back. "Perhaps it wasn't your proudest moment taking advantage of her misplaced affections, but I promise you that was not what led to her death."

Her words eased the burden that had placed heavy chains about his shoulders just as the door opened to readmit Anders and a rueful-looking Danny.

"My presence is surplus to requirements," Danny said wryly. "Zahara and Brighid have everything in hand. I am unwanted." Then he must have caught the look Anders gave Gideon because he grinned suddenly and clapped his hands, rubbing them together when they met. "Oh, someone wants me? Where to, gentlemen and do I need my sword?"

Chapter Eight

It was as well Danny took his sword and a handful of his men as an escort too, since they were unfortunate enough to run into another drunken brawl of soldiery. The men of Colonel Sandys and Sir William Russell had yet again come to blows in the street.

Danny used his men and his authority to good effect, having the host of the alehouse which had been serving ale after curfew arrested for doing so.

"We should do here what the Dutch do and have *doe den tap toe* each evening," he said when they were finally free to move on. "I'll talk to Philip about it. If not, I fear we'll have the hosts and hostesses of half the taverns, alehouses and ordinaries in Worcester under arrest before the week is out."

"*Doe den tap toe?*" Gideon asked. "What is that?"

"Turn off the taps," Anders translated.

"Exactly that," Danny concurred. "The Dutch send drum and fife to march through the towns they garrison to play 'taps' so the tavern keepers and their ilk know to turn off the taps on their kegs, stop serving beer and send the soldiers back to barracks. The Dutch," he said thoughtfully, "are a very well-organised people. Pragmatic. I admire that. If I weren't English, I would very much like to be Dutch."

They found the path between Martin's Gate and Glovers Street and Gideon quickly realised that even with lanterns, there would be little they could see at night. With much reluctance, as he wished to progress the matter as fast as he could, Gideon agreed that Danny should leave a guard on the path at either end to keep people from it until they could make a proper inspection the following morning.

He was turning away from a final look at the scene, as Danny issued the needed orders when the lantern light winked mutedly on something on the ground. Picking it up he found it was a pewter button, still attached to some shreds of black wool that he could see were slightly matted with blood. He studied the button which was shaped like a bead and had a small cross-cut design opposite the shank, wondering why it looked so familiar.

"What is that?" Anders asked.

Gideon showed him. "Brighid's cut did more than just draw blood."

"We look for a man who is missing this button? It is a shame it is not more distinctive."

Anders' words unlocked a memory.

"Perhaps it doesn't need to be to point a finger for us," Gideon said, "I saw buttons identical to this on the doublet that Nehemiah Fisher was wearing. Sir Philip will confirm as much, I am sure. We must ask him."

Sir Philip had returned to The Talbot by the time they got back. Gideon took a seat at the table between Lord and Shiraz. Danny was already heaping a dish with food. Zahara returned from taking supper to Christobel and Brighid and as she sat beside Kate, Anders asked her a quick question, nodding at her reply.

"I've sent word to Samuel Sandys," Lord told him, fingers dripping with some dark red sauce as he ate. "You should no longer be considered guilty of the murders since other women were attacked in the same way when you were firmly in my keeping. He might, of course, choose to cast aspersions upon my caretaking, but I think it more likely he will allow your innocence. He needs my goodwill. He is finding I make a fine ally in his cause against the intransigent policies of Sir William Russell and would see it as unwise to endanger that."

"Does this mean I'm no longer your prisoner?" Gideon asked.

"You are no longer counted amongst the damned," Lord assured him. "*Nimble jugglers that deceive the eye, dark-working sorcerers that change the mind, soul-killing witches that deform the body, disguised cheaters, prating mountebanks...* No, you are now adjudged soul-pure and restored as a penitent redeemed by grace." He lifted a finger. "However, there is one caveat I place upon that. For your safety, I must insist you keep company at all times. I do not trust that all in this city will be willing to accept your innocence."

"I'm already struggling to see how I can both arrest Joan Fisher's husband and secure her goodwill on your account, which will complicate matters," Gideon protested.

Lord cocked his head.

"You think Reverend Fisher is the murderer?"

Gideon produced the button attached to its matted cloth and set it on the table. It was Kate who commented first.

"You found that where Christobel was attacked?"

Gideon nodded.

"And that," Lord jabbed a finger towards the button, "is the same as Nehemiah Fisher was wearing running down the front of his doublet on Thursday evening."

Kate picked it up and wrinkled her nose at the blood.

"It's a common style," she said. "But the small design on the top is perhaps less so. I would be reluctant to hang a man on this alone."

Lord pushed the button towards Gideon. "Tomorrow being a Sunday, you must to church with your loyal servant Thomas. To offer thanks that, as Joseph before you, you have been delivered from Pharoah's dungeon."

Gideon wasn't happy with that prospect, but he put the button away and allowed himself to be drawn from his troubles by the brilliance and humour of what passed for table talk in Sir Philip Lord's household under the sway of its master and his lady. It was, Gideon knew, a large part of their strength that they could step aside from whatever the issue of the day might be and find—no, create a small place of joy and brightness. Closing the shutters firmly on the darkness beyond, they were, for a short time, at peace.

Which meant he went to bed as they all did, without the weight of cares too heavy to stand as a barrier against sleep. Even Danny, having gone with Anders to be sure that Christobel slept well, came yawning to bed and made no mention of cards.

Sunday morning dawned and Gideon had barely dressed when Lord arrived in his servant's guise.

"Are you sure this is wise?" Gideon asked. "As you have said, some will remain convinced of my guilt. Fisher might well be one."

"I neglected to mention that when I was with him yesterday evening, Colonel Sandys received representation from Nehemiah Fisher. He took on the role of Moses to Pharaoh and demanded that you be released. Of course, by then word had spread that another woman had been attacked whilst you were detained."

"But why…?" Gideon tailed off his question unfinished. The obvious answer was that Fisher knew Gideon was innocent because he was guilty.

"I also had no chance to tell you what I learned sitting in the Youngs' kitchen whilst you supped with them," Lord went on. "There was talk of the reverend and his wife being less than happy about their son marrying Phoebe Young. Joan Fisher, it seems, thought them a poor match in personalities and Nehemiah regarded poor Phoebe as coming from too lowly a background."

"Would that be grounds for murder? He could simply have broken the arrangement off. Phoebe would have been delighted."

"Indeed so, but Ezra—according to servants' gossip—was much enamoured of Phoebe Fisher and is cast in his father's stubborn mould, if not more so."

As they left the inn, Gideon realised that the last time he had been in any church with Sir Philip Lord it had been for Lord's wedding to Kate. When they entered Nehemiah Fisher's church Gideon was struck by how different that church in Oxford had been from this one. On the outside, they could belong to the same tradition. But within, the walls here were plaster-plain and where, perhaps, delicate stained glass had previously graced the high windows, now there was ordinary glass in most, though gorgeous colours still filtered in from what had once been a side-chapel.

When the Reverend Fisher appeared, he bore no sign of any injury and no additional bulk of bandaging was discernible. He wondered if Brighid hadn't cut as deeply as she believed she had.

The Book of Common Prayer was followed to the letter, but Gideon could feel grudging participation at some points from much of the congregation. Those attending were, as the Youngs, what Dudd Dudley's friend had called 'the middling sort' of men. Those who earned their livelihood with their hands as craftsmen—clothiers, glovers, hosiers, hatmakers, cabinet makers, coopers and cobblers. They were men of some education and strong opinions. Opinions that Fisher both reflected and helped to shape in his sermon.

When the time for that came, the hush in the church was as if a hungry crowd awaited admittance to a meal. Fisher stood before them on the floor of the church. There was a hard glint in his gaze, one Gideon recognised for he had seen it often in his father and despite himself, he shivered.

"Ephesians, chapter six, verse twelve. *For we wrestle not against flesh and blood, but against principalities, against powers, against the rulers of the darkness of this world, against spiritual wickedness in high places.*"

There was an indrawing of breath across the church and the tension was palpable. These people had not come for spiritual comfort. They were here to be fired up with righteous anger and they knew they were going to be well provided.

Gideon recognised much of what followed. He had read it in various pamphlets and printings and heard the arguments rehearsed in discussions and debates. Some of the more moderate views he wholeheartedly agreed with. Fisher was a clever man. He avoided saying anything against the king, making his entire sermon about Biblical rulers who had been defeated and overthrown and allowing his audience to draw what they would of a modern parallel. He spoke much as he had to Gideon over supper, of God sending deliverance to his oppressed people and he reminded them that, like the wise virgins, they must keep their lamps filled with oil and be ready.

After the service had finished Gideon kept in his place as the church emptied around him. To his relief, it seemed he hadn't been recognised as the suspected murderer dragged through the streets two days before. But then he was dressed differently, and his sober and pensive mien probably didn't fit whatever notion most there might have of what a murderer should be like.

ELEANOR SWIFT-HOOK

"*Blessed be the Lord, who hath delivered you out of the hand of the Egyptians, and out of the hand of Pharaoh.*" Nehemiah Fisher strode over from where he had been speaking to a group of his parishioners, his voice ringing across the church. Heads turned and Gideon's heart picked up its pace. "I didn't think you would come. But God is indeed marvellous, and you have. Praise be!"

Gideon feared that Fisher would embrace him, but he satisfied himself with gripping one shoulder.

"You should be careful," Fisher went on, his voice low now. "The Midianites send their spies into our camp. It is best if we don't seem too friendly. Take your leave and send your servant to my house within the hour, I shall have something for you."

But Gideon wanted answers.

"How are you so sure I'm innocent? Others seem less so. Colonel Sandys is convinced of my guilt."

Fisher released Gideon's shoulder and lowered his head.

He was going to confess, surely.

"That is why I am sure of your innocence," Fisher said, his eyes ablaze as he looked up again. "You were condemned by Pharoah. And it is the way that God works to show his chosen through persecution."

Gideon bowed his head as if in acceptance. Then, on an inspiration, reached out and clapped Fisher above the elbow, squeezing his shoulder on the side he had not lifted his arm. Fisher nodded and gave him a slight smile.

"Send your man to my house. We'll meet and talk later. I'll tell your man where." Then he turned and strode back to his waiting parishioners who were talking amongst themselves, with one or two sending distinctly dark looks in Gideon's direction.

"His shoulder isn't injured then," Lord observed in a low voice.

"No. But…"

"Something isn't right?"

"I don't think he is the murderer," Gideon said. "I think the buttons are a coincidence, a chance purchase from the same seller. But not Fisher, then who?"

"Murderer or no makes little difference to what we need to do. His entire sermon was a call to arms against the king and strongly

98

suggested some immediate action." Lord shook his head. "That means we have to keep as we are with him regardless of whether he was involved in the murders or not. There is an inn nearby, you can wait there. I'll go to his house and see what he has to say."

The Rose and Crown on Foregate was a fine inn. Sir Philip Lord performed his servant's task of arranging food and drink for his master, before slipping out of the stableyard door.

As he ate, Gideon found his thoughts turning over all he knew about the murders. If not Nehemiah Fisher, then who had killed the two women and attacked Christobel? He went back to the beginning, starting with the women themselves. Was there some common thread that bound them together apart from being on their own in places that were secluded?

The obvious point, especially in light of what Brighid had heard the attacker say, was that both Ursula and Christobel were involved with encouraging the women of Worcester to help prepare the defences for a siege. But Phoebe Young hadn't been one of those women. She'd been a true daughter of her father.

Then it struck him that Joan Fisher had called Phoebe 'flighty'. Did that mean she was perhaps getting up to things outside her family's knowledge? Could it be she was involved in some way with the women who were helping with the defences? After all, she had been bold enough to send a message to Gideon. And what it was that Phoebe had wanted to tell him about William Richardson's men?

The remains of his meal were still on the table when Lord returned and set to with enthusiasm in finishing it off.

"I had to wait for a while. The reverend was occupied." He spoke between mouthfuls, voice lowered so it wouldn't carry beyond Gideon. "We have a meeting to attend later today at the sign of The Swan on Baker's Street. I'll have Danny bring some of the company so if there are enough of the conspirators, we can take them *in flagrante delicto*."

Gideon stared at him in horror and had to make a conscious effort to keep his voice subdued.

"If we are to have any chance at all of getting the information we need about Lydia Kelley from Joan Fisher, that would be a bad idea. I would be top of the list of suspects."

Lord looked thoughtful and swallowed his mouthful.

"Not if you and I are seen to be arrested along with the others. Then perhaps, I in my rightful guise, could visit Goodwife Fisher and offer the safe return of her husband in exchange for the information she holds regarding the whereabouts of her mother." He sat back and smiled. "That would work well I think, especially now you are convinced he is not a murderer. I would be willing to let one rebel go free, although he would need to be removed from his benefice. We really cannot allow such enthusiastic preaching against myself and our men to persist."

"You are missing one important point," Gideon said. Lord ate some stewed fruit and tilted his head slightly in interrogation as he did so. "Joan Fisher might feel that it would be placing her mother at risk—if she is indeed even still alive—to betray her whereabouts to someone willing to threaten the life of her husband to obtain the information. For all we know, she is more fond of her mother than of her husband."

"If she is indeed even still alive," Lord echoed quietly. "But I regret you may be right. After all, Goodwife Fisher could simply deny her mother yet lives, even if she does, or send us on a wild-goose chase. All of which makes my job much harder as I promised Sandys, I would sweep up the malignants in his city." He spread his hands in defeat. "Very well, we will go as we are and see how the land lies. But I want as many names from this meeting as we can muster between us. I cannot afford to let such an opportunity go by with nothing done."

"When is the meeting?"

"At half-seven this evening, which suggests to me it will not be a long one, as curfew is at sunset and that will be less than an hour after. I am sure these conspirators will not wish to draw attention to themselves by being out after curfew."

"If they are conspirators," Gideon said. "They might just be meeting for prayer and Bible reading."

"I am sure that will be the excuse should anyone in authority chance by," Lord agreed, "However if that were the case the reverend would not be having me collect your invitation for you." He reached into his fob pocket and produced a small coin, pushing it across the table to Gideon, who picked it up and studied it.

It was a token of the usual kind that popular taverns and inns might issue to their customers to make up for the universal shortage of small change and to ensure they would return to spend again. This one had a swan on it on one side and the other—where the value of the token might expect to be found—was blank.

Gideon pocketed it. As a way of identifying someone, it was anonymous. Such tokens were ubiquitous, and if one had been issued without its obverse stamped by mistake, who was to know that had any special significance?

"And now we should return to The Talbot so I can realign my appearance with my true identity. Alas, I have matters I must attend to this afternoon, whereas you may take your leisure and spend the hours in meditation and contemplation as is meet for the sabbath."

They left the inn and the street was quieter than usual as it was Sunday. For some reason, Gideon found that thought enough to bring a surge of nostalgia for his old, settled life. A life where there were difficulties and troubles, but which had been within bounds predictable and secure. When he knew each week that he would attend the same church and each night sleep under the same roof. He wondered if he would ever know that life again.

"How do you live like this?" Gideon asked as they walked. "From inn room to lodgings, from tent to begrudged quarters, from abandoned ruins to stolen houses? Where is home?"

Lord glanced at him as if wondering the origin of such a question.

"I've not had a home in the way you mean it since I was a child. For me, it is people that make a home, not buildings or possessions. I come home to Kate wherever she may be."

Perhaps that made sense for a man like Lord, but Gideon was not at all sure he felt the same.

When they reached The Talbot, Lord vanished to his room to get changed and Gideon was about to follow him upstairs when he was hailed from the common room.

"Mr Fox. Mr Fox, sir."

Gideon turned, one hand on the bannister rail. It was one of Danny's men. He stepped off the stair as the man approached him.

"Mr Fox. Colonel Bristow asks if you would do him the kindness of attending upon him right away. He said I should tell you it is an urgent legal matter that he would appreciate your help with. I have a horse ready and waiting for you if you would…?"

Of course, Gideon went.

Chapter Nine

"It's neither urgent, nor a matter for a lawyer," Gideon protested. Danny was cheerfully unrepentant.

"I consider it urgent," he said. "Who better than a lawyer to offer a cool head in judgement?"

They were standing on top of the fortifications on some kind of platform built to hold a group of guns. Behind them were the old walls of the city and in front, the rolling Worcestershire countryside.

"My *judgement* says that you are both being childish." Gideon was struggling to believe that Danny thought having a bet with Dudd Dudley to settle their disagreements was a matter which needed his attention. Especially such a bet on the sabbath.

Danny had the grace to look sheepish.

"You don't have to work with the man," he said. "If you did, you'd understand. I suggested the bet so I could dispense with having to argue the depth of every ditch, the angle of every salient and scarp, the width of every berm, the number of gabions for each cannon and even the correct placement of the guns—though he has mostly stopped opposing me on that since Scarlett always accords with my choices." Danny broke off and lifted both his hands in frustration. "I have forever to put right whatever he's decided needs changing and ordered so in my absence."

Gideon was incredulous.

"And you thought the best way to resolve the matter was to have a bet, with the winner being the one who will oversee the rest of the fortification work and the loser relegated to an assistant?"

Danny tilted his head and then nodded.

"Yes. Oh, and the loser has to say nothing to the winner for the next full day as well so there can be no debates or arguments."

"What do you need me here for?" Gideon asked. "I assume you've challenged Dudd to a game of Piquet?"

Danny wrinkled his nose, his freckles emphasising the expression.

"Not exactly," he admitted.

If the situation hadn't been so serious Gideon would have found it comical. Two grown men unable to work together, resorting to schoolboy methods of resolving the issue. Though, he supposed, this being Danny it was probably a better alternative than the more obvious one of his calling Dudd Dudley out with swords. Gideon gritted his teeth.

"Then what have you in mind?"

"A duel. No, it's not what you think. A duel with cannon."

"You are going to shoot at each other with artillery pieces?"

Gideon was near despair.

"Of course not," Danny said, as if even to think of taking his words in such a way was ludicrous. "Philip wouldn't forgive me if I killed Dudd, or there'd be no problem at all." He gestured out over the fields before the earthworks. "Do you see that broken-down barn?"

It was a ruined structure perhaps a mile and a half away. Gideon, misliking where this was going, nodded reluctantly.

"We each have three shots. Whoever gets the closest or hits it the most with their three shots wins."

Gideon knew little about artillery, but he knew that accuracy was not a strong point for most over that kind of distance even if the ball might travel as far or further.

"And where do I come in?"

Danny took off his hat and scratched at his scalp before replacing the hat again.

"You're my adjudicator," he said, avoiding Gideon's gaze.

"I'm—?"

"The idea is that you, Scarlett and someone who Dudd appoints will judge the wager. You won't know which guns we each fire— even we won't know until we begin as we have agreed to toss a coin for who gets which battery—so you three record which shots hit the barn."

"And if none do?"

Danny looked askance.

"If none do then Dudd Dudley deserves to win," he said sharply. Then he sighed. "If none do then you have to decide which shot came closest. That is why we have three judges, so there can be no tie if it comes to a difference of opinion."

"If Lord knew you were doing this, he'd—"

Danny looked up at the sky.

"If Philip knew I was doing this he might fire me from one of the cannon. Yes. Yes. I know. That's why I asked you and not someone who holds a military rank. They'd be duty-bound to tell Philip about it." Danny spread his hands as if in defeat. "I need your help. Please. As my friend and someone I can trust."

It was an appeal Gideon knew he had to honour. Danny had stood by him in friendship more than once. He looked out over the peaceful fields.

"What if one of your cannonballs kills someone?" he asked.

"There are no houses in any danger unless Dudd decides to fire in completely the wrong direction and not even he is that stupid." Danny looked thoughtful and frowned. "Well, I don't think he is."

"And people in the fields?"

Danny waved a dismissive hand. "I've had my men run a sweep over the area to clear it. We need to practice fire anyway. Who knows when Waller might appear over that very horizon?"

Gideon realised he was hearing the beginning of the justification Danny would use with Lord. He also knew from experience that for every logical argument he put forward Danny would muster two against. It struck him that if Danny had become a lawyer, he would have been a ferociously successful one.

"Alright. I'll do it," he said, not troubling to disguise the grudging reluctance in his voice.

Danny grinned and thumped him on the back.

"I knew I could count on you. Come with me."

He led the way along the crude walkways that connected the gun placements. At one point there was a group of men working their way along the ditches with a cartload of wooden stakes, sharpened at each end which they were setting to point out.

"Storm poles," Danny said, seeing the focus of his attention, "I wanted abatis but get storm poles. That is the story of my life." He shrugged theatrically. "At least we have chevaux-de-frise for the roads, as we are not allowed to do anything else to them since it might upset the citizens."

Gideon tried to look as though he understood as they came to another bastion—or was it a bulwark? Either way, it was an angular pointing platform on which cannon had been placed to threaten the peaceful and empty fields. However, even his inexpert eye could see the presence of hills nearby was a significant challenge to the defensive strength they offered. But, Gideon supposed, that was more about the placement of the city than the fortifications themselves. He was sure that whatever could be done to mitigate the threat would have been arranged. Danny was not a man to overlook anything.

Dudd Dudley stood by one of the cannon with two men. One was a small, prematurely balding man in his thirties and the other a man who Gideon recognised as the loud-mouth bluff officer from Sandys' supper table on their first night in the Worcester. Danny performed the reintroductions quickly.

"Captain Humphrey Beaumont you will remember Gideon Fox, he is a lawyer. Gideon, this is Ned Scarlett, master gunner and the chief cannoneer of the Worcester garrison."

Gideon noticed Danny neglected to mention Dudley but the man himself seemed unconcerned as if it was a given everyone would know who he was.

"Good, then we have our adjudicators," Dudd said and rubbed his hands together, clearly delighted at the prospect of the contest ahead. "I'll have you eating your words, Bristow, you wait and see. I know you've been pouring lies into the ears of Colonel Sandys and Sir Philip about my work. Well, this will show everyone once and for all which of us is the better man."

"I've not told a single lie about you," Danny protested. "Oh, wait. I described you once as the son of a baron rather than the *bastard* son of a baron. My apologies for that."

Dudd snarled and gripped his sword before Beaumont put a restraining hand on his arm.

"He's not even a proper gentleman, Dudd. His father was a tradesman." Beaumont said the last word as if it was an inherited deformity.

Gideon was beginning to see that some kind of resolution needed to be reached between these two men or blood would indeed be shed, their antipathy rested on such deep foundations. Perhaps Danny was wise in making it into a relatively harmless target shooting contest and that the weapons chosen for the task were great engines of war. The sheer scale made the thing, win or lose, an unmistakable public display to the world which perhaps offered a stage big enough for Dudd's sense of self-importance whichever way it fell out.

The only problem was that the outcome was far from certain. Danny might indeed be the better cannoneer of the two but over such a distance, luck would surely play a huge role. He had listened to Danny in the past, when challenged over the utility of cannons on a battlefield, waxing on about how between 'point blank' and 'best random' there was almost no ground.

"You do the calculations, set the elevation, then pray," he had said. "Although it helps if you know the personalities of your guns."

But Gideon also knew what kind of a gambler Danny was. He would never make such a wager unless he was confident he stood a very good chance of winning it—a chance he would have calculated out to the smallest fraction, no doubt.

The three judges were to take a sighting place on some outlying high ground the locals called Wheatsheaf Hill, where Danny had been building a fort, with lines of communication and defensive ditches going back towards the city.

"Then let's get this done," Danny said stiffly. "We'll see who is the better man to match Waller if he comes."

Armed with a borrowed perspective glass, Gideon was escorted up the hill along with his fellow judges. From the fort on its brow, they had a clear view over the countryside to the contested ruin. Beaumont also had a perspective glass from somewhere which Gideon discovered when Scarlett cleared his throat.

"You're not supposed to be looking at the batteries to see who has taken which, sir."

Gideon, who had been feeling his usual admiration for modern miracles seeing the ruined barn as close as if he could reach out and touch its walls, lowered his glass. Beaumont was looking outraged.

"What are you implying?" he demanded.

Ned Scarlett met the angry glare.

"Nothing at all, sir. I was merely reminding you of the rules we agreed we'd all keep to."

If Dudd had thought Scarlett was supposed to be a neutral judge in this wager, Gideon realised, then he was badly misled. It was clear that the cannoneer was as partisan for Danny in this as Gideon himself.

There was a brief volley of musket fire. The signal that the competition would begin.

"They'll fire alternately, sirs. We just have to record which we think is the closest." Scarlett reminded them.

Gideon kept his perspective glass trained on the ruined building as the first of the cannon shots boomed over the countryside and birds flew up from the nearby trees as it echoed like thunder. If it went anywhere near the building Gideon couldn't see it.

"There, sirs," Scarlett said, and Gideon lowered the glass just in time to see a small plume of earth and mud about sixty yards past the barn and wide to the left.

Before the echo of the first shot had fully died away there came the second from the other battery. It went over the barn and landed perhaps ten yards closer than the first.

There was some delay as, presumably, whoever was firing their second shot was making new calculations. Then the roar came and this time the shot was beside the ruin but to the right.

Scarlett tutted, implying that he regarded a lateral miss of that degree as an amateur mistake.

This time there was an even longer delay before the next shot and the ball ploughed into the ground in line with but well short of the ruin. Gideon took stock and decided that so far, the third shot, for all it had made Scarlett wince, was the one closest in distance to the ruin.

But there were the final shots to go.

The crash of the cannon broke the quiet of the afternoon and a small explosion of mud erupted from a hedge at the left and well beyond the target building. Whoever was manning that battery, the third shot, wide as it was, would still be their best and it was closer than any of the others.

Waiting for the final shot, Gideon was glad he had no notion who was firing which. He knew if he had done so he wouldn't be able to be so certain which shot had come closest and might well be debating with himself that one of the others was the more accurate. Now he wondered if he should be hoping the last shot was closer or more distant than that third one.

The final boom of sound broke the regathered stillness. Barely had the tiny puff of smoke appeared on the line of fortifications before the walls of the city, then a piece of the decaying barn roof crashed down. Whoever had fired that final shot was indubitably the victor.

Gideon closed his perspective glass and turned to his co-judges.

"The last one hit and was the only one that did," he said, and Scarlett nodded.

"Nonsense." Beaumont was shaking his head vigorously. "It was simply a coincidence that part of the barn collapsed at that time. While you were distracted by that, I saw the ball land over there." He waved his hand vaguely. "I say the third shot was the closest, without a doubt."

Scarlett's eyebrows had climbed up to the point from which his hairline had receded.

"I'm with Mr Fox on this," he said, doggedly. "The final shot hit the barn."

Gideon held up his hand.

"Perhaps we should talk to Colonel Bristow and General of Ordnance Dudley and see if they agree the last shot hit the barn."

Riding back, Beaumont pulled ahead of the escort. Scarlett, beside Gideon, shook his head. "He knows full well who fired which shot, sir, and that is why he has come up with this excuse."

They found Danny looking tense and Dudd wearing a huge grin, having just heard Beaumont's decision.

"Bad luck, Bristow," Dudd was saying. "Sad that bit of the barn falling off just so you thought you had hit it. Had me fooled at first too."

Danny ignored him and crossed over to Gideon as he and Ned Scarlett swung down from their horses.

"What did you see?" he demanded.

"The last shot hit the barn, sir," Scarlett said carefully. "The ball flew true, and part of the upper wall was knocked off."

Gideon nodded. "The last shot was the only one to hit," he agreed.

"Preposterous," Dudd barked, "If Humphrey says it was a miss, it was a miss. He saw the ball land in the field. You two were just distracted by some tumbling masonry, perhaps loosened by the vibrations from the cannons firing."

"Un-bel-ie-va-ble." Danny spoke each syllable separately, from between clenched teeth. "I wouldn't have thought even you would sink that low, Dudley." His hand had slipped to his sword and Gideon had a frisson of fear before Danny seemed to come to himself and release his grip. "Two of the judges say one thing and one the other. That means I have the majority verdict and so I win."

Dudd scowled.

"Are you accusing Captain Beaumont of lying, sir?"

"Whatever he saw, we're still left with the fact two of the judges saw things differently," Danny said. Then he seemed taken by a new thought. One that pleased him. "But since there is such a dispute, I propose that we call this attempt void," he grinned at Dudley. "And repeat it."

Gideon felt his heart sink.

"As the issue is that two of the judges aren't expert enough to tell for sure what is a cannonball and what is not," Danny went on, "we should be the judges and they should fire the guns."

Gideon gaped in horror. He had never held a linstock let alone fired a cannon and knew nothing of the calculations needed to decide the angle of elevation of the cannon to travel the right distance in the right direction. Danny had taken leave of his senses.

Dudd Dudley looked from Danny to Gideon and back again.

"A lawyer? A lawyer against an experienced officer? Ha!" He made an odd burbling sound and repeated it a few times until Gideon realised he was helpless with laughter.

Danny stood smiling happily and Beaumont looked a little perplexed. Whatever Ned Scarlett felt was impossible to read, he stood face grave and said nothing.

"Very well," Dudd said when he could speak again. "We'll do it, Bristow. But afterwards you must not complain as it is you who have chosen these terms." Then his expression changed. "And no consulting with your lawyer before the wager is run. Humphrey will have to do this on his own, so will your man."

Danny spread his hands and adopted an innocent look.

"I have complete faith that Mr Fox will manage very well with no advice from me." He sent Gideon a warm and happy smile. "Now, we should take the horses out to the fort and leave these two so they can make the toss for the guns. Here." he flipped a coin at one of the men as he crossed towards Gideon to take the reins of his horse and mount it"

Gideon felt sick. Why was Danny doing this?

He stared at the coin in the soldier's hand and then looked up at Danny, who gave him another reassuring smile, then turned the horse and rode off with Scarlett and Dudley.

"Sirs, who will call?" The man with the coin tossed it in the air.

"I call heads," Beaumont said before Gideon could speak.

"Heads it is, sir. Which side do you want to take?"

"The right side, of course." He laughed. "Same as Dudd. He told me it has better placement and gun crews." Beaumont sent a gloating look towards Gideon. "Do you want to fire first or second, Fox? Or shall we toss for that too?"

"I am content to follow you, captain," Gideon said, not caring either way. He could see no way he could win this and was bewildered at what Danny expected of him.

Gossip had spread fast because by the time Gideon reached his artillery battery, they already knew he was coming. The men by the guns greeted him with conspiratorial smiles.

It dawned on Gideon that though they couldn't say so the regular cannoneers were rooting for Danny as much as their commander Ned Scarlett was doing so. They would all have seen Dudley and Danny in action over the past few days and know by now which of the two they preferred.

And that was when it came to him.

"That last shot," Gideon said. "Can you set whichever gun fired it to the same position?"

The grin that brought to the face of the man in charge of the battery split his face in two. "Of course, sir. I kept the calculations from each shot. If we do get besieged, it'll help with my range finding."

Gideon watched as the gun crew worked, sponging out the barrel, putting the cloth-wrapped charge of powder into the mouth of the cannon and ramming it home. Then the heavy ball and finally a couple of handfuls of straw, compacted by the ramrod, as wadding to hold it all in place.

The cannoneer in charge handed off the linstock with its curl of burning match to Gideon, gesturing him to keep a few paces distant from the gun. Then he used a slender prick of metal to push through the touch hole, both to ensure it was clear and to puncture the bag of powder beneath. Finally, he filled the touch hole with powder from his flask and stepped back.

"There you go, sir. She's set up just as Colonel Bristow had her."

Then Gideon had to wait.

He was to fire second.

It seemed an age though was perhaps only ten minutes, before the cannon on the opposite battery fired. Gideon realised that from here it was harder to tell where the ball went than from a sideways view but the mocking cheer from his own gun crew told him that Beaumont's first shot had been something of a disaster.

It was hard to fathom why. The gun crews were capable of getting close to the target without any outside help. All Beaumont had to do was leave it to them...

Which, of course, being who he was, he would never do.

Which, of course, Danny had known—just as he had been sure Gideon would do exactly that. It was an extra good fortune that Gideon had the battery Danny had used, but even if he hadn't, the gunners left to themselves would do better than Beaumont. The truth was Danny knew and trusted his men. Beaumont, like Dudley, would always think he knew better.

The cannoneer beside Gideon cleared his throat.

"You can give fire now, sir, when you are ready."

Gideon glanced at the linstock and its burning match then at the cannon and finally at the cannoneer who gave him a brief nod of encouragement. He stepped forward.

"Have a care!" the cannoneer shouted. Gideon brought the lit match down to the small pile of powder heaped over the touch hole and his ears rang with the noise of the cannon firing.

For some reason, he found he had a grin on his face. A schoolboy's delighted grin at being the one to make the cannon roar, and as his hearing was restored, he realised the men about him were cheering. They had hit the barn again.

Two shots and nearly an hour later, his gun had hit the barn once more and even the shot that missed had, he was assured by the men about him, come closer to the building than even the nearest of Beaumont's shots. This time not even Dudd Dudley could try to make out that the barn had crumbled by itself.

Feeling buoyant and flushed with a success that wasn't at all his own and entirely the work of Danny Bristow and the capable cannoneers, Gideon headed back to meet with Beaumont and the three judges. But there could be no doubt—the wager was won.

Chapter Ten

"You're late," Lord greeted him, leaning against the door by the stable yard, once more clad as Thomas the servant, as Gideon got back to The Talbot.

"Danny—"

Lord held up a hand. "Enough said. 'Danny' is an adequate explanation for any variation from expectations. He stands as the wild card in the deck, there to throw sand in the face of fortune."

That suited Gideon just fine as he had no wish to explain what he and Danny had been up to that afternoon, or to describe Danny's jubilation when Dudd Dudley was forced to concede. Although he had tried hard to wriggle out by claiming that as nothing had been in writing the whole wager was invalid. That had been Gideon's opportunity as a lawyer to convince Dudley that his word when given in front of witnesses was as good as his signature. It had been satisfying to see Dudd realise he had been defeated and stomp off angrily, with Beaumont in his wake.

It was only as he and Sir Philip Lord headed away from the inn at a brisk pace that Gideon realised the real reason Lord had no wish to hear any account was that he already knew. The tide of military gossip would have flowed upstream to reach him, borne faster than the thunder of the cannon. However, what Sir Philip Lord did not know officially, Sir Philip Lord did not need to take action on. Gideon had no doubt, Danny would be hauled over the coals for his behaviour, but in private.

The streets of Worcester were quiet, but there was an odd sense of tension in the air that hadn't been there before. Apart from the occasional group of soldiers, anyone on the streets had their heads down and walked quickly, with purpose. Now and then loud bursts of heated conversation reached them from houses. A door slammed and Lord lifted his head like a hunting dog scenting its prey.

"There is something afoot here," Lord said softly, *"By the pricking of my thumbs, something wicked this way comes*. Perhaps our meeting will cast some light upon it."

The Swan was an establishment which catered for the sort of craftsmen and tradesmen who formed the majority of Reverend Fisher's congregation. As they approached the door, a man who had been standing beside it slipped in ahead of them. From below or nearby there came an occasional thump. The sound had Lord cocking his head and from his expression, Gideon had a feeling he knew what the cause might be.

It stopped as they entered the alehouse.

It was a Sunday and whereas in London after church the alehouses became places of political debate here there were only a handful of men to be found. The hostess, a dour-looking and dumpy woman who seemed ill-suited to the role, bustled over to greet them. When Gideon showed his token, she gave him a suspicious look and asked him to wait, before she disappeared through a door at the back of the room. Presumably, as he was a stranger, she wanted to make sure he was indeed welcome and not some chance individual who had improperly come by a token. When she returned it was to gesture to the door behind her.

"Through there down the stairs." Then she turned her attention to one of the other customers.

Lord raised an eyebrow and Gideon led the way through the door and found the stairs at the end of a short passageway, lit by a hanging lantern. The thumping sound had begun again and was now louder. It came from a room below.

Reverend Fisher was just coming up the stairs as Gideon reached them and he gave a taut smile.

"I was worried you wouldn't come. I've been telling everyone about who you are. Have you eaten? No? Then once we are done here you must come home with me and take supper. Unless the curfew troubles you? Then that is what we will do. Now, come and meet the others."

They went down the stairs and the thumping got louder. Then Fisher opened the door at the bottom of the steps and revealed the source.

A small printing press was set up in the cellar. Each time a sheet was printed, the page had to be pushed home beneath the pressing plate and it made a distinctive thump. The room was bustling with men who were cutting and preparing pages or hanging up freshly printed ones to dry and as they entered one of the men left clutching a bundle of papers. He nodded at Fisher before heading up the stairs.

"Nearly done now," one of the men operating the press said as he lifted out another sheet. "That'll be a thousand. Enough for the town *and* the troops."

Fisher rubbed his hands together and looked at Gideon and Lord.

"This is God's work, my friends. Fitting for the sabbath."

Lord had picked up one of the printed sheets and read it, his expression unchanging. Then he handed it to Gideon, who felt his blood chill at the words.

To all gentlemen, and other inhabitants of the City of Worcester

As many of you as are sensible of the danger of your religion, your persons and goods, and the privileges of your Corporation, are desired to declare yourselves sensible of them at this opportunity. It being my errand (by the help of God) to rescue them from the oppression of your present governors. And I promise that all such as shall appear willing to welcome my endeavour shall not only be relieved of free quarter, but protected to the utmost of my power.

May 29th, 1643.
William Waller

Gideon looked up at Fisher, hoping his expression reflected more of the zeal he wished to project than the horror that was in his heart.

"Waller is coming?"

"He will be marching from Gloucester tonight with his entire army to take the ungodly by surprise and bring liberation to us here in Worcester. *For it shall come to pass in that day, saith the Lord*

116

of hosts, that I will break his yoke from off thy neck, and will burst thy bonds, and strangers shall no more serve themselves of him: but they shall serve the Lord their God."

"Amen and amen!"

There came a chorus from the dozen or so men present.

Lord stepped forward with such a blaze of light in his eyes that Gideon feared he was going to forget himself and denounce them.

"*And the Lord said, I have surely seen the affliction of my people which are in Egypt, and have heard their cry by reason of their taskmasters; for I know their sorrows; and I am come down to deliver them out of the hand of the Egyptians.*"

"Amen to that," Fisher said, nodding with approval.

As if not to be outdone two or three of the others produced Bible verses about liberation from bondage and the chorus of amens swelled. Then Fisher put his hand on Gideon's shoulder.

"Friends, brothers in Christ, this is Gideon come to deliver us from the Midianites. He has infiltrated their camp and stands ready to act with us."

Every eye in the room moved to look at Gideon, who wondered what it was he was being set up to achieve.

"Brethren," Fisher went on, "we all know that John Porter who brings us so much news from the heart of our oppressors' confidences, had been willing to act on the eve of this day of liberation. Being at the right hand of Sir William Russell he would have cast our enemies into disarray. But Russell is not returned, and the day is upon us. I have prayed to God that we might have another, and God has answered our prayers."

Fisher paused then nodded his head as if agreeing with their thoughts.

"Yes. As Gideon with the Midianites, as Jael with Sisera, as Judith with Holofernes, so will this Gideon free us from our oppressors by severing the head from the body." He turned to Gideon. "God has placed you in the midst of our enemies so you can strike at their heart."

It took Gideon a few moments to catch up and realise what he was being asked to do and the rush of horror must have made his skin sallow. He tried to take a breath but choked and coughed.

Then before he could recover Lord spoke from beside him in the passionate tones of Thomas.

"Sirs, let me be the one to strike the blow. I am often in the presence of the son of Belial who leads them. I am a body servant to Sir Philip Lord and have been a soldier, I would have no problem being with him as Ehud was with Eglon." He put his hand on his thigh where a long knife hung to underline the point.

There was silence in the room and Gideon realised he was the only one present who had been shocked at the idea. But Fisher seemed oblivious and releasing Gideon he turned to Lord, who had his head bowed as if in prayer.

"Thomas, you are poorly named for there is no doubt in you at all is there? You shame us all here with your devotion," Fisher said. "But this is the task appointed to Gideon, although you may aid him in it."

Feeling as if he must surely be having a bad dream from which he would awake to find Danny pulling on his boots, Gideon shook his head.

"You ask—"

"I ask nothing," Fisher said, rounding on Gideon, eyes blazing. "It is God almighty who asks this of you."

"I—" Gideon caught Lord's gaze briefly and faltered. Then he, too, bowed his head and answered honestly. "I will always do what God asks of me."

After that things seemed to progress in a blur from which Gideon stayed apart. He was introduced to the other men, but their names slipped away from him, although he was sure Lord would be noting them down in a ledger at the back of his mind. The men congratulated Gideon and addressed him with respect, as if he had already performed the deed, they now expected of him. He nodded, smiled wanly, and tried to answer them as best he could. Then the talk turned to Waller coming, some plans that were in train to undermine the defences, condemnation of the women helping on the earthworks and prayers said, before, finally, he was walking from the alehouse with Fisher. It was only then, out in the fresh air, he seemed able to shake the malaise that had gripped him.

"May I speak with you, sir?" Lord was beside him and his expression, invisible to Fisher, was urgent. Gideon stared at him, then realised.

"You need to get back," he said quickly. Lord gave a nod and Fisher frowned.

"There is a problem?"

"I am supposed to attend upon the man of whom we spoke," Lord said, twisting his lips in distaste. "If I am not there, it will lead to questions being asked."

Fisher nodded.

"Then you must go. We need nothing to get in the way of our affairs. God go with you, Thomas, we shall work together for our liberation from the bondage of our oppressors. Here," he pushed a bundle of the printed pages into Lord's hands. "See if you can deliver these to the army."

Lord nodded vigorously and turned to Gideon.

"As the Lord watched over Daniel amongst the lions, so he shall watch over you, sir."

"Amen," Fisher said. "Amen to that indeed."

Then Lord was gone, his form lost to shadow before he was more than a few paces away, leaving Gideon wondering if he should be reassured or troubled by that parting sally, the meaning of which was plain. Danny would be sent to be close by to the Fishers in case he was needed.

"Are you sure it is wise for us to be seen together?" Gideon said although the empty streets made it unlikely unless someone peering from a window into the twilight caught a glimpse of them.

"The way from here is safe enough," Fisher said confidently, "It is not far, much in shadow and away from the main streets. Besides, there is a matter I am hoping you can help me with which I would address you over supper."

Gideon could only speculate on the issue Fisher might wish to raise with a man he had just charged to commit murder. But then if he thought his own case was difficult Sir Philip Lord, having offered to assassinate himself, was now in the unenviable position of needing to curb the plans against his troops whilst not revealing that he knew of them. To do so would be to close the only open door he had to discover his true heritage. Unless Gideon could achieve something at this supper which would unbind Lord's hands.

"And here we are," said Fisher as they reached his door. "*But thou, O God, shalt bring them down into the pit of destruction: bloody and deceitful men shall not live out half their days; but I will trust in thee.* It is for the best if we do not speak of your special task to my wife or my son, such things are for the chosen few."

And that was something of a relief to Gideon who had no wish to even think about it, let alone try and talk sensibly about such a notion as if he agreed with it.

They were barely through the door and into the parlour of a comfortably furnished house, before Joan Fisher appeared, her face anxious.

"Oh, it is you, Reverend Fisher," she said, but in a tone which suggested she had hoped it might be someone else. She managed a tight smile for Gideon. "And Mr Fox is here too." Then her attention went back to her husband. "Ezra…" Somehow, she managed to put an entire message of meaning into the name, because Fisher straightened up and nodded.

Gideon was painfully aware there was a domestic crisis unfolding but of what nature he had no idea. Politeness demanded he should quickly withdraw, but he hesitated before speaking the needful words. The problem was that this supper was most likely going to be his one chance to speak to Joan Fisher.

In the event, he was saved as Fisher put a hand on his arm.

"I apologise, Mr Fox. I must go out again for a short time. You will wait for me?" Good. My wife will entertain you in my absence and please do not wait upon my return to sup, I am uncertain how long I may need to be..."

He turned away sharply and strode off, shutting the door behind him, and leaving Gideon with Joan Fisher.

"Please come through," she said, her tone stiff.

Gideon realised he was being as much of a boor as Dudd or Humphrey Beaumont. It shocked him that he could be reduced to such behaviour in pursuit of any goal, no matter how worthy.

"No. I'll go. You have matters you need to—"

"Please, Mr Fox." Her voice cut over his. "I would be grateful if you would stay. The Reverend Fisher won't be long, I'm sure."

Gideon acquiesced in the face of her insistence and inclined his head.

"If you're sure that's what *you* wish," he said carefully.

She smiled then, a fraught smile.

"It is. I would much appreciate the company."

Any suspicion that he was a murderer had not reached this household.

The room set out for supper was modestly furnished, but with everything of decent quality. Gideon took the seat he was offered.

"You will excuse me whilst I arrange for the meal to be served," Joan Fisher said and bustled off. But it was almost half an hour later when she returned. The food was brought by a young woman who then fetched a sewing basket and set it in the corner of the room.

"Please don't mind Patience, she needs the light," Joan Fisher said, though Gideon decided that her presence was more down to proprietary than the need to sew.

The meal was well cooked and as he ate, Gideon wondered how to open the conversation onto topics more onerous than how clement the weather was being and how well Fisher's sermon had been received.

"...for it is most certainly true that we know not the hour," Joan Fisher was saying piously. "I think God's will can be hard to discern and I know the Reverend Fisher spends many hours in prayer to try to understand. It's a huge responsibility placed upon him."

"Sometimes things happen that seem by chance and yet might be God's will," Gideon said swiftly, seizing his chance. "For example, was it by chance or God's will that I took the wrong street and was able to protect a household near the docks from saltpetre men?"

"God's will, I am sure," Joan Fisher said, nodding.

"There was an old woman there who told me that your mother was the sister of Sir Edward Kelley." Gideon watched her face as he spoke, but she seemed not to think there was anything untoward about his words.

"Yes, that's right," she said, nodding. "My mother had a lump of gold she said he'd given to her after his first experiment with alchemy. They were close as children. She was very fond of him, and my Uncle Tom." Joan Fisher smiled then, the first proper smile since Gideon arrived, remembering happier times.

"The old woman told me that she thought your mother was still alive," Gideon prompted.

"Oh no," Joan Fisher said, shaking her head. "My mother passed away seven years ago. I went to her funeral in Baddersleigh. She'd gone there to live with my Uncle Tom. You see, he bought a big house there with the money he brought back. Some from abroad and some he'd been paid by Dr Dee. My mother was proud that her two brothers had done so well for themselves." Then the smile faded. "I didn't see her after she moved away, the Reverend Fisher didn't approve of her or my uncles."

"Did you know your uncles?"

"I never met Sir Edward. He must have died around the time I was born. But I knew Uncle Tom from childhood. He would come to visit and bring presents and tell tall tales to myself and my brother and sisters." Her face fell a little. "Of course, that was before the fever. It carried them all back to God along with my father and left just me and my mother. We would have been hard-pressed had Uncle Tom not stepped in then to help us."

Gideon was about to ask if her uncle still lived but there were sounds of footsteps and raised voices in the passageway. A door slammed, and Joan Fisher got to her feet quickly. The anxious shadow was back on her face.

"Please excuse me, Mr Fox. I think my husband and my son…"

She slipped from the room without finishing the sentence, leaving Gideon in turmoil. This was the information he needed, and Joan Fisher seemed happy to provide it. But now her menfolk had returned, and he would be unlikely to be able to pursue the topic when they joined the meal.

The scream had Gideon on his feet and at the door barely had it closed behind Joan Fisher. But as he opened it, she staggered back into him, and he had to catch her. Her hands gripped at his arms and her gaze found his, full of unspeakable anguish. Then she slumped against him.

Gideon realised that where he held her about the waist something warm and sticky was oozing over his hand. She had been stabbed. For a terrible moment he thought she was dead, but he realised she was still breathing. Lowering her to the floor, he looked over to where the maidservant, Patience, had dropped her darning and stood hands pressed to her mouth as if to stifle a scream.

"Attend to Mistress Fisher," he told her, his tone sharper than he intended. But it served to bring the girl over at a run as Gideon opened the door and stepped out into the parlour, his hand on his sword.

The room was unlit and the door to the street was open. Gideon tripped over a bundle on the floor just in front of it. The bundle made a sharp gasp and Gideon realised that it was a man.

"Ezra." The voice was as thin as a breath and belonged to Nehemiah Fisher. "God forgive me. Ezra."

"Are you alright?" Gideon crouching down.

"Ezra," he repeated. Then with a sudden strength, he gripped Gideon's wrist. "Promise me you will stop him. You must stop him. The church. He will have gone back to the church. You must—"

The grip on his wrist slackened abruptly and Fisher's final breath escaped with a whine, and he lay still. Somewhere in the house, Gideon could hear two servants asking what was wrong. A dog was barking further down the street and then there were running feet.

Gideon pushed himself up and gave chase down the dark street.

It had started raining. Not heavily, but with steady persistence. The clouds made the night seem even darker, although here and there a tattered shred of cloud lifted to expose the moon just entering its final quarter.

The church stood in brooding silence, its bulk seeming ominous at night, set in its tiny churchyard and pressed about by houses. Gideon entered by the little side gate, as he had when he found the body of Phoebe Young. Now, as then, there was no one visible and the lone tomb stood quiet. Without conscious thought, Gideon drew his sword and made his way with stealthy steps along the side of the church to the door which stood ajar.

Inside he could just see a faint glow as if of a single candle and a voice murmuring in prayer. With the reassurance of his sword in one hand, Gideon pushed the door open a little more hoping to be able to see what was within—who was within.

The hinges squeaked in protest.

It was not a loud sound. But it was enough.

The murmur of prayer ceased.

Gideon quickly pushed the door wide and strode into the nave, then he froze in horror as the meal he had just eaten rose into his throat.

Lit by the flame of a single lantern the body of Phoebe Young had been laid naked on the stone flags, her innards exposed by a large butcher's cleaver which lay gleaming and bloodied beside her. The sight and the stench made Gideon recoil, retching. Which was when Ezra Fisher attacked him from the shadows.

Stripped to the waist, covered with blood, Ezra had armed himself with an iron bar. He held it in one hand, the other arm had its upper part swathed in strips of gory linen. That first blow just missed Gideon's head, but landed on his shoulder, numbing his arm so the sword slipped from his hand as his fingers lost all sensation. Gideon drove his good elbow back hard and felt it connect as Ezra gasped. He followed that up by turning fast and pummelling fists and feet into the other man. But Ezra was already gone, and the bar swung up again from the side, Gideon catching the lift of it in a shadow, had scant warning to hurl himself down and roll away.

His right arm was still useless, but he landed beside his sword and snatched it up into his left. Now, for the first time, he understood why he had been made to practice basic movements with both hands. He was as clumsy with the blade as a novice, but he could defend himself and parried the next assault.

Ezra snarled and lunged. This was savagery in its purest form and Gideon had to fight fire with fire. Ducking under the iron bar, he placed his booted foot precisely where he knew it would do most harm. Ezra grunted—but he must have slipped so far into his state of demonic bloodlust that pain meant nothing. Without pause he swung the iron bar at Gideon's head.

Ducking again, Gideon used his momentum headfirst towards Ezra's chest, smacking solidly in his solar plexus. As the breath rushed out of Ezra's lungs, Gideon smashed at the arm that held the iron bar. The bar went flying and landed with a satisfying clatter of metal on stone.

Ezra released an unearthly howl that made Gideon's hair stand on end. For a precious moment, Gideon was frozen as Ezra dived past him and snatched up the blooded butcher's cleaver that had been left beside the devastated body of Phoebe Young. With seemingly inhuman agility, Ezra bounded up again to hack at Gideon with a wild swing.

That time, Gideon only just avoided the scything sweep of lethal metal, but his left hand seemed to be remembering more of its sword practice the longer it held the blade, and he pushed Ezra back by dancing the point towards him. The greater reach of the sword meant he could keep the slicing cleaver at a distance.

Slick with sweat himself, Gideon tried to disarm Ezra, who was panting like a dog. But he underestimated the man's sheer desperation and overestimated his own ability to fight wrong-handed. It was the unfamiliar use of his left hand that meant he was not fast enough to reposition after a feint—and Ezra got within his guard. Gideon swiped desperately, catching the cleaver at the base of its blade and forcing it from Ezra's grip, but leaving his body open as he did so.

Ezra dropped his head and fastened his teeth to Gideon's wrist. Shrieking with excruciating pain and horror, something inside Gideon seemed to fall away. The same dark tide that flowed through Ezra had finally caught Gideon in its vile wash, transferred somehow by the bite. Dropping his now useless sword, Gideon threw himself kicking and screaming onto Ezra, bearing him to the ground. Then he seized Ezra's head and bashed it against the stone of the church floor.

Again.

And again.
And again.

Chapter Eleven

It took, Danny told him later with clear admiration in his eyes, three men to prize Gideon from Ezra Fisher.

"I kept telling you he was dead, but you didn't hear it. Christ, Gideon, you have a savage streak in you." He said it with a kind of proprietary pride. The truth in the words made Gideon sick to his stomach.

Danny had the body of Phoebe Young discreetly removed and the church cleaned up by his men before any of the local people should see it. It was, Danny told him, a matter of military necessity as it could cause unrest for that kind of horror to be amongst them just as Waller descended upon the city. Gideon was glad as it meant no one else needed to bear the full burden of what Ezra Fisher had done. And the burden was great. In removing the body of Phoebe Young from her parent's house on the eve of her funeral, Ezra had killed them both.

Anders was called upon to tend Joan Fisher and Lord ordered her moved to The Talbot where he had now emptied the other rooms of any remaining guests and created it as his headquarters. There were more of Lord's men there too when Gideon arrived, the regiment having been called inside the walls and dispersed to pre-planned quarters in the city.

When Anders came to treat Gideon's wrist, arriving just as Zahara finished her work doing so, Gideon asked him if Joan Fisher would live. Anders would only say that was much too soon to be sure and refused to be drawn into speculation. On the other issue Gideon was grappling with, he was more forthcoming, but even less able to give a satisfactory answer. It was plaguing Gideon why Ezra had taken Phoebe's body and cut it open.

"I do not know why," Anders admitted when Gideon pressed him. "Perhaps he was truly possessed."

The truth of the brutal murders would be known, but any inquest into what had happened was, of necessity, now delayed by warfare. Sir Philip Lord appeared briefly when Anders had gone as Zahara was plying Gideon with a soothing remedy that tasted of honey and spices.

"You seem to have found your murderer by the simple expedient of almost being his victim," he said in greeting. "I would chastise you for that, but I think you have taken enough punishment. Danny tells me you fought heroically."

"I spoke to Joan Fisher, before… Well, before that happened," Gideon said, keen to change the subject. He would never come to terms with having been reduced to such brutality. "Her mother is dead but was living with her brother's family in a house he purchased with money some of which he got from Dee. A place called Baddersleigh. If Joan Fisher survives, we might learn more."

Lord's expression changed as Gideon spoke and his jaw tightened.

"Baddersleigh is perhaps ten or twelve miles from here. Right now, it might as well be in Muscovy. We are about to become besieged and although I sent Shiraz to Oxford with word for the king and the princes, I'm not hopeful they will send speedy relief. We are here in Worcester for as long as General Waller requires us to be. After that… Well, after that despite *all the impostures, the prodigies, diseases and distempers, the knaveries of the time, we shall see all…* You have done well."

"I suppose this means you'll now arrest those who were at the meeting?"

Lord looked at him oddly.

"I already have," he said.

"You already have?" Gideon echoed, incredulous.

"Why did you think I left you when I did? John Porter too—he was one of Russell's penmen. I was right it was a clerk betraying us, but wrong as to whose clerk it would be."

Lord was gone before Gideon could respond.

Exhausted in body, mind and spirit, he gave in to Zahara, who insisted on his drinking another cup of her honey remedy. Gideon crawled into his bed sometime after midnight—but he alone of Lord's men was able to do so. The rest were preparing for the siege that was about to be forced upon Worcester.

He woke when it was still dark, to find Danny looking for something in his possessions.

"We have company," he said blithely when Gideon sat up. "If you're quick, you can come and see how it all begins. Waller will send someone to summon us to surrender. Then Sandys will tell him where he can stick his summons. But done in the most polite, flowery and formal language you can imagine, with trumpets, drums and flags thrown in to make it all look pretty."

Gideon rose quickly and winced as he dressed. His right arm was functioning, but moving it was painful as the shoulder was bruised. His left wrist was wrapped with the dressing and bandage Zahara had applied.

They left the inn, and the predawn air was fresh. In the streets about them, the city slept uneasily in its multiple beds, but its soldiers were already active. Tramping feet broke the stillness and shouted orders woke the citizens of Worcester to their plight.

"Of course, Waller has taken the high ground we couldn't control, which means I'm going to have to work hard to keep him at a distance," Danny said. Then talked happily of his plans to do so, apparently oblivious to the fact that Gideon had no idea what half the words he used meant.

When they reached the Sidbury Gate, Lord was already there leaning on a parapet. Beside him Sandys used a perspective glass. Lord straightened up as Gideon and Danny approached and made a gesture to where shadowy shapes could be seen moving in the fields.

"*Hang out our banners on the outward walls; the cry is still 'They come:' our castle's strength will laugh a siege to scorn: here let them lie till famine and the ague eat them up*, or more likely in this case our army arrives to threaten their rear."

"He has brought his full strength, I think," Sandys said. He sounded on edge.

"My scouts took some of his men in the night," Lord said. "He has some three thousand with him."

"And guns?" Danny asked, but in a way that told Gideon this was for Sandys' benefit and that Danny already knew the answer.

Knew it and had acted on the information to the best of his ability already.

"And guns. Eight guns," Lord agreed. "None of the variety that will make our lives too miserable. You can hardly force march with heavy siege pieces. But I've no doubt we will hear from them anyway as soon as the day gets going."

He put a hand on Sandy's shoulder and that was when Gideon realised that the colonel was suppressing a terrible anxiety. After all, he wasn't a professional soldier, and this was his first siege. As acting governor, the security of the city rested on his shoulders, and he would be accountable to the king for it. Men had been broken, tried and even executed for making bad decisions as governors under siege.

"We can hold," Lord told him, lifting his voice so the men about would hear. "We have provisions in hand of vittles and munitions. Our walls are braced by the fine work of General of Ordnance Dudley and Colonel Bristow. The malignants within the population have been uncovered and your troops and mine stand trained and ready. You need only to say 'no' when summoned and half the work is done. The king will not forget his loyal city of Worcester and will send to relieve us fast as he may."

Lord sounded so confident that Gideon wasn't surprised to see Sandys' shoulders lift and his spine straighten.

"The summons will come soon?" Sandys asked.

Lord glanced at the paling sky and back to where the ranks of men could now be seen broiling over the ground that yesterday had been the site of Danny's wager.

"Very soon. I think after his efforts with the disaffected here, Waller may even have some hope you will accede. I made sure no one got out to take him word last night, so we may have the delight of surprising him."

The sun began to lift itself over the horizon as Waller set out his army. Parading for the benefit of the people of Worcester, showing his strength. As they moved into place, a group of three mounted men came towards them. One carried a flag of truce, all were unarmed, and their leader was resplendently dressed. They rode up to the gate as close as they could approach it, kept at hailing distance by Danny's chevaux-de-frise. The horizontal poles studded with sharp wooden stakes had been pulled across the road to fill the gap in the defences.

The man at the front of the trio had a good loud voice and he called out the summons, offering that the entire garrison could march out with weapons and colours, unharassed, were Sandys to surrender immediately.

Sandys' expression was tense and focused, Lord's relaxed and mildly curious as if having only an academic interest in what might transpire and Danny's was oddly eager, perhaps anticipating with enthusiasm the challenge of mounting this defence. The regular soldiers on this gate were from Sandys' regiment and they pointed their muskets down at the trio as if they were an assaulting force about to overwhelm them, not unarmed men under the protection of the laws of war.

When it was clear the man speaking had finished, Sandys shouted back.

"You're not at Hereford. You'd better be off."

"That wasn't flowery," Danny said softly. "It wasn't even polite."

And indeed, the trumpeter himself seemed unimpressed.

"Such an answer is most uncivil, sir," he called. "Not one I can take back to my general. I would have a proper response."

"You have my reply, now be off with you," Sandys shouted. Then, clearly feeling he had said all that was necessary, turned on his heel. "To work, gentlemen. Captain Beaumont, this is your gate to hold."

Captain Beaumont.

Humphrey Beaumont.

Gideon's stomach dropped with a sudden foreboding.

The captain had been keeping back as the summons was issued and rejected but now made an elegant bow to Sandys and stepped up to the parapet as the acting governor strode off. Lord exchanged exasperated looks with Danny, then turned and followed Sandys. Gideon heard raised voices as they went.

Danny looked disgusted.

"You'll have to excuse me, my work calls," he said, then clapped Gideon on the shoulder before taking the steps down at a run.

Gideon stayed where he was. It seemed Waller's emissary had meant it when he said he wouldn't leave without a better reply. He sat his horse unmoving, flanked by the two unarmed men who had escorted him. Beaumont's men jeered as he demanded again that he and his general be treated with respect and accorded a proper and decent response to the most generous offer Sir William Waller had made to the people of Worcester.

"By the laws of war," he called in a powerful voice, which Gideon thought worthy of a town-crier, "I am entitled to a civil answer to take back to my general."

"You're the lawyer." Gideon jumped as Beaumont addressed him gruffly. "Is he right?"

Gideon had no idea. He could only draw on Danny's words and Lord's reaction.

"I believe so," he said.

Beaumont nodded to one of his men.

"You had better tell the colonel or we'll be here all day with this man. I think he'll stand there until the trumps of judgement and probably blow them himself."

There was a ripple of laughter from those standing duty and the man hurried off. When Sandys returned, he was alone and in a truly foul mood.

"What is it, man?" he shouted down. "What the hell is the matter with you? Why are you still here? Don't you understand simple English? You have my reply. Begone!"

The trumpeter sat even more upright in the saddle, his face puce with outrage.

"You, sir, are a rude, ignorant—"

Beaumont made a sharp gesture at the musketeers beside him, his meaning clear. Gideon opened his mouth to shout a horrified protest, but his voice was drowned by the sharp explosion from a musket.

Gideon could see nothing right away, as the gunsmoke blew into his eyes. Then he saw the man still in the saddle, clutching at a brilliant red hole in his thigh before he tumbled to the ground.

This, he was sure, was not supposed to happen. It was against all convention for anyone under a flag of truce to be shot at.

But Sandys seemed pleased, he slapped Beaumont on the back, flipped a coin at the musketeer who had fired the shot, then stalked off as if that was finished business.

The two men with the wounded trumpeter had helped him back onto his horse. They were retreating to their army followed by jeers and catcalls from Beaumont's men as Gideon left the gate. He was sure Lord would have heard the shot and probably already have some account of the event, but he also doubted whatever Sandys or his men might say would reflect the truth of what had occurred.

Lord had indeed clearly heard some account because Gideon encountered him on the way back to the inn, issuing curt orders. He saw Gideon and called him over.

"Fox. I need a letter to Waller, presenting my personal apologies on the dire necessity of the shooting of his man, explaining that the man was rude and objectionable and declined to take back the message he was given. That he refused to leave when told to do so, thus forfeiting the privileges bestowed by the flag of truce he bore."

Gideon opened his mouth to protest, then closed it again. He could see from the tightly reined fury in Lord's expression that he was simply doing what needed to be done to avoid making a bad situation even worse.

"Yes, of course," he said, wondering if he could write legibly with his arm as it was.

"Ask Kate if she will pen it. I'll sign it as soon as I get back."

"Is there anything I can—?" Gideon broke off, suddenly uncertain what exactly he was offering.

Lord studied him.

"Can you hold a sword? Fire a pistol? I need an honest answer, or you would endanger us all."

Gideon hesitated, then shook his head. "Perhaps, in extremis."

"Then you will do me the favour of remaining with Kate. If there is an extremis that is where I need you to be." Then Lord turned and strode away, calling to one of his captains as he turned to receive a message from another of his men.

Gideon went back to The Talbot. He reached the door, nodding to the men guarding it, just as Zahara emerged with Anders and Brighid. All three were burdened with bags.

"We need to be with our soldiers," Zahara said and as her hands were full, stood on tiptoes to brush Gideon's cheek chastely with her lips. Then anticipating his concern, shook her head. "You need not be worried. We will be well protected by Captain Greene."

Her words were abruptly drowned by the boom of gunfire. Danny must have decided to start his work discouraging Waller from approaching too closely to the city. Zahara left Gideon, with a further smile of reassurance over her shoulder, then hurried away after Anders and Brighid.

It was, Gideon thought, the men who were supposed to go away to fight and the women keep safe at home. But today Zahara was the one risking her life under gunfire. And since Lord would have made sure Argall Greene and his men, as the strongest unit of infantry, were at the weakest point in the defences, if Waller tried an assault to storm the city there would be a good chance she might be caught up in the fighting. Forcing his feet to carry him into the inn, he reminded himself that she knew the risks better than he did. She had lived this way long before they ever met.

Inside the inn, the common room had become a war room. Two tables pushed together held a large and detailed plan of Worcester with its completed fortifications marked. One of Lord's men was updating it to match a sketch just handed to him by a messenger. A sketch that Gideon could see was in Danny's distinctive style, representing the way Waller was positioning his troops and guns. He realised this plan would be kept updated at all times so whatever Lord needed to know, when he needed to know it, the information would be here, in one place.

A voice made Gideon turn to see Kate coming down the stairs slowly, taking one step at a time with Christobel beside her.

"...he is a physician, so, of course, he would say you must stay here. But I promise you we have much work to do. I will need your help. And here is Gideon." Kate stepped from the stairs and crossed towards him. "I hope Philip wasn't too brusque with you. He told me he was going to be ordering you to stay here. I think he feels you have done quite enough fighting already." She softened her words with a smile.

"He's probably right," Gideon agreed. "I couldn't even wield a pen today let alone a sword."

"Whereas I am more than willing and able to help out," Christobel said, her frustration evident. "Danny has shown me everything I need to know to help the cannoneers fire a gun. I could even serve as a matross, but it seems I am still not permitted outside. I had to wait until Anders had gone before I dared leave my bed."

"Well Anders did say that the injury you received could lead to you becoming faint for the next few days," Kate pointed out, her tone kind but Gideon heard in it a repeated refrain. "It wouldn't be helpful if you collapsed whilst trying to swab out a gun." she put her arm around the younger woman's shoulders. "Besides, if you were out there you would undoubtedly distract Danny from his work. It has always been the same for me with Philip. When he is working, and I am with him I try to ensure he knows I am safe, so he is not distracted by concerns for my safety. And as I said, there is enough for us both here that needs doing."

"Talking of which, Sir Philip wanted me to ask you to write a letter," Gideon said.

"You really should call him Philip, you know Gideon." Her eyes sparkled. "After all, you call me 'Kate'."

Gideon flushed and avoided her gaze. He had tried before to move to a place where he felt comfortable using Lord's given name but somehow it had never felt right. And yet with Kate, who was the daughter of an earl, he found he had no issue doing so. Somehow, she made it easy.

"The letter is for General Waller," he said, evading her comment. "He sent under a flag of truce to ask the city to surrender and Captain Humphrey Beaumont took it upon himself to have the man shot."

Christobel's eyes went wide, and Kate made a tutting noise.

"You had better tell me what happened and what Philip wants me to say to Sir William."

It was as Kate had written the letter and was drying the ink, Lord himself strode into the common room in company with both the Sandys brothers, Lieutenant Colonel Davies and half a dozen of the other senior commanders. Dudley was there but Danny was noticeable by his absence.

Lord graced Kate with a smile and Gideon and Christobel with a nod between them, as he crossed to the map and the other men joined him. Gideon was too far away to see much but Lord's voice carried across the room. Explaining where Waller's men were and what he thought they should be doing. The men with him were attentive. He was, after all, a renowned military commander and in the face of real danger, these men, most of whom were not career soldiers, were willing to listen to what he had to say.

After he finished there were a few questions and Dudley began complaining about the placement of the guns, but Lord cut him short by the simple expedient of holding up his hand.

"Waller is currently digging in here and here. He holds Digilis to the south and is spreading East. I believe if we made a sortie from St Martin's Gate, we could roll up that eastern advance and force his men back onto his centre."

"But the ground out there now is pretty treacherous for cavalry," one of the commanders protested.

"It will get more so if we don't prevent them from digging it up. We can have the guns focus fire there and put more of your men, Colonel Sandys," he nodded at Martin Sandys as he spoke, "on the walls and earthworks to keep a steady rate of musket fire. That will make them keep their heads down, then we bring in the cavalry to sweep from the north."

"Surely we should be trying to drive for his heart, not hack at his extremities?" the same man protested.

"*Do not cry havoc, where you should but hunt with modest warrant*," Lord told him patiently. "If we had the strength for that we would not need to keep within the walls. I regret defeating Waller in open battle is not an option available to us. But if we can bloody his nose—or to maintain your analogy, colonel—cut off a few of his fingers, we might speed his departure."

The colonel subsided with a vague nod of agreement.

"We have six hundred horse." Lord smiled. "The exercise would do us good, not to mention boost morale across the city."

"You speak as if it's a foregone conclusion," Sandys protested. "What if Waller sends men to reinforce his flank?"

"This is a sally, not an initiation of battle. We go in and withdraw. By the time Waller is aware we are there, we should be pulling back."

There were more questions of a similar kind, and the officers were divided between those who were excited at the thought of a raid on the enemy and those who saw it as a foolhardy risk to men and horses.

Then Samuel Sandys, who had been studying the map as if it were the entrails of slaughtered beast from which he could predict the future, straightened up abruptly. In the end, the decision was his as acting governor.

"You are certain this can be done?" he asked, looking directly at Lord.

"I wouldn't have suggested it if I were not," Lord assured him.

Sandys gave a curt nod.

"Then we do this, but on one condition."

"Which is?" But Lord's expression told Gideon he already knew what caveat Sandys would be placing on it.

"You will command the cavalry and lead the sally."

Lord responded with a brief bow.

"Of course, colonel. That was always my intention."

Then there were orders given to move musketeers from one part of the defences to another. Issues were raised and either addressed or dismissed according to their importance and the gathering was done. As the commanders left to return to their duties and carry out their new instructions, Lord looked over to where Kate sat with the letter in front of her.

"*Behold I see the haven nigh at hand, to which I meane my wearie course to bend.*" He crossed the room as he spoke, pausing to drop a kiss on her upturned face, then picked up the letter and read over it. "Thank you, my love. Although these are words which should never have needed to be written. Men like Beaumont are a curse." He picked up the pen and dipped it in the ink, scrawling his confident and flamboyant signature over the bottom of the page beneath Kate's neat hand.

"Would it help if I sent a letter to Sir William myself?" Kate asked. "I got to know him quite well in those terrible days after White Mountain. He was part of Queen Elizabeth's personal guard, he and Ralph Hopton. They were such good friends back then. It's so sad that now they face each other on the battlefield rather than stand together as they once did."

Lord considered her offer and then shook his head.

"If it were some mistake or accident then I would think it fitting, but this…" He flicked the paper with one finger. "This isn't even stupidity. It's malice. Bad enough that I must put my name to it, I wouldn't have yours dragged with it."

"God willing the poor man survives or there really will be an issue. One that will reach the ears of the king."

Lord sighed.

"That would be—"

The man who burst in was breathless and Lord was halfway across the room to meet him before he was more than a couple of paces inside.

"What is it?"

"There's an assault being made on the Friary Gate, sir. Colonel Bristow said—" Lord didn't break his stride and was through the door taking the messenger with him.

"Philip was never much good at saying goodbye," Kate said, then she turned to Christobel. "You don't need to worry. Danny is more than capable of mounting a defence with or without Philip to hold his hand."

Gideon crossed to the plan of the city and found the Friar's Gate, a pulse of relief going through him as he confirmed that it was nowhere near where Zahara was with Argall Greene's company.

This not knowing and not being able to do anything was pure hell.

Chapter Twelve

Two hours later a messenger came from Lord.

The man brought updates to the plan of the siege works on the city map and told them the assault had been repulsed with heavy losses to the attackers and slight to their own defenders. He wore a grin as he reported.

"The Schiavono let them get right into the mouth of our guns then blew them to perdition," he said cheerfully. "It was raining arms and legs on their friends below and that was enough. They took off like the devil was on their heels."

"And Colonel Bristow?" Gideon asked.

"Oh, he had the guns stuffed with bags holding bits of rubbish and stones and metal, so it was like a blast of hail. Ripped them to pieces. You should've seen it." he finished gleefully, "A red mist hanging there."

Gideon found himself incredibly glad that he hadn't seen it and not for the first time wondered how Lord and Danny, neither of whom lacked compassion or care for their fellow man, could bring themselves to think up such evil. He had to remind himself that their own lives—his life, Zahara's life—would have been at hazard had they failed to turn back the assault. But something so horrific, barbaric and inhuman?

Kate's hand touched his arm and he turned to see understanding in her eyes.

"It is a terrible thing. But think. Had they not done so, many more would have been wounded, maimed and killed—on both sides."

It was hard to hear, hard to understand. Hard to want to understand a world where such brutality was necessary. To Gideon it was hollow. Empty excuses justifying the unconscionable. But then war was unconscionable in any form. Not for the first time he wondered if he truly belonged with Lord and his people.

"Christobel," Kate said, her gaze not leaving Gideon. "Would you be kind enough to take Gideon up to see Joan Fisher?"

"If I must," Christobel said. She seemed undisturbed by the account from the messenger and more so from finding her forced confinement burdensome.

"Philip is insisting Joan stay here as much for her protection as for her recovery," Kate said. "I spoke with her first thing. She has no family left in Worcester now and people will be vile when they find out that her son was a murderer. As it is, the Sandys are looking for ways to try and show she knew what he was about and was covering for him. My impression is otherwise. Besides, Anders tells me she is far from out of danger from her injury. He has done his best but if the wound becomes corrupted..." She trailed off. Gideon knew she must be thinking that it was not so long since she was in that same place herself.

"Anders is an excellent physician," he reminded her.

"He is." Kate gathered her composure swiftly. "Joan Fisher seems to me to be a kind woman. Her enquiries were first for you after she asked about her husband and son. It seemed to me she took the news of their deaths as a relief beneath her natural grief. There is a story there, I think, of much suffering and sadness. She asked to speak with you earlier, but I wanted to give her a chance to rest first."

Christobel led the way upstairs and Gideon felt Kate's gaze upon his back as he went.

"She tries hard for us," Christobel said. "But sometimes I wish she wouldn't as it means I have to try hard as well." She glanced at Gideon over her shoulder so he could see her wry smile.

"Kate is one of those people who brings out the best in those around her," Gideon agreed. "So is Sir Philip. They are, I think, well-matched."

"Isn't she some years older than he is?"

It wasn't something Gideon had given much thought to before, but yes Kate had to be four or five years Lord's senior which meant... "Good grief, she must be almost *forty*."

"But you wouldn't think so, would you? *Age cannot wither her...*" Christobel sounded thoughtful. "I'd like to be as Lady Catherine is when I am her age."

They had reached one of the bedrooms and she tapped on the door before going in, then returned soon after to open it for Gideon.

"Widow Fisher is awake and will receive you," she said.

Widow Fisher.

It was strange how much that changed her status both legally and socially. Suddenly she had privileges that as a wife she never had. She was now an individual under the law in her own right, no longer subsumed under her husband's legal identity. Gideon wondered if that would make things easier for her or more difficult.

The room was not typical of most sickrooms Gideon had ever visited. He was used to red drapes and stifling heat, but this was a normally furnished inn room and the window had been opened to let in light and air. He wondered how healthy that could be as every physician he had ever met before spoke against it.

The open window also let in the steady thunder of Danny's guns, joined in their hellish chorus by voices from Waller's lines as his artillery pounded the earthworks. Eight guns didn't seem many, and none were heavy siege pieces, but well used they could still force a breach. And there were three thousand men with Waller, more than twice as many as currently garrisoned in Worcester.

Martha was sitting beside the window repairing a stocking. She scooted to her feet as Gideon entered, to sink back as he gestured to her to carry on. He wondered whose stocking she was mending. Then he realised his abstracted thoughts were akin to Danny's chevaux-de-frise—to fend off the unwanted reality of having to face the woman whose son he had killed. That he'd had no choice made it no easier.

With an effort of will he turned to face her.

On the bed, looking small in its largeness, her face with little more colour than the plain linen pillow she rested her head upon, lay Joan Fisher. She seemed to have shrunk since he last met her. But when she saw Gideon, she held out a hand to him.

He stepped forward and took it.

"I am sorry for your loss." The formal words of condolence sounded empty.

"I believe you indeed are and so I am glad to see you," she said, her tone sincere. "I owe you, my gratitude. You saved my life. Lady Catherine told me that you—that Ezra…" Then she faltered and a single tear escaped her. "I apologise, sir. You see, to me, that name still brings me memories of an innocent little boy, not—not what he became."

"You knew what Ezra—?" Gideon struggled to think how to say it without causing her more distress.

"I knew what he had become, but I never imagined…never thought…" Her voice was a thin whisper of the jovial woman he had known her to be before. "I saw how his father's words altered his mind. Turned him so he no longer listened to me as I was just a woman. He began to speak more and more of the violent passages in the Bible. Then, once he started working for William Richardson, he learned to be violent too. That made him quicker to lash out—at me, the servants, even poor Phoebe once, as much as he adored her."

"Richardson?" Gideon was taken aback. "He worked for William Richardson, the saltpetre maker? But your husband..." He recalled Nehemiah Fisher declaiming against Richardson as a sinner.

Joan Fisher was nodding.

"My husband was angry because Mr Richardson had said he did not want Ezra working for him anymore because a man who could not govern his temper was no use in a business, though I never did find out what it was Ezra did to make him say that, but I can guess. There was something that changed in him. Some days he would answer every question with a verse from the Bible. I suspect that was why Mr Richardson dismissed him. Nehemiah said it was just an excuse and Mr Richardson didn't want to pay Ezra what he should be due once his apprenticeship was done."

And that, Gideon realised, maybe explained why Phoebe had written to say she had something to tell him about the saltpetre men.

Joan Fisher reached out and gripped Gideon's hand with a claw of cold fingers. "Before God, I promise you I didn't know what Ezra had done. I didn't know he was the one who killed that poor

Mistress Markham or dear Phoebe. Or that he attacked Mistress Christobel."

Gideon believed her denials. He was certain from her demeanour that had she known she would have spoken up and tried to prevent what happened.

"But Nehemiah knew, I'm sure of it now," she said, and a tight anger crept into her tone. "Overnight he became a most desperate man, looking for desperate solutions. I asked him what was wrong, but he refused to tell me. When Mistress Markham died, he said it was surely God's vengeance for her immoral behaviour, persuading God-fearing women to behave like men. And you may not believe this, but I overheard him telling one of his friends that he thought you should kill Sir Philip Lord."

Gideon didn't have the heart to tell her that her husband had indeed asked—no, assumed that of him. Instead, he spoke to comfort her.

"No one will hold what your husband and son have done against you, I am sure."

That brought a faint smile to her lips.

"Oh, perhaps not before the law, but they will all say I knew—that I must have known."

"Sir Philip will protect you," Gideon assured her.

"How can he protect me when he is gone from the city, and I have to remain?" She shook her head sadly.

Gideon was at a loss. The unfairness of it was clear, but he knew human nature well enough to know Joan Fisher spoke the truth. Then he remembered.

"Your uncle, did he have children? Do you have family in Baddersleigh?"

A small flame of hope lit the wounded woman's eyes, then faded.

"My uncle is an old man in his seventies, but I have a cousin, younger than me, although he is married and surely wouldn't want another dependent."

Gideon spoke without thinking. "But you will have inherited your husband's house and wealth? Or do you have another son?"

He regretted it instantly as it cast a silent pain into her eyes.

"God saw fit to bless us with four children but now he has called them all back to him, one by one. And Nehemiah owned nothing. The house was with his benefice, and I will be evicted when a new minister is appointed, I am sure."

Christobel, who had been standing by the door, came over then and sat on the side of the bed.

"You need not worry. Sir Philip Lord will see that you are established in your own home wherever you may wish to be."

Gideon nodded in agreement. Just for the name of the village she had already spoken, the place where he might find some clue to his heritage, Lord would pay that price willingly.

A little of the shadow lifted from Joan Fisher's face and she gave a small nod and closed her eyes. "You are most kind to me," she murmured. "I have no notion why you should be."

Christobel passed a hand over Joan's forehead and her expression became a frown.

"I'm not certain," she said, in a low voice, "but I think..." Her expression tightened and she spoke a little louder. "Martha?"

Martha looked up from her sewing. "I'll bring Lady Catherine," she said.

Christobel nodded. "After all this poor woman has been through," she murmured. "It just seems so unfair."

When Kate came, she took one look at the woman in the bed.

"Gideon," she said, "send someone to fetch Anders."

He took the stairs at a run. Before he reached the bottom, he had decided to go himself. He could send one of the waiting messengers, but they might be required for military matters. The man by the plan of the city pointed out to him where to find Argall Greene's infantry. Once outside, Gideon's path was blocked by a large group of soldiers, marching from one part of the walls to another, faces grim, some pale with fear. Most would have seen some action in the war but there were still many fresh recruits for whom this was their baptism of gunfire. But there were also veterans to hand. He stepped aside as Roger Jupp rode past at the head of a familiar company of cavalry.

Jupp acknowledged Gideon with a brief lift of his hand as he trotted by. "Have a care for yourself, Fox and wish us good hunting."

"God keep you," he called after Jupp. "God keep all of you."

Several of the men riding behind Jupp gave a ragged cheer at that. Unlike most of the other soldiers, they looked neither excited nor afraid. They held themselves with confidence and an edge of anticipation. They were Lord's men, and they would be fighting with him, so they would acquit themselves at their best.

Gideon's way lay in the opposite direction to theirs. He knew he had to head towards the castle, to the point where the city walls and the new fortifications met the River Severn. That was where Sir Philip Lord's foot were placed holding the defences opposite Digilis.

Digilis.

Lord's voice, clipped and curt as he pointed to places on the map.

Waller is currently digging in here and here. He holds Digilis to the south…

It was where the main body of Waller's men was to be found. The 'centre' on which Lord and Jupp were about to push back the eastern flank.

The weakest point of the city's defence.

And Zahara was there.

Suddenly Gideon found himself running. The sound of gunfire that had been a steady backdrop to the day flared in intensity and the roar of voices yelling made his blood freeze even as his heart hammered harder.

The gunfire came from where Zahara would be.

They recognised him at the wall and let him through. He had to clamber ladders and walkways and then he was on the defences. Beside him a row of Greene's men were reloading muskets with curt movements, needing no commands and with a speed which was impressive to see. One of the men saw Gideon and without pausing called to him.

"You should keep back, sir, it's hot work here."

"Where's Dr Jensen?" Wherever Anders was Zahara would be, he was sure.

The man was lifting his musket to rest it in an embrasure between the gabions. He nodded his head towards a large house that was close enough to the walls to be under their shelter but far enough that the earthworks had not fully embraced it. Shots were coming from the upper rooms and Gideon realised it was being used as a firing platform for more musketeers.

"He's in there, sir, but I'd not—"

Gideon didn't wait for the man to finish.

The gun smoke with its acrid bite of sulphur was thick enough to sting his eyes but swept aside with the stiff breeze. Beside him the river flowed on, oblivious to the human conflict on its banks. Gideon scrambled down a steep slope, ignoring shouts from behind him and ran past an old outbuilding, across the remains of what must have once been a pleasant walled garden, to reach the house. There was a sudden ragged volley of musket fire from the other side of the house, answered. It was impossible to know which was friend and which was foe.

Someone had taken the door off its hinges to use it elsewhere. Inside the detritus of daily life was scattered over the floor. The linen press had been pulled open and all the sheets and other household items pulled out. It reminded Gideon, painfully, of Wrathby Manor and how domestic felicity so quickly turned to chaos and brutality. Then, in a flash of insight, he understood why Sir Philip Lord had no wish for a building and a plot of land to become something he might think of as home. He had seen too much of this—inflicted too much of it.

"What the hell are *you* doing here?" Argall Greene glared at him, looking identical to the time Gideon had first met him in Banbury. He wore the same morion helm over his close-cropped hair and the same old leather buff, but now over that was a bright peacock-blue sash and his coat, where visible, was the same blue as all Lord's men wore. His tone was, if anything, even more unfriendly than it had been that time and his dark brown eyes smouldered like coals with restrained fury. He had his sword in one hand and, disturbingly, there was blood on it. That must surely mean he had been in close quarters to the attacking force. Behind him were two men, both with muskets.

It wasn't hard to read the true reason for his bristling hostility. All of Lord's men knew that Gideon was someone close to their commander and all felt he was less capable of defending himself than the least of them. They saw him as someone to be protected, someone they had responsibility for and risked answering to Lord for failing to do so. In the general course of things, Gideon took care to avoid putting the men or himself into the place where it happened. But he had no choice and no time for Captain Greene's finer feelings.

"I need to find Dr Jensen," Gideon told him.

"He is about to leave," Argall said, expression unaltered. "In there." He gestured with the bloody sword. Then he jerked his chin at the two men with him. "Go and make sure this gentleman, Dr Jensen and the women get back into the city. I don't want to have anyone else to worry about." He shifted his gaze to Gideon. "When you get there be sure you tell the Schiavono some bastard just took away the damn guns that were supposed to be protecting us, and this place is about to become a battlefield."

A shout came from upstairs.

"Here they come!"

Gideon felt his heart drop away in freefall and Argall's jaw tightened.

"Ah, shit!" He made the word carry a full burden of anger, frustration and concern. "Just get the hell out of here Fox, you hear me?" Then he was off at speed.

Gideon needed no second bidding himself.

He went through to the room Argall had indicated and nearly ran into Anders who was coming out, supporting a man with a leg in splints.

"Gideon? What are you—?"

"I was sent by Lady Catherine. She thinks Joan Fisher needs you."

Anders frowned. "You should not have come. I will go to Mrs Fisher as soon as I am able. We need to leave. Please, if you can, persuade Zahara. I have to get this man—"

147

"I'll see to it," Gideon promised. "You just go."

Anders glanced back as he headed for the door, slowed by the burden of the man he was supporting. Inside the room, Brighid must have just finished packing Anders' bag and was securing it with buckles. Then with a quick nod at Gideon, she picked it up and followed Anders out.

The room itself had until recently been a comfortable parlour of the kind one might expect to find in any well-to-do house. But now the furniture had been pushed aside and the windows were broken so that men could put the barrels of their muskets through them. Well-padded chairs had been overturned to provide makeshift gabions. As Gideon entered the men at the window fired a volley and began reloading, stepping back so their places could be taken by those who had loaded weapons ready.

Zahara was in one corner crouched beside a man who was lying in a tumble of red-soaked linen. There were two other, unmoving, figures nearby.

Crossing to Zahara in three quick paces, Gideon dropped into a crouch beside her. She was holding the hand of the man in both hers and talking softly to him. His eyes were locked on her gaze and his breathing was shallow and ragged. Gideon didn't need a physician's skill to know this man was dying.

He didn't understand the language Zahara used, or what words she said, but there was something of peace in the man's face, despite its dreadful pallor.

"We need to go," he said as gently as he could. Zahara's gaze switched to him. She seemed unsurprised that he was there.

"I am staying with Benjamin," she said, her voice low. "As long as he needs me here."

Gideon's throat tightened in panic.

"Then we will have to take him with us, we cannot—"

"No. He needs to lie here." She must have seen the desperation flood his face because she lifted one of her hands from gripping that of the dying man and brushed her fingers against Gideon's hand. "You go. I will not be long," she said softly.

He could see from the calm certitude in her eyes that she would not leave before the man died. Outside there was a sudden roar, the sound of hundreds of men giving voice to encourage themselves and their fellows and there was a rattle of musket fire as Argall Greene answered them.

"Hah!" One of the men who had been firing through the window made a contemptuous sound and one of the others laughed. From this Gideon concluded they had managed to dissuade the attackers.

He looked back to Zahara, her eyes closed and her lips moving softly in prayer. The man whose hand she held was still dragging rasps of breath into his body, but they were weaker than they had been even when Gideon first arrived. He realised Zahara had been right, it would be a very short time before he had gone.

Gideon wondered then how many times she had sat like this, bringing comfort to someone she barely knew on behalf of those who couldn't be there. The oasis of peace she cast about her drew him in and despite the renewed clamour of battle outside, he felt strangely calm and secure.

Without really meaning to he closed his own eyes and added his prayers to hers and for some reason despite the fact they used different words and addressed a different idea of God, it felt right in his heart. It was a stillness that brought him back. When he opened his eyes Zahara was looking at him. Her soul seemed in her gaze and Gideon knew without having to ask or say anything that she too had felt their communion. The man had died amid their prayers because he lay now with his face free of pain or care. Zahara folded his hands on his chest and closed his eyes.

Gideon wanted to draw her into his embrace then and there, but the door was flung open, and Argall Greene strode in.

"You still here? For the love of God—"

"That is why we are still here," Zahara told him, rising and Gideon rose with her. "But now we will go."

Greene looked from her to the dead man and the anger seemed to leave him like a cloud lifting.

"He was a good man. Thank you." Then he turned and called to those lining the window. "We give'em hell one more time, boys, then we withdraw. I'm leaving a few surprises. Soon as we get the damn guns sorted again, they'll regret it."

That last defiance prompted a ragged cheer from the soldiers. Zahara picked up her bag as he was speaking. Gideon took it from her on his good shoulder. If they had to run and scramble, he didn't want her to be encumbered.

And that was when the first cannon shots hit the house.

Chapter Thirteen

A scream followed the shattering sound and Gideon's immediate and unworthy thought was to wish from his heart that whoever had screamed might be dead because he knew if not Zahara would want to tend them.

Greene swore then lifted his voice.

"Give fire!"

The volley must have come from every man in the house and the noise was as loud as a cannon.

"Withdraw!" Greene yelled. "Let's get the hell out of here, boys!"

He paused by the parlour door long enough to grab Gideon and Zahara by one arm each and propel them ahead of him.

"Keep in the middle of my men and run," he instructed.

They ran back through the house and met others coming down the stairs and out of the other rooms. Gideon realised then that perhaps half of Greene's full strength in men had been holding the house. Another cannon shot hit but this time, to Gideon's relief, there was no scream.

"Someone was hurt...?" Zahara was asking the men coming down the stairs, "Are they...?"

"It was Ricco. He's gone," one of the men with a heavy Italian accent to his French, told her. Gideon saw her lips moving in a brief prayer as they ran with the flow of men for the door.

"Withdraw in good order." Greene's voice carried over the new sound of shouting and musket fire from the other side of the house. One or two of those who had been sprinting ahead slowed to keep with the main body.

Gideon with Zahara beside him had barely made it halfway to the earthworks when a rolling thunder of musket fire came from one side. A small group of musketeers had pushed around beside the house and managed to take a position which commanded the ground between the house and the defensive works to which they were retreating.

151

Zahara grabbed his free hand and then they were running together towards the small stone-built outbuilding Gideon had passed on the way there. It lay along the wall that encircled the house's grounds and was sheltered by the house itself from the worst of any attack from the far side of it and would give them safety from this new threat. Beyond it were bushes and a couple of straggling trees partly uprooted by the digging of earthworks, then a stretch of more open ground before the ditches of Danny's outer city defences began.

There were shouts, more shots and a high-pitched scream as Gideon followed Zahara into the safety of the building.

The first thing he noticed was the smell. Even over the stench of powder smoke, it was acrid. Inside, it was a small room, perhaps four yards deep and three wide. There were the remains of a low hearth and a hole where there had been a chimney. Perhaps it had once been a brewhouse, laundry or bakery, now it served as a dovecote for pigeons to roost in its roof. That explained the stench, although the birds themselves had been scared away by the fighting. The space below the roosts served to hold some of the spades, hoes and other tools that would be used to maintain the garden. These were protected from pigeon droppings by a wide shelf that jutted out from the top of the wall and would also serve as a platform to reach the pigeons.

Gideon risked a look outside and made little sense of what he could see. There was a fog of gun smoke shrouding the area and sounds from the house of shouts and cheers. He could see figures running away from the house but had no notion who they were until Zahara pulled him away from the door.

"Captain Greene was driven back. The enemy is in the house and those men running past, they are not ours. It is not safe for us to go anywhere now."

As if to verify her words, a stark rattle of musketry was followed by a shout to withdraw from a voice that was too deep and harsh to be Argall Greene. A figure suddenly filled the door and Gideon drew his sword with one hand and thrust Zahara behind him with the other. He would have run the man through when another sporadic volley of musket fire came from the earthworks and the soldier staggered and fell, lying still just outside the door.

No more followed, perhaps put off the attempt by the death of their comrade on the threshold. But the musket fire continued from both sides unabated, with now and then the skit of a bullet hitting the building. And that was when it dawned on Gideon with the force of a gut punch. He and the woman he loved with all his soul, were stranded in the middle of a battle.

Zahara seemed to know when that realisation hit home, perhaps his breathing had changed, or his muscles had grown tense, but she drew him to her and reached up to brush a stray hair from his cheek, then placed her fingers against each side of his face so he had to look into her eyes.

"When Captain Greene tells him what has happened, Daniel will reposition the guns and that will force the men in there to leave the house," she said carefully. "We will be alright." Then she smiled and he realised she was just as afraid as he was and drew her close in his embrace. She wrapped her arms around him, and he drew comfort from her and knew she was taking the same from him.

It was like being caught in the middle of a thunderstorm, only instead of pelting rain, there was a hail of deadly musket balls.

"All that could take some time," he said, trying to keep his voice steady. He knew, as she knew, that they were in danger every moment they stayed there. "I wish I'd thought to bring something to eat and drink, then we could have dinner whilst we wait."

"You might not have thought to do so," she said, "but in my bag is a half loaf of bread, an apple and a water flask." Then she wrinkled her nose. "But I'm not sure I want to dine in this place. The previous guests were not well brought up."

Gideon laughed.

They made themselves as comfortable as they could. Moving the gardening tools to have a space free from pigeon deposits, they discovered a solid ledge behind. When brushed clear it offered a seat of sorts—if they sat pressed together. For a while, they stayed thus, sheltered in each other's arms, the sounds of war so close about them and yet seeming to Gideon as if in a different world to the one the two of them occupied.

After a time Zahara murmured some words.

"You are praying?"

She nodded.

"I pray for all the men out there. Those on both sides. That God will care for them."

Words came to him from his childhood. *Love your enemies, bless them that curse you, do good to them that hate you, and pray for them which despitefully use you, and persecute you.* He must be a bad Christian, he decided, as he couldn't pray for those who were shooting at them and placing Zahara in peril.

"I hope this war ends soon," he said.

"The Schiavono says that if this lasts another year, or if we cannot take London in that time, he thinks the king will not be able to win."

"What will we do if the king loses?" he asked, not expecting an answer.

Zahara gave a small shrug as if it was a matter of little account.

"The Schiavono will leave England again."

Leave England. Become an effective exile. Did he really want that? Then Gideon realised, suddenly, how little that meant anyway. If he stayed with Lord, there would always be a war. He would always be part of the fighting. Even if they survived this one, there would be more sieges and more battles. A cold desolation settled over him.

"Is there no end to war?" he asked. "How can Sir Philip keep fighting? Is there not a time he stops and calls: 'Enough!'? I feel as if we're trapped in it with no escape."

There was no answer and he regretted having spoken. They were not words for this time and place where they were indeed trapped. Then Zahara answered.

"I think, perhaps, he will stop when he has no cause to fight. That will be when he can find peace in his own heart—when he can let go of the past. I hope that time will come soon."

"And until then we are trapped with him?"

Zahara reached up and drew Gideon's head down to her, lips meeting lips, and her lips parted. In wonderment, like a pilgrim before the altar of a saint, he closed his eyes and tasted her sweetness and when she pulled gently away, he opened his eyes to find her gaze full upon him. The same wonder and discovery that he was lost in reflected there.

"I used to feel," she said softly, "as if my heart was trapped like a bird in a cage. But with you, it is as if it can fly again."

Her words reached into Gideon's chest and unlocked something there. Unbelievably, in the midst of war and carnage, with the thunder and rattle of gunfire all around, he discovered true peace and joy. It was as if he had been on a long journey and finally come home.

He drew her close, her head under his chin.

"Marry me, Zahara," he whispered. "Marry me by whatever form, rite or ritual you choose, but please, marry me."

He felt her breath catch and he stood on the edge of a precipice as she hesitated. She looked up at him and he knew from her eyes that it wasn't anything about him or anything between them that made her hesitate. It was a barrier within herself. And as she gazed at him, he saw that crumble and fall away.

"Yes," she said simply. "I will."

The roar from the direction of the house swallowed her words. Zahara turned in Gideon's arms, her body suddenly tense and hard beneath his hands where before it had been relaxed and soft.

"They are trying to storm the earthworks," she said. "Daniel must be moving the guns back."

She had no need to explain further. The movement of the guns, whilst it would lead to their eventual rescue, also meant that the Parliamentarians would see this as their last chance to penetrate the city's defences having gained the advantage of the house, knowing that once the guns were trained on them, they could not hold the position for long.

It also meant their small outbuilding would no doubt become a forward shelter in the advance.

Zahara stepped free of his grip, picked up her bag then pulled on Gideon's hand.

"Run!"

He resisted her pull. "But we will be—"

He was speaking to empty air. She had gone through the door. Mind blanked with fear for her, Gideon had no choice but to follow. They were perhaps fifty yards ahead of the men who were charging behind them as Zahara pushed through the bushes, running faster than Gideon had ever imagined a woman might despite being burdened by the bag she carried, and his long stride only gained on her as she slowed to clamber over the first of the fallen trees.

They were together as they stumbled into the shallow ditch at the base of the earthwork and Zahara pulled Gideon down into the mud with her.

"My God, why did you—?" Gideon heard the taut fear and relief come out as anger and stopped himself from speaking.

"There was no time to explain," she said. "There is none now. Trust me. We must move."

She rose to run, and a man landed in the ditch right behind her, his musket reversed in his hands which he was swinging, like a club. Gideon barged Zahara aside, so she stumbled back, knocking into her assailant as the blow swept in. Gideon caught his arm, blocking the musket and drove a boot hard into his groin. Drawing his sword as the man fell forward, face down, Gideon drove it hard through his spine.

There was no chance to consider his action. Another man had landed in the ditch—an officer—levelling a pistol at Gideon's head. At that range, it could not miss. But even as he could see the finger tightening to bring his death, a billet of wood smashed the officer's arm aside, so the pistol fired into empty air. Gideon lunged to put his bloodied blade through the man's chest.

Zahara met his gaze, her eyes wide and he realised it had been she who had swung the billet and saved him. He could see the anguish in her eyes and wanted nothing more than to draw her close and take that from them, but instead, he snatched up her bag, took her hand and started running with her along the ditch.

Now he could hear the return of musket fire and even the clash of steel, as men came to hand-to-hand fighting. He realised then why Zahara had run from the pigeon house when she did. Whilst the men streamed across the open ground in their swarming assault, they would not have been firing and the defenders would be aiming at them. It had been the best chance they had to escape. That was an unwelcome reminder Zahara was more experienced in matters of war than he. She had seen the opportunity and taken it.

"Gideon!"

A shout from above made Gideon look up. Unbelievably he saw Danny's face, grimed with powder smoke, peering over the parapet of the defence work about two yards above the ditch they were running along.

"Stay there," he called. "I'll get you out as soon as I can."

Under the shelter of the repositioned guns, whose voices suddenly thundered over their heads, Gideon drew Zahara into the protective circle of his arms and pressed them both into the muddy slope of the ditch. It seemed to be a small eternity that they were stranded there, clinging together, trusting the skill of the man defending the ramparts above them to ensure none of the enemy could come close enough to do them harm.

The guns were still firing when the ladder appeared, sliding down towards them. Gideon braced it so Zahara could climb and when he saw her hands being taken by Danny to help her, he made his own rapid ascent.

"You may be pleased to know that Argall Greene is having his entire month's pay docked for leaving you two behind," Danny said cheerfully, between the firing guns. "To say Philip was furious would be a bit like saying a gale is a light spring breeze."

Zahara shook her head.

"He didn't mean to do so. I will speak to the Schiavono."

Danny looked doubtful.

"You can try. When he gets back. He had to lead the cavalry sortie to clear the east side of the city. If he succeeds, we can bring more men across to the south here and play a bit more havoc with Waller's intrepid assaults. Oh, look." He pointed back to the house they had fled, which now had flames shooting from its windows. "I think we'll owe William Berkely a bit more than a letter of apology now. That was his house and all his worldly goods." Danny sounded happy. "Waller's just lost his best chance of breaking into the city. I would have destroyed the house before if I'd thought there was any risk that the guns would be moved."

"Why were the guns moved?" After all that he and Zahara had been through because of it, Gideon wanted to know.

Danny gave him a wry look.

"You have to ask? Why do you think? Because Dudd bloody Dudley thought he knew better than me when my back was turned." He put a hand briefly on Gideon's shoulder. "I'm glad I got you out or I'd be on zero pay for the rest of my life. First for not attending adequately to your rescue and second for murdering Dudley. But now you'll have to excuse me, with the house slighted beyond any use to the enemy I need to reposition these guns again." He turned to order two of the musketeers to escort Gideon and Zahara back to The Talbot.

Kate saw them come into the inn and rose from her seat where she had pen, ink and paper and a small pile of documents set out. The relief on her face was obvious.

"I was so worried, and Philip was too," she said, crossing over to them and embracing Zahara, despite the splattering of dried mud that covered her clothes. "He would have looked for you both himself but had to lead the sortie."

The tale of their rescue took little telling. Then Kate gripped Gideon's hand as if she wished to reassure herself, they were both there and alright.

"Please excuse me, Lady Catherine. I'll get changed," Zahara said, bobbing a curtsy to Kate and smiling at Gideon before she headed for the stairs.

"It must have been frightening," Kate said when Zahara had gone. "I'm glad you took good care of each other. You are both precious to me and Philip."

Gideon was lost for what he should say to that.

"Now I have embarrassed you," Kate said, sounding contrite.

"No. Not at all. I mean—" Gideon broke off wondering what he did mean. He took refuge in formality. "I'm honoured by your esteem, and I assure you it's mutual."

Kate smiled. "That's good because it makes it easier for me to ask if you would assist me in getting this work done." She gestured to the papers on the table. "There's any amount to sort on local affairs, and word arrived yesterday that poor King Louis has died in France, so there is much that must be done now to secure Philip's French interests."

Gideon felt a new chill of concern. Saint-Léon-du-Moulin, the beautiful house and prosperous holding Lord had in France might be at risk.

"You look worried and there is no need to be," Kate assured him. "Philip is careful in his investments and the new *éminence* thinks highly of him. But there are things we need to do to secure it all."

"Then as soon as I have changed," Gideon promised and then he remembered. "Is Joan Fisher...?" He hardly dared to finish the question.

"Anders thinks the affliction was of her mind not her body," Kate told him, resuming her seat at the table and picking up the pen. "Joan is sleeping peacefully again having eaten a thin broth and taken all the medication Anders says she should have. Christobel is sitting in with her, or I would have had her help me. But poor Martha was so exhausted, I sent her to get some sleep. She is such a sweet and loyal girl."

As Gideon changed his clothes, he noticed the shadows lengthening as the achingly long day came to a close. He hoped the guns would stop at sunset, presumably they would have to when it was no longer possible to see what they were shooting at. But there was the certain knowledge that they would start up again tomorrow. Worcester would face another day of pounding guns, sorties and assaults, of death and horror.

How long did sieges last? Gideon recalled that Reading had been besieged for over two weeks before it finally surrendered. But he had heard of sieges that lasted months. The thought of weeks or more of pounding guns made him feel weak. And then how might it end? Would they be forced to surrender? And after how Waller's trumpeter was treated, would they even be accorded honours of war and the right to march out unmolested? And what if one of the assaults succeeded despite Danny's guns? He knew the one he had been involved in had come close and had it not been Argall Greene and his men holding the defences there, the entire city could have been overwhelmed from that one breach. He had a sudden image of the horror he had seen at Kineton. The screaming women and children being cut down by men who were lost in a savage blood haze.

It was in a sombre and darker mood than he had left Kate that he returned to her. She frowned when she saw him and gestured to the other chair at the table and pushed a few of the documents towards him.

"Zahara has gone to sit with Christobel, she will come down in a while. Perhaps you could make a start on reading these…"

An hour later the sound of many hooves on the cobbles of the stable yard and shouts announced the return of Sir Philip Lord.

Kate rose to hurry to the door, Gideon with her. But Lord came in before they could reach it. He was filthy and stank of black powder, there was blood staining his buff, breeches and boot down one leg and his hair was matted with it too.

"I see our fox has escaped the hounds," Lord said, glancing at Gideon. "Zahara too?"

Gideon nodded and Lord picked up Kate in both his arms, lifting her from the ground and turning with her as if in a dance so the careful gathers in her taffeta skirts spread out like the bell petals of a flower.

Lord laughed up at her as he lifted her high. "*Glorious is my love, worth triumphs in her face.*" Then he set her gently down on her feet and took her hand to kiss it chastely. "Much as I wish to do so, I would not press you to my bosom as I stand," he told her. He saw where her gaze fell and shook his head. "The blood is not mine, I promise you."

"You were successful?" Kate asked.

"What can I say? *David went out, and fought with the Philistines, and slew them with a great slaughter; and they fled from him.* Yes, we were successful. More than we had any right to be, but then we did have the advantage of surprise. I think their soldiers had it in mind we would just sit like bees in a bottle and make no attempt to remove them from their holes, hedges and stolen houses."

"Is everyone safe?" Kate asked.

Lord turned back to the door and called through it.

"Jupp? Did anyone fall off his horse on the way back?"

Roger Jupp appeared looking as sweaty and filthy as his commander. He swept off his hat in a flourishing bow for Kate and gave Gideon a brief nod.

"Olsen lost his horse," he said. "But he found one of theirs which he swears he likes better. Berne has a cut to his sword arm and Stolar's pistol had a hangfire and nearly took one of his toes off. But we've no one to bury today. Where's Dr Jensen?"

"He and Brighid are with Argall," Kate explained. "He will be back shortly, I'm sure, as he has a patient he needs to check on. But Zahara is here, she will look to our men."

"I will fetch her," Gideon said and went.

Zahara was just coming from the room where Joan Fisher lay and smiled when she saw him.

"I heard horses," she said.

"Sir Philip and Roger Jupp are back with the Company. There are two men injured."

Zahara nodded. "I will fetch my bag and come and tend them." Then she hesitated, looking shy. "Have you told the Schiavono and the Lady Catherine that I—that we—that…?"

He had no idea what she meant. Then he did and felt mortified that he hadn't understood her right away.

"About us? About our getting married?"

She reached up and touched his face, searching it with her gaze. Her eyes were troubled. "You have not changed your mind?"

Gideon thought his heart might break from his body at the pain in her words and without conscious thought, he drew her to him and held her close.

"No. Never." He whispered fiercely. "I love you. You are the key to my lock, the spring to my winter. You complete me."

She looked up as he spoke, the shadows gone from her face.

"*The love of thee has taken so strong a hold upon my heart and upon my soul, that, though my head were separated from my body, my love for thee would still survive*. We will tell them together," she said. "After this siege is done."

Gideon let her go with more reluctance than he had ever known before. It was as if they had just opened the door onto a secret garden, but now must wait for even snatched chances to walk in it together.

He wondered how it was Kate and Lord endured it.

How any mere mortal could.

Chapter Fourteen

Supper was late. An hour after dark.

The guns had fallen silent and the silence itself was loud as Gideon made his way downstairs having changed. The scrape of pen on paper, the soft crackle of a log in the hearth. Voices regained their lost volume.

The whole household assembled to eat together. Only Shiraz was absent, having taken word of the siege to Oxford, and Martha, who was once more sitting with Joan Fisher.

Christobel, freed from Anders' restrictions on a special dispensation, had been taken by Danny to see the guns' firing and the might of Waller's army that his hard work had done so much to keep at bay. They returned wreathed in smiles, arm in arm, with Christobel talking excitedly about the bright explosions in the darkness, how the smoke and flame shot together from the mouth of a cannon, and of being permitted to fire one of the guns. Danny looked oddly absent every time he glanced in her direction, which he seemed to do a lot.

Gideon waited until Christobel had finished her excited description, before taking the opportunity to ask his question.

"How long will the siege last?"

Lord cut into his pie as he replied. "Tomorrow Waller will intercept a message supposedly from Oxford which will purport to put heart into us trembling and timorous defenders, telling us to be of good cheer because Lord Capel is marching to our relief and will be here by the second day of June at the latest."

"And is he?"

"Good grief no. Capel, I am sure, has far more important things to do than rescue us who need no rescue. We could sit here for the next month if need be, as we have shown today. Whereas I think Sir William will be getting worried letters from home speaking of Prince Rupert and Bristol in the same panicked paragraph."

Gideon thought about that.

"You believe that Waller will just up and leave?"

Lord nodded and helped himself to more of the vegetables which had been roasted and served with rosemary.

"Waller has seen how sharp our teeth can be and wouldn't relish the thought of being pinioned between us and a field army." The confidence with which he spoke seemed to warm the atmosphere.

"Will we be staying here when they have gone?" Christobel asked.

"I will be wanted elsewhere I'm sure, but I have some business nearby so we will for a short time."

Kate set her cup down and her hand reached out to rest on the back of Lord's.

"That is all for the future," she said, then smiled at Anders. "How is Joan Fisher?"

"Better than I might have expected," Anders said. "Since she was told Sir Philip will help her, that has given her hope where before she had only despair. She has been speaking of cousins she has nearby and—"

"Cousins," Danny burst out, making Gideon jump. "You said cousins—of course. She's too young to be Kelley's sister. She's his niece?"

Lord narrowed his eyes and Danny subsided. It was not so surprising he had worked that out. After all, he had been with them at Mortlake.

"Whoever she might be," Anders said, doggedly ignoring the interruption, "she is the better for the hope she has been given. But it will still be a few days yet before I can be sure she will live to enjoy those hopes being brought to fulfilment."

Which was a sobering thought.

Kate clearly decided they had spoken enough of such things and turned the conversation to other topics.

It was later, as Gideon said goodnight to Zahara before her door that a cold thought crept into his mind. He turned back to her as her hand was on the latch.

"Did you know what Danny was talking about?"

She nodded.

"Widow Fisher told me who she was and what you had asked her. Christobel knows too."

It was as if a shadow wrapped the air between them.

"What will he do when he knows the truth?"

Zahara didn't ask who or what he spoke of, she studied his face in the light of the candle she held as if trying to read the reason he asked.

"He will still be himself," she said simply. "Nothing that *matters* will change."

Gideon took that assessment to bed and found the question troubled him enough to keep sleep at bay. When Danny finally appeared, glowing visibly with happiness he was still wide awake. For once, and to Danny's obvious and immense delight and surprise, it was Gideon who suggested they play cards.

Having gone to bed late, Gideon was woken with all Worcester, well before dawn when the guns began again. Danny, of course, was long gone. Pausing outside the room where Joan Fisher was recovering, Gideon heard voices. Zahara and Joan. He moved away quietly not wanting to disturb their conversation.

Once he was downstairs, Kate was quick to capture him to assist her, as Christobel had gone out with the women to help on the defences. His ability to write was somewhat restored even if the letters were perhaps less perfectly formed than he would have liked. The work they had to do was fully engaging but as the morning progressed Gideon noticed the war map was updated a lot less than it had been on the previous day.

Kate must have noticed him glancing across at it, because she got up to study it critically, her brow drawn into lines.

"It seems to me that Sir William is not making so much effort today. He is still using his guns but apart from a half-hearted push here he seems content to leave us be for now." She touched the map at the same point as Gideon had been caught in the fighting yesterday.

The mystery of Waller's inactivity was solved when Lord appeared mid-morning with both Samuel Sandys, his brother Martin, Lieutenant Colonel Davies and two of the most senior commanders of Worcester in tow. Leaving them by the map table he dismissed the other men there and strode over to greet Kate.

"I need to borrow your clerk," he told her, but his gaze was on Gideon. "If I may?"

"Of course," she said, "although I expect to be recompensed for his loss."

Lord smiled into her eyes and took her hand to kiss the fingers before he released it again. "You may name your price," he told her.

She lifted her eyebrows and smiled then picked up one of the ciphered papers she had been working on for most of the morning and handed it to him.

"I was going to have this brought to you, but as you are here…"

He took it and read, his expression growing serious as he did so. Gideon had no idea what was in it, but he could see where Danny had made some detailed notes on it, presumably before he went out and Kate had continued his work.

Lord's eyes widened a little as he read.

"Thank you, my lady, thank you indeed. For this, you deserve a new gown."

"And Danny?"

"Danny," Lord said, folding the page neatly and slipping it into his coat, "looks terrible in a gown, but can have one too if he wishes." He turned to Gideon, who was already on his feet by then and put a hand on his good shoulder.

"How are your arms now?"

"I can hold a sword and pistol," Gideon told him. "I managed well enough yesterday."

"That's good to know, but I was more hoping you might be able to wield a pen."

Gideon gestured to the page he had just been writing. "Or that too."

"With me then, if you please, Mr Fox." Which was a fair warning that it was Colonel Sir Philip Lord who required his services and Gideon should conduct himself accordingly.

The small group by the table had been watching Lord and wore disapproving looks.

"Is it wholly appropriate for your wife to be writing her letters here?" Samuel Sandys asked as Lord rejoined them with Gideon in tow.

Lord lifted a brow and cocked his head.

"Is her presence a distraction to you?"

Sandys must have caught the edge in Lord's tone because he shook his head and coughed awkwardly.

"No. Not at all. I was merely thinking it must be dull for her to have to listen to us."

"Lady Catherine is deeply absorbed in her letters," Lord assured him. "Indeed, here is one of them." He reached into his coat and pulled out the folded sheet Kate had just given him and held it out.

Frown deepening, Sandys held up his hand to ward the paper away.

"There's no need—"

"I insist," Lord said, implacable.

Gideon felt pity for Sandys, he knew too well what it was like to be on the receiving end of Sir Philip Lord in such a mood. Sandys had frozen at the hard glitter in Lord's gaze, taking the paper from him as if it were a venomous snake, holding it at arm's length as he unfolded the page.

"I say, that is—that really is—" Martin Sandys started to object, and it was his brother who silenced him, looking up from the paper in shock.

"But this means—where did you get this?"

"It was intercepted by one of my men last night."

Martin Sandys tried to peer over his brother's shoulder to read and Gideon caught a look from Kate who dropped a wink before returning demurely to her work.

"What is it?" Davies demanded.

Lord took the paper out of Sandy's hands and waved it like a fan.

"This, gentlemen, is an order from Waller to one of his captains garrisoned at St. Johns to requisition as many boats as he can find along the river to ship the wounded back to Bristol."

"So?" Martin Sandys said, confused. "It tells us noth—"

Samuel Sandys made a noise that reminded Gideon of an irritated horse.

"It says the boats must be acquired immediately and be ready to depart by this evening at the latest," Sandys said as if explaining something obvious, even though only he and Lord seemed to grasp the implications. "If it were just about sending the wounded to Bristol there would be no need for such a stringent time limit. No. This tells us Waller means to go and from what that says," he pointed to the paper, "he means to go soon. Perhaps even tonight."

Gideon felt a lurch of hope and relief so powerful he felt the world swerve and had to grip the table. The siege was going to end. To end soon.

"There's no doubt this is genuine? Not some ruse to mislead us?" Davies asked.

Lord gave a nod of confirmation.

"The cipher is one Waller wouldn't want to be broken and I am sure he doesn't know it has been. This is no ruse. Besides I had intelligence this morning that Waller is sweeping the countryside for horses and anything portable of value. I regret that means our own assessments might fall short this month, but that had already alerted me that he is intending to leave soon and is grabbing what he may before he goes, this is confirmation. The question is what do we do with the knowledge?"

"Why do anything?" Davies asked. "If we're sure he's going, what difference does it make?"

Gideon was wondering the same thing himself, but in his present role knew better than to ask. It was Samuel Sandy's who answered.

"Think about it. If he leaves as he came, he will depart under cover of darkness, planning to be in Gloucester by dawn with us little the wiser that he's gone until then. If he shows he is withdrawing, we can harry his retreat."

"That's true," Lord said. "Besides, he fears Lord Capel is approaching. I suspect he will depart tonight so there is no opportunity for Capel to force him to fight with us right behind him."

"Why would he think Lord Cap—?" Martin Sandys was not so well informed as his brother who lifted a hand to silence him.

"What did you have in mind, Sir Philip?"

"I will explain. But before I do let me be very clear on one thing. If word escapes that the siege is being lifted, we will be faced with a prematurely exultant citizenry and a soldiery who will not be on their guard. As long as Waller is without the walls, he remains a real and present danger to the city. He is an excellent commander and, as we have seen, an opportunist. If he marks any sign of weakness, he isn't going to let it pass just because he has plans to depart. Make no mistake, gentlemen, I will put my sword through any man who allows this information to be known outside of this room" There was a sudden chilling of the atmosphere as he looked at the other five men one at a time. "Is that understood?"

No one spoke and Lord gave a small nod of satisfaction.

"I had anyway intended to see if we could shake loose a few apples from his orchard as he tried to do with us, this news makes that notion more relevant." Lord picked up a paper that was already on the table. Gideon recognised it as the sheet he had seen being printed in the cellar room of The Swan. Waller's attempt to persuade the people of Worcester to rise in his support. "We have access to his printing press. I think we could provide notice to the waverers in Waller's troops that they would be welcome to join the king's army here in Worcester."

Samuel Sandys pulled a face.

"If it worked, could such men be trusted?"

Lord shrugged.

"The point about those who might turncoat, colonel, is not so much to recruit for ourselves as to deny men to the enemy. If any apply and you shouldn't want them, I will take them. However, I don't expect a flood, maybe not even a small trickle. The real impact will be upon the spirit of the men. They are already setback. This was supposed to be a second Hereford and instead, we have barred their way and bloodied their noses. If we then start offering largesse and promises, it makes us seem even stronger to them."

Sandys rubbed his chin and then nodded a few times, his expression thoughtful.

"I like the notion of returning Waller's offer. To slap his face."

Gideon was tasked with writing up a draft document, while Lord outlined succinctly what they would need to do that day and in the night to come if Waller did indeed raise the siege.

Outside the guns kept up their seemingly endless bombardment. *If I can get the artillery set right we can keep him at arm's length.* And Danny had done so. Perhaps when the guns fell silent tonight, they might not be needed tomorrow.

Gideon completed his writing and read over it, satisfied it met what he had been asked to do. It was the same phrases Waller had used but repurposed to offer the Parliamentarians sanctuary in Worcester. He got to his feet and Lord, who had been leaning on the map table, straightened up.

"I think we are done then, gentlemen. Let's see what Mr Fox has composed."

He took the paper from Gideon, read it to himself then handed it to Samuel Sandys who nodded approval as he finished reading. "You have turned Waller's own words against him. He will hate that."

"I have some people at The Swan, Fox," Lord said. "Take this to them. They know what to do."

Gideon went accompanied by one of Lord's men. On the way, it dawned on him that the reason Lord wanted that secret press and none other used to print the letter was to send another, more profound and subtle message to Waller. The press would be distinctive in its printing style and by using it Waller was being told that his network in Worcester had been uncovered and broken.

On the way back from The Swan, stepping step aside to allow a marching troop to go by, Gideon found himself beside a bookshop. A brief pang of nostalgia engulfed him, nostalgia for happier days in London when he would indulge himself looking through the booksellers around St. Paul's. He glanced inside, thinking that if the opportunity arose, he would like to return and see what the bookseller had on offer. Through the open door, he caught sight of a painting hanging on the wall and froze, staring. Then drawn by a force he couldn't resist, stepped inside so he could study it more closely.

It was a painting in a heavy frame of a seated old man with a child standing beside him. The man was Dr John Dee. He was pictured in the rose room of the house in Mortlake. A mirror behind him reflected the hearth and its eagle and rose plaque. Dee wore his scholar's robes. On his lap, he was holding a book upon which could be seen his *monas hieroglyphica* symbol. Beside him stood a child of perhaps five or six. She was shown dressed in a dark turquoise gown which matched well the colour of her eyes. Her hair, where it was visible before being drawn back under a small and neat French hood, was as white as Dee's beard. Gideon could see the curve of the hood was embroidered with tiny crowns. In one hand the child held an opening rosebud—a Tudor rose as the petals within were revealed as both white and red. A thorn had drawn a drop of blood from her finger which sat on the white petals like dew.

Chapter Fifteen

"Can I help you, sir?"

Gideon realised he was staring at the picture so intently his lips were slightly parted. Closing his mouth he swallowed and turned to the bookseller, dragging the shreds of his scattered wits together as best he could.

"That painting, where did you come by it?"

The bookseller gave him an odd look then frowned and peered short-sightedly at the picture as if seeing it for the first time. "Oh yes. It was one my father acquired. I inherited it along with the business. He was fond of collecting oddities. I suspect he bought it cheap in a public sale. He attended them often in search of books. I think it's supposed to show Dr Dee with one of his daughters."

Gideon swallowed hard not wanting to comment on what he thought it depicted.

"How much would you be willing to sell it for?"

The bookseller looked at him.

"This is a *book*seller's," he said, helpfully.

"Yes, I know it's not a book, but I would like to buy it," Gideon said.

The bookseller's eyes narrowed. There was something in his expression that troubled Gideon. He was not sure if it was cupidity or nervousness.

"You're not a local man," the bookseller said. "You're with the army?"

"I am a lawyer and yes, I'm with the army," Gideon told him, thinking it would add weight to his status. Then instantly wished he could unsay it as the bookseller's lips had tightened. This man was clearly one who didn't welcome the presence of a Royalist garrison occupying his city.

"Then you may have it for ten pounds."

"That is outrageous. I could buy a horse for less," he protested. "I will give you five."

The bookseller's jaw was set.

"That is my price, sir. I'll not negotiate."

Gideon opened his mouth to object, but he knew there was no point and closed it again. He could always seize the painting and walk out. The bookseller couldn't prevent it, especially as one of Lord's men waited outside the door. But it would draw attention to the painting and that had to be avoided. For the same reason he had no wish to have Sir Philip Lord himself linked to the painting. Word would spread like wildfire that the man at the right hand of the acting governor had bought a painting and what it looked like. Whereas Gideon making a purchase would not be remarked.

He pulled out his purse and emptied it on a table, poking his finger through the pile of coins. "Two pounds, fourteen shillings and thruppence," he said. "That is all I have on me."

Scooping up the coins, the bookseller pulled a face as if he had a bad flavour in his mouth. "Ten pounds, if you want to take the painting with you."

Exasperated, Gideon agreed. "Very well. I will leave you the money as a deposit on the purchase. You will give me a receipt to acknowledge that and to confirm you are selling me the picture for the price specified. We will both sign it. If you wish, we can make two copies, and each keep one. I will be back within the hour."

"You *are* a lawyer," the bookseller said as if he had doubted the claim before.

Gideon nodded wearily. "I am," he agreed.

He supervised the painting being taken from the wall, carefully wrapped and placed in a locked bookcase ready for his return. Then, with the receipt in his pocket, he hurried back to The Talbot. The problem was he didn't have the rest of the money needed to redeem the painting.

He stopped at the door of the inn as he saw Danny and Christobel approaching.

They seemed caught up in each other's company, walking with an escort of two of Danny's men. Danny threw back his head and laughed whilst Christobel was grinning hugely. It struck Gideon that if he and Zahara faced issues in contemplating marriage, those confronting Danny and Christobel were even more profound. But if that thought troubled either of them, he could see no sign of it.

Then inspiration struck. Dismissing the man who had escorted him to The Swan, he waited for them. The two were still smiling when they reached Gideon.

"And here we have a man with something on his mind," Danny said, his tone light but his expression growing serious as he studied Gideon's face. "Personal? Professional? Philip? All three?"

"Can we talk—apart?"

Danny glanced at Christobel, who gave a little shrug.

"If it is men's talk…"

Gideon shook his head quickly. "It's a matter I am happy to bring to you too," he said. "It touches you more than most and you might be able to help."

"But not Philip?" Danny asked.

"Not yet," Gideon said.

That had them both intrigued and Danny looked thoughtful.

"It seems dinner may have to wait then. If we step inside, Kate will want to know why we aren't at her table, and I take it you would prefer…? Then, come with me."

Danny led the way across the stableyard and into a large room attached to the end of the stables where the horse furnishings were stored at one end and bales of fresh straw and hay and sacks of oats at the other. He had a quick word with the ostler and slipped him a coin, who nodded and called a boy from the room, closing the door as they both left.

Christobel walked across to the hay bales and made herself comfortable sitting on them, gesturing to others beside her.

"Take a seat, they are not at all uncomfortable to sit on."

"Maybe not for you with that bum roll under your skirts... What? You're not wearing one?" Danny had to dodge, laughing, as Christobel took a swipe at him.

"You should be careful what you say," she warned him. "Or you will be wearing mockado and buckram for the rest of your life."

Danny clutched at his breast.

"Be still my mercer's heart, a woman who knows how to stiffen the very marrow of a man."

"Your *marrow*?" Christobel arched her brows in mock surprise.

Gideon, who had taken a bale beside Christobel, cleared his throat and Danny turned to face him, hands pushed behind his back and with an expression of feigned innocence like a schoolboy caught out in wrongdoing. It was impossible not to laugh and Gideon made no attempt to resist doing so.

"You two," he said when he managed to regain his equilibrium, "are—"

"Unbearable company?" Christobel hazarded.

Danny pulled a face at her. "Delightful company," he insisted.

"I was going to say made for each other," Gideon said and the sudden awkward silence that followed both confused and embarrassed him. "I only meant… I mean…"

It was Christobel who leaned forward and patted his shoulder.

"It is quite alright. It's us. Not you. But what did you wish to tell us?"

Gideon produced the receipt and told them about the picture and the deal he had struck with the bookseller. When he was done any humour there had been before was gone and both looked thoughtful.

"We *have* to have that painting," Danny said.

"I don't understand it," Christobel said, and Gideon looked at her in surprise. She lifted a hand as if to wave his surprise away. "No. I mean I don't understand why this bookseller…" She peered at the receipt. "This Peter Dingley wouldn't let you take the painting. That you had so much money on your person to be able to give him there and then, should surely be enough to reassure him that you will have the full amount. He could have offered to deliver it, so you were spared the walk back to his shop." She frowned at Gideon and Danny was also staring at her nonplussed. "Oh for—It is obvious that neither of you two does much shopping. You seem poorly acquainted with the behaviour of such tradesmen. Believe me, having run a large farm I know these things."

"What are you thinking?" Gideon asked, still uncertain quite what point Christobel was trying to make.

"I am thinking that his behaviour is strange for a man who wishes to make a sale." She reached for her purse and was looking through it. "I have a bit less than a pound. Danny, how much money have you with you?"

"Only small coins. Perhaps ten shillings together," he said, then stopped. "Oh, and this." He stood up and pulled a fat gold coin from his fob pocket, holding it between thumb and finger. "A triple unite, fresh from his majesty's Oxford mint."

Christobel's eyes were round.

"I had heard they were striking these, how did you come by one?"

"The king," Danny said as if that was explanation enough. "I've kept it since for luck."

"Well, it's lucky you have it now," Christobel agreed. "If we take this to the bookseller, I'm sure we can persuade him to part with the painting and say we will pay the rest later."

"I'm not sure he will," Gideon said, thinking of the tight refusal to negotiate that the man had shown.

Christobel wrinkled her nose at his doubt. "I know how to deal with such people. I am good at striking a bargain."

"You should believe her, Gideon," Danny said and took Christobel's hand to help her rise from the bales. "I'd like to have some dinner and if we're quick I might just manage it."

"Do you have the time to do this?" Gideon asked, remembering belatedly that Danny was one of the key elements of the city's defence.

"I can't see this is going to take very long and as General of Ordnance Dudley has himself gone for dinner it's safe enough," Danny said. "He is dining with his dear friend Beaumont. I doubt he'll be back until mid-afternoon at the earliest. Without his interference, Ned Scarlett is more than capable of handling anything that needs doing. As long as I'm back before Dudd is so I can keep him from giving Ned orders that he has to obey, it'll be fine."

It took them very little time to get to the bookseller's. Inside the shop, nothing seemed any different to Gideon from his previous visit. Except the bookseller was absent.

"Perhaps he's gone upstairs for dinner," Christobel suggested.

Gideon pointed at a door at the back of the shop.

"We could go and see—"

"Danny!" Christobel's voice was sharp, and Gideon spun around. Danny had turned faster, and his sword was already drawn. The man who held a pistol probably assumed that gave him complete mastery of the situation, but Danny didn't hesitate, lunging even as he turned. The finger that tightened on the trigger was that of a dying man. Danny's sword passed between his ribs and through his heart even as Gideon was still drawing his own blade. The pistol fired as the man fell back, lying still on the floor.

There was a terrible silence.

Gideon, sword half-drawn, stared at the shelves where the man had concealed himself, trying to make sense of what had happened and why. Danny was already moving quickly around the room making sure there was no one else there, then he came back and put his free arm briefly around Christobel as if to reassure himself she was alright.

"He was hiding," Christobel said, her eyes wide. "As if he expected someone."

"If he was expecting someone," Danny said, wiping his blade clean before restoring it, "I don't think it was me."

Gideon crouched beside the dead man. It was not someone he had ever seen before.

"Perhaps we are reading too much into this," he said. Maybe this man came to rob the store and we interrupted him."

The door to the street was flung open from the outside and Danny moved to bar whoever might come in from going further, his sword back in his hand.

"What the—?" The man who burst in was a soldier and he looked from the sword to Danny then stepped back lowering the pistol he held. "Colonel Bristow, sir. We heard a shot and..."

"You did," Danny agreed. "I want men front and back of this building. Make sure no one enters or leaves"

"I'll see to it, sir." The soldier closed the door again.

"I'll check upstairs." Danny headed to the door at the back of the shop and vanished through it, Christobel following.

Gideon crossed the room to the bookcase where the painting had been placed. It was still locked and securely so. He was trying to find a way to open it when he heard Christobel's voice from above.

"Mr Dingley? Are you alright?"

By the time Gideon got up the stairs, Danny and Christobel had untied the shop owner. He was on the floor of his parlour and pulling a gag from his mouth. He looked terrified and for some reason, the sight of Gideon seemed to fill him with fear afresh.

"No," he said, pulling a key from his pocket, holding it up as if it was an amulet to ward off evil, then pushing it into Gideon's hand. "Take the picture. Take it and go."

Danny shook him by the shoulder.

"What happened?" he demanded, his tone sharp enough to cut through the man's fear. "Tell me, or you'll be made to tell in the castle."

"Yes, yes, of course." The bookseller couldn't speak fast enough. "I did nothing wrong. A man came into the shop two or three weeks ago and gave me that picture. Told me I should hang it where it could be seen and if anyone showed interest in it or asked to buy it, I should keep them in the shop and send a boy to ask for Mr Skinner at The Black Cock. He said he wanted to talk to the man who did so as it might help him find an old friend. That's why I had to ask such a high price, so the gentleman would have to come back with the money."

"Why not tell me this when I asked to buy it?" Gideon demanded, his anger rising.

"The man, Mr Skinner, said he wanted to surprise his friend and he'd only pay me if I said nothing and told him when someone came—and then he…." The bookseller buried his face in his hands in despair. "He said how easy it was for a bookshop to catch fire." Gideon could see where the cord used to bind Dingley's wrists had left deep marks. He supposed he should feel some sympathy for the man, but none seemed to be forthcoming.

"So what happened?" Danny demanded, shaking the man again.

"I sent word to The Black Cock. When Skinner came, he—he was furious I'd let you leave. Threatened to kill me. Left me as you found me here. He said when someone came to untie me, I was to give a message to Sir Philip Lord—a message to add to the one he would leave himself."

Gideon's blood chilled. The nature of Skinner's intended message was clear. If Gideon had come alone, if Danny had not been who and what he was…

"What was the message?" Christobel asked.

"He said to tell only Sir Philip, no one else."

Danny gave a hollow laugh.

"Your friend Skinner is dead, Dingley. I killed him. Now, if you don't want to wind up dead too, you will give me the message."

The bookseller swallowed hard, his skin the colour of cheap tallow.

"I was to tell Sir Philip Lord that Sir Nicholas Tempest intends to complete the work his uncle began."

Chapter Sixteen

As a colonel, Danny wasn't without his own influence, resources and men in Worcester, so he acted quickly to do what needed to be done even before Lord was informed. Besides, as Danny said, Worcester was a very small city and Lord had very long ears.

They were careful to make no mention of a painting and, clutching Danny's triple unite, Dingley was silenced with threats of a prolonged stay in the castle were he to mention it. There had been a thief. That was all. Thankfully Colonel Bristow had been visiting the shop at the time. Gideon had seen Dingley was capable of dissembling, he had little doubt the bookseller would keep silent, aware he was lucky not to face much worse consequences for his part in what had happened.

Of course, the man who had been staying at The Black Cock left nothing behind in his possessions that might give any clue as to who he had been or where he was from. He would be buried under the name of Skinner, whether it was his or not.

The landlord at the inn said he had arrived some two weeks before. He'd been no trouble at all, kept himself to himself and not spoken to anyone except a few regulars, none of whom knew him. The only information any could offer was that he had spoken with an accent that betrayed northern origins and had said he was in Worcester to further his business. What business that was he never mentioned. Seeing as he caused no trouble, was generous with his gratuities and seemed a decent man, the landlord had not pressed him about it.

"He must have been one of Tempest's men," Danny said as they returned to The Talbot an hour after they had left it. "Not one I'd ever met."

There was little more that could be done. Worcester was under siege and until the fields around the city no longer sprouted soldiers, that had to be the priority.

As if to bring that home, as they arrived back at The Talbot Danny was intercepted by a runner from Ned Scarlett saying he was needed urgently. Dudd Dudley, it seemed, had returned and, over dinner, came up with some notion of flooding part of the earthworks from the Severn to create a moat. So it was left to Gideon and Christobel to give an account of events to Lord.

The remains of dinner were still set out on the table even though it was mid-afternoon. Lord had arrived back only shortly before them. Kate had been sitting with him as he ate. He saw Gideon come in and gestured at the plates and dishes.

"Return'd so soon! Rather approach'd too late: the capon burns, the pig falls from the spit, the clock hath strucken twelve upon the bell; my mistress made it one upon my cheek: she is so hot because the meat is cold. Please sit, belated ones, sit and eat."

Putting the wrapped painting on the table, Gideon held a chair for Christobel, then took one himself.

"Your mistress didn't wait for your return," Kate said severely. "She has long since dined with Zahara and Anders."

Gideon found a plate of cold meat and some bread and decided to be satisfied with that.

"And how do you know that it is you I am referring to as my mistress?" Lord asked, narrowing his eyes at Kate. "Or do you forget you are now my wife?"

Kate smiled at him.

"A woman can be both," she said. "But I think Gideon and Christobel have something of moment to impart, so perhaps we could save that discussion for another time?"

Lord stabbed some food on his plate with his knife.

"Gideon and Christobel wish to tell me that Danny killed a man in the booksellers who was trying to shoot them with a pistol."

"There was a trap set," Gideon said, unsurprised that Lord's long ears had already heard an account of the events. "It was meant to catch whoever you sent to investigate here." It was the only thing that made sense. The Covenant would have realised that tracing the Kelleys, Dee's known close associates, would be one of the few paths left open to Lord. Inevitably, sooner or later, he would have sent someone to Worcester or come himself. The question was if the trap was fully sprung or if there was more.

Lord pushed his plate away and filled his cup from the jug then sat back.

"I don't have too much time," he said. "Tell me."

So Gideon did, with Christobel adding to the narrative whenever she thought it appropriate. It didn't take long and as Gideon finished with what they had discovered about the man calling himself Skinner, Lord reached over and pulled the wrapped painting towards him.

"Sir Nicholas Tempest. Why does a threat from him not fill me with terror?"

"His man nearly killed me," Gideon protested. "Had Danny not—"

"But he did," Lord snapped. Then he lifted his hands in apology. "You're right, it never does to forget that it's not he that we face but the might of the Covenant." As he spoke, Lord used his eating knife to slice the twine holding the wrappings and then unfolded those to expose the painting to view. But before he lifted the final sheet he stopped and held a hand out, towards Christobel.

"Come. Let us look at this together," he said. "This concerns you as much as me."

The expression on Christobel's face was stark as if she had been drowning and Lord had lifted her head above the water. Tears sprang suddenly to her eyes, and she quickly hid them by turning her head as she got up from her seat and went around the table. Without a word, Kate rose from her place beside Lord and, smiling at Christobel, stepped aside so she could sit.

Gideon had examined the picture enough not to need to peer at it again. Instead, he studied the three who did. Kate stood with one hand on Lord's shoulder and one hand on Christobel's and looked between the identical heads of white hair. He knew the moment she registered what it was she saw in the painting because her face was suddenly drawn by an emotion Gideon could not identify and her hand tightened on Lord's shoulder. Lord himself showed nothing as he gazed at the painting, but Christobel gave a little gasp and her hand went to her mouth, eyes wide.

For what seemed a long time none of them spoke, then Lord folded the paper back over the painting with extreme care as if it were something too precious to leave exposed.

"So now we know," he said softly.

"I joy, dear mother, when I view
Thy perfect lineaments, and hue
Both sweet and bright..."

He turned to Christobel taking her hand in both his, protectively.

"I should have said this before, but perhaps it is better now as we have Gideon and Kate to bear witness. Whatever comes of this, whatever we may or may not discover in the future of our heritance and heritage, our past and our parentage, mutual or otherwise, I hold you as my sister now and henceforth and would be honoured if you would hold me likewise your brother."

Christobel's mouth moved as if she wanted to speak but lacked the air to do so, then she gulped back a sob. Yet she was smiling, with tears making her eyes brilliant.

"I would like nothing more," she said at last.

Kate must have seen the emotion was at risk of overwhelming Christobel completely because she clicked her tongue.

"You are both in good company. Danny has a sister, Anders once told me he has three and even Martha has a brother who ran away to sea. That only leaves me and Gideon siblingless. Should we be jealous?"

Which made them all laugh. Then Lord got to his feet.

"I would that I could delay, but I'm out of time. I promised both the Sandys I would take such cavalry as we have available to stop Waller stripping the countryside of horses and valuables. I think they're mostly concerned for their lands at Ombersley, so if it is at all possible, I will oblige them with a foray to the north if I can. We might gather some intelligence of Waller's intentions in the process."

He dropped a kiss on Kate's cheek and left the room, calling for those of his men he had left in the common room as he headed out to the stableyard.

After he had gone Christobel turned to Gideon.

"If Lady Catherine will forgive me, I would like to go to see Danny, would you escort me?"

Gideon had no chance to reply.

"Of course you should go, and I'm Kate. But if you're going to Danny for goodness' sake, take some of this food with you. As long as I've known him, he forgets such things as eating when he's working and if he is being irritated by Dudd Dudley then lack of food will make him even more intolerant." She began gathering some of what was left on the table. Then sent for a linen wrap and a basket so Christobel could carry it before she was happy to let them go.

Following Christobel from the room Gideon glanced back. Kate had uncovered the painting on the table in front of her and gazed at it an expression of unspeakable sadness on her face.

"I don't understand Sir Philip," Christobel said as they left the inn.

As someone without family himself Gideon thought he did.

"Sir Philip will have meant every word he said," Gideon told her. "And having spoken, he will never go back on it."

"I know." She walked on in silence for a few paces. "If I'm truly to think of him as a brother I should perhaps try to neglect his title a little, but it is hard." Christobel looked sideways at Gideon. "You feel that too, I think?"

Unable to answer or explain, or even to open the box of the why of it for himself, Gideon just gave her a small nod and carried on walking.

Danny was with Dudd Dudley and Ned Scarlett. Scarlett's face and bald head were as red as his name with frustration. Danny was clearly just as riled.

"This is loosely compacted earth," Danny snapped. He kicked at the platform built on the earthworks they stood on with his heel. "If you remember, I fell down when one you built collapsed. If you cut a path to the Severn, you'll be letting the force of the river through, and these banks weren't designed or constructed to take that. It could all be swept away. If you're building dikes strong enough to hold the pressure of running water, you build them with that intent from the first and add wood or stone facings. I know this for a fact. I've helped design and build them enough in the Low Countries."

Dudley shook his head. "You're just afraid to try it," he sneered.

Danny's hand moved to his sword.

"Can wood facings be made?" Gideon asked quickly, stepping forwards to stand between the two.

Danny looked at him as if he were speaking an unknown language.

It was Scarlett the cannoneer that answered. "We have palings that could be, maybe, made to serve. Would need work and time though."

"How long?" Gideon asked.

Scarlett shrugged. "That depends on how many men we have to spare to prepare them. Without taking from those we need on the defences, a day, maybe two or three."

Gideon lifted both his hands and spread them. "Then that is the answer."

He hoped Danny wasn't too lost in his fury. He hoped he had spoken to Sir Philip that day. He hoped Dudley wouldn't balk at a delay.

"There," Dudd Dudley slapped Gideon hard on the back. "A man of uncommon sense. Eh, Bristow? You can have your damn facings—then you'll have no reason to protest my experiment."

For a moment Gideon thought Danny hadn't spoken to Lord, didn't know, hadn't followed his reasoning as the same taut expression remained. Then, slowly, Danny nodded as if conceding something huge.

"Very well," he said, his voice so tight it was hoarse. "Make the facings then."

Dudd Dudley was jubilant.

"At last, you see sense. Good God, if I'd known all it would take was a few bundles of sticks. Scarlett. Show me these palings."

Gideon stood where he was as Dudley strode off calling for his men and demanding that all who weren't required on the defences be made to report to him. The cannoneer glanced at Danny who gave him a brief nod, then hurried after Dudley.

The three of them stood in silence then Danny let out a slow breath.

"Christ, Gideon, you've got a very cool head on those shoulders," he said softly. "I'm deeply in your debt and so is Dudd Dudley. I was going to call him out."

"But what happens in three days when the facings are made, and he wants his mad scheme tried?" Christobel asked.

Of course, she didn't know.

Danny smiled at her and bent his head to whisper in her ear. Her eyes widened and she looked at him with delight as he straightened up, speaking loudly enough for the men nearby to hear. "We'll rest the guns to save powder in half an hour. Keep them ready in case Waller shows an interest in prosecuting a fight." He looked out over the countryside which had been already dug up into primitive siegeworks by Waller's troops as they built shelters for themselves from the rain of lead the city was spending on them. Here and there spadefuls of upflung earth testified to the fact that Waller had kept any word of his possible impending departure as much from his own men as from the enemy.

Christobel glanced at Gideon then tugged on Danny's arm. "There's something I need to tell you. It was why Gideon was kind enough to bring me here."

Gideon took the hint and took his leave. He returned to The Talbot and as he walked through the door of the inn Kate called to him, her tone sharp and urgent with excitement.

"Gideon, come and see what Zahara found."

The two women were sitting by a window. The painting was face down on the paper it had been wrapped in, its back exposed. He dropped onto the bench seat beside Zahara returned her warm smile of greeting and studied the back of the frame.

The painting was on canvas but had been mounted with a wooden backing which had then been covered with thick paper. That had been peeled away and now, Gideon could see the back panel was set in grooves and designed to slide open. It would provide a small hidden storage space between the painting itself and the back of the frame. Kate swiftly traced the point of a knife around the edge of the mounting at the bottom, where linen strips had been glued to hide the sliding panel.

"Zahara noticed that there were two layers of these strips. As if the back had been removed and replaced at some point," Kate said as she worked. "This false back and seal looks to me as if it is not as old as the rest of the frame. See? The wood was stained somehow to make it darker. If there is anything inside, it wasn't placed there at the time this was first framed. But it was so well concealed that whoever owned this before it was hung in the booksellers for Gideon to discover, most probably had no idea there was even a compartment hidden there."

When she was done, she glanced between Gideon and Zahara.

"Do you think we should look?" he asked.

Zahara was shaking her head.

"We should keep this safe and show it to the Schiavono when he returns," she said. "It is his by right."

The implications hit Gideon hard. "This might mean we have something the Covenant are not aware of—or are not aware we might have."

Kate nodded and Zahara turned the painting over. The girl holding the rose was looking out of the picture, directly at the viewer and Gideon realised the artist had captured perfectly the quality of the gaze that both Lord and Christobel possessed. Dee, on the other hand, sitting in a high-backed chair, his beard long and as white as the girl's hair, was looking at her. Gideon felt a shiver creep along his spine and knew a sudden pity for this child. Her fate foreshadowed in the drop of blood the rose had torn from her finger.

"I think we should put this away until the Schiavono returns," Zahara said again as if sensing the uneasiness the picture seemed to be causing him.

Kate nodded and quickly rewrapped it, using some twine to hold it together.

"I spoke to Joan Fisher," Zahara went on as Kate was finishing the knots. "She told me that she knew little of how her uncle fares nowadays save that he still lives. Her husband refused to let her visit him in Baddersleigh—or even her mother when she was alive. Reverend Fisher thought the Kelley brothers to be evil dabblers in the occult because of their use of alchemy. When she went to her mother's funeral seven years ago, it was her first and only visit there." Zahara paused and looked at Kate who nodded. "She said there was a woman at the funeral, some years younger than herself but already prematurely white-haired. She did not know who the woman was and did not discover her name."

Gideon felt as if all the breath in his lungs had been sucked away.

At that moment the guns fell silent.

Chapter Seventeen

Sir Philip Lord did not come back to the inn that evening and neither did Danny. Christobel returned bearing news from both, saying not to wait for them as they did not expect to return now until they had seen their unwanted guest, Sir William Waller, from the premises.

A captured messenger revealed that Waller had issued orders to his officers to begin preparations after dark so the army could march at midnight. They were to leave fires burning to try and convince the city garrison they were still there. Already the boats he had commandeered were taking the Parliamentarian army wounded downriver to catch the tide to Bristol.

Kate was suffering from one of the occasional and debilitating bouts of pain her injury had left her with, so Anders insisted she rest and take supper in her room. He helped her to retire and Zahara went with them. Without Kate, the idea of a household supper at table had evaporated. Christobel went to take hers with Brighid who was sitting with Joan Fisher allowing Martha to rest.

Shiraz was still absent, not yet having returned from Oxford, so Gideon thought he might be eating alone, but Anders returned to join him, lines of fatigue on his face. The Dane's company always lifted Gideon's spirits. Perhaps because whilst the others laboured to take lives, Anders was striving just as hard to save them.

"I looked in on Joan Fisher," Anders said as he sat down. "She has shown no further signs of decline and now seems well set on the path of recovery."

"If so, it is through your skill," Gideon told him.

Anders nodded. "My skill and God's grace. Talking of which, Lady Catherine tells me that the siege should end soon, possibly even tonight. I hope that is so, but it seems unlikely. The men out there have been digging in and seem to me minded to stay."

"Some communications captured strongly suggest that is so," Gideon assured him.

"Then that is good news." Anders used his knife to lift the pie crust and peered curiously at the contents, before cutting into it. "I'm glad we will not be required to endure the rigours of a long siege that would have us eating dogs or rats."

"Until the troops are gone, I think we have no grounds for complacency," Gideon said. His own worst fear was that despite what Lord had said about the cipher, they were being made the victims of the same kind of deliberately misleading stratagem as Lord himself had perpetrated upon Waller. "I just pray to God that it is indeed over."

He took the thought to bed, and it was in his prayers as he lay awake in the dark. He thought he would struggle to sleep, the uncertainty and the desperate hope clamouring loudly in his heart. But sleep must have claimed him nonetheless because he woke just as dawn was beginning to lighten the sky to find Danny, still dressed and filthy, sleeping on the bed beside him, mouth slightly open and giving the occasional soft snore.

His tousled hair was loose with no hat to provide it even a modicum of restraint and his freckles clear against the pale linen of the pillow. One boot was still on its foot, the laces loosened as if Danny had been in the process of removing it when he fell asleep. The fact that Danny, the lightest sleeper Gideon had ever met, didn't stir as Gideon got up, dressed and quietly left the room, was a profound testament to his state of exhaustion.

Outside the silence was deafening. The only sounds that reached him were the normal sounds of a city yawning and stretching itself to face a new day.

The first person he met as he made his way downstairs was Shiraz, who was coming up them. Shiraz greeted him as they passed, with a nod and the slight lift to the edge of his lips that was for him what in another would be a beaming grin.

"I am glad to see you safely returned," Gideon said, meaning it. Then he wondered as he went on down the steps if Zahara had told Shiraz of their plans to marry. So far, he had seemed accepting of Gideon, but would this be going too far? He held Zahara as closely as he might a daughter or younger sister. If anyone felt the barrier of faith was too high, it would surely be Shiraz and without his blessing, Gideon knew Zahara would never be happy to wed. He pushed the troubling thoughts aside as best he could.

When he reached the common room, Lord was sitting alone at the big table, the plan of the city and a cup of wine before him. A jug stood to one side in easy reach. He looked up as Gideon approached, yes over brilliant.

"*What pity 'tis, so civil a young man should haunt this debauched company?*" he gestured to the map. "As you can see the city remains, but the besiegers are quite gone."

"We won?"

Lord nodded.

"We won. Or more accurately, we didn't lose. There might be victory celebrations in Worcester today, but there was no true victory in seeing off an army that shouldn't have been here in the first place. We didn't defeat Waller, we merely persuaded him to leave us alone."

"Isn't that what any successful defence is in any siege?"

Lord leaned forward to pick up his cup. His hand trembled slightly, and Gideon realised he was either quite drunk or utterly fatigued—or most likely a combination of the two.

"You undoubtedly have the right of it," Lord agreed amicably. "More to the point, in this case, I think we can be sure Waller will not be back in the foreseeable future, so perhaps that is something worthy of celebration." He gestured to the jug. "Join me, we can toast victory together. "*Now are our brows bound with victorious wreaths; our bruised arms hung up for monuments; our stern alarums changed to merry meetings; our dreadful marches to delightful measures.* And now we are free to ride to a merry meeting at Baddersleigh."

And that was when Gideon realised that Lord was drunk not because he was celebrating his victory, but because he was afraid of what he might soon discover.

"We don't have to go," he said. "It can be enough to know what you know and leave the rest as—"

"No!" Lord brought his fist down hard enough to make the cup dance and the wine within splash redly over the map. Then he sat back again in his chair and drew a shuddering breath as if it took an effort of will to bring himself back under the tight reins of self-command. "I made an oath," he said. "In Oxford. The day I wed Kate."

"You haven't been so troubled by this before," Gideon said. "In Howe, in Mortlake—you wanted to know, to find out, to press on. What has changed?"

"What has changed?" Lord echoed. "What has changed is that before it was all academic—dry parchments and history. The worst of it fell on me. Whatever I might find, whatever revelation there might be, it was just myself who would bear that consequence. Myself, whose life is already surrounded by hornworks and ramparts, palisades and chevaux-de-frise. The worst I had to face was a possible slight to my no doubt overweening self-esteem were I to discover it was all some wild fancy and far from being of royal and imperial descent, I was nothing more than plain Philip Nobody, the illegitimate son of a bawdyhouse keeper and one of his bawds. But now…" He shook his head and pulled the cup to him and drank down the remains in it. "But now it seems I also have real people to confront, not just names on paper. I'm no longer the only one who will be affected by whatever we may find."

"You mean Christobel?" Gideon hazarded. "If so, I am sure she will deal well with whatever the truth might be."

Lord put the cup down and nodded a few times.

"Christobel, of course. Yes."

But not only Christobel.

Then Gideon realised. The expressionless gaze in the painting. A white-haired child, her innocent finger pricked by the thorns of a Tudor rose.

"Your mother," Gideon said and saw Lord's whole body tense. He stopped then. To go on would be placing his profane feet in a sacred nemeton. So he fell silent and waited. Lord was gazing sightlessly at the map in front of him.

"My mother," he agreed in a different voice from before. "I find…" He stopped and swallowed. "I find that whilst I may have some notion of what it means to be a brother, I am not at all sure what it might mean to be a son. You see I have never been called upon to be one before."

Gideon wondered what words there were to answer that, what words could ever fill the void where a normal childhood should have been—where a mother, a father had belonged?

"I am sure," he said carefully, "when it happens, that you will know how."

Lord was still staring at the map.

"That is what Kate said too."

His finger moved to trace the lines of the city wall, then he looked up and met Gideon's gaze.

"Enough of this, I think. *If the Head Himself deny, shall not the Family comply? — But lose not heart, nor droop amain, thy sinking Lord will rise again.*" As he said the last words, he pushed himself to his feet. "I will need to sink and sleep an hour and then rise again and we will set out for Baddersleigh. As much as I would like the luxury to spend my time on my own affairs, the affairs of princes always take precedence and if we don't go today, whilst the Sandys and the city are in celebration, I fear we may not get to go at all."

Gideon watched him walk to the stairs and hesitate briefly as he set his foot on the bottom step, but then he went on, no trace of unsteadiness visible. Much as Gideon wanted to go to Baddersleigh as soon as was humanly possible, he found himself hoping that Sir Philip Lord would not be awake in an hour, or even in two.

In the end, it was nearer to two hours than one when Lord reappeared. Danny had emerged shortly before him, hollow-eyed and yawning, but ready to be restored by a good meal. By then Zahara, Shiraz, Christobel and Anders were all up and had breakfasted. As Danny ate, he recounted the adventures of the night, which to Gideon seemed to have involved a great deal of chasing around and little actual fighting.

"Did any of the soldiers desert Waller for our cause?" Gideon asked, thinking of the printed letter that he had helped craft.

Danny shrugged.

"I've no idea. We were on the move a lot—and I mean a lot."

Which was when Lord came downstairs with Kate, who seemed much recovered. Lord was immaculately clad in the blue and silver of his command. All signs of fatigue, except a shadow under his eyes, were subdued beneath the diamond carapace of his self-control. Under one arm he carried the wrapped painting.

"Since I know full well that all of you are of a curious disposition it seemed best to have this settled before we go," he said, setting that down on the table.

Anders, Danny and Shiraz had never seen the picture before, so Lord allowed them a short time to examine it as Gideon explained how they had come by it. Shiraz nodded as if something made sense to him that had not before. Danny pointed at the painting.

"I'm sure I've seen that before. I just need to think where."

Anders stared at the child in the picture then looked from Lord to Christobel and back.

"That is…?"

"That is my mother, yes," Lord said. "And, we are to assume, some relation to Christobel as well. Blood will out, as they say." Gone was the hesitancy and dread. The brief rest had restored his hard edge. "Now, let's see what secret this contains."

He turned the picture over and Gideon put a hand on it before he could begin to work on the back panel. This felt wrong. Exposing a man who had enough of that from his enemies. Lord glanced up at him, frowning.

"You don't need to do this here," Gideon said. "You can take it somewhere private. Just you and Kate and Christobel."

Something changed beneath the sea ice of Lord's gaze.

"Speculation about whatever this contains will be common gossip in this company for the foreseeable future. I would rather we did it here and now."

"And Christobel?" Gideon asked.

The owner of the name spoke up. "Christobel is of the same mind. Honestly, it is like living in a nest of starlings." Her words held affection not rancour and she smiled at Gideon. "But you are kind to consider it for me and Philip."

Philip. She had crossed that Rubicon and Gideon felt a sudden flood of warm pride on her behalf.

"If we are agreed?" Lord said. No one dissented and he returned to his task and drew the wooden board free of the painting's frame.

Inside was a document bag that had been carefully flattened to fill the space available. Lord lifted it and laid it carefully on the table. The seal on the ties was the *monas hieroglyphica*. The symbol adopted by the Covenant.

There was a date on the seal—MDCXXV.

"In that year," Lord said, tapping the table beside the seal. "I turned sixteen. I'd been branded a traitor and was no longer in the country. Christobel you'd have been what? Seven? Eight? And the man who presumably left this in the booksellers for us to find, young Sir Nicholas Tempest, would have been all of three or four years old."

"That's it," Danny said, suddenly. "That's where I saw it before. Hanging on the walls of his father's house in Durham. Newhall."

Lord nodded. "I have a feeling young Sir Nicholas wasn't privy to its deeper secrets." As he spoke, he pulled open the top of the bag, before sliding the contents out onto the table. There were two carefully folded documents one much older than the other. Lord picked up the older of the two and unfolded it.

"What have we here? A list of my antecedents going back to the deluge? *And Zadok begat Ahimaaz, and Ahimaaz begat Azariah, and Azariah begat Johanan, and Johanan begat Azariah...*" He broke off as he saw what the document contained, and his eyes narrowed. "No. It is the opposite. A list of those who I would extirpate from existence if they still lived. Only this is the old list so this—" He quickly opened the newer of the two and a feral smile twisted his lips. "This is the current list, or close enough."

"So what is it?" Kate asked, frowning.

Gideon was reading the neat legal Latin phrases of the older document and his blood chilled.

"This is a contract, a compounding of individuals to a single cause, a—"

"A covenant?" Lord suggested gently.

There was a momentous silence.

"Christ," said Danny.

Gideon lifted the older document which included amongst other names and signatures that of John Dee himself.

"This is a copy of the original Covenant," he said. "It says each signatory is to be given one so each none could deny or betray it."

"It is genuine?" Lord asked.

There was no doubt in Gideon's mind. He had worked with enough legal archives and viewed enough such contracts even if they were far from being such a compact as this and were personal transactions of inheritance or marriage, conveyancing or copyhold. He even recognised some of the fifteen signatures. Some were of great men, names that he was shocked to see there. But others, such as Dee himself, were much lesser luminaries of the time.

"I believe this would stand in any court as proven," he said, knowing the effect his words would have. He pointed to some of the signatures. "There are many other examples of these on other documents of the era for comparison."

Lord put the newer version beside the first.

"And this?"

Gideon frowned as he studied it.

"The words of this are different, I would need to take time to compare the two. But, yes, I would say this is genuine too."

"Whoever left this painting with the bookseller didn't know these were hidden inside," Christobel said.

Lord shook his head. "These are too powerful in my hands. They hold the names," the sudden brutality of his tone revealing the depth of his hatred, "of the men I will kill."

That was met by a brittle silence.

It was Zahara who broke it.

"There is no need for that," she said quietly. "You do not need to feed the flames further. *Why do you stay in prison when the door stands open*?"

The silence that followed her words was of a different order and Lord's eyes went wide. Gideon knew a rising warmth of love and pride. She was right. The bloodshed of the Covenant, and its life-twisting ways, held them all prisoners of hate. Lord let out a shuddering sigh.

"You are the voice of my conscience," he told her. "But let us see the names of those I must confront. They have been faceless and in shadow for long enough." And he picked up the more recent of the two documents and spread it out over the old.

The most obvious difference was that the names appended to this newer document were of a different order of men than those on the first. Most were names Gideon had not even heard of, though Sir Bartholomew Coupland and Sir Richard Tempest were both on it as was the name of Bacon and Sir Gilbert Brandon. He traced his finger over them quickly, then stopped. There was only one name apart from Bacon of any substance.

Lord saw where his finger rested.

"Fulke Greville, the then recently created Baron Brooke—the man who owned and rebuilt Warwick Castle and was reputedly the richest man in the nation during his lifetime."

Gideon looked at Lord. "We met his son in Warwick Castle, Lord Brooke. He recognised my sword."

"I heard Lord Brooke had been killed at Lichfield," Christobel said, frowning.

"He was. But Lord Brooke wasn't Greville's son," Lord corrected. "Just his adopted heir—a cousin or second cousin I believe. Fulke Greville never married."

"Oh, but he did." Kate had been investigating the document bag and had pulled out another, much smaller folded sheet and was studying it. She set it out on top of the others.

"Who," Danny asked, reading it, "is Margret Coupland?"

Lord frowned.

"Before I read this, I would have said she was the first wife of Sir Richard Tempest, mother of Nicholas and Henry, and sister to the late unlamented Sir Bartholomew of that name, but…" He turned to Gideon, his face now puzzled. "What is this?"

Gideon was already studying the odd document and trying to follow its clauses.

"It is a form of contract between Sir Fulke Greville, Sir Richard Tempest and Sir Bartholomew Coupland regarding Margret Coupland. It is not so much a contract of marriage as…" He tried to think of how to express it. "A contract of concubinage."

The whole table stared at him.

"You need to explain in simple words," Lord said. "Then even we who are not lawyers may understand."

Gideon wondered what to say. The document was nothing he had seen before.

"I'm not sure I can," he said. "This is a contract by which Margret Coupland would be the mistress of Sir Fulke, even though she was to be married to Richard Tempest as soon as she was with child. That child would be raised as Sir Richard's own. In return for which Tempest received the sum of one thousand pounds and the freehold of Newhall in County Durham. It is dated from five years before the seal on the bag."

Lord gave an explosive laugh.

"Ha! Tempest sold his marriage bed for advancement and—" He broke off and his expression changed. "And Sir Nicholas is not even a Tempest at all. I wonder if anyone has told him?"

"Did Margret give her permission?" Christobel asked. "Surely she had to sign it too?"

"I don't see why," Lord said. "These men thought themselves above the law of the land—they were busy creating a new order. A new world. New laws based on what they saw as God's newly revealed truth. Is it not in the Bible that Moses inflicted leprosy on Miriam when she criticised Moses for taking a second wife? Did not the kings and patriarchs have *pilegesh*? Did those women have any say in the matter?"

Gideon recalled what he had found in Dee's notes in the Cotton Library and was sickened.

"Don't you remember?" He was unable to keep the revulsion from his tone. "The angels told Dee and Kelley they should share their wives. Dee spoke of it as some kind of a sacrament—as a new matrimonial-like licence instructed to him by God, and for Dee alone."

Lord nodded slowly. "It seems," he said, "we have some notion now of the man who moved and shaped. New world. New religion. New rules. In his mind, and probably in the view of the Covenant, Greville was taking on the mantle dropped by Dee. The same exemptions and the same privileges that Dee had enjoyed would fall to him."

"But why bother with any form of fake legality?" Danny asked. "If this man Greville wanted to bed Coupland's sister, he didn't need a contract."

"Perhaps because he didn't see it as fake," Christobel said. "He believed in it. If they ever came to power, then this 'matrimonial-like licence' would be made valid and legal."

"But why not just marry Margret Coupland himself?" Danny said. "Why the duplicity of a secret concubine?"

"Perhaps there was some impediment to such marriage," Lord suggested. "Or perhaps he just wished to indulge his satyr impulses with a veil of legal—"

But Gideon no longer heard. He had just read to the end of the document, and it was as if the walls of the room began closing about him.

"Gideon? Are you alright?"

Kate's voice seemed to come from a great distance and then Zahara was beside him and the world returned.

Lord was studying the document and now looked at Gideon with a troubled expression.

"Archibald Lennox signed as a witness."

Gideon nodded and swallowed before he could bring himself to speak.

"My father. It makes no sense. He was so strict in his beliefs. He would surely never have condoned..."

"We cannot help who our parents were or be held accountable for their deeds," Kate said, placing her hand over his.

Lord pushed himself to his feet.

"It's getting late in the day. We need to be away. All this," he gestured at the documents but included in it the ramifications of all they raised, "will have to await our return. We don't have the luxury of time right now. Danny, Shiraz, we need horses and the carriage as Kate is coming with us."

Zahara, who was beside Gideon, stood up shaking her head.

"I must stay. There are those here—Widow Fisher and others—who need care."

Gideon turned to her thinking to ask her to reconsider, but Lord was already speaking.

"Very well, you will stay, and Shiraz will stay with you. The rest of us will go."

As everyone rose Zahara leaned in and kissed Gideon's cheek

"You will be back by this evening," she said softly. "The Schiavono has said so. This is not something I can help him with as you can." Then she smiled and leaned in again to whisper in his ear. "We will tell them at supper tonight."

The warmth of that thought was enough to banish the ice that his discovery had set about Gideon's heart.

A short time later, with an escort of ten of Lord's men and Kate in the coach, they set out from Worcester for the village of Baddersleigh. As they rode, Lord explained that Baddersleigh Priory had once been a monastic house and was now both home to a certain Thomas Kelley and of a Royalist garrison under one Captain Young.

The official reason for Sir Philip Lord's visit was to ascertain the state of the garrison in the aftermath of Waller's presence in the area. Although being secluded in the Malvern Hills and much protected by that seclusion, Lord told them, there was always a risk that Baddersleigh might still have suffered from Waller's attention in his final broad sweep of pillage before he retired.

It was the first of June and summer was already spreading her blue skirts in the cloudless sky above them. They travelled quite fast despite the need to accommodate the coach and had reached the outskirts of the village by dinnertime. The Priory itself was a walled and fortified house that Captain Young had improved with some basic earthworks.

"I think if Waller's foragers did come this far, they would have been disappointed," Danny said as they reached the gates. "But there's no sign they did."

Sir Philip Lord's name was watchword enough to persuade the men on the gates to permit them entry. Soon after they were handing off their horses to members of the garrison and Lord was helping Kate down from the coach as the men of their escort were taken away to receive refreshment.

The house itself was not of the more convenient or conventional modern kind. It was built around two sides of a courtyard with one wing being a half-timbered construction, with brick below, timber beams with plaster above and casements with small diamond panes set in lead. The other had an older stone footing for the ground floor, but the two floors above it were built from brick, with wide clear windows. It looked to Gideon as if a giant hand had taken two different houses and pushed them together at ninety degrees, making an equal-sided L shape around what might once have been a small cloister but was now an elegant courtyard.

They were greeted by a man who introduced himself as Lieutenant Saddler. Saddler took them into the house through the main door, which was guarded by two men. Inside was a surprisingly spacious entrance hall with stairs up to a short, boarded, gallery.

"We were not told to expect anyone from Worcester," Saddler explained. "If we had known…"

"There was no time to send word in advance," Lord told him. "If I could speak, perhaps to Captain Young?"

It made sense that Lord would speak first to the military men in charge, but so far Gideon had not seen much sign of the house having any civilian occupants at all.

"Wait here, sir, I will find him." Saddler left them and went back through the main door which he closed behind him—and locked it.

"What the—?" Gideon stared at the door.

Danny and Lord were beside it, swords in their hands. Then moving to check the other doors which were also locked. Concerned, Gideon drew his blade and even Anders had his sword drawn.

"Welcome to Baddersleigh Priory, Sir Philip."

On the landing above them stood a young man Gideon had never seen before, with dark brown hair, a straight sharp nose and a narrow chin. As he spoke, the space on either side of him was being lined by eight men with muskets, their barrels trained on those below.

Gideon was suddenly profoundly glad that Zahara had chosen to stay in Worcester. He heard Danny curse softly and beside him Lord was very still.

"You have my gratitude," the man on the landing went on. "You have brought my wife with you."

Chapter Eighteen

"Don't be ridiculous, Tempest," Lord said, taking two strides towards the stairs, his tone commanding. "The Worcester garrison knows we are here, and we're expected back this afternoon. If I fail to return, you'll be hunted down like a rabid cur. Whatever folly you have committed so far, I'm willing to overlook it. If you take your men now and go, you need not fear pursuit. Apart from anything else, I have no time to chase down random malignants."

Gideon had a glimmer of hope that Lord's approach might even work. Then the young man straightened up.

"And miss the chance to make you suffer? The chance to reclaim my wife and to cut the balls off the man who took her from me?" He gave a mirthless laugh. "You don't seriously expect me to do that? You're supposed to be clever."

"If you harm me or any of my people, there will be nowhere for you to hide afterwards," Lord told him. "That is not a threat, it is simply a statement of fact—and one I can do nothing to ameliorate since I will not be there to stop it from happening to you. I am offering you the opportunity to avoid the biggest mistake of your life."

Sir Nicholas Tempest shook his head and the hate distorting his face sent a shiver of chilling dread down Gideon's spine. This man intended to kill them all.

"You're wrong. The biggest mistake of my life was trusting Daniel Bristow," Tempest said coldly. "But I'm not the only one. He cozened Mags as well and turned on him, and he did the same to the Covenant too."

Danny remained unmoving and expressionless, sword useless in his hand. Useless, Gideon thought bitterly, because no matter how good he might be as a swordsman, he could do nothing to defend against the muskets trained on them.

"Colonel Bristow, believe it or not, was trying to save you from Mags," Lord said. "You were never anything other than a rung on the ladder to Francis Child. That is all any of us were."

"Oh really? So where does stealing my wife fit in with that?"

"He was obeying my orders, as he has been from the first time you met him. So that is at my door, not his." Lord pushed his sword back into its scabbard. "I'm the one responsible for all your ills. Keep me here, do whatever you wish with me—you have no need to keep anyone else. And, if you do, I will give strict instructions that nothing is done against you no matter what you might do to me."

Gideon heard Kate's breath shudder and wondered if it was as hard for her to keep silent as it was for himself.

"If I had my way," Tempest said, his voice taut, "I would order these men to fire then come down there and cut up whatever remained of you and 'your people' myself. But I'll have to save that pleasure for later. There is someone who needs to speak with you first and unfortunately you arrived on the one day he required to be absent. Don't worry, he will return later and you'll all be dead before you are even missed in Worcester. Now, put your swords in a pile by the door."

Gideon saw a muscle twitch in Lord's jaw. The only sign that betrayed him.

"You seem to put much faith in those men—although from all I have learned they have no particular care for you." He paused and when he spoke again, Gideon knew the note of warning wasn't meant for Tempest, although his gaze remained solidly on the man. "*He that knows great men's secrets and proves slight, that man ne'er lives to see his beard turn white.* It is dangerous indeed to know too much about the Covenant and speak of it."

That made Tempest frown.

"I'm not loose-lipped," he snapped, and Gideon realised then that Sir Nicholas wasn't a clever man. That thought gave him the first true thread of hope since the musket barrels had appeared on the landing rail. Then Tempest's next words ripped it away.

"I'll give you a count of five to bestow your swords in a pile or you will face the consequences here and now."

"No!" It was Christobel who had broken under the unbearable strain. "I'm the one you want. Let the rest go and I will even come willing to your bed."

Gideon saw Lord's features tighten and Tempest's face twisted into sudden and utter contempt.

"You think too much of yourself. You're my wife. My chattel. I may do with you as I see fit." His voice caught then on a shred of real emotion, and for a single moment, Gideon glimpsed the dark and bottomless well of pain behind his anger. "I was too kind to you before and you rewarded me with betrayal. Now, the swords. One."

Christobel opened her mouth, but Kate had seized her arm with urgency and wrapped her into a close embrace, whispering something Gideon couldn't hear.

"Two."

None of the men moved. All taking their lead from Sir Philip Lord as Gideon was himself.

"Three."

Lord stood like a stag at bay, then he turned and strode back to the door, loosening the strap on his baldric and swinging it from his shoulder as he went. He placed the sword on the floor and let the leather straps drop on top of it. He bowed his head as if in prayer. Then turning, he lifted his voice giving it the cut of command.

"Gentlemen, put your swords with mine."

If there had ever been a test of Lord's authority over him—over any of them—Gideon knew this had to be its ultimate expression.

It was Danny, whose skin beneath his freckles had gone white at Tempest's last words to Christobel, who moved first. Slamming his sword home, he stalked to the door and undid the buckles before throwing it down with Lord's. Then he turned and sent Lord a look that might have withered a lesser man. Anders walked over and undid his belt to slide the frogging from it before refastening the belt once the sword was free. He then bent to lay it with the others before stepping aside and following Danny back to the middle of the room to stand with Lord.

Lord was looking directly at Gideon. "Do as I say, Mr Fox. This is no time for heroics or mutiny."

Gideon met his gaze and read the clear message there.

Trust me.

He turned and walked to the door, undid his sword belt and left it lying with the others.

Tempest lifted his voice. "You can take them now."

The side doors opened, and men filled the room like a tide, sweeping them apart. Gideon saw with some small gratitude that Kate and Christobel seemed to be taken away together. Danny had vanished already. His last glimpse of Lord was with hands bound, walking from the hall as if of his own will and direction. Then Gideon himself was being manhandled roughly along one of the passageways, behind Anders. They were taken up a narrow flight of stairs and another then pushed into a small room which had a barred window. There, ungentle hands searched him, removed his knife and took his purse, before he was thrown to the ground. The men left, locking the door behind them.

Gideon stayed where he was, eyes closed in prayer. He prayed that whatever might befall himself, Zahara would remain safe, that Shiraz would keep her so. He prayed for Kate and Christobel's protection, and he prayed for the strength to endure whatever he must. Then he picked himself up, strangely grateful that the worst he had suffered so far was bruising from the overzealous fists of the men who had brought him there.

Anders was already on his feet. "Are you alright?"

The room was furnished as a regular bed chamber, perhaps for a youthful guest or a servant, with a truckle bed and a chest, a chair, with a chamber pot tucked away beneath it. The casement window was open by the small amount the bars across it allowed and the walls were whitewashed plaster.

"I am as alright as any man might be in our position," Gideon said, crossing to the window. They were on the top floor of the house with two below them. Even had there not been bars on the window, perhaps originally put there to prevent a child from falling out, it was too far to the ground to contemplate escaping that way. "Are you?"

Anders nodded.

"Do you think our lord and master has a plan?"

"I got the impression he had."

"Let us hope so, my friend. It is too late to learn to swim when the water is up to your lips." Anders studied Gideon's face as if appraising him. "There is something I would ask if not betraying too many secrets. I know that Sir Philip is not as other mercenary commanders—or even as other men—and I have eyes that tell me Mistress Christobel is, somehow, his kin, but this talk of some covenant and Sir Philip's and Mistress Christobel's ancestry…" He shook his head slowly. "This morning most of what was shown and said meant little to me. I was content to wait for things to unfold in due course. But now it seems my life might be forfeit because of it all and I find myself more than a little curious as a result."

Gideon realised with a shock that it hadn't crossed his mind Anders didn't know. Lord would have been aware of that, yet still, deliberately included Anders. Perhaps it had been his way of showing the esteem in which he held the physician. That was when it struck Gideon like a hammer in the chest that Anders might be the last friendly face he ever saw.

Anders must have taken his silence the wrong way because he frowned.

"If you consider it best that I do not know, I will understand. Speech is often repented, silence never."

"No, it's not that," Gideon said quickly. "If Lord—" He stopped himself. They might never meet again in this life, but it felt right that he took the step anyway. "If *Philip* allowed you to be present then he wished you to know. I was just wondering where to begin."

"Perhaps with 'who is Sir Philip Lord?'" Anders suggested.

"It is who others believe him to be that matters," Gideon said. If nothing else telling the tale of it would keep them both from dwelling on the dire situation in which they found themselves. He lowered himself to the truckle and gestured Anders to the chair. They might as well be as comfortable as the circumstances allowed.

"Maybe I should begin where I first found out. You were there too, the night Philip and I went to Howe Hall…"

It made more sense to tell the tale as he had lived it. Beginning with the hidden room in Howe protected by a lock in the form of a chequerboard puzzle where he'd first seen a Tudor rose on the breast of a Hapsburg eagle. Below that room, another airless chamber where the monstrous offspring of Queen Mary and King Philip, whose concealed existence had inspired the story of Caliban as Prospero had been inspired by John Dee, had been kept to grow to adulthood so as to found the bloodline of which Sir Philip Lord was the culmination.

Then he spoke of discovering a sword after the battle beneath Edgehill akin to both Philip's and the one Danny had later stolen from the Covenant, and the way Lord Brooke had reacted to it with recognition in Warwick Castle. How he had unearthed John Dee's spiritual diary in the Cotton Library in London, which spoke of communications with angels, together with plans that revealed a secret chamber beneath Dee's old house at Mortlake. The secret chamber matched the descriptions of the fabled tomb of Christian Rosenkreuz. There he and Philip had discovered the clues that pointed to the Kelleys in Worcester, the finding of Joan Fisher and Gideon discovering the picture in the booksellers.

It took some time to tell. Anders asked the occasional question. When Gideon reached the end, he looked thoughtful.

"If I had not myself been witness to some of those events and known you for a man of integrity, I might doubt you speak the truth," he said at last. "But an honest man does not make himself a dog for the sake of a bone. So, there are those who believe—and it may even be true—that Sir Philip Lord has a strong claim to the throne of England?"

"That's the problem," Gideon agreed.

"A pretty problem indeed," Anders said. "I am not surprised there are those who would rather he was dead. He would not be an easy man to try to shape to their desires. But he has all the attributes a monarch might wish for—he can lead men, he can administer lands and organise armies, he is a skilled diplomat and as much a philosopher as a warrior and he even looks the part more than many. So why would he not want it for himself on his own terms?"

Gideon gave the answer Philip had given him.

"He knows the price of such power, both for himself and for those about him."

Anders met Gideon's gaze and tilted his head in consideration.

"I have admired the man for many reasons," he said. "But to have both the wisdom and strength of mind to refuse such temptation? I do not think another man in the same place would be able to do so."

"He sees the Covenant and all its works as evil," Gideon said. "I think that helps."

"Do you think it is one of the Covenant leaders that Sir Nicholas is waiting for?" Anders asked.

"I don't think he would take orders from anyone else."

"Then perhaps we have some grounds to hope," Anders said. "After all, you have just explained how the Covenant has a vested interest in Sir Philip, which gives him some power with them. And I consider him a formidable negotiator."

A sudden volley of shots from outside shattered the false calm of the afternoon. Anders stood quickly and moved to the window.

"There is nothing to see. Perhaps it was just a training exercise."

Gideon nodded, his pulse racing. Better to believe that than the unthinkable: that one of their own had just been killed. It cast a pall over the room and pushed Gideon back into his dark thoughts until Anders broke the corrosive quiet.

"Do you think Mistress Christobel is Sir Philip's sister?"

"I don't know. But he has declared her to be so."

"So I heard and am glad for that. They both need some family."

"Do you have any brothers or sisters?" Gideon asked, remembering what Kate had said.

"I have three sisters," Anders told him. "All younger than I. Kirsten, the oldest and a most talented artist. Sofia, always with her head in a book, always learning and studying and Margrethe…" He broke off, a look of fondness filling his features. "My sister Mette was not born for this world, but she enlightened all who she encountered. She was so often ill, so often…" He looked back to meet Gideon's gaze, his eyes holding sorrow. "She was the reason I became a physician. But I have not seen them since I left home. I made a mistake and as a result, my parents found out I was not the son and heir they wanted me to be. I was disowned. Not in public as that would have been a scandal but disinherited and told to leave and never go back."

Gideon shook his head. He knew he had struggled himself to accept Anders as the man he was, one who loved other men and not women, but surely his own family…?

"I am sorry to hear that," he said. "It is your family's loss."

"And mine. But it is what it is, and it is in the past. What about you? Your family?"

It seemed very strange that in the time they had known each other, they had never touched on such personal ground. But it felt right to do so now. Gideon shared his story of a less than happy childhood as an only child under the stern gaze of his ferociously unyielding Presbyterian minister father and the warmth and joy his mother had brought to his life despite that. And as the long afternoon began to dip towards twilight, they shared memories of happier times.

"I wonder if we will be fed," Anders said after they had fallen silent again. "Or perhaps we are to be left here untended all night."

Gideon heard the sound of heavy footsteps on the boards of the passageway outside the room. He got to his feet and Anders rose from the chair and moved to stand so they were facing the door together.

The man who came in had two soldiers behind him. He was in his thirties, and looked as if he wore mourning attire. Golden blond hair was set in fashionable curls over his shoulders and a sword hung at his thigh. Gideon had seen him once before in London talking to Ellis Rushton just before someone tried to kidnap Ellis. One of the Covenant's archangels—Gabriel.

What was it Lord had said? *Oriel was the treasurer, Raphael was the archivist, Michael was in charge of the armed forces and Gabriel of the others who served.*

"You. Sit." Gabriel pointed to Gideon, who quickly dropped onto the chair, then the blond man turned his attention to Anders.

"Who are you and what is your connection with Sir Philip Lord?"

Anders made a polite bow.

"I am Dr Anders Jensen. I serve as a physician and surgeon with Sir Philip's regiment."

"Then why are you here today?"

"I was ordered to attend Lady Catherine. She finds travel difficult, and I was to be available if she needed me."

"Sir Philip takes his regiment's surgeon to see to his wife's inconveniences?"

"I do as he asks. He is my employer," Anders said, his tone bland. "He pays well, and he pays on a regular basis."

"And that is your sole concern in Sir Philip's affairs?"

"Of course. I do what I am paid to do."

Gideon was surprised Anders could act a role so well. Then realised that it was something a physician was called upon to do more frequently than one might first think when considering the profession.

"Tomorrow we will discuss your future employment," Gabriel told him. "I am sure we can come to an arrangement that will suit us both."

Anders made another bow. "Thank you, sir."

Gabriel gestured to the chair where Gideon was sitting.

"Alright. Your turn. Get up."

Gideon got to his feet, changing places with Anders.

"So, who are you and what is *your* connection with Sir Philip?"

Gideon felt his pulse rise sharply. There was something in the way the too blue gaze was studying him that left him feeling profoundly uncomfortable.

"I am Gideon Fox, a lawyer. I'm employed by Sir Philip to handle the legal and administrative affairs of his company." He realised what he had said and corrected himself. "I mean his regiment. It—it is also a mercenary company."

"Indeed," Gabriel agreed. "That is primarily what it is. Mercenary." The scrutiny continued. It was as if Gabriel was sure he had met Gideon before and was trying to place him. "What is your relationship with Sir Philip Lord?"

"He is my employer. I was ordered to accompany him here today because he told me there might be some documents he required to have authenticated."

That made Gabriel's eyebrows rise.

"Is that so? And have you authenticated other documents for him before this?"

Gideon felt the sweat breaking out over his shoulders and beading at the top of his brow. He had clearly said entirely the wrong thing, but he was at a loss as to how else he could explain his presence.

"I—"

"Oh, come now, it is hardly a difficult question. Has Sir Philip shown you any documents and asked you to authenticate them or—?" Then he stopped and his expression became one of discovery as if something occurred to him that had lurked at the back of his mind.

"What did you say your name was?"

"F—Fox," Gideon stuttered, convinced now that he was doomed.

"That's not your real name, is it?"

Gideon said nothing. If he admitted to having lied, he would be revealed as Gideon Lennox, the man the Covenant had tried to kill. Perhaps, he now realised, that was because of his father's involvement in the document by which Sir Richard Tempest agreed to allow the first Lord Brooke exclusive access to his wife until a child was born. He opened his mouth unsure what to say but then the decision was taken from him.

"You're Gideon Lennox, raised by Archibald Lennox the preacher and your mother was—"

Raised by…

Something in Gideon gave way, he stepped forward, hand lifted to strike and one of the men with Gabriel moved between them hand on sword.

"You leave my mother out of this," Gideon snarled, his world cascading about him like the cutting shards of a broken mirror.

Raised by?

"I was going to say she was regarded as one of the most beautiful women of her generation. Old Lennox did well out of it, not many of his age and profession get to marry the daughter of a baron."

A baron?

212

A wash of relief went through Gideon. This man was mistaken.

"My mother, sir," he said, coldly, "was the daughter of a goldsmith in Newcastle. Orphaned young and given much help by his guild until she was of age to marry." But even as he said the words, he found himself thinking of the old swivel ring his mother had given him saying it had been her grandfather's, the crest on it worn away...

Gabriel's eyebrows rose.

"Is that what she told you? Well, I suppose she had little choice. I will assume that was the story Lennox put around anyway. She was an heiress at the time. It was a shame your grandfather remarried and had a boy child in his dotage. Disowned her. Your life would have been different. Coupland was supposed to keep you close when you were sent to him, but he said you had been killed by Sir Philip. I'm glad to find he was mistaken."

But it had been Coupland who had tried to kill him.

"I'm not—"

"You are wasting your time denying it," Gabriel told him. "You *are* Gideon Lennox, and you *are* a son of the Covenant."

Gideon opened his mouth to press his protest, but Gabriel was already leaving the room. He paused on the threshold and looked back.

"I regret the need to confine you both here tonight, gentlemen, but it is temporary. Sir Philip Lord has been most amenable to my offer and that means that I need to set in place certain arrangements so we may all leave here tomorrow. I shall have another bed provided and see you are brought food and wine." His gaze stayed on Gideon as if looking for something before he went on talking. "Tomorrow you will begin new lives because tomorrow this nation will embark upon a new destiny." And from the catch of pride in his voice, Gideon decided he believed it.

"I do not pretend to understand what he meant," Anders said as the footsteps receded. "What do you think?"

Gideon said nothing. His mind, his heart and his very soul were in turmoil. Enough of his world had already been taken, broken and changed over the last year. This was too much. This tumult ripped away his last rags of certainty and turned his knowledge of who he was inside out, sweeping away the vestiges of his essential self, leaving him clinging naked to the sharp rocks of an unbearable reality, defenceless against the rising tide of despair. Then from somewhere deep within, beyond the raging maelstrom, he heard Zahara's voice.

I used to feel as if my heart was trapped like a bird in a cage. But with you, it is as if it can fly again.

He drew one breath and then another.

The fixed star in his firmament still shone.

Zahara's love. His love for her. Whoever he was, that would never change.

She was safe in Worcester and somehow, he had to return to her.

"What do you think?" Anders asked again as Gideon tried to orient himself on this new shore where he had been swept by the cataclysmic tide of revelation.

"Uh…"

"Do you think Sir Philip will agree to join these men?"

"I'm not sure," he said, his wits returning and gathering as he spoke. "If it meant saving all our lives, I believe he would agree."

He knew if Philip bound himself by that he would bear it stoically. As he had borne not knowing who he was, who his parents and their parents were.

Now Gideon understood the full weight of that burden himself and knew the poison it drove through the veins.

Chapter Nineteen

When the door opened again, a little over an hour later, they had been reduced to a rising moon as their sole means of illumination. Gideon assumed it would be the promised extra bed or perhaps some food and drink. He hoped for the latter as he hadn't eaten since the brief breakfast taken soon after dawn.

But instead, it was a group of soldiers who, without any explanation, bound their wrists then hustled them from the room and downstairs. After Gabriel's words, it was a surprise to be so roughly manhandled, but there was no opportunity to protest it. Perhaps, Gideon thought bleakly, whatever Philip had promised he had already reneged on or simply withdrawn.

The room they were herded into was once, a century before, the refectory for the priory. It was a long, high-ceilinged room, with a floor of flagstones of dull grey slate and lit by two, large, hanging candelabras. The hall was patterned with geometry. Square-panelled oak wainscotting lined the walls, above most of which were square mullion windows or wooden panels each containing a lozenge. Some held long faded heraldic devices, perhaps those of previous prioresses or maybe some of the benefactresses of the religious house this had once been.

One of the two long walls boasted a large hearth and on each side of the fireplace, stood a suit of archaic armour that once might have been worn on the battlefields of Crecy or Agincourt. Old weapons were pinned to the walls, a sword that was six-foot long from point to pommel, crossed halberds, an arrangement of daggers and even a crossbow which was set beside a musket with a broken lock.

At the far end from where they entered was a balustered gallery or balcony that had presumably been added by the subsequent, non-monastic owners, which was also panelled below its balusters. A long oak table had been pushed back against those panels and the benches that were meant to serve it had been set under the

windows on the wall opposite the hearth. These were occupied by
a few soldiers Gideon assumed belonged to the garrison.

As they walked the length of the room Gideon's heart leapt into
his mouth. Two women had appeared on the balcony and were
being pushed into seats at the front of it by the soldiers escorting
them. Kate and Christobel

Gideon and Anders were hurried up the stairs to the gallery. At
the top Gideon was pushed down to sit on the boards. Beside him
was a bench, beyond which were three chairs, set by the
balustrade. The chair nearest Gideon, just past the bench, was
empty and beside it stood a small rectangular table on which was
a jug of wine and four cups. Christobel was seated on the next
chair and Kate beside her. Behind them stood two men,
presumably set to guard them but whether in their protection or as
prisoners—or both, Gideon was unsure. A few feet behind the
soldiers was a door that, presumably, led to more accommodation
in this wing of the house.

Kate looked towards him and sent a brave smile. But Christobel
sat grey-faced and stiffly erect as if she had a spear thrust down
the length of her spine. Anders had been pushed to sit beside
Gideon, so he was right by the stairs up from the hall. Sitting close
to the well-spaced, decorative balusters at the front of the gallery,
Gideon had a good view of the hall below.

More soldiers were coming in. He counted thirty and then
stopped. It must surely be the bulk of the garrison, Gideon
assumed. He wondered where the owner of the house, Thomas
Kelley, and his family might be. The soldiers took seats on the
benches, their conversation reaching him in snatches.

"...lost it completely. Shouting and raging. I never heard the like
and..."

"...skin him alive when they find out what he's done...."

"...mad for blood, and who can blame him. His own wife and..."

"Sport is sport. I put my money on already..."

Gideon felt sick as he began to see the picture the comments
were painting. Beside him, Anders leaned closer. "They are saying
Sir Nicholas and the Covenant gentleman had a falling out over
something, but they must have resolved it because the Covenant

216

man has gone somewhere tonight to make arrangements for us all to travel tomorrow and left Sir Nicholas in charge in his absence."

"But what would they—?"

"Shut up."

The casual blow from a musket butt of a man standing behind them was hard enough to daze Gideon and he closed his mouth.

The answer came to him in the painful aftermath of the blow. Christobel. If Philip had sold his soul to the Covenant, it would only be because he had been able to use it to purchase the lives and freedom of all those who depended on him. Philip would never abandon Christobel after what he had said. The Covenant would surely not see that as too high a price to pay for Philip's willing cooperation with their plans. But Tempest was obsessed with her and hated Danny for what he saw as a betrayal. He would be furious to be told that he could have neither his wife nor his revenge. Surely Tempest wouldn't dare to cross Gabriel? To challenge the might of the Covenant itself?

Some men came through the door at the back of the gallery. One was Sir Nicholas Tempest and with a shock, Gideon realised that his own sword, the one he had found on a battlefield, was now by Tempest's thigh. With him was the man who had introduced himself when they arrived as Lieutenant Saddler and two others who also seemed to be officers. Tempest took the remaining chair. He sat alongside Christobel who had become a marble statue of herself. The three officers sat on the bench, Saddler himself was right beside Gideon.

The officers were already the worse for drink and were making crude jokes and speculating as to how Kate had acquired the scar on her face, after all one marked the face of a whore. Gideon's fists tightened. He wanted nothing so much as to silence them. But Kate bore it stoically, ignoring them.

Christobel continued to sit scouring-stick straight, her gaze fixed on the space in front of her and when Tempest tried to engage her in conversation, she turned her head and sent him a look so venomous that he flinched and turned his attention back to his fellow officers. Gideon saw Kate reach for and grip Christobel's hand and murmur something in her ear, which the younger woman

217

seemed not to hear. After witnessing Christobel step away from her past and blossom in confidence, it made Gideon feel sick to see her like this.

There was a commotion at the far end of the hall and Sir Philip Lord was brought in. Despite having his hands bound in front of him he seemed to be making the task of his captors far from easy. But once they had forced him into the hall, Gideon saw his demeanour changed. He drew himself up to his full height and—far from resisting—strode forward to stand before the gallery, choosing to stop at a point where he had no need to lift his chin more than a small amount to look up at the occupants of it. He was clad only in a shirt and breeches and was still wearing his boots. With no hat, his hair was straight and loose, and it lay on his shoulders the colour and lustre of pearl. His gaze went to its homing and fixed on Kate as if she was the only person present in the whole room.

Then, when he held her gaze in return, he lifted his voice, trained to carry on a battlefield and even over the clamour of men echoed by the walls, he could be heard.

"My Lady Catherine, I am glad to see you. I trust you are in good health?"

The noise in the hall that had risen at his first appearance, fell away in the wake of Philip's words.

Kate bathed him in a serene smile, the cost of which Gideon had no wish to know. She was sending him the gift of her strength and letting him know that she would not permit any to weaken him through her.

"I am well, sir," she said simply, her voice steady and strong.

Lord made a deep courtly bow to her that even lacking the use of his hands maintained every appearance of grace.

Sir Nicholas Tempest rose to his feet and clapped in ironic applause.

"Huzza, huzza! Such a performance."

"I normally charge," Philip said. "However, today is my day for charity. I will let it pass. But, please," he held up his bound wrists, "do not ask me to juggle." That earned him some laughter from around the room.

"You lack only the motley to make a most excellent fool," Tempest said with contempt.

"I would rather be counted a fool for my wit than have men consider me one for the lack of it." Philip replied. "There are those who have no need of motley to show their true colours to the world. They need only to open their mouths." That won more laughter and even the odd derisive cheer aimed at Sir Nicholas.

"This is not a game," Tempest shouted, and the hall fell silent again. "But we can make it one if you insist. A game of swordplay."

"You are challenging me?" Philip sounded delighted. "Then I accept, provided I am allowed one of my hands returned. The other I am happy to have tied behind my back. If I win you release me and mine, if I lose—" he broke off and shrugged. "Fighting you with one hand tied behind my back?" He shook his head. "I won't lose."

Pandemonium broke out. Some baying for Philip's blood for insulting their colonel and some demanding to see such a fight right away. Tempest dropped back into his chair, leaned over to the officer sitting beside him and said something in his ear. The man nodded and got up, pushing past those guarding Gideon and Anders and making his way down the stairs.

Gideon feared he was being sent with orders to dispatch Philip, but instead the man kept on across the length of the room and went out of the door at the far end—the same door Gideon had entered by.

"Do you accept my challenge?" Philip lifted his voice again above the hubbub. "I am offering you a clear advantage—you may even choose which of my two hands is the one restrained."

That set the room off again and the men about Philip had to stand firm to keep some of those he was angering at bay. Gideon realised that most of the soldiers had been drinking, perhaps Tempest's way to keep them on his side. But it meant the room was a powder keg and Philip held a lit match.

Tempest stood up to lean on the balustrade at the front of the gallery, lifting his hand for a silence that was slow to come.

"There is no shame," he said as soon as he could be heard, "in refusing to fight a man who is known to have no honour. A man who sells his sword to the highest bidder and hides his vile nature behind cheap speeches. There will be a duel, as I have promised."

Those who lined the room, standing against the walls or sitting on the benches gave a cheer.

Gideon felt sick. They would cheer cock fights with as much enthusiasm. He wondered, who Tempest was going to pitch against Philip? And suddenly found himself transported in time back to a barn in Yorkshire. There, in a setting not so different from this, he had been made to fight for his life and that of Zahara. The memory sent shards of ice through his veins.

Then the officer who Tempest had sent out returned. With him were two of his soldiers and Danny Bristow. Gideon's relief was profound. When he and Anders had heard the volley of musket fire, a dark corner of his heart had been convinced that Danny had to be the target they were aiming for.

Danny, like Philip, had been stripped to shirt and breeches, and his hair was an untidy tawny mop over his shoulders. He had bruises on his face and his hands were bound behind him, but he held his head high and his gaze swept the room impartially, before settling on Sir Nicholas.

Gideon glanced along the gallery to where Christobel sat, carved from marble and his heart ached for her. Where Kate had the right to stand openly with Philip, Christobel would know that to let her feelings for Danny be revealed would place him in greater danger. There could be little, surely, to inflame Tempest more than the knowledge that the wife he seemed obsessed by should have given her heart to the man that Tempest deemed his most bitter personal enemy. Gideon saw Kate close her hand over Christobel's, lending her strength and understanding. But Christobel's face remained a brittle mask.

The men escorting Danny pushed him to stand alongside Philip and it was hard not to notice the differences between the two men. Philip was taller by almost a head, his whole body in proportion, longer limbed and with the elegant, perhaps even arrogant, bearing of a man sure of his status. Danny was shorter, though a little above the average height of the men around him, his shoulders were broader than Philip's and his limbs more sturdy. His stance was not as elegant, but like that of a hunting dog, holding himself always as if ready to move.

By the briefest glance and nod, Gideon saw Danny tell Philip that he would follow his lead. It was not needed between the two of them, men who knew each other's ways and worked so well together that one could be the limbs of the other. But it was, like Kate's smile, a reassurance and reminder for Philip that he was not alone and could count completely on those about him. It was also, Gideon realised, a sign of the absolute faith that they had in Philip—and that both Danny and Kate did, somehow bolstered Gideon's confidence. *We have all been here before*, it seemed to say, *we can get through this too.*

"Gentlemen," Tempest straightened from leaning on the balustrade and made a broad gesture towards his prisoners, "I give you Sir Philip Lord, traitor to his nation, the vulturine commander of rapacious men, bringer of suffering, misery and death as he profits from war and force-feeds the foulness of the dregs of every nation in Europe and beyond down the gullet of England. And Daniel Bristow, a debased creature who lies and schemes his way into the good graces of honest men with the sole intention of betraying them, who stoops at nothing, not even the theft of another's wife, if it serves his ends. Two men with the integrity of whores and the honour of murderers and thieves."

The silence was complete now. Gideon expected Philip to step forward and make some cutting remark or a clever witty riposte to silence and belittle Tempest as he had so easily before. But he said nothing. He didn't even deny the charges heaped upon him or point out that—

Gideon struggled to his feet, ignoring the hands trying to push him down, unable to keep silent.

"Sir Philip Lord has his knighthood from the king's hand. Is that the mark of a traitor? He was exonerated not pardoned—"

It was Philip who silenced him, cutting and dismissive. "I have no need of a canting clerk to speak in my defence, Fox. You should be down here with us." He gestured to the cleared space. "*Lawyers are good rapier and dagger men; they'll quickly dispatch your money.*" That brought laughter from the room below. "Now I've had enough of it. You are no longer in my employ."

"I—I only—" Completely taken aback, Gideon felt the colour flood his face as he was thrust back on the floor by the man who had hit him before. He had not expected to be thanked, but he had thought—what? How exactly had he expected Philip to respond?

Anders leaned closer, taking advantage of the fact all eyes were on the men below.

"You cannot stop what is going to happen," he said, his voice a whisper. "What is play to the cat is death to the mouse, the strongest among the weak is the one who doesn't forget his weaknesses." Then he straightened up before Gideon could even think of a reply.

But Anders was right. All Philip had done was thrust him out of the line of fire after Gideon had tried to step into it.

"You see the ingratitude of this creature?" Tempest was contemptuous. But the jeers were half-hearted and the men becoming impatient. Tempest might have won them over with drink and the promise of entertainment, but he would only hold them if he delivered.

Would he ask for volunteers to take on Philip or Danny? Offer a prize to the man who defeated one of them? It would give them some chance if so, although if they had to fight all comers, they would eventually be exhausted. Or did Tempest have a champion he intended to call?

"Alright," Tempest shouted and held up both his hands as if in surrender to the demands. "There is nothing more to say. You will both fight."

"If there is to be any fighting then surely the women do not need to witness it," Philip said.

"There will be fighting, and the women will stay," Tempest insisted, although his officers looked uncomfortable at that.

"Who?" It was Danny's disdainful voice. "Who do you want us to fight?"

That brought an odd breathless hush to the hall and Gideon's heart wedged in his throat, beating too hard and too fast.

"You mistake me," Tempest said. "Or perhaps as you always did, you underestimate me. I meant you will fight each other."

Philip groaned as if in exasperation rather than despair.

"Surely you can do better than that?" Then, unbelievably, he laughed.

"Get on with it." A voice from somewhere in the hall, the call picked up by others.

"Very well, if it will amuse you all," Philip spoke across them. "Colonel Bristow and I will fight. If you would be kind enough to release our hands so we can better hold our swords rather than with our teeth."

There was laughter for that and calls of appreciation.

But Tempest wasn't done.

"Oh, I am sure the two of you can put on a fine display. I have seen Bristow's dancing steps before. But this will be a fight to the death."

The room spun around Gideon. *Oh God, please no, not that.* He had thought Tempest might seek revenge by humiliating the two, but he had never for a moment believed he would go so far, against the will of the Covenant itself.

Philip Lord's gaze was Baltic.

"Your masters will not approve."

"I need no one to approve," Tempest said, spitting the words. "I am my own man."

"Then I refuse. I will not play your game. You cannot force me to fight. If you want an execution, do the deed yourself or set up another firing squad."

"If I think for one moment," Tempest went on, as if he hadn't spoken, "that either of you is not fully engaging to try and kill the other man then I will have one of your men put to death. One of the eight in the barn, perhaps—"

Eight? They had come with ten. Suddenly Gideon was sure he knew what the volley of musket fire had been.

"—or we could start with one of the two here." Tempest nodded to the men behind Gideon, but it was Anders they pulled roughly to his feet. "Take him outside and hang him."

Gideon hated himself for being glad it was Anders who was chosen, glad that he would live a little longer, glad that he was not to have his life snuffed out for no reason dangling at the end of a rope. The men began pushing Anders towards the stairs when Philip's voice stopped them.

"That would be a terrible waste of a good physician. Very well. I hear your stick, Sir Nicholas, what is your carrot?"

At another sign from their commander, the men pushed Anders back to his place beside Gideon. He sat, eyes closed, lips moving in silent prayer and a bead of sweat running down his face.

"You need a carrot other than your survival?"

Lord laughed.

"I would have thought by now you would have understood I do not hold my life that highly. I have risked it every day of my adult life on the battlefield or off it. I suggest that you give your word that whoever of us wins will be free to take all my people—those here and those in the barn—and leave unharmed. Those are my terms if you wish to see us fight and one of us die. Otherwise, you may hang them all and I'll still not fight, because I'd not trust you to let them live anyway." The steel in his voice left no one in any doubt that he meant it and a clammy coldness seemed to press against Gideon's skin. "I need your word before all these good men, who will bear witness to it."

There was silence in the room, absolute silence. Gideon felt the tightening of an invisible noose about his neck as sweat prickled across his body. The gaze of every man present was fixed on Sir Nicholas Tempest.

"I hear what you say." Tempest sounded dismissive. "You have my word. Now you fight."

The room erupted in cheers.

Their swords were brought and laid on the table that had been pushed back to the panelled wall beneath the gallery. Those guarding Philip and Danny cut their bonds. Both men began rubbing the circulation back into their hands and moving into some simple movements to loosen the muscles that had been constrained and were about to be stressed to the limit. Then, being given their swords, they made practice movements with them, appraised by those watching as bets were made and taken.

Glancing at the women, Gideon saw they were being offered wine. Kate refused with a shake of her head, but Christobel took the cup woodenly. Gideon didn't see her drink any, she just held it in her free hand, as if unaware that she did so. Her other hand now gripped Kate's, the knuckles white.

Beside him, Anders stirred.

"Do you still think our lord and master has a plan?" he asked softly. "Or is this all extempore?"

"I have no idea," Gideon admitted.

"Then all we can do is hope."

Tempest, Gideon noticed, had downed an entire glass of wine and begun another. He was talking to the officers beside him, one of whom seemed less enthusiastic about what was happening than the other two. Then he shut his mouth like a rat trap and stared at the two men below him with undisguised hatred. Gideon knew then that whichever of the two might win, and whatever he might have promised, Tempest would not allow the survivor to leave alive and he shivered, although the room was pressingly hot.

Philip stood still in the centre of the hall facing the gallery with Danny beside him. They were alone in the arena of the hall where once nuns had gathered to eat and pray with the quietude of religious life.

Silence descended.

Lord made a sweeping bow towards Kate then lifted his sword in salute.

"*Set in thy tail a blaze,*
That all the world may gaze
And wonder upon thee…"

He spoke lightly but Kate blanched and lifted her chin. Her eyes held a sudden sparkle of unshed tears. Whatever message Philip had given her it wasn't one she had wished to hear. Gideon saw her mouth three silent words, and of the two of them, it was Philip who could not sustain it and looked away.

"That the best you can do? No maudlin words of affection?" Tempest wore a sneer. Gideon wondered how much he had been drinking. "What about you, Bristow? No last adulterous thoughts to share about my wife?"

Danny's eyes smouldered, and his jaw muscles worked but he said nothing.

"Such a shame," Tempest said, his voice pitched to mock sympathy.

That unlocked Danny's voice.

"You are the only one who brings shame to her." Then he closed his mouth as if not trusting himself to say more.

Tempest's dark eyes glowed like embers in a fire ready to catch.

"Enough delay," he snapped. "Fight!"

And that was it.

Chapter Twenty

Danny made a bow, lowering his head as he did so, his message clear to Gideon, but Philip met him rising from the bow with a shake of his head that most would have missed and none about them have understood even if they marked it. Gideon felt his heart constrict.

In that brief exchange, Danny had offered his life and Lord had refused him. Sir Philip Lord had decided Danny should live and he would die. It was his final order and from the tight expression on Danny's face, Gideon wasn't sure it would be obeyed.

After that, the formal salute felt ironic as they crossed blades.

"*Fino alla morte*," Philip said the words clearly.

Even with no Italian Gideon knew that phrase: *to the death*.

Danny inclined his head. "*Fino alla morte non si sa qual è la sorte.*"

Anders, who had learned his physician's skill in Padua, translated softly. "Until death comes, we do not know what fate holds."

Philip laughed and without warning lunged, drawing an instant parry from Danny as the fight was joined.

As the swords met, it was obvious even to a barely competent swordsman like Gideon that this was no ordinary duel. These were two great swordsmen at their work. Gideon had never seen Philip fight outside of the wild melee of battle. Now it was plain that he was a man born with a sword in his hand, trained to it by some of the finest swordsmen of a generation past.

But Danny was a master. He had been apprenticed to the science as to a trade.

He barely seemed to move his feet, effortlessly cutting and parrying, sometimes deflecting from the guard of his hilt with the flick of his wrist, then moving to counter with no more than a lift of his arm. Philip moved more. Like quicksilver, he darted in and out, exploiting any chance, just as competent in his parries and ripostes.

For a time it appeared to Gideon that the two could keep this up forever. Neither seemed to show the fatigue they must both surely be suffering after the physical demands of the night before, chasing Waller's men from Worcester and the all too brief sleep each had managed after that. It was Danny who, discerning a weakness in his opponent's guard, struck through like a snake. Only the sheer speed and agility Philip possessed saved him from more serious injury although the sword point nicked his earlobe, splitting it open like a ripe plum and spraying blood everywhere, far more than Gideon would have imagined such a small place could provide.

"First blood to me."

Danny had stepped back as he spoke, but Philip seemed not to be mindful of any of the graces of chivalry and, blood dripping to stain his shirt, instantly pressed his attack past Danny's blade. Had it been any other man the fight would have been over then. Danny barely even moved. A swivel of his hips meant that it was just the sleeve of his shirt that was ripped as his blade caught and deflected the lethal thrust. As they renewed their fight it was Philip who appeared to Gideon to be giving ground.

It was about then that he became aware there was disruption happening outside, voices and running feet. Tempest must have heard it too because, keeping his eyes on the combat below, he beckoned Saddler to him and spoke into his ear. The lieutenant nodded and hurried through the door at the back of the gallery.

There was a sudden shout, which pulled Gideon's divided attention back to the fight. Danny had drawn more blood in a cut to Philip's arm. But just as it seemed Danny was free to press home his advantage Philip kicked over a suit of armour so that Danny had to jump aside and barely avoided a cut to the sword arm that could have incapacitated him.

There was surely no possible room for anyone to accuse either man of not fighting to his best extent to bring down the other. Gideon looked across at Tempest to see he was leaning forward in his seat and his face was twisted with an ugly emotion. Beyond Tempest, the two women sat like statues, hands linked. Though each must surely be praying for the man the other loved to be the one to die, even that would not divide them before their enemies.

The noises outside had grown louder. Gideon glanced to the door behind which the sounds were escalating, then they were drowned out by a cacophonous clatter that dragged Gideon's eyes back to the fight he didn't want to watch at all.

Danny had snatched a long dagger from a display on the wall as he passed, bringing the rest of the knives and swords crashing to the floor in an untidy heap. He sprang aside to avoid it and spun like a dancer as he did so, briefly facing the gallery and making a spectacularly crude soldier's gesture towards Tempest, thrusting his arm upwards so the room erupted in coarse laughter. With the inimitable grace that characterised everything he did, Philip Lord leapt over the pile, taking advantage of Danny's distraction to capture himself a dagger too.

The fight was renewed with increasing ferocity. But Danny was now the one who struggled more, being pushed back step by step, towards the gallery. It seemed he had miscalculated in switching to sword and dagger, a style Philip clearly favoured. Until, backed to the wall and finding himself with nowhere else to go, Danny leapt onto the table where the swords had been laid, right below the gallery itself. Gideon now had to peer down through the balustrades to see him. Philip tried to cut at his legs and feet, but Danny avoided that like a sword dancer, kicking out. To cheers from their audience, Philip joined him on the table.

Then everything changed.

As they clashed, Philip dropped his dagger and jumped. Danny stepped in, lifting him, adding his strength to the upwards leap. Philip caught the gallery's balustrade rail with his free hand, his feet finding purchase at the base of the balusters. Even then it might not have worked if Christobel had not acted. She rose and turned fast, hurling her wine cup into the face of the man already moving to intercept Philip, with a musket coming to bear. The liquid made the soldier flinch and pull back and the cup caught him hard on the bridge of his nose.

Using the precious seconds purchased for him, Philip swung his legs over the rail. Sir Nicholas, slowed by drink, finally realised his danger and got to his feet, but Philip drove an unstoppable fist into Tempest's gut. Then he pulled the other man up, sword blade pressed against his throat. It was only a moment later that the men about Sir Philip Lord and his victim were bristling with weapons, but it was a moment too late.

"Back!" Philip snarled, his lips pulled up in feral anger to reveal his teeth. "Stay back, or he dies."

Gideon's stomach twisted. This was not going to play out well. One of the men was already preparing to shoot, and below, Danny was alone and exposed to a crowd of armed men whose mood was ugly. He glanced at Anders, who nodded and the two of them rose, turning on the men guarding them, although Gideon knew it would be more distraction than effect with their hands bound.

What might have happened next would never be known because the door at the back of the gallery burst open and the man who had been bringing his musket to bear on Philip made an odd gulping sound and collapsed, an arrow in his spine. Another man had dropped as the rest reacted, turning towards the door at the back of the gallery, and a third died even as he shifted his aim to the figure clad in black who stood there bow in one hand and a cluster of arrows in the other, drawing and firing in a single fast, repetitive movement.

Shiraz.

He moved to cover the hall below, three arrows left in his hand, as the men behind him filled the gallery. At first Gideon thought Shiraz had brought soldiers from Worcester and the house was taken. But then he realised these were the same men who had ridden with them in escort that morning and there were only seven of them. This was not so much a relief as a rescue. They were still in grave peril and badly outnumbered.

Someone sliced the bonds on Gideon's wrists, and he turned to where Philip still held Tempest, in time to see Christobel helping Danny over the balustrade. Danny swept her into his arms as soon as his feet were on the floor. Then Christobel turned in the shelter of Danny's arms and spat full in the face of Sir Nicholas Tempest. As she did so something caught Gideon's eye.

"My sword," he said, pointing at the familiar hilt currently half hidden by the bottom of Tempest's coat.

"Take it," Philip told him. "Sir Nicholas will have no future need for it." He shook the man in his grip like a terrier with a weasel.

By the time Gideon had the sword belt free and was putting it on, Philip had pushed a struggling Tempest into the care of two of his men, who were binding his hands. The soldiers below in the hall were impotent to intervene. Those men Shiraz had freed had gathered pistols and muskets and the means to fire them in their passage and three of them now trained musket barrels on the men below whilst Shiraz dissuaded any from stepping on the stairs by the simple method of putting an arrow through the throat of the first who tried it.

But it was a temporary standoff, they were not in sufficient strength to fight through the men. The garrison here was more than five times their strength.

"Gentlemen," Sir Philip Lord lifted his voice to reach those below. "You have all done your duty in striving to detain us, but we have the person of your colonel in our keeping. If any attempt is made to attack us as we leave, he will be the first to die. Now you may like him as little as I do, but I think you might find it difficult to explain his death to your officers." He gestured to where the two who had been on the gallery with Tempest lay bleeding. One was still alive and clutching at the wound on his arm, the other was either unconscious or dead. "Although these two might not be the ones you are answering to in future."

Then he turned and issued swift orders to the men with him.

"We withdraw in good order. Colonel Bristow, lead off. Shiraz, you have our rear, Mr Fox and Dr Jensen, please keep the women close in our centre and defend them with your lives."

The retreat, even if in good order, was an inglorious scurry.

They left the balcony crossing the room beyond where Gideon had to assist Danny and the men with him to force a passage. Another room and then another led to a back staircase. There Kate stumbled and groaned with pain. This was far more walking, let alone running than she could sustain. Gideon lifted her in his arms and carried her. and even when she protested that she could manage, he refused to set her down.

"We will go faster if I carry you," he insisted, and she didn't ask again.

Down the stairs to more rooms below and along another passage. From the sounds behind him, where Gideon knew Philip was side by side with Shiraz as their rear guard, fighting was becoming more intense. They hurried through some of the workaday rooms and finally outside. They rolled a heavy water butt to block the door, then they had to go around two sides of a small cloister to reach the stableyard. Shiraz had left a man in the stables and the horses were furnished and waiting. Those pulling the carriage had been made ready, so it was the work of little time to yoke them to the vehicle.

Someone lashed Tempest to the powerful black gelding Shiraz rode, a mount well used to having two riders since Zahara was often pillion. By the time Lord and Shiraz had arrived, Danny had everyone by their horse and Kate with Christobel in the carriage.

They set out in the darkness at speed, the moon giving little benison being just past its first quarter. Herding all the other horses from the stables before them, to stymie any pursuit, they made it through the gate as the men garrisoning the house began firing at them. A saddle emptied, beside Gideon, but no one he saw stopped to see if the man lived.

Once free of the walls Gideon knew a wash of relief. It wouldn't be an easy night ride back to Worcester, but they had done worse. The mad chase from Warwick when he and Kate had been rescued, for example. Now he rode behind the coach with Anders, aware they were to be the final line of defence for the two women if all else failed. Although he had seen Kate and Christobel given a loaded pistol each and both knew well how to use them.

They were barely away from the village when it happened. A shout from Danny then shots from the front. The flashes were blindingly bright. There was no good ground to take the coach off the track and by unspoken mutual consent, Anders and Gideon moved to put themselves on either side of it as it came to a halt.

There was a sudden dreadful silence and Gideon peered through the dark to try and see what was happening but beyond shadowy shapes, he could tell nothing.

"Sir Philip?" Gabriel's voice. "What is this about? You gave me your word—"

From closer than he had realised Gideon heard Philip curse. Then he lifted his voice in reply.

"I gave you my word on the condition that none of us would be in any way molested. I feel pretty molested right now. Do not accuse me of breaking my word when yours was shattered into fragments first."

"I have no idea what you…" Gabriel trailed off. "Whatever has happened it can be made right."

"I think not. I have Tempest as my prisoner. Let us pass and do not pursue us and I will release him unharmed. Now tell the man I speak the truth, Sir Nicholas, or you will be short a digit."

"It is true," Tempest's voice was a squeak.

There was a strong silence.

"I would preserve Sir Nicholas if I could, but you matter much more to the Covenant than he does. I cannot let you pass."

Gideon knew what Philip would say to that, what he had no choice but to say, and what would happen then.

Something within Gideon revolted. There had to be another way to fight this. A way that didn't end in blood and death.

"No," he shouted.

Suddenly, the word 'fight' lost its swordlike shape. It became again what it once meant to Gideon in his previous life—the battle of argument and debate. It was as if some inner prompting was reminding him of who he was and what he was. With that memory came the knowledge which placed the weapons he needed in his hands. He knew what to do and exactly how it needed to be done.

This was his battle, and he could win it.

"If you don't let us pass there will be no more Covenant," he called. "We have the Tempest copies of the original and the new Covenant. Neither the king nor his parliament would tolerate a secret compact of men within the state which aims to seize power. That is treason. Your Covenant is a plant that only thrives in darkness and shadows. Imagine how it would be if we exposed it to the light of public gaze? If we fail to return to Worcester the person who holds those copies will see the documents reach the men who need to see them—men on both sides of this war. But only after printing many copies of the Covenant and its signatories so the people may know."

This time the silence had a different quality and from close beside him Philip murmured, "I promised Kate a new gown, what would you have?"

Even if the question had been in earnest there was no chance for Gideon to reply before Gabriel called out.

"I don't believe you, Lennox. If ever you had sight of such things, it would have been from your guardian. The Tempest documents are safe in Newhall."

"They were once. They were within a picture of Dr John Dee and a child holding a Tudor rose. That is where we found them."

That was met by an appalled indrawing of breath that was loud enough to carry and a moan of outrage from Tempest.

Gideon went on quickly. He listed some of the names which, unbelievably, had been on the old, original, document, names that would cause a scandal even today if they were known to have been associated with such a project. "I told you I was with Sir Philip to authenticate documents, and those I have authenticated. They would stand in any court of law, be it convened under his majesty's justices or those loyal to parliament."

He stopped speaking to a silence that was broken only by the snuffling of the horses and the chink of harness in the dark.

When Gabriel spoke, there was something new in his voice. It was no longer mocking or dismissive. "How did…?"

"I found the picture in a bookseller in Worcester."

From the dark came a groan of pain. "Dear God, the Tempest boy is such a fool. I told him someone would come to Worcester, I never expected..." Then Gabriel's voice changed. "Lennox, listen to me, you have no idea what you are doing or even who you are. We will do this another way. I presently hold the whereabouts of certain documents I know Sir Philip is most interested to have sight of. If you come with me now and I leave Sir Nicholas in the

234

safekeeping of Sir Philip, I will allow you access to them both. After that," he paused as if unsure what to say. "After that, if you still wish to make public those documents that you hold, I will not stop you. The only way forward I can see now is through persuasion. Sir Philip has already agreed with much I have said, I will show you the rest and you will tell him the truth of it."

"You have shown little care for the life of Tempest in the past." Danny's voice called from a short distance ahead. "Why should we trust that you have any care for it now?"

"Things have changed, Mr Bristow, and you had a hand in their changing. By taking the life of one of our number in London, you altered the balance of power within the Covenant. Now all the surviving sons of the Covenant are highly regarded and considered most precious."

All? For God's sake how many—?

"I will do it," Gideon called before he could talk himself out of it.

"You do not have to," Philip said quickly, his voice low. "We can use those copies of the Covenant to negotiate our safety."

"We could," Gideon agreed, "but then you will never know what is in the documents the Covenant holds. It would be a lifelong standoff and neither side would feel safe to move from that."

"I have lived thus far without knowing, I am sure I can survive the rest of my life in such ignorance too—more happily than I would if anything happened to you."

"You made an oath."

That was met by silence.

"The hazard is not that extreme," Gideon lied. "The two copies of the Covenant you hold, and Nicholas Tempest will secure me. Just be sure to keep him alive."

The moon gave enough light that Gideon could see Philip lower his head in acceptance.

"Very well. You have my trust in this over any other man. But you had better return to us or Zahara will never forgive me even if I could ever forgive myself."

Zahara. *We will tell them at supper tonight.* He had promised to return, and he was breaking that promise. But he knew in his heart this was the only way things could ever end without bloodshed and chaos raining down on them all.

"Zahara will understand why I'm doing this," he said, knowing he spoke the truth.

Philip's head moved again, and Gideon saw he was looking towards the shadows that concealed Shiraz.

"Just remember, the Lord will be watching over you," he said softly.

As Philip called out to arrange with Gabriel how they would proceed, Gideon found Anders beside him.

"I will come with you, my friend," Anders said. "I think you—and perhaps Sir Philip too—will need a witness. Someone who is not as closely caught up in this as the others. The Covenant have no reason to kill me, and it may even suit them to have an uninvolved witness."

"But I can't guarantee your safety," Gideon protested.

"When I was in prison in Paris you fought to free me," Anders said. "Now, tell me you would have left me to rot in that cell had Lady Catherine's fate not also been in jeopardy, and I will ride to Worcester."

Gideon shook his head.

"It would be a lie if I said that, though you tempt me to lie to save you from this."

"Ah no, my friend, you of all people know that it is better to suffer for truth than to prosper by falsehood."

After that, it took less time than Gideon would have thought.

One moment he was hearing a whispered "God keep you safe," from Kate and feeling the brief weight of Danny's hand on his shoulder, the next he was riding through the night in the alien company of the blond-haired Covenant man called Gabriel, aware that somewhere behind him Shiraz would be shadowing them silently, and behind that the weary entourage of Sir Philip Lord was heading for Worcester and safety. Whatever happened now, they were safe and that left Gideon with a sense of relief despite his own peril.

All safe except Anders.

The two of them rode amid a large body of cavalry which had the discipline to travel in silence through the night, except where communication might be essential to ensure everyone made a turn or when they needed to ford a stream.

They had been riding for over an hour when Anders spoke quietly. "You do realise these are Parliament's men?"

"Or Covenant men," Gideon suggested. "The Covenant seems to support both factions as it suits them."

When they eventually reached their destination, it was a small, fortified house. At one end was an old tower and the house itself was built onto that like the nave of a church might be to a church tower. But that was all the impression Gideon was able to gather before he and Anders had been encouraged to dismount and Gabriel joined them.

"Have you eaten this evening? No? Then I will arrange some food for you. We can talk as you eat and you will need to decide whether you wish to sleep before we do the work you are here for."

As he spoke, he was showing them into the main part of the house which was furnished in a style that made Gideon think it had barely been updated since the turn of the century.

"Whose house is this?" he asked as he looked around.

"It is mine," Gabriel told him. "Through here, please."

They were ushered into a comfortable room set out with a table and the embers of a fire still glowing in the hearth. A small clock was set on the wall with its weights hanging down and a bookcase stood in the corner but was too much in shadow for Gideon to see what treasures it might hold.

Gabriel gave orders for them to have food brought, then taking a seat at the head of the table, gestured to the place on his right and left. Gideon took the right-hand side and sat down.

"Where are Thomas Kelley and his family?" He asked as Anders moved around the table to take his place. It was something that had been troubling him since they arrived at Baddersleigh.

"Hale and well," Gabriel assured him. "Thomas is an old man. He was not happy to remain in his house once it was garrisoned. He has gone to stay with one of his daughters."

"Then where—?"

"You may ask me whatever you wish," Gabriel said, cutting across him. "Before you do, I would ask you something."

Gideon met his gaze.

"I'm not in the habit of sharing my thoughts with a man whose name I don't know. The only name I have for you is Gabriel and that, as I understand it, is a title, not a name."

There was no hesitation.

"Of course. My name is Sir John Drake, my mother was Katherine Dee, daughter of Dr John Dee and, like you, I am a son of the Covenant, although unlike you I have been raised to know that from birth."

In this evening of revelations that was a small thing to learn. Gideon thought back.

"There was no 'Drake' on the Covenant list of signatories."

Gabriel—or Drake as he claimed to be—smiled tightly.

"No more is there 'Lennox', but that means little."

It didn't seem the time to mention that if not a signatory to the Covenant itself, Archibald Lennox had signed as a witness to a document of theirs. So instead, he asked, "And being a son of the Covenant, means?"

Drake held up a hand.

"Please. I will answer all your questions, I promise, but after you have answered just one of mine."

"And that question is?"

"I would know what you believe the Covenant to be and how you perceive it? Please speak honestly."

"What I believe the Covenant to be?" Gideon echoed the question as he gathered his thoughts. "Very well. I believe it to be a conspiracy of men seeking power to inflict their view of how things should stand upon the world, with no regard to the human cost of achieving that end. Men who are so ruled by the power of ideas, they have forgotten that their ideas are grinding the bones of innocents and even children in their mill—have forgotten, or else simply do not care."

Lowering his gaze, the golden-haired man gave a small nod.

"I fear that we may well stand guilty as charged."

238

Chapter Twenty-One

With a world-weariness he had not shown before, Drake looked up to meet Gideon's accusatory glare.

"You make the point, and you make it well. But it is not the past that matters now, it is the future."

"On the contrary," Gideon said, hotly. "The past matters. I've seen what the Covenant has done to Sir Philip. I've seen you harassing and threatening a friend of mine in the streets of London. I've seen the chamber where a child was raised in darkness in the bowels of Howe Hall. I read the contract of concubinage by which Margret Coupland was traded like a broodmare. I have just witnessed the atrocities of Sir Nicholas Tempest and I was nearly killed by the manipulations of that man's uncle last autumn." He shook his head, suddenly wondering why he had come here. "*Ye shall know them by their fruits. Do men gather grapes of thorns, or figs of thistles?*"

Drake held up both hands as if in surrender.

"The Covenant was born of desperate men praying for a remedy to circumstances that threatened to overwhelm all they held precious. God answered those prayers. An infant came into their keeping against all conceivable odds, giving legitimacy to their plans and providing the path to achieve them."

"Legitimacy?" Gideon made no effort to hide his contempt.

"Yes," Drake insisted. "Men like my grandfather had a vision of a world no longer torn apart by Catholic, Lutheran, Calvinist or any other sect. One bound in a new universal religion that would embrace them all. It would be governed by enlightened men whose spiritual wisdom came directly from God and his angels. My grandfather and others in the Covenant had communication with great thinkers all across Europe, some of whom were men of power and influence. But for that they needed a ruler with a legitimate right to govern much of troubled Europe and a creed that could unite Catholics and Protestants. My grandfather was told by those he later learned were angels, that through the child would come that ruler."

"Then these conspirators," Gideon said, sickened but keen to progress the story, "took the malformed child of Mary Tudor and Philip Hapsburg and raised him as if he were a dog to be bred from?"

Drake's lips tightened. "She was indeed seen as a monster."

"*She?*" Gideon felt his flesh prickle. Why had he assumed the child would be a boy? Perhaps because having seen the room in Howe Hall he had struggled enough to think of a man being made to live there—but a woman?

"Yes. The child was a girl, Princess Mary, and she was simple, with little understanding. To begin with, she was raised as a child of the family she had been placed with, but as she grew older, she became ungovernable and was given to violence. She was sent to somewhere she could be cared for but kept securely and apart. I promise you that she was as well treated as she could be. She wanted for nothing. But her guardians struggled regardless."

"She was kept locked up in a lightless room," Gideon protested.

"Mr Lennox, do you think such a child born even today would be treated any differently? Have you seen how those in Bedlam are kept?"

What he said was so appallingly true, that Gideon found his teeth clenched tight. With an effort, he unlocked them. Across the table Anders had lowered his head as if in pain.

"Go on," Gideon said, stiffly.

"Then Queen Mary died. That was the time the Covenant had its first major internal dissent. Some believed with Elizabeth on the throne things had changed and the Covenant should be dissolved. Those were the men who were more concerned about their personal positions of power than the broad vision of the Covenant. Some supporters renounced their interest, but the Covenant was already too powerful for them to dare denounce it. Even my grandfather considered stepping away, doubting the spirits who told him the child would bring forth a line of great rulers. He had great hopes of the queen and spent hours in her company trying to persuade her to our vision. Ultimately to no avail."

Drake shook his head in regret.

"When Queen Elizabeth reached forty, it became clear she would never marry and produce an heir. The succession was yet again an issue. There was a real risk her cousin, Mary of Scotland—a devout Catholic—might succeed her. The ideals of the Covenant and the unity it promised were once again most pressing."

"I thought the Covenant was neither Protestant nor Catholic?" Gideon said.

"Then you are misled. It is both and more than both," Drake said. "But Mary of Scotland would never have countenanced its aims."

"Neither did Elizabeth of England." Gideon lifted a hand. "No matter. You have this story to tell, so tell it."

"My grandfather realised he had been wrong to allow himself to be distracted from what he had been told he should do. By then Princess Mary was in her late teens but could never be viewed as a candidate for the throne, so a viable heir had to be—" Drake broke off, clearly struggling to find the right word. "A viable heir had to be provided. But the leading men of the Covenant were unwilling to be the one to marry themselves or their sons to her, even with the golden prospect of fathering a line of kings one day. That was when it was decreed Covenant marriages could be clandestine as long as the documents were impeccably witnessed."

"So who—?" Gideon found his tongue revolted against even asking and he had to swallow before he could go on. "Who *married* her?" He tried to push from his mind the thought of what that word encompassed in this case.

"At the time all this was happening, my grandfather had just been bereaved of his first wife. A sure sign from God that he should be the one who did so." Drake cleared his throat before adding. "He was deemed of suitable status as he came from royal blood himself, being a direct descendant of Rhodri the Great. It was not a marriage to shame the princess. The Covenant saw he was recompensed well for the responsibility."

"He was *paid* to?" Gideon's voice clashed with Anders'.

"I have known such young people," Anders said with an uncharacteristic surge of anger. "My own sister…" He stopped, hands tightened into fists, needing to master himself before he went on, his fury and disgust plain. "If Princess Mary was similarly afflicted, she could not have given consent to marriage in any meaningful way."

Drake had the decency to look abashed.

"I can only repeat they believed God was on their side in it—and who are we to deny that? These things happened that made the impossible possible. That is surely the definition of a miracle."

Gideon was about to say he didn't see how any Christian could conceive of such actions being blessed by God, but before he could, there was a tap on the door.

Drake rose and opened it to see who was there, then pulled the door wide to admit two servants bearing food and drink. After they had gone Gideon's stomach demanded that he eat. Drake watched him and Anders do so, until Gideon pushed his plate away, glad that the gnawing ache in his midriff had finally been satisfied.

"And a child was born?" Gideon felt suddenly weary and wanted this telling to be done.

Drake poured three cups of wine and pushed one each towards Anders and Gideon then picked his own up and nodded.

"Yes. She was called Mary Elizabeth. Sadly, her mother had a difficult delivery and never recovered. She died the following year. Mary Elizabeth was raised by a Covenant family as if she were their daughter and so she believed herself to be. There was nothing to mark her out in the way her mother had been. She had no sign of her mother's infirmities or distinctive colouring. I am told she much resembled my mother."

"She was completely normal?"

"By all accounts. Beautiful, quick-witted, charming, vivacious."

"That sounds—"

"Another miracle. A sign that the Covenant was indeed blessed by God in its work. To cut a long tale short, events transpired that my grandfather went to visit Emperor Rudolf. He took all his family and Mary Elizabeth travelled with them. They went for many reasons but not least was to fulfil a promise my grandfather had made to the emperor's father, Maximilian, that one of his bloodline should be the ruler the Covenant had been promised."

Gideon recalled then Philip's voice reading from Dee's book in the house in Mortlake. *Oh, Maximilian! May God, through this mystagogy, make you or some other scion of the House of Austria the most powerful of all...*

"The emperor was much taken by Mary Elizabeth, and he was a man who, like his father had before him, had been secretly embracing the ideas of my grandfather and the Covenant for some time. He prized alchemy and other mystical arts. Even so, my grandfather thought it was the charms of Mary Elizabeth herself more than the idea of fathering a divinely mandated heir that made him agree. The emperor was not restrained in his affections. There was a clandestine marriage. Though secret it was well enough witnessed that any son born would have been heir to the emperor and have a strong claim to the English throne on Elizabeth's death. The original plan was he would be raised under Dee's tutelage to become the ruler who the Covenant had been promised and his rule would usher in a new golden age. Unfortunately, the plan fell at the first hurdle. Just before they met my grandfather was called upon by the angels to rebuke Rudolph for his behaviour. It had soured their relationship from the first."

Thinking of what he had read in the documents in the Cotton Library, this was not surprising to Gideon. But it struck him then that there had been no mention of any of what Drake was telling him in those papers.

"How do you know all this?" he asked abruptly, "Are there records of what occurred?"

Drake smiled.

"I wondered when you would ask that. My grandfather was a meticulous man, a scholar down to his fingertips. He recorded it all in a ciphered journal which the Covenant has in a secure place where none may chance upon it. Sadly, whilst we know he also kept a spiritual diary and another for his regular household accounts, those were not entrusted to our care and have long since been lost."

Gideon wondered if he should mention that he knew where the spiritual record—or part of it—was to be found, but Drake had already returned to his tale.

"Unfortunately, whilst Emperor Rudolph had seemed completely committed to the notion of a reunified Christendom and as much a man as my grandfather for prophecies and miracles, he proved not so willing to face the consequences in real life. In the end, the emperor banished my grandfather after the Jesuits accused him of necromancy and heresy."

"And Mary Elizabeth?" Gideon asked, wondering how it was that the human element was always disregarded. Not one of these men had considered how the intelligent and vivacious Mary Elizabeth, still only in her mid-teens, felt about it.

"She stayed with her husband. Rudolph had many lovers, both men and women, and she was treated as another such by his court. For a time, he showered her with gifts and, if not publicly acknowledging her as such, treated her as his consort. Then she became pregnant. At which point, for whatever reason, the emperor decided he had no wish to engage further with the Covenant. It was as if the stark reality of the child being born overwhelmed him. He destroyed his copy of the marriage documents and sent Mary Elizabeth home to England in the company of Thomas Kelley. Tragically, it was winter. In the snow and ice, the coach she was travelling in had an accident and overturned. She was injured and went into early labour. She died days later, from the injuries she had received in the accident, leaving a baby girl who, against all expectations, survived."

"Another 'miracle'?"

Drake smiled, acknowledging Gideon's cynicism. "Yes. Another miracle. Truly. Thomas Kelley took her to my grandfather, who convinced my grandmother to accept the infant as if it were her own. My grandfather called the child Madinia, and she was born with hair as white as—"

"As white as her son's?" Gideon suggested.

Drake nodded. "I was going to say as an angel's, but yes, as white," he agreed, "as her son's."

"I have heard nothing yet to change my opinion of the Covenant." Gideon said. "Old men pressing the weight of their failed dreams onto the next generation."

"But that is precisely what I am striving to prevent from happening in the future," Drake insisted. "It is why I am here talking to you and why—"

"Let us finish with the past," Gideon said brusquely.

Drake's smile this time was forced.

"The past. Yes. Though now we are in a past that runs to the present." He put his elbows on the table and steepled his fingers. "Those were the years when men of standing were looking to the end of the reign of Queen Elizabeth and fearing all she had achieved might be pulled asunder. Remember this was the time of the Babington Plot, the Throckmorton Plot and others. The queen was aging and it was by no means certain that there would be a protestant succession. Fulke Greville was amongst the richest men in these islands at the time and well known for his piety, so when he stepped forward to offer leadership of the Covenant, he was supported by many." Drake spread his hands. "His influence changed the direction of the Covenant. He was less tolerant of Catholics than my grandfather—he was a man who had fought with Henry of Navarre."

"The Covenant no longer promoted Rosicrucian ideals?" Gideon wondered at that, knowing that Philip had spoken of the strange beliefs he had been raised to.

"On the contrary," Drake said, "Lord Brooke, as he would become, saw that as the way to teach what he believed in. He used his wealth to encourage the spread of the Covenant teachings and there were many small groups or lodges set up around the country as a result. Secret, loyal and committed to our ideals. Lord Brooke was not a narrow man, far from it. But the *political* direction of the Covenant was shifting. It began to shed any European aspiration and became about England. Some years before my grandfather died, Greville was anointed his successor. To confirm that, he secretly wed Madinia who was then of legal age being twelve."

Twelve years old. It might be the minimum legal age, but Gideon could think of few nowadays who would condone wedding a girl so young. He tried to set that aside to focus on the other, equally terrible aspect of this.

"But why the need for secrecy? It's not as if there was any impediment on either side. Why not acknowledge his marriage openly?"

"Perhaps had circumstances been different he might have done so," Drake said. "But you must recall that there was at that same time a crisis of succession and the Covenant was yet again being broken on the rocks of factionalism. Until that had been resolved it was deemed better to keep the marriage a secret. Some felt with Elizabeth's death it was the perfect opportunity—perhaps their best and only one—to step into the open and through Madinia claim the throne. Then there were those who said it would never work, that the nation had endured enough of women rulers, that we were still at war with Spain so an heir with the Habsburg name would garner no popular support, and that to make the attempt would be little short of suicide for them all. My grandfather's voice might have made a difference, but he was a very old man by then and vacillated too long. Events overtook them and to the approval of most, King James became king of England."

"But they still didn't abandon the Covenant?"

Drake spread his hands.

"A few. But those who held firm believed this was a test—the last and greatest test and that the time would come if they remained true." He sat back and smiled. "Then, when a strong and healthy son was finally born, the first such in the bloodline, it was the vindication of the faith of those who stood loyal to the Covenant— a sign that our time was finally coming. Greville named the child after his long-dead friend, the man he had always most loved and admired—Sir Philip Sidney. My grandfather lived just long enough to see the child born. In the last notes he wrote for the Covenant, he said that the natal chart he had calculated showed this child to be the one they had awaited who would fulfil the aspirations of the Covenant when the time was right."

"And that son was Sir Philip Lord." Gideon recalled the beauty and grandeur of Warwick Castle, the home where Philip should have been raised and should now own, the perfect setting for a man of his brilliance, elegance and exquisite taste. And it would have been his had this not all been done behind curtains and with whispers.

"Yes. But as that needed to remain secret, he was given into the care of the Couplands, so he could be kept a long way from London, although his father maintained a strong interest in Sir Philip's education, which was conducted to the highest principles."

"Secret? But why?" Gideon demanded. "There was no encumbrance, no prior commitment. No crisis of succession. What was the excuse this time?"

"Because questions would have been asked about his wife." Drake's tone had exaggerated patience as if it should be obvious. "At the time Greville was seeking to secure place and influence at King James' court. It would have been inconvenient, to say the least, were even a hint of improbity to have reached the King's ears."

Inconvenient.

"But whoever she might have been, in the eyes of the world she was seen as a daughter of Dr Dee," Gideon protested. "Where is the problem with that?"

"My grandfather, by then was regarded as a controversial figure and generally deemed of ill-repute. He was said to have been a conjurer of spirits, a worker of sorcery—and King James was a man who loathed and feared such things."

Which made sense of a sort, but still reeked of these powerful Covenant men seeking excuses and giving no regard to the young woman and her child at the heart of their machinations. It was as if they saw the entire project as something aside from their lives, rather than central to them. As if the people caught up in it—the young women of the bloodline and their children—were not flesh and blood but pawns on a chessboard to be moved around for whatever political advantage and sacrificed to expediency, until one could reach the far side of the board and be made queen or king.

"So why was Sir Philip presented to King James to catch his eye? How did that help further the ends of the Covenant?"

Drake had been leaning forward and now sat back in his chair as if a little deflated.

"My understanding is it was not something planned by those who ruled the Covenant. Sir Philip was brought to court to further his education."

"That wasn't what happened though, was it?" Gideon recalled Philip speaking of King James. "He was offered up on a plate to the king."

His words made Drake shift uncomfortably.

"What happened wasn't intended. It happened to be when Prince Charles was away in Spain with the king's beloved favourite the Duke of Buckingham, expected to return with a Spanish bride. The country was all but ruled by Buckingham at that time and he was widely hated even by those who courted his patronage. When it was seen that the king was drawn to Sir Philip, others than the Covenant were quick to push him forward. He was everything the king admired in Buckingham, but younger, more beautiful, more athletic and in addition, he was much more intelligent and well-educated—both traits the king was known to appreciate. Lord Brooke was furious. But there was little then he could do without declaring his relationship. Others in the Covenant regarded it as a good thing and encouraged it. They thought it would bring them power and influence."

Drake lifted his cup and sipped some wine before going on as if his throat was dry.

"Of course, things did not turn out well. On his return, whilst outwardly pretending amity, Buckingham secretly arranged for Sir Philip to be removed from the game in a way that left himself uninvolved. Too subtle for Buckingham acting alone, but who helped him we never found out. It was a clever play."

The turn of phrase made Gideon's fists clench with anger. It truly was a game to these men. Because of that, he didn't bother to tell Drake that he had uncovered the truth of it. Lord Coke had been the man who Buckingham had turned to. He had ensured Philip wound up exiled as a traitor, abandoned alone on an enemy shore at the age of fifteen and left to fend for himself.

"In all this, you haven't told me what it means to be a son of the Covenant," he said instead.

Drake nodded.

"I was coming to that. You see Madinia had one child then proved barren. When Sir Philip was four years old, he fell gravely ill with a fever and for two weeks it was in God's hands whether he would live or die. The Covenant was thrown into turmoil. It was recognised that we needed to look for other ways the aims of the Covenant could still be enacted in some form even if the bloodline was lost. One result of that was to encourage the publication of the pamphlets planned to prepare the ordinary people for the new revelation in religion—the Rosicrucian manifestos. It would not have been safe to publish them here so it was done in German, with the certain knowledge they would come here. More effort was put into the secret lodges Lord Brooke had established scattered about the country, so whatever might happen the ideals and ideas would be preserved. Finally, to provide the strength of leadership needed, it was agreed to create a *real* fraternity—a secret band of brothers, men united by blood, from whom the future leaders of the Covenant could be drawn. All these aims needed to be approved so there was the need for a new charter."

"The second Covenant," Gideon said, trying to recall the odd phrases he had seen in it.

"It removed names no longer active and brought in those who were willing to step up and take on the mantle of responsibility for the Covenant's new aims."

"And this 'secret band of brothers', they were conceived under the same kind of deeds of concubinage as the one I saw for Margret Coupland?"

Drake pulled a face at the word and Gideon's tone of evident disgust.

"The form of these unions had both Biblical and Covenant precedence," he insisted. "The angels themselves had condoned such to my grandfather. There was nothing wrong or salacious about them. Indeed, they were acts of benevolence. Lord Brooke saw what he was doing as a sacred duty. He provided generously for those who accepted. No man was compelled or forced into it."

"No man," Anders echoed gravely. "What of the women? The women who were made to sleep with one man and marry another, did they have no say in the matter?"

A shadow crossed Drake's face. "It is true that not all were happy with the arrangements. Indeed, it was after a major argument on the topic at a meeting of the Covenant in London that Lord Brooke was murdered. But no fingers are pointed, and history records it was a disgruntled servant who did the deed. Anyway, following his death, the faction that sought to unpick the Covenant and end all that had been done, began to grow in dominance. As no successor had been anointed by Greville, we no longer had a single leader. We had the four archangels. When one died the remaining three would choose his successor." Drake spread his hands. "I think you know the rest."

Gideon was trying to distance himself from what he was hearing, trying to imagine he was listening to this being recounted about another man, trying hard not to think what Drake had said in Baddersleigh Priory. *You are Gideon Lennox, and you are a son of the Covenant.*

"Who are—? I mean, how many—?"

"Sons of the Covenant? There were five of us, but since last month only three are still living. Being a young man of quality in this age is a dangerous state. We are required to fight in this war, and it has taken its toll. Ironically those two who died did so in the same battle fighting on opposite sides. And that is why we who remain are now seen as most precious to the Covenant."

"And no daughters were born?" Gideon asked. "No sisters to that band of brothers?"

Drake narrowed his eyes in response to the edge of anger Gideon had been unable to keep from his voice. "If there were, they are daughters of their present houses, raised and honoured as such, but I have heard of none, and they are not recorded in the Covenant archives."

Philip's words from a conversation soon after they met slipped unbidden into Gideon's thoughts. *It would be damnably awkward to wake up having spent the best hours of the night in the throes of lust, only to learn I had just done so with a previously unknown sibling.*

Gideon swallowed hard.

"You, Sir Nicholas Tempest and—and I, are all 'sons of the Covenant'?"

Drake nodded. "And as I am one, I know how that feels and I know the responsibility the Covenant has for each of us." He went on seemingly unaware of the fire of fury Gideon was fighting to suppress. The thought of his mother being bound like a chattel to the man his father had been just to provide the appearance of decency for what she had been made to endure. Hurled from a loveless bedding to a loveless, lightless, marriage. Yet somehow despite that, despite who Gideon was and all that he must have represented to her, she had loved him unconditionally. Gideon's fists tightened.

"But things are changing in the Covenant now," Drake was saying. "Our last Michael was found dead in the Thames two months ago. Sir Philip's man, Bristow, wounded our last Raphael. He never recovered and died five weeks past. Tempest is not fit for any such role, but you—you would be perfect as our next Raphael, our archivist. And if Sir Philip is willing to accept what I already offered him, the chance to give Parliament a legitimate candidate to be king, then the three of us can concur on his choice of appointment to be Michael. I suspect that would be the dangerously intelligent Colonel Bristow."

It was too much. Gideon hammered both his fists hard on the table, rattling the dishes and cups, then pushed himself to his feet.

"No." He shouted the word. "Can't you see what this is? Can't you see the warped and twisted way this has been wrought? Can't you see how wrong it all is—and has been from the first?" He was shaking with anger. Anders, too, was on his feet.

Drake seemed unperturbed. He lifted his cup from the pool of wine it now sat in and produced a kerchief to mop that before setting it down again.

"I didn't create the Covenant. I don't approve of all it has done and I am not trying to justify it. You are not alone in your feelings.

The Couplands and the Tempests and their faction had come to believe that the only way forward was to destroy it all. To kill Sir Philip and any of the sons of the Covenant they could lay hands on, except Sir Nicholas of course, to wipe out any claim it might have to current or future legitimacy and to cover their own historic involvement with it." He gestured to the chairs. "Please be seated again. After all, you came here to talk of these things, difficult as they are for you to consider."

Gideon remained standing, his head pounding, and he flinched when Anders reached out and rested a hand on his shoulder.

"Let us sit and listen to the man," Anders said. "We need to hear the end of this if only because we need to take it all back to Sir Philip."

His words broke the spell and Gideon sat, but Anders walked around the table to stand beside him. A steadying presence lending him strength, calm and assurance.

"So let us hear the end," Gideon said, biting off the last word.

Drake sipped from his cup before replacing it carefully.

"Right now," he said, "the Covenant is spread across the country, men on both sides of this war, a handful of note in most towns—more in each city, who come together secretly in mutual aid. They accept a different view of God to most, the Rosicrucian hermetic view that has been revealed to us in the Covenant through men like Dr Dee. Yet in good faith, they still worship according to their conscience or social necessity in their communities. They help each other as brothers in a family might help each other and they recruit with care to grow our strength." He spread his hands helplessly. "That is not going to stop happening now. It spreads without any consent except that of each local lodge. However, it means that there are those of substance in every sizable community who would acclaim Sir Philip as their king. That— backed by the power of the army of Parliament placed in his hand—would secure the kingdom, end this bloody and pointless war and usher in a new golden age such as we have never enjoyed as a nation before."

"He has no desire to be king," Gideon said. "I understand why, and I would never press him to it."

Drake stared at him, clearly struggling to understand.

"Don't you think he has the makings of a great king? His existence itself is a miracle many times over, and his timely presence in England now, when so much can be accomplished, is surely proof that God is with us in this. He would bring peace and glory to England."

Gideon wondered how to reply to that.

"But can't you see that isn't what would happen? Have you been so blinded by what you have been told you don't understand the way people would view it—would view Philip?"

There was a strained silence then Anders cleared his throat.

"No physic will cure a body that is corrupted," he said. "You cannot build something strong on rotten piles. A good handicraft rests on a golden foundation." He paused and shook his head. "I came as an impartial observer. As such, I say to you, your Covenant is long dead. You and your fellow 'archangels' are trying to keep the breath in a shambling corpse."

Drake said nothing, his expression suddenly cold, his gaze veiled.

"Fortunately, it is not for you two to make the decision." He pushed himself to his feet. "I promised you sight of the documents that prove this. There is an ahnentafel and the proven copies of the documents that validated each marriage and witnessed each birth." He walked to the bookcase and unlocked the doors to remove what looked like a Bible. It had a lock to hold the covers closed, but when Drake set it on the table and opened it, Gideon saw it had been hollowed into a storage place for documents.

"There," Drake said, gesturing to the documents. "Read what you will. All is open to you."

Gideon lifted them out one at a time and studied them, Anders looking over his shoulder. From the feel and look of each, the style of writing and the seals, he knew that Drake was not lying. Either these were genuine, or they were clever forgeries that would deceive any.

"Where are the originals?"

"They are concealed in a place of complete safety. Secure and inaccessible until they may be needed." Drake smiled. "*Trophaeum Peccati.*"

"The trophy of sin? I don't—?"

"It's not important now. Such matters we can talk of once all is established and they need to be redeemed."

Having taken his time to examine each document and what it said, Gideon carefully returned them to their hiding place and closed the cover before handing it back to Drake who locked the book and returned it to its shelf, closing and locking the doors to conceal it again. There was nothing new in what the documents contained, but word by word and line by line they confirmed all Drake had said.

Gideon needed time to think, time to consider it all, time to work out what he needed to do and...

"It is late," Drake said, stepping back from the bookcase. "I have rooms prepared for you and we can talk of this further tomorrow. Then I will set you on the road back to Worcester as I gave my word. In the end, it is not for you or me to decide what to do. It is for Sir Philip alone."

Gideon was shown to a comfortable guest room that he didn't have to share with Anders. It had a feather bed and a washstand. The window had no bars obstructing it. He didn't feel he was in much danger by sleeping. After all, if Drake planned to murder them, he could order it done with ease. Although Gideon had a strong feeling that murder was the last thing on Sir John Drake's mind that night. Like Gideon, he had much too much else to think about.

Chapter Twenty-Two

It was not the dawn that woke him.

It was a soft tap on the door. Someone not wanting to attract too much attention from a still-sleeping household.

Wondering if it might be Anders who wished to discuss what they had learned, or perhaps Drake seeking to have another attempt to persuade Gideon to his cause without an inconvenient sober-minded Dane to counter what he might say, he pulled on his stockings and breeches to present a semblance of decency. He was walking, shirt clad, to the door when the soft taps were repeated.

The door opened on quiet hinges.

Standing on his threshold stood a woman in her later middle years. She had skin as clear as porcelain, the hair that was visible from beneath her coif was the colour of pearl and her eyes were a brilliant turquoise. She looked uncertain as he opened the door, as if unsure of her welcome. Then she smiled tentatively, and Gideon saw the shades of both Philip and Christobel in the angles and planes of her face.

"I'm so sorry to wake you, but may we talk?" she asked, her voice soft and entirely unlike either of those her face resembled.

Gideon realised he must be staring and that his mouth had come slightly open. He closed it again and nodded.

"Yes, please—I mean, of course. I will dress and—"

Her smile gained a little warmth. "I don't think at my age I would be compromised from being alone in a room with my stepson."

Her stepson? Gideon wondered who she meant. Then it hit him, and he was unable to move, breathe or even to think.

"Are you alright?" Her voice seemed to come from another continent, one where things still made sense and the world was as it had always been. "I thought you knew, John said…"

Gideon drew a gasp of air into his aching lungs.

"Yes," he said, "yes, I knew, I just—"

He was unsure how to finish so moved aside to allow her in. She was shorter than Christobel, but not tiny, a little below the height of most women Gideon had met, but she walked with a proud and upright carriage that told him she was not cowed by her world, whatever might be found in it.

She took a seat in a chair that was set by the window, spreading her modest blue wool skirts. Gideon brought over a stool so he could sit with her.

"This must all have come to you as a terrible surprise," she said. "I was brought up to know a little of the strangeness, only recently John has been able to tell me the whole of it. I am Madinia Greville, though my name as a child was Madinia Dee."

Gideon got to his feet.

"This is wrong. It should not be me meeting with you, it should be—"

"My son, or perhaps my daughter?"

"I don't think it is for me to…"

"You believe I might try and add my persuasion to what John would have you do?"

It shocked him that she had seen so quickly into his heart. His expression must have answered her because she shook her head.

"You are very like your father," she said, as if in explanation, and Gideon was shaken to realise she wasn't talking about Archibald Lennox.

Whatever he had imagined Philip's mother to be, it was not this quietly confident and self-contained woman that the child, with her finger torn by a Tudor rose, had become.

"I am sorry if this is hard for you, but I wanted to speak with you first because, you see, until recently I had believed both my children dead. If I had known they lived, nothing on this earth would have kept me from them." She paused, her hands tightening as if she was gripping her courage to speak. "They first told me my son had died when he was four of a childhood illness. Then, by chance, a decade later, I learned that had been a lie. I would have gone to find him then, but he was accused of treason against King James. The man I sent to take him a message returned to say my son had been murdered in the Low Countries on account of that accusation. Another lie." The sudden stark tears lingered briefly like crystals in the corner of each eye then ran unheeded down her face. "And my daughter, my beautiful daughter, I was told, had also died, overlain by a wet nurse when I had a fever after she was born. I held each of them for perhaps an hour and gave them that once each of my milk. I think," she said, her voice wistful, "I would have been a good mother."

Gideon had no words to speak to that. At least his own mother had been able to hold him, nurse him, nurture him in his childhood and keep him in her arms until she had no choice but to leave him.

"They are brother and sister then?" he asked, his voice a hoarse rasp.

"Philip," she said as if she hadn't heard Gideon speak. "They told me he would be called Philip. He was the son of my husband. But after Philip, no more children came and eventually my husband stopped visiting me. Then I met John's father when I came to live here. He was my brother-in-law, of course, so there could be nothing between us even though we both knew there was from the moment we set eyes on each other. But when my sister Katherine died, we became close—too close. We loved each other, you see." She blinked the tears away and looked at Gideon as if seeing him for the first time. "You must understand how it was. We knew we had to keep it secret, knew how dangerous it was, but with a baby that was impossible. I never loved my husband, but I loved Christopher. He died before our daughter was born. It was a riding accident, and then they took her from me too— although at the time I believed that had been God's doing." Her eyes misted a little but then she fixed her gaze on Gideon and it was as vivid as before. "What did they call her?"

"Christobel," he said, his heart numb.

"Christobel." She smiled and said the name again. "For her father, of course. And no, I'll not ask you to tell me of my children, that wouldn't be fair though I would fain hear of them, how they look, how they sound, what they enjoy reading, what they like to do and all the thousands of small things that make us each who we are and unique." She leaned forward and reached for his hand in an impulsive gesture. "I only have one thing I would ask you Mr

257

Lennox and that is, do my children hate me so much for what has happened to them that they would not want to meet me?"

Gideon stared at her in incomprehension.

I made an oath. In Oxford. The day I wed Kate.

She studied his face and as she did so, the lines of anxiety seemed to smooth. She nodded and gave a small smile as she released his hand and sat back.

"Thank you. I had to know. I wouldn't want to walk unwelcome into their lives." She got to her feet then. "John is not a bad man, but he is a misguided one, although there are many in these troubled times—and I like your Danish companion, he was kind to me when I found I had chosen to knock on the wrong door. What was it he said? Children are certain sorrows, but uncertain joys. He is a wise man, wise and kind. It gives me great hope to see that my son surrounds himself with such men as Dr Jensen and yourself."

Gideon rose with her. A hundred questions thronged in his mind, but none seemed to matter anymore. Except one.

"What should I tell your children?"

Madinia Dee smiled at him with the mischief of the child in the painting dancing suddenly in her eyes.

"You need tell them nothing. I've decided that whatever John may wish, I will come with you to meet them both."

She left then as quietly as she came, and Gideon had barely finished dressing properly before he was summoned to breakfast. He encountered Anders on the way, who greeted him by leaning in to speak quietly.

"She is a formidable woman, I think. It is a shame she has been made to hide away for so long."

Gideon found himself thinking how much Philip's mother reminded him of Kate more than Christobel and he wondered how they would all find her. She had seemed confident they would be free to leave, and she would be permitted to ride with them. Gideon was unsure.

He and Anders were served a small meal of freshly cooked frumenty, together with some of the leftovers from the previous evening, in the same room as before. As they ate, Gideon's eyes were drawn to the locked bookcase with its secrets. He wondered what Philip would decide when he was given the full story. Then he realised he was wrong to wonder. There was nothing in any of it that would change Philip's mind.

Just as they finished eating John Drake came in, dressed as ever in the mourning black he always favoured. An affectation or…? *He died before our daughter was born. It was a riding accident…* With a flash of insight, Gideon understood that it was for his stepfather, the man he had probably thought as a child to be his true father. Was it that Drake suspected it had been no accident? That the Covenant didn't wish to risk more illegitimate claimants who might become pretenders in a world where their king ruled?

"You will take my proposition to Sir Philip?" Drake asked. "I know you will not endorse it, but I believe I can trust you to present it fairly and, having spoken with him myself yesterday, I believe he may have the vision to see further than you do with it."

"He ended my employment as his legal advisor rather publicly yesterday evening," Gideon said. "That means I am free to offer what you say without the need to express my legal counsel."

"And that is the best I can expect. I'd hoped you might see…" Drake trailed off and then gave a tight smile. "There remains, then, the transaction. I am willing to provide copies of the ahnentafel—though not a proven copy of course—if Sir Philip wishes. Indeed, should you want, you may come and make the copy yourself under my promise that you would be free to leave after. In exchange, I would want the documents he holds. I will give him his heritage if he restores to me that which might harm the Covenant."

"And Sir Nicholas?"

"He was to be restored to me when you were restored to Sir Philip. Or is Sir Philip indeed not a man of his word as the rumours of him suggest?"

"He is a man of his word. More so than most," Gideon said but struggled to see how he would persuade Philip and Danny—let alone Christobel—to allow Nicholas Tempest to go free once he was safely back in Worcester. That was solved for him in the next sentence Drake spoke.

"Good. I will approach Worcester as close as I may, then Dr Jensen here can go and fetch Sir Nicholas. I will wait with my men to escort him back and let you return when he is with me. I merely wish to ensure he is safe, not detain you."

The ride to Worcester was not as leisurely as the one to Baddersleigh had been the day before. This time, Gideon and Anders were making the journey with a troop of Parliamentarian horse, through territory that was held by the king's men. The only real disappointment for Gideon was that Madinia was not in their company. He had to presume that despite her brave and determined words, John Drake had refused her permission to ride to see her children. He almost asked, then realised that perhaps Drake didn't know they had met and he decided to say nothing.

In the end, there was no need to approach Worcester. They were still in the Malvern Hills, in the land that was not claimed too hard by either side when they saw the blue and white cat's head banner of Sir Philip Lord fluttering in the breeze. He had drawn up his horse in a line on the brow of a hill so they could be seen from a distance and the message sent clearly that this was no ambush.

Drake halted his troop, which was outnumbered three to one or more, at a distance that would allow them to make a rapid retreat if it was needful should the cavalry on the hill show any sign of advancing.

"Dr Jensen, if you would be kind enough to ride and present my greetings to Sir Philip and ask him to send Sir Nicholas back alone. You may tell him as soon as I see Sir Nicholas riding out, he has my word I will allow Mr Lennox here to ride forward too."

Anders made a brief bow to Drake, as much as he could on horseback, then reached over to grip Gideon's hand before putting the little chestnut mare into a brisk canter towards the blue and white banner. They saw him ride up the hill, his medical bag strapped behind him on the saddle. The ranks opened to allow him in, then closed again behind him in a solid wall. Gideon shielded his eyes, looked for and found Roger Jupp, then saw Danny beside him, perspective glass in hand trained upon them. He smiled, knowing that for Danny it would be as if he was standing right in front of them.

THE CAVALIER'S OATH

The wait seemed to go on much too long. Even the usually phlegmatic Drake appeared to be becoming concerned. The first trace of a frown was beginning to etch itself on his brow beneath the golden curls when the line of horses parted again and Sir Nicholas Tempest began to ride down the hill, kicking his horse into a trot.

"I had better let you go then, Gideon." There was a note of regret in Drake's voice that Gideon felt was nothing to do with the plans he had discussed. Drake held out his hand. "God keep you, my brother, whatever comes of this," he said, and Gideon briefly gripped the proffered hand, then turned his mount towards the line of blue and silver clad cavalry.

Brother.

He felt sick.

Sons of the Covenant. Drake was his brother. So was the man riding towards him who would have seen him dead.

It was inevitable that the two passed in the middle of the valley, but it was not inevitable that they needed to pass closely or that Sir Nicholas would rein in and block Gideon's passage. He was unarmed so Gideon let him do so, wondering if, after it all, he was going to apologise.

"I want you to give a message to that whore who is my wife," Sir Nicholas snarled. "Tell her I will never free her to marry her lover and if they have any children they will be as base born as she is." He jerked his horse's head around, clearly planning to ride on, but Gideon caught his bridle.

"On the contrary, *brother*," he spat the word with contempt, hating the truth of it. "You are going to free her as soon as you can, because if within three months the marriage is not annulled by you declaring it unconsummated I will make sure the world knows that *you* are base-born and have no right to the lands and title you have inherited."

"Your word against mine," Tempest snapped.

"Not my word," Gideon told him. "I have the document signed by Sir Bartholomew Coupland, Sir Richard Tempest and Sir Fulke Greville trading your mother to be a concubine whether she wished it or not. That is what I will make public if you do not

261

release Christobel. I have no doubt you can persuade the Covenant to use their influence to get it done speedily. They would not want that document made public either."

The hatred in Tempest's eyes seemed to sear into Gideon's soul before he pulled his horse away and rode off.

Gideon watched him go. Such was the power of the pen, able to make and unmake a man. Then, satisfied he had done what was needed, he carried on towards the line of cavalry on the hilltop, cheers welcoming him as he put his horse up the last slope.

A couple of minutes later Olsen was yelling and banging him on the back and he had a grinning escort to where Sir Philip Lord awaited him standing with Anders and Danny by their horses. Kate sat on a portable chair beside Philip, and Christobel was behind her. On Kate's lap was the open Bible case Gideon had last seen Drake returning to the book cabinet before they had retired for the night and in Kate's hands was the ahnentafel. Wondering, Gideon dismounted and crossed the last of the distance on foot.

"Anders was given a parting gift by a mysterious benefactor," Philip said, gesturing to the Bible case as Gideon reached him. "It's amazing how copious his medical bag seems to be. But he tells me he's not at liberty to say who that benefactor might be. It was bestowed upon him on the sole condition that he kept silent on that point. In it is all I need to break the chains that have held me bound these long years." Then Philip looked at him half way between amusement and delight. "And it seems I have a younger brother."

Brother.

The word took the breath from Gideon's lungs.

He hadn't thought it through. Of course, as much as he was brother to Drake and Tempest, he was brother to Sir Philip Lord.

He must have looked thunderstruck because Philip reached out a hand to steady him.

"I know it is bad, but it could have been worse," he said gravely. "You could have discovered you were Danny's brother."

The laughter released him, and Philip stepped forward, pulling him into an embrace, thumping him on the back. It was some minutes later before the laughing and embracing finished. Kate said how she liked the idea of having Gideon as a brother-in-law, and Danny retorted that brother or no, Gideon had been in law for quite a while already. Which made more laughter.

Gideon resided the urge to chastise Anders for the incredible risk he had taken carrying the Bible case. He knew how the Dane must have come by it. He was just wondering if he should broach the subject, so Anders would have no need to break his word, when a shout went up from the line of cavalry still guarding the hilltop.

Philip and Danny were on horseback at once and Gideon followed, suddenly afraid that something had gone terribly wrong.

But there was no sign of Sir John Drake, Sir Nicholas Tempest or the cavalry troop they had been with. The only riders in sight were heading towards them at a steady pace. A man on a broad-backed black gelding with a bow at his saddle and a young woman riding pillion behind. The sight made Gideon's heart rise and grow to fill his entire chest. But with them were two more riders, one clearly a servant, but the other was an older woman in a blue gown riding side-saddle on a pearl white mare the colour of her unbound hair.

Madinia had come.

It was Philip who moved first, putting his horse into a canter then a gallop, the wind trailing his hair behind like a white Oriflamme as he streaked down the hill. Danny murmured something incoherent then he pulled his horse around, calling for Christobel. Gideon hesitated. Then he set off down the hill.

Philip reined at the bottom of the slope as if unable to go on. Stopping beside him, Gideon saw his face. A parched man caught up in the vision of a waterfall, hardly daring to believe it was real and afraid that a sudden shift in the shadows and sunlight might snatch it away.

The four riders were still crossing the field towards them, and Philip slid from his high horse to stand and watch them come.

Before the four had covered more than half the distance that remained, fast hooves came from behind. Danny's horse stopped beside them. Christobel sat behind the saddle with her arms wrapped tight about Danny. Her expression, one of wonder and her gaze fixed, as her brother's, on the small, neat figure on the milk-white mare.

It seemed to take an eternity for the approaching riders to cross the final field, but then, unexpectedly soon, they were there. Shiraz brought his horse to a halt and the servant stopped with him. Gideon caught Zahara's gaze, and she sent him a smile as the pale woman on her pale horse continued on alone.

Philip started walking—running forward. He was beside Madinia as she was gathering her reins to dismount. Reaching up, he lifted her from the saddle to place her on the ground. Then stepping back, he dropped to one knee, careless of the wet grass and the mud, sweeping off his hat as he did so. He bowed his head for his mother's blessing.

She placed her hand upon him, and no one heard the words she said except her only son as she bent to place a kiss on his brow. Then he rose and brought her into the shelter of his arm—giving by that, the promise of his ongoing protection. She was looking up at him, her smile that of someone restored to health after a long malaise.

Slipping down from her seat behind Danny, Christobel walked towards them. Uncertain, hesitant, as if not sure whether or not she might be welcome or belong. But her mother stepped forward, walking, then running a pace or two, to embrace Christobel and draw her into the circle that was now a family.

Gideon's throat closed up at the sight of the three of them standing together. Philip with an arm around each of the two women who, in turn, held each other tightly, as a lifetime of pain and separation faded as frost fades in the sun. And, as they looked and touched and talked, slowly the disbelief was melting into unalloyed joy and healing laughter.

A cheer came from behind and Gideon glanced back up the hill to where Sir Philip Lord's men stood. Kate was with them, supported by Anders, her smile so brilliant it was clear to Gideon even at that distance.

"Not a dry eye in the house," Danny said, his tone wistful. He was sitting his horse with a misty-eyed look and rubbed impatiently at something that gleamed on his cheek. Then he

264

reached out and plucked Gideon's sleeve. "I think you might be wanted."

Following Danny's gaze Gideon saw Shiraz lift his chin as if beckoning. Gideon put his horse into a trot to cross the short distance between them. Zahara must have insisted on riding with Shiraz to find him, unwilling to sit quietly by when he might be in danger, and his heart swelled at her courage and her love. Instead of Gideon, they had found Madinia, setting out on her brave pilgrimage.

When he reached the black gelding, Zahara smiled with the gentle joy that was always her special greeting for him and him alone. But before Gideon could say anything, Shiraz reached over and grasped his wrist. Confused, but unresisting Gideon let him do so. Shiraz pressed his hand against Zahara's, then gripped the two together. His expression was earnest, his meaning plain. She had told him their secret, and he approved.

Something shifted deep within Gideon's chest as Zahara's smile deepened and her soul danced in her eyes. He reached over to lift the woman he loved from her pillion and onto his own saddle.

"If you would like," he told her, "from now on we will always ride together."

Zahara wrapped her arms tightly about him, her head turned to rest on his shoulder.

"I would like that very much," she said.

Sir Philip Lord's voice reached them, lifted in verse.

"*Love, all alike, no season knows nor clime,*
Nor hours, days, months, which are the rags of time.
We have ridden so far and now we are all come home…"

Author's Notes

This book is dedicated to you.

You have stayed the course and been with Gideon through all his adventures with Philip Lord. You have fought battles, endured sieges, solved murders and unravelled the dark conspiracy of the Covenant that reached its grasping arms from the past. Thank you for doing so. I hope the journey has given you enjoyment in full measure. If it has, and you are willing to do so, please take a moment to let me know. Leaving a review means so much and takes so little time.

Some of the key events and people in this book are drawn from history and as far as possible I have had them all be in the place history has placed them at this time. How they behave and what they say is my invention.

The collection of urine-soaked earth by saltpetre men for use in the production of munitions was a common grievance of the time. It was even one of the issues listed in the Grand Remonstrance list of grievances by Parliament to King Charles I. Ironically, Parliament itself would pass a law soon after which removed the legal protection Gideon quotes from those areas under their sway, making it fully legal not only for just about anywhere to be dug up, even inside a house, and for householders to have to lend their carts to carry the soil produced if required. However, in practice, poor people were already abused in this way and the legal requirement to make good damage done was often honoured in the breach.

The events around the siege of Worcester itself are portrayed closely to the historical record. Colonel Samuel and Martin Sandys were there and the opening encounter with Waller's trumpeter, the assaults and sorties made were much as I described. There was indeed much friction between Russell's and Sandys' men. Waller did send the printed letter I quote into the city by his agents to try and stir disaffection—though, to the best of my knowledge, none was sent back.

Dudd Dudley was a real person who was indeed General of Ordnance for Prince Maurice and may well have been responsible for modernising the defences of Worcester, although I am not sure if he was in the city at the time of this siege or not. He seems to have been a larger-than-life character, overconfident and far from risk-averse, whose schemes often didn't work out, but I probably do him something of a disservice in the pages of this book.

The Fishers, Youngs and Ursula Markham were all my creations as is the story about them.

I don't know for sure that the women of Worcester were active on the walls with the men before and during the siege, but it seems likely they were as some were reported killed during the siege and at the end of June the women of the city of were said to have gone out in organised and flattened the siegeworks raised by Waller's men to make it harder if he should return.

The Kelleys were born in Worcester, and little seems to be known of their origins beyond the fact that their father was called Patrick Kelley. The history of Sir Edward, who was John Dee's scryer and became a renowned alchemist in his own right, is well recorded. Once Thomas Kelley left John Dee's purview he seems to drop from historical sight and their sister Elizabeth (or Lydia) likewise. Katherine Dee equally vanishes from history shortly after her father's death having nursed him in his final years. Drake, father and son, are my creations as are Baddersleigh village and priory and Drake's house.

John Dee had a daughter called Madinia, about which little is known except the date of her baptism in February 1590. She too vanishes from the historical record and has always been assumed to have perished along with Dee's wife, Jane, and some other siblings in an outbreak of plague in Manchester in 1605.

Fulke Greville, 1st Baron Brooke, is a man about whom a large number of myths have been spun. He was, amongst other things, a soldier, a politician and a writer. Best known for his 'Life of Philip Sydney' but he was also a poet and even wrote a play that was never performed.

He is claimed by some to have been a leading Rosicrucian, (perhaps even their first Grand Master and also the founder of freemasonry) and by others to have been Shakespeare (and by some to be all three). He was phenomenally wealthy for his era, much involved in politics through most of his life and was murdered by a servant who felt slighted by his will in 1628 when he was seventy-three.

Lord Brooke had a magnificent tomb built in the Collegiate Church of St Mary in Warwick which cost a small fortune to construct and on it had placed the words '*Folk Grevill Servant to Queene Elizabeth Counsellor to King James Friend to Sir Philip Sidney. Trophaeum Peccati.*' There have been claims made that radar investigations have shown the tomb contains boxes which purportedly hold proof of his Shakespearean writing—or perhaps some other secret documents.

Finally, I wish to be very clear on one point.

As a writer, I take such tales and speculation and weave them into the fabric of my stories. But the final result, even if it owes much of its form to history, is still only a work of fiction.

There may have been many conspiracies and secret cabals in this era, but The Covenant is my invention. Any historical figures I have dragooned into its ranks, whatever else of weal or woe they might have done in their lives, they are completely innocent of that.

Please note that even if the story puts muddy footprints here and there upon the historical record, I have done my best to respect its integrity and avoid distorting it.

You can follow me on Twitter @emswifthook or get in touch with me through my website www.eleanorswifthook.com where you can find more about the background to the book including the origins of the various quotations in the text and learn about my upcoming projects.

As this is the last book in this series, I would like to say a few brief thanks.

Thank you to my publisher Richard Foreman at Sharpe Books for taking a chance on Philip Lord and to Tara there for her assistance.

Thank you to those of my fellow authors who have given me so generously of their time and effort in supporting and encouraging me.

And thank you to the English Civil War Society who touched match to powder and sparked my passion for the period many years ago.

Printed in Great Britain
by Amazon